PRAISE FOR *STARS*

"Ann Marie Stewart writes with immeasurable spirit as she probes the deep currents of faith and love. Abby McAndrews tells her compelling tale of family grief with truth and admirable humor. *Stars in the Grass* is a powerful novel that will light your way."
—Alyson Hagy, author of *Boleto* and *Ghosts of Wyoming*

"In this remarkable novel, Ann Marie Stewart explores the aftermath of tragedy with intelligence, grace, and subtle humor. *Stars in the Grass* is a story of great loss, but also of great hope. A beautiful, haunting tale, it is one I won't soon forget.
—Ann Tatlock, award-winning author of *Once Beyond a Time*

"*Stars in the Grass* reminds us that even when we think God has forgotten us, we're forever on His mind. Ann Marie Stewart's writing is outstanding and her voice captivating. I fell in love with this intriguing novel from the first page."
—Bestselling novelist Kate Lloyd, author of *Leaving Lancaster,*
Pennsylvania Patchwork, and *Forever Amish*

"Ann Marie Stewart's beautifully crafted prose depicts a family in deep turmoil as they walk through a dark valley. . . . Told in first-person narrative by nine-year-old Abby, Stewart gets her voice just right as a precocious child thrust into the world of grief. A thought-provoking and sensitive look into the different paths each family member travels in the aftermath of tragedy, the role of God and faith along the path, and the way time wraps its way around this family until they each can embrace the truth and move forward."
—Elizabeth Musser, bestselling author of
The Long Highway Home and *The Swan Hous*

Stars
in the
Grass

a novel

Ann Marie
STEWART

SHILOH RUN PRESS
An Imprint of Barbour Publishing, Inc.

Print ISBN 978-1-63409-950-9

eBook Editions:
Adobe Digital Edition (.epub) 978-1-63409-952-3
Kindle and MobiPocket Edition (.prc) 978-1-63409-951-6

Special thanks to Shaunna Bohan for contributing to the discussion questions.

Cover photography: Jolena Long, www.joliemaephotography.com

Published by Shiloh Run Press, an imprint of Barbour Publishing, Inc., P.O. Box 719, Uhrichsville, Ohio 44683, www.shilohrunpress.com.

Our mission is to publish and distribute inspirational products offering exceptional value and biblical encouragement to the masses.

ECPA Member of the
Evangelical Christian
Publishers Association

Printed in the United States of America.

DEDICATION

Dedicated to Julia Marie Stewart
No matter how far you travel you'll always be close to my heart

ACKNOWLEDGMENTS

Nick Harrison for always believing in this story and me
Chip MacGregor, agent, for always challenging,
encouraging, and offering sage wisdom
Barbour Publishing for their energy and inspiration
Acquisitions Editor Annie Tipton for listening to Abby's voice
Holly Lorincz and Joanne Simmons for their insightful editing
Beth Greenfeld and Kitty Eisele, my writing group
Fred Ricker, John Enloe, and Bruce Stewart, all Clock Docs
Michelle Albanese, for her unfailing support, encouragement, and GPS
Gilda Carter, a friend who loves unconditionally
Barb Boughton, my friend and sister in Christ
Lori Galloway, for sharing her journey to hope
on the anniversary of her daughter's death
Shaunna Bohan for helping with Discussion Questions
The Writers Center, Bethesda, Maryland
Lake Forest Park Presbyterian Church who made God's house
feel like home
Marvin Wayne, for medical information in Blaine, Washington
The Pink Brains Book Club, my favorite book club that never
actually bowled
Will Stewart for supporting my writing
Julia Stewart and Christine Stewart, our beloved daughters
Charlie Baxter, my UM professor for "Seeing from the Balcony"
Alyson Hagy for continued friendship
and support beyond being my UM professor
Bill and Ruth Roetcisoender, I love you both so much
James Scott Bell, Lydia Harris, Catron Enloe,
Robert Burroughs, Sherry Larson
My heavenly Father who carries me now and forever

PROLOGUE

I spent the better part of my childhood sitting on a pew in the balcony of Bethel Springs First Presbyterian Church, listening to my dad's long vowels as he preached on predestination. Sandwiched between my older brother, Matt, and my little brother, Joel, I counted bald heads, doodled on church bulletins, and studied the stained-glass Jesus.

Reverend McAndrews was godlike and mysterious. Definitely not the same man who read to us from Dr. Seuss, ran through the sprinkler on steamy Ohio summer afternoons, or smiled as we played hide-and-go-seek in his Father's house.

Though I can't remember many of his three-point sermons, I have other good memories. One Sunday during a hymn, Matt and I sang loudly, changing the words to our liking, "Gladly, the Cross-Eyed Bear," and crossing our eyes for added effect. When we sat back down, I rested the hymnal on the railing and fanned myself by riffling through the pages. Then it happened. Onto one of the fifty-one shining bald heads below, I dropped the hymnal.

It clapped to the floor, and then in the congregational hush, Mr. Ludema winced in surprised pain. I only looked down long enough to see necks craning up toward the balcony and then turning toward my father and then back to the balcony. Dad squinted to see Mrs. Ludema as she nursed her husband's head and then looked up at the cause of the disruption. Me.

Dad stared at me for fifteen seconds. I know because I counted every one of them. I did not look away; instead I memorized his thick sandy hair fringed with gray streaks. I couldn't see his eyes because the sun was reflecting on the lenses of his glasses. His mouth was closed, his thick jaw tense. The congregation waited for the Reverend McAndrews, and so did I. At last he said, with a nod to the balcony and a sigh, "And the Word has come down from on high."

During responsive reading, his voice rose and fell so predictably, I was nearly lulled to sleep unless I pulled out a pencil to sketch the hills and valleys. "'O give *thanks* to the LORD, for he is *gooood*,'" Reverend McAndrews read from Psalm 136. His voice grew louder and the pitch higher until the word *Lord*, where he paused and let it fall off to a low, soft, long, concluding *gooood*. We echoed, "For his steadfast love endures for ever.'" After repeating it twenty-six times, what I thought everlasting was the psalm itself.

I did not question the psalmist's message until I was nine and Matt was fifteen and we crossed a crevasse of pain. It took struggling through that jagged blackness of doubt and fear for the girl in the balcony to finally consider the words, and to really connect with the man in the pulpit and the woman at the organ.

My mother looked just like Jackie Kennedy. I don't know if our former First Lady could play the organ, but my mother could *not*, despite the expectations of the elders of BS Pres. (Such an unfortunate acronym, but one this preacher's kid enjoyed flaunting.) The organ faced forward, so my mother's back was toward the congregation, which could have been symbolic considering her reluctance to play the role. Though my mother's keyboard technique lacked beauty and grace, her speech did not. My mother's voice was soft and gentle, full of intricate words she shared, always believing in expanding her children's vocabulary at every opportunity. Nothing about her projected strength, but I would learn she had enough for all of us.

The summer before I turned ten was *idyllic*—until August 3, 1970. At the time I didn't know what that word meant, not having heard it in a sermon or one of Mom's vocabulary lessons. But it perfectly describes a time when I thought the world was safe and good things lasted forever. What I couldn't know then, but try to remember now, is how fragile and delicate are the moments we most treasure, and if they break into pieces, repairing means seeing anew.

ONE

We rushed upward into the night sky, lifted by an unseen force. The higher we climbed, the cooler the air, the fainter the smell of hot dogs and cotton candy, and the softer the music from the merry-go-round below. With my arms outstretched, I traced a wide curve, embracing a crescent of beach fires, twinkling lights, and dimming pink sunset. Birch Bay was black, nearly invisible, the people now dots on the landscape. I leaned against Dad's shoulder and stared up at the stars. Then we crested the top and plunged downward.

After a dizzying return up, the Ferris wheel slowed and then stopped, leaving us hanging in the sky.

"What happened?" I asked.

"They're letting people off at the bottom. The ride's over."

Now with each lurch we measured time; my stomach sagged in disappointment. I could see my brothers swinging below at ten o'clock. Kicking my legs up and down, I tried to make our carriage rock back and forth. Was it really over? Each time the wheel stopped, more riders dismounted. And then it was our turn, and the man unlocked our lap bar. As we left the amusement park, I turned to see the carriages filled and beginning another circle, like hands on a clock.

"Joel rode the Ferris wheel," I told my mom as we returned to our campfire.

"I rode with Matt," Joel burst out, looking up proudly. Joel's "wiff" instead of "with" always made me smile. But not Mom, who turned to Dad and gave him a scolding look.

"I'm *fifteen*, Mom," Matt reminded her, his arm around Joel.

"But *he's* only three," Mom answered.

"It's safe, Renee. There was a safety bar across his waist," Dad explained. "You worry too much."

I gazed back at the Ferris wheel spinning in the distance, a moving spiderweb in the sky. Mom dug into the grocery bag and pulled out marshmallows, Hershey's chocolate, and graham crackers.

After s'mores and storytelling, Joel fell asleep, cradled in Dad's arms at our campfire on the beach. We lay in a circle, our feet to the fire like spokes, our heads pillowed against beached driftwood, the sound of the waves lapping the shore. The air was warm and still, and I wished we could stay there forever. Washington felt so far from Ohio and yet so familiar beneath the same canopy of stars.

"Vega, Antares, Altair, Arcturus. And there's Polaris—the North Star," Dad said, outlining the dotted sky. "'He determines the number of the stars, he gives to all of them their names,'" Dad added gently, not in his minister voice. Poking the fire with his stick, Matt kicked up a hot flame. Sparks sputtered and crackled.

"Cygnus is the swan." Dad traced his fingers along a band of dots, connecting stars into shapes. I blurred my eyes, trying to see a swan, though it looked more like an umbrella. "And that is Pegasus, the winged horse." He drew what looked like a hairy spider. I could only find the Big Dipper.

The warmth from the fire made me blissfully drowsy and I closed my eyes. Mom played with my hair, running her fingers through it before letting it trickle downward, just how I liked it.

"Gossamer," she said softly.

"What's that?" Matt asked.

"Something delicate." Mom closed her eyes and breathed in deeply. "Sort of how this night feels."

"Gossamer. . . ," I whispered, trying it on for size.

✳

The next day at Birch Bay, after digging for clams, building sand castles, and splashing in tide pools, we headed back to our car, strolling the remaining crescent of beach. Joel picked up a long piece of seaweed tethered to a rubbery ball and dragged it behind him, leaving a trail in the sand. He was slowing, the time for his afternoon nap long past. Now the tide was coming in and we were running out of beach, so we shifted to the narrow strip of sidewalk between the surf and the road, the tide pressing us on the right, cars inching along the road on our left. Whenever we strayed too close to the road, Mom gently nudged us back toward the beach.

"Go to Bossy Cow!" Joel whined.

"We're not there, Joel," Dad said. "We can't stop now. Just keep walking, buddy." The Bossy Cow, a diner at the tip of the crescent, served the best shakes. Thick, muddy chocolate milkshakes Joel could never finish.

We walked in slow motion, in no hurry to get anywhere, Joel's pace becoming ours. Even now I wish we had stopped. Like an unwound clock. Time never ticking forward.

"Bossy Cow?" Joel asked again.

"No Bossy Cow, but how about some boats?" I looked to Mom, hoping she'd agree with my suggestion.

"Oh, all right," she said, seeing Joel clap his hands in excitement. Joel and I had discovered the diamond-shaped caramels covered in white chocolate with an almond for a sail. We crossed the street to the Sea Shoppe to buy half a pound. Matt wanted to play in the game rooms, but Dad said it was time to get back to our campsite. I savored a boat, first licking off the white chocolate, then relishing and finally chewing the caramel.

"Carry me, Matt," Joel asked, dropping his *r*'s but not his chocolate sailboat.

"C'mon, Joel, just a little farther." I pulled him along by his wrist, avoiding the sticky candy in his fist. "Mom, Joel's tired. He's too slow."

"Matt, please?" Joel begged, his polite "pwease" making his whining endearingly effective. "Mattie, Mattie."

"Hop on board, little buddy." Matt bent low so Joel could jump on his back. They looked like such a pair, Joel's head resting on Matt's shoulder, his arms around Matt's neck.

"He's going to fall asleep and let go," Mom warned as Joel's eyes closed.

Dad stepped forward. "I'd better carry him."

"Me and Matt." Joel yawned.

"C'mon, Dad, he wants *me*," Matt argued. "I won't let anything happen to him."

"Mattie, Mattie," Joel agreed sleepily.

But Dad pried him off Matt's back and stretched out his arms to lift Joel high in the air, Joel's back blocking the sun's rays. Dad's smile was warm and his eyes so tender. He lowered Joel as if he couldn't resist giving him a hug. Joel's legs wrapped around Dad and his arms circled his neck, his head nestled beneath Dad's chin.

I've heard that people block out traumatic moments, but I remember it all. The line of cars was moving slowly, like a processional, until a blue Chevy lurched free and swerved off the road. In the filmy haze of that afternoon, it almost looked like the car was heading straight toward us in slow motion.

My mother screamed and pushed me out of the way and I stumbled backward, but with enough time to see the car hit Dad, tossing Joel into the windshield and away. Then all I could see was the car.

I remember the Washington license plate and the broken windshield with spidery veins across the glass.

I remember the driver, a woman who jumped out of the blue car, screaming, "I'm so sorry. I just don't know what happened. I missed the brake. I'm so sorry. I'm *so* sorry!"

I remember my mother screaming, "Where is he?"

I remember people helping my dad up. I remember him walking, then wincing in pain as his leg buckled beneath him. He stood again and hobbled, searching for Joel.

I jumped up and ran for my dad.

"Abby!" Mom screamed as she crossed the line of cars now at a standstill. I caught up to Dad and followed him, gripping the back of his T-shirt. He staggered toward a group huddled around something on the road. Everybody was pushing Dad away until he yelled, "I'm a minister!"—his ticket to join the circle—and then they all just let him through.

Matt was already there with the group, his fists balled up against his sides. He was shaking his head.

"Let me through! Let me through!" I could hear my mother scream. I turned to see someone holding her back. There was something we weren't supposed to see. Something Matt had already seen.

Joel lay on his back. He looked asleep but so different from the way he slept on the beanbag chair in our family room at home. There was blood on the road. Was it Joel's? I knelt down as my dad touched Joel's damp forehead and whispered to him. I wanted Dad to make Joel open his eyes.

"He's bleeding," Mom moaned as she burst through. "Where's he bleeding? Where's he hurt?"

I studied the growing pool of blood and realized it was coming from Joel's ear. Matt stared as if straight through Joel to the pavement below.

"Somebody call an ambulance! He's bleeding!" Mom cried as she stood to plead with the growing audience. And then Mom saw the woman from the blue car. "You hit my son! It was *you*! *You* hit my son!"

Dad grabbed Mom's arm to keep her close, away from this woman who stood crying, clutching the hand of her little girl. Maybe it was the sight of the little girl holding her mother's leg, sobbing in fear. Mom turned and knelt back down.

"He needs a doctor," she whispered.

"Don't touch him!" Dad warned and Mom gasped. "Not yet," he said more gently. "Just don't move him right now." Dad put his hand on her shoulder.

Mom caressed Joel's arm and brushed the hair from his forehead. "Oh Joel," she said, crying. "It's all right. Mommy's here. It's going to be all right. Open your eyes, Joel." As she pulled her stained hand away, I saw the blood she couldn't feel.

The strap on Joel's overalls had slipped off his shoulder, and I pushed it back up. Then I remembered I wasn't supposed to touch him. Where was the ambulance? Dad took off his T-shirt and put it over Joel, as if he needed it on that warm summer day.

Right then I knew something was very wrong. "He'll be okay, won't he, Dad?" I asked.

"He's my son," Dad said to someone hovering over us. But not to me. Still, I was satisfied with the answer. Dad had always taken care of everything. "We have to do something," Dad said, his voice hazy, as if a cloud had suddenly covered the warmth of that day. He looked around at the growing congregation. "We have to get him to a hospital."

"He's not breathing, John. I don't think he's breathing!" Mom exclaimed as Dad bent over and listened.

"Is there a doctor?" Matt yelled and then ran through the

growing crowd, even stopping at the cars stalled in the train of traffic. "We need a doctor! Are you a doctor?" Matt banged on car windows as he ran farther and farther away from us.

"Heal him, God," Dad said softly. I thought Dad should remind God that He had a Son, too. I really wanted to pray with him, but the only thing I could remember from Sunday school was the Twenty-Third Psalm, which began with "The Lord is my shepherd" and had that scary line about the valley of the shadow of death.

A fire truck, the sheriff, then finally an ambulance arrived in quick succession. A woman with red hair kept repeating, "He was in his dad's arms." One officer took her aside to question her while another officer talked to the woman from the blue car. The men from the white ambulance broke our circle and dispersed the crowd, then huddled over Joel, blocking our view. Not a minute later, one man stepped back and announced, "He's got to go *now*."

"I want to go with him," Dad said as a man in a uniform placed Joel on a cot in the back of the wagon.

"Don't leave me, Dad!" I cried, choking on the forgotten melting caramel.

"I've got to go," Dad said as he released my grip.

"I'm going, too," Mom cried.

"Your husband's been hit," one officer said, pointing to Dad, who stood with his weight on one leg. "He needs to go with your son, ma'am," the man explained. "You can ride in the sheriff's car with her." He pointed at me. Mom stood, slack-mouthed, as they helped Dad into the ambulance.

"Where's Matt?" I asked, suddenly feeling strangely alone. I looked across the faces and trail of cars. "Where's Matt?" I repeated more urgently. "Wait for Matt!" I screamed, but nobody was listening.

"Where are they taking him?" Mom asked, and then I realized

we didn't know the way. We were strangers here. And where was *Matt*?

"St. Luke's," the officer said, "Bellingham." But where was that? They slammed shut the back of the ambulance.

As the siren screamed and the wheels turned, I saw Matt running to catch the ambulance, knowing he had been left behind.

And suddenly it was over and they were gone, leaving Mom and Matt and me standing there in the summer sun, by the side of the road, which was so very hot on our bare feet.

TWO

I've always wondered if Joel heard our prayers as we stood over him on that sidewalk.

When we arrived at the hospital, we ran into the emergency room looking for Dad. A nurse at the main desk took us to a waiting room, where we stood around until a doctor arrived. Mom studied his face and then slowly shook her head as she backed away from him.

"No, no, no!" she said, louder and louder, as if she could make it not true.

"I'm sorry, Mrs. McAndrews." And then the doctor turned to Matt and me. His eyes looked sad.

"No!" Mom cried out. "Don't say that. He was just here! He was fine! The car wasn't going that fast!" Her voice pleaded as she gasped for breath.

"His head struck the windshield and then the road," the doctor continued. "The brain injury was more than he could survive. He never suffered," he added, as if that would make us feel better.

Matt slipped out the door and I didn't know if I should go to him or stay with Mom. Mom sat down and began to sob so loudly I couldn't hear myself cry.

Joel is dead, Joel is dead, Joel is dead. I couldn't believe it. I started shivering, and I couldn't make myself stop. Was it my wet bathing suit or was the hospital so cold? I smelled like salt water. My hands tingled and I shook them back to life.

"Where's my husband?" Mom's voice was paper thin.

"They're treating his leg," the doctor answered.

Mom stood shakily and staggered. I rushed to steady her.

"Oh, Abby." She wrapped her arms around me. I held her and she held on to me, and I never wanted to let go of her again.

The doctor waited and then escorted Mom into the second room down the hallway. He talked with Mom and Dad in Joel's room while Matt and I sat outside the door on folding chairs. I could feel wet sand grind against smooth metal. When I took Matt's hand, he didn't pull away.

I watched the sterile black-and-white clock on the wall, the second hand circling and the minute hand shifting almost imperceptibly. I could anticipate each subtle movement. How long would they stay in there?

When the minute hand had moved more than seventy-two times and I had stopped counting, the door opened.

A doctor pushed a man in a wheelchair. It was my dad in a blue robe, but not really my dad because he didn't seem to notice us. I don't know what he was staring at. I started to say something, then closed my mouth.

"Dad," Matt said as he slid his hand from mine and stood. But Dad didn't turn. At last Matt put his hand on Dad's shoulder and Dad turned to look. That face is the one I don't want to remember. A rope of fear tightened across my chest. I could hold Mom's sadness, but Dad's grief was overwhelming. He seemed broken in a way I wasn't sure could be fixed. The clock behind Dad now read 4:27, and then the hands blurred with my tears as I watched them wheel Dad down the hall.

I wanted the day to be over. But then again, if the day was over, my brother was really dead. Today Joel had been alive. If only we could go backward, our afternoon would be morning and we'd wake up and Joel would say, "Get up and play with me, Bee!" and this would not be happening.

When we returned to the cabin, Mom rummaged through our suitcases, laying out Joel's clothing on the bed. The little suit from the wedding, another pair of overalls, a few shirts and shorts.

"I don't know," she said. "I just don't know."

Neither did I. What was she doing?

"They asked what we wanted him to wear. . ." Her voice drifted off. I picked up the suit and threw it back in the suitcase. Definitely not that. Then Matt removed the shirt with the scratchy tag on the back. We were left with a T-shirt and Joel's blue overalls.

That night we went to bed with our clothes on. Now there were just four of us. This was our family. I closed my eyes and then quickly opened them, staring at the ceiling for so long my eyes felt dry. My stomach growled. We hadn't eaten since the candy, but I wasn't hungry. My mind would not stop. Oh, to sleep and never wake up.

"You're having a nightmare!" Matt whispered as he shook me awake later that night. "No!" I cried out in a strange voice, the memory of yesterday rushing back. I had fallen asleep? I actually fell asleep even though my little brother had just died? How could I have fallen asleep?

In the other room my mother wept, a soft, haunting moan, accompanied by the unfamiliar sound of my dad's low, muffled sob. Whenever my eyes adjusted to the darkness, I could see Matt on the cot nearby, his eyes wide open, staring straight ahead. Somehow I wanted it to be a shared secret that we were all awake. As if that could be a secret.

Dad wouldn't leave Joel in Washington, so the congregation sent money to have Joel's body transported by train back to Ohio, and

Dad would ride with the body. Mom had to drive Matt and me all the way home. Our same bags were loaded into the same purple station wagon, ready to return on the same roads, yet nothing was the same.

I needed to say good-bye to Dad, but he'd left early that morning. It seemed Dad couldn't leave Washington fast enough, but how could he go without saying good-bye? Suddenly good-byes seemed so much more important. *Gossamer*. Life was so delicate.

Our car felt empty. Mom in the front, Matt in the middle, and me lying in the back. Matt never talked, and I had yet to see him cry. Mom was silent, too, her eyes locked on the road, occasionally blinking hard as if to stay awake, or sometimes to hold back the tears. If I could have read their thoughts, I wouldn't have. My sadness was enough for me alone.

"I feel sick," I said, after two hours on the highway.

"Crawl up here with me and look out the front window," Mom suggested.

The front seat was Joel's special place. Joel always sat on her lap or curled at her feet. That was not my place. I climbed into the middle seat and sat next to Matt, then cranked the window open and hung my head out like a dog.

I reached forward and flicked on the radio only to hear about a war I didn't understand. All those unfamiliar words and acronyms that didn't want to be explained, *Cambodia* and *Kent State* and *Tet Offensive* and *North and South Vietnam* and *POWs* and *MIA*. Those casualties were too far away to comprehend. Especially when my own battles seemed more real.

When we hit eastern Washington, the temperature soared to one hundred and four degrees, and we were so miserable we had to peel ourselves off the sticky vinyl seats. We rolled the windows up and sweated until we were wet, then rolled them down so the wind cooled us. "It's evaporation," Matt explained dully. Was it this hot for Dad in the train with Joel's casket?

We didn't ask, "How much farther?" or "When are we going to get there?" After all, would getting home make anything better?

This was the end of our first family vacation. With Dad's sister getting married and Grandpa's heart attack, the timing was right for Dad to go home. I had looked forward to standing under the Peace Arch, where I could straddle the border of Canada and America and say I had stood on foreign soil. But life had turned from happy to sad as easily as heading west and returning east. We had left for a wedding and were returning home to a funeral.

I imagined how the journey would be if Joel were still with us. I considered his toes tickling the rear window as we lay in the back of the station wagon. In Montana, when we drove by a bear and a baby cub in the forest, I wondered what Joel would have said. I did a double take when I saw a small boy in overalls with a diaper-fattened bottom, thrown in the air and caught by his daddy. In the Dakotas, we stopped at a roadside park, but I didn't want to play on the swing set. There were too many preschoolers. When we bought groceries in Wisconsin, I instinctively looked for Cap'n Crunch with Crunch Berries and Hostess CupCakes. But by the time we hit Ohio, when we returned to the car, I stopped counting to check if we were all there.

It was all about split seconds. One followed by another. And we couldn't make them go backward. If we had known, we never would have gone. We would have unpacked the station wagon and said, "Not this year." Or we could have played longer on the beach, or we could have skipped buying the candy. I could have stopped complaining for the length of a heartbeat. I could have held Joel's wrist a split second longer.

I thought about that a lot, and it made me wonder about

God. And about what He stops and what He doesn't. And I know it's not because He can't. My dad preached about a good and loving God who can do anything, but now I didn't know what that meant.

THREE

I wish someone had put away his toys. The blocks set out like roads running through the living room were lonely without his beeping and buzzing cars. His color crayon drawings of Curious George covering the coffee table were silent without his narration.

Matt ran up the stairs and I heard a door slam and music blare. Mom walked through the house as if seeing it for the first time. I followed her path until she stopped at the back door, where she knelt down and bowed her head. Was she praying? I stood frozen in sunlight.

"It's his fingerprints." She traced a circle in the air in front of the glass door. "All over the glass. Look. It's Joel."

Smudges everywhere. I could picture Joel standing at the door waiting for Dad, waiting to call out, "Daddy's home!" as he pressed his nose and hands against the window. No warm circle of breath remained, just fingerprints everywhere.

Mom took charge of planning the memorial, alone. Her mind was focused. She gathered pictures of Joel—as many as she could find for a third child. She looked for color. Matt's and my childhood pictures are black and white, but everything about Joel was in color.

On the day of the funeral, I wore yellow and sat in the balcony. If it were July 12 instead of August 12, 1970, Joel would be with me drawing pictures. Someone said they'd never seen a casket so small. I'd seen dozens of funerals because when Dad delivered a eulogy, Mom played the organ, and we sat in the back pew. I was probably more prepared for a funeral than anybody, but I'd never seen one for a child or for someone I loved. This time, it was *my* family surrounded by men in black suits and women with quiet voices.

I spied my best friend, Rita, and her mom, Miss Patti, and that made me want to cry. I scanned the pews looking at all the people who loved Joel and cared about us and could find almost everyone. But Miss Mary Frances and Uncle Troy were noticeably absent.

Uncle Troy is not really my uncle, but that's what we call him. He lives three doors away and is married to Miss Mary Frances, and don't ask me why we don't call her *Aunt* Mary Frances. She's my piano teacher and Uncle Troy is the head usher, a huge, imposing man with thick, black-framed glasses and a broad chest that makes him look like a bear. But I think he's the sweetest man at Bethel Springs Presbyterian because he gives Matt and me a round peppermint candy every time he hands us our bulletins.

In the dog calendar I hang over my bed, I renamed the dogs with the names of people I know. The big old Great Dane is Uncle Troy and the wiry dachshund is Miss Mary Frances. They make quite a pair.

The kids in the neighborhood are kind of scared of Miss Mary Frances. They think she's too particular about her plants and crabby about our noise. Mom lovingly refers to her as *eccentric* or *peculiar*. She was once the junior high band director, handing out brass instruments to the girls, claiming they were gifted with a high tolerance for pain. "Childbirth," she explained as if she herself had delivered three or four kids. She's tough and demanding, but I know her differently from all the Sundays I spent in the church library, hidden beneath her worktable, curled up with a book at her feet, when I was supposed to be in Sunday school or church. The Israelites worshipped in a tabernacle tent, but my church tent, a fellowship hall tablecloth, hid me from anyone who might turn in a kid playing hooky. Where was she when I needed her?

The organist was a stranger, hired from out of town so that on this rare occasion Mom could sit in a pew.

The pallbearers filed in, moving the box slowly to the front, and I found Uncle Troy holding one end. I wondered if the box felt heavy or whether Joel was now even lighter than his thirty-one pounds. Joel would want out. My heart raced. *No box should be that small.* Someone had asked if I wanted to draw a picture or write a note to slip inside, as if I wanted to think of Joel trapped below the ground with only my shabby artwork or a message he couldn't read. He wouldn't like being in a box forever and ever. I secretly hoped Dad had slipped him out of there and put him safely somewhere else. Surely Dad would have known what to do.

The church was warm and my gold polyester jumper felt scratchy. It was all I could do not to roll my knee-highs down to my ankles. I took short, shallow breaths of sticky August air, but the balcony seemed short of good oxygen. What a horrible day for a funeral. Funerals should be in winter. Cold. With snow on the ground. Funerals should be for old people. The whispers of consolation were true, *"Nobody should outlive their own child. . . . He was so young. . . such a good boy."*

Joel *was* a good boy. It was Joel who sang the loudest in the preschool choir, dropping his *r*'s and *l*'s. *"Jesus wuvs the wittle ones wike me, me, me. Wittle ones wike me, sat upon His knee. . ."* It was Joel who asked, "Where's *God's* mommy and daddy?" and it was Joel who let go of helium balloons, explaining, "They're for *God.*"

The stranger in the pulpit talked about many mansions. Maybe Joel was playing hide-and-go-seek in his. But was anybody else Joel's age? I hoped he wasn't lonely.

Sun streamed through the stained-glass window of Jesus, with His pierced hands reaching out toward me and the seven children at His feet. Was Jesus opening His arms to my little brother? Was Joel running to Him?

I used to check how many kids were in the window, to see if anyone had run away. But I didn't know why anybody would leave someone who looked so kind. Today I re-counted the children. Though the number stayed the same, it looked like somebody was missing.

A black limousine waited for us. I slipped in behind the driver, who looked like he was paid not to smile. I hoped Matt would climb in after me but Mom followed, sliding her long legs into the roomy interior. Dad and Matt sat in the front. A chain of cars lined up behind us, flicking on their lights as if we'd become separated on the four-mile drive from church to cemetery. No one spoke.

As we drove into Shady Springs Cemetery, I looked out the limousine's tinted windows to see a green tent and chairs. We emerged from the black car into bright sunlight to find a dark pit. I had never been to a graveside service.

A man I didn't know said words about a little boy he didn't know, and I can't remember any of it. Matt was silent, staring out at the field dotted with tombstones. I could read a few nearby. Millers, Smiths, Hughes, Wilmoths. None of them were our family names until now. Polly, Jonathon, William, Sarah. For some reason it was their first names that made me sad, and I didn't even know them.

I heard them crank down on a handle, and the little box lowered into the ground. My heartbeat quickened. The box disappeared. Someone passed out a few roses. Joel always picked the neighbors' roses and brought them to us as gifts. Now we were supposed to give them back. Mom's hand trembled as she dropped her flower into the hole that swallowed my brother. When she gasped, Matt took her arm. My father stood behind them. He coughed to disguise his groan. Dad looked unfamiliar to me—so old and bent. When it was my turn, I kept my flower. No more death upon death.

Before we went back to the car, Uncle Troy took me aside. I looked around for Miss Mary Frances. Why wasn't she here? She was more than just my piano teacher; I always thought she considered me the child she never had.

"I have something for you," Uncle Troy said as he opened his car door to show me a red helium balloon. His big fingers fumbled with the knot until he had the string loosened. Then he handed it to me.

"You know what to do." He pointed upward. "This one's for Joel," he added softly. Together we watched the balloon clear the branches of the great oak tree, rising slowly until it became a dot in the sky, and then nothing.

✳

Our house was filled with families and food and words, but I felt lonely and slipped out the alley gate and into Rita and Miss Patti's backyard. Rita was my best friend; our houses stood side by side, like twin sisters.

Now Rita and I climbed down beside the house and played the game of Life under her front porch while everyone at my house played death. Through the latticework, I could see the legs of Bethel Springs come and go. Car doors slammed, voices murmured, *"Let us know what we can do. . . . I'll be over this week. . . . You need any help. . . Must be so hard for the kids. . . ,"* followed by what I knew to be hugs with the obligatory *pat pat pat* to signal *Let go now.*

After most of the guests had left, we still hid out in our fort. Miss Patti's screen door slapped shut. I heard her support hose scratch together and her shoes squeak above my head as she shuffled along. I was probably supposed to leave, but I didn't want to.

"You girls want some dinner?" she drawled in her thick

chocolate-milk voice after knocking on the side of the house and pausing respectfully.

Rita was a girl of few words. She turned to me, raising her eyebrows. I nodded and she shook her bobbed head as if her mom could see her answer. "We don't wanna get out, though, Mama," Rita added, as if reading my mind.

"That's why I brought it to *you!*" Miss Patti said, her vowels long and warm.

When I was little, I asked Mom why Miss Patti talked funny, and Mom said she was from the South. At the time I thought that odd because Rita said they came from *North* Carolina.

Miss Patti bent slightly to slip a plate under the deck and above the latticework. Rita reached back up for our glasses of milk. As Miss Patti shifted her feet, the deck groaned under her weight.

Rita's mom was fat. Since her name was Patti, there was the inevitable neighborhood rhyming chant *Fatty Patti, Fatty Patti.* I heard *Fatty Patti, Fatty Patti* in my head even when I didn't want to think it. I just hoped I never accidentally called her that.

I even asked Mom for a new word, anything not to call her *fat*, but Mom wouldn't play the word game with me unless I told her why. Matt looked up words in the thesaurus and found *corpulent* and *obese*. I thought they sounded much worse than *fat*. Finally he suggested *rotund*.

But Rita's mom was not just a *little* fat, and she wasn't rotund; she was *enormous*, and I told her so when I was going on five. It was no surprise to her—neither my observation nor that I would actually tell her. She had been kind enough to take Rita and me to the movies. There were no seats in the theater that fit her, so she brought her wheelchair and scooted up to where I sat on the aisle.

"You're big," I said, frowning.

"Yes, I am," she said very seriously, nodding in agreement.

"I mean, you're *huge*," I continued. Rita leaned forward next to me as if she needed another look at her mom.

"Yes, Abby. I am," she said as respectfully as if I had asked, "Are you Rita's mother?" Maybe she sensed I was just a curious four-and-a-half-year-old, or maybe she didn't want her daughter to lose her best friend. Or maybe she appreciated honesty.

"How'd you get so fat?" I asked, as I opened my box of Dots, pouring out two orange ones for Rita and holding out my empty hand for a trade of her Raisinets. Miss Patti paused and then leaned closer to me as if this was a secret for only the two of us.

"I have a monster gene."

I paused mid-Raisinet. This was something new. I had never heard of a monster gene. If someone could make being fat sound positive, Miss Patti sure could.

"A monster gene?" I pursued.

"Every once in a while, in my family, one generation has one enormous person," she continued. "I'm it," she added matter-of-factly as she picked up her soda. "Seems some of us just grow and grow and grow. Unusually large," she added before taking a long drink of Coke. I turned to Rita, who shrugged. I tried not to cringe, but the thought of a monster gene growing and growing and growing, blowing up like a balloon, scared me. Miss Patti held out her hand for a Dot.

"Yellow, please."

"How do they weigh you?" I asked, imagining her teetering on our little bathroom scale.

"Two scales. I put one foot on each." I looked down at her two swollen feet as I sucked on a red Dot, my favorite. "I just add up the total of the two scales," she concluded.

"Just how much *do* you weigh, anyway?"

"Well, let's see," she said, studying me before she winked. She seemed less willing to share this part of the secret. "Guess," she said at last, with a smile. "Just how much do you think, Miss Abigail?"

I had weighed thirty-nine pounds for the last three months. Even when I jumped on the scale I couldn't get it to stick on forty.

"Seven hundred and thirty-nine thousand pounds," I blurted out with little calculation. I loved big numbers as much as big people and so I shot high. Miss Patti considered this for a minute, respectfully giving credence to my outlandish guess.

"Well, at last count I weighed four hundred and eighty pounds. I can only hope it's gone down or I might be half a grand."

"Hmmm." I nodded, almost disappointed with the truth. Miss Patti grinned and put her arm around me as *Mary Poppins* began. Her hand was as soft as Play-Doh and she smelled of pine like her kitchen. Oh, how I loved her. "I think you're *more* than half grand," I said with a smile.

Apparently Rita did not have the monster gene. I used to check her daily, but Rita remained one of the shortest, smallest, and skinniest kids in our school. And if Rita was embarrassed of Miss Patti's size, she never let on. Maybe because in so many ways Miss Patti was the kind of mom everybody needed.

Today she was just what I needed. As well as her offering of macaroni and cheese.

"You girls want anything else?" she asked from above. I looked at Rita and shook my head.

"No, Mama, we're fine," Rita answered. I swallowed half the cup of ice-cold milk and took a bite of the mac and cheese. Miss Patti's macaroni and cheese is full of real cheese and butter, and it slides down your throat in warm and comforting gulps. I haven't tasted better macaroni and cheese.

"You girls thinking of having a sleepover?" Miss Patti suggested. My eyes went big and we nodded to each other.

I pointed to my house and shrugged my shoulders.

"Could you call her mom?" my spokesperson asked, vocalizing our shared wish. And I began hoping beyond all hope that Miss Patti would say yes and convince my mom to say yes and give me the gift of one night away from everything Joel. One night away from the longing to remember and the fight to forget.

FOUR

Mom had painted the beadboard ceiling of the porch a pale blue to look like the sky. Lying on the porch swing, I surveyed her world without clouds. Nearby, a few old quilts hung on a rack for cooler evenings and brisk mornings when Mom and Dad did their *checking in with one another.* That's what they called it when they had their private chats on the porch. They hadn't been checking in with each other for some time.

Back and forth, back and forth, the swing swayed. Five more minutes at the candy shop. Maybe I shouldn't have asked for candy. Did I walk too fast? If I had held his hand, then maybe it would have been me and I wouldn't be here today.

Or maybe, worst of all, maybe it happened because there were days I wished Joel had never been born. I stopped rocking and sat up, nausea overcoming me.

Guilt is even worse than fear. Guilt gnaws and makes me wonder if I have the flu. But I knew I couldn't take medicine or hug the toilet and have my mother massage my head with a cool wet rag. I was in this by myself.

If one bad thing can happen, I knew we had to be careful. Dad left every day for a few hours, running somewhere all by himself no matter the weather. Was he safe? I didn't like the boys Matt was hanging around with. Would he get hurt? And when Mom got in the car, I wanted to go with her in case something happened. I didn't want to be left alone.

Rita ran up the front steps holding an envelope I immediately recognized to be the annual school letter. I usually counted down the days until school ended each spring and then ironically the days until it began each fall. Then I begged for a new outfit and all new school supplies and couldn't wait to find out which teacher I had. Not this year.

"I got Mrs. Clevenger!" Rita said, waving the envelope proudly. "Who do you have?"

I shrugged. "I don't think Mom's gotten the mail."

"I'll get it," she announced as she ran back down the front walk and opened our mailbox. I knew I had Clevenger or Simpson. More important to me was whether Rita was in my class. "Can I open it?" she called out, waving the envelope like a banner, her excitement so unfamiliar. This was as enthusiastic as Rita got, her smile surrounded by her new haircut, which looked like someone had stuck a bowl on her head and cut around it.

She didn't even give it to me; she just ripped it open in our front yard. I think that might be illegal. "Clevenger!" she called out. "We're in the same class!" She ran back up the front walk and sat down beside me on the swing. "See, here's where it says it. Clevenger," she said, pointing at the name as if I needed proof.

"Okay." I smiled slightly. At least *she* was excited.

"Aren't you glad?" she asked. "We're in the same class. Just like in first grade!"

"I'm just not quite ready for school," I tried to explain.

"I don't like it when summer ends either," she sympathized.

Rita folded the letter, put it back in its envelope, and handed it to me. I felt like she wanted to ask a question, but she didn't know what it was; and I wanted to help her out, but I didn't know the question and probably not the answer either.

Four days before the dreaded first day, Mom went up and down the grocery aisles of Food Mart and I followed in her shadow.

Her hollowed eyes seemed too full to hold more sadness. She mechanically pushed the grocery cart past rows and rows of food, up and down the aisles, her heels clicking on the gray linoleum. I looked for a good time to tell her what was bothering me, but I never found it. When we got in the checkout line, Mom's grim stare suddenly turned to grief, and I looked around to figure out what had happened or who or what she'd seen.

"I don't need this stuff," she whispered to me, biting back the tears, her hands outstretched over the groceries, her fingers holding air and quivering. She looked shocked. "I was just shopping like usual. That's all. I didn't think," she said, as if trying to convince me. Mom was fragile. She was falling apart, and I didn't know how to help her.

Mom backed out of the line, then pushed her cart behind a rack of bread, hidden, as if unsure where to go next. She grew flustered, blushing as she studied the cart's contents.

"I'll have to put these things back," she said. "I can't believe I did that." Mom began yanking out specific items and stacking them in the place where Joel used to sit in the front of the cart: Cap'n Crunch with Crunch Berries, a bag of orange circus peanuts, a new bottle of orange shampoo, the Bugle chips he liked to stick on his fingers. "We don't need these things," she whispered. The word *anymore* hung unspoken as she blinked back her tears.

There was no more talk as we hastily went down and up the aisles, returning the items made unnecessary by Joel's absence. I kept my head down but looked out the corners of my eyes to see if anyone thought it strange we were undoing our cart. As we left the store, our load was smaller, but it didn't feel lighter.

The dreaded bad day arrived, my first day of fourth grade.

"Do you think people will ask lots of questions?" I asked, sitting on Matt's bed in my pajamas.

"I dunno." He shoved his gym clothes into his backpack. How I used to envy that backpack, wanting so badly to be big enough to have lots of homework to carry around.

"What should I say?"

"I dunno, Abby," he repeated.

"I don't want to go," I said.

"Then don't." Matt was developing a contradictory nature. At least that's what Mom called it. *Contradictory* or *antagonistic*. New words for a new season.

"You know I don't have a choice," I reminded him, slowly dragging up the sheets on his unmade bed.

"Look, I don't have all the answers, Abby," he said quietly. I looked away. "You go to school and figure out what you have to do."

"Will you be home after school?" I asked at last.

"No, I have football."

"And then you'll come right home?"

Matt didn't answer. That meant no.

"Matt, please?"

"Mom'll be home."

"Yeah," I agreed, realizing she wasn't enough anymore. Just as we weren't for her.

"You'd better get out of those pajamas," he scolded. I nodded and went back to my room as he swung his backpack over his shoulder and headed downstairs without me.

Mom didn't buy me a new lunch box or pencils or pens or a new outfit or even get me new hand-me-downs for the first day of school. And I didn't ask for them. I dug out a few dresses from last year and hoped they still fit, even though nothing really fit anymore.

By the time Mom called for breakfast, almost everything I

owned covered my bed and floor and I was back in my pajamas. I wanted to hide underneath the blankets and sleep all day.

"Abby, the bus'll be here in ten minutes," Mom yelled from the bottom of the stairs. "Come and eat!" I traced my fingers along the chenille tracks of my bedspread. Joel used to run his cars along the pattern as if it were a highway.

I shouldn't leave Mom alone all day. I didn't need all the first day introductions, rules, and the stacks of papers for Mom to sign. And if I didn't go the first day, everybody might just forget all about firsts and leave me alone on the second day. But then again, maybe I'd be the only new person on the second day and I'd really stand out. The third day was probably the best day to start.

By now the kids were lining up for the bus, holding new tin lunch boxes, looking down at their new clothes, and talking about who had which teacher. They were excited to be in a new grade. They were glad to be a year older. They'd go to school and come home to a snack instead of to a mom who may or may not have gotten dressed that day or to a dad who seemed like a stranger.

"Abby! Come down *now!*"

I really thought about pulling on my clothes but crawled back in bed instead. When the bus honked, Mom opened my door and gasped.

"Are you sick?"

"I don't know. I just don't feel very good."

I wasn't very good at lying, and so I hoped this semi-honest answer would pass. Her hand was cool.

"You don't feel warm. Is it your tummy?" Mom sat down on the bed and smoothed her hand over my hair. Well, maybe it *was* my tummy or my head or maybe it was all of me. But somehow I knew she'd never understand what made me sick.

"I could drive you. Dad won't need the car."

"Still?" I asked, thinking that if we went back to school, he should go back to work.

"Dad's taking a sabbatical."

Sabbatical had something to do with the word *Sabbath*, the day of rest. How ironic that a man whose calling demanded working on the day of rest, needed a sabbatical to rest.

"Should I bring you a glass of orange juice or something?" She stroked my arm.

I shook my head. Orange juice wasn't going to fix anything. Suddenly her hand stopped.

"Abby, what's with all the clothes on the bed?" She stood up and surveyed the room, then looked at me with a frown. "This whole morning thing doesn't have to do with being embarrassed about what to wear, does it?"

"No. I don't care what I wear." Did she think I could be that silly?

"Are you *really* sick, Abby?" she asked, biting her lip.

"I didn't say I *was*," I answered truthfully.

"But. . . ?" Mom began.

"I said I didn't feel good and I *don't*," I repeated. "I don't feel very good."

Mom gently peeled back the covers. "If you're not sick, then you need to go to school."

"You don't understand." I pulled the sheets over my head.

"No, I don't. I don't understand anybody and I can't fix anything, but *somebody* has to keep going, and today that somebody's going to be *you*." And with that, Mom grabbed a jumper and a blouse from the heap and tossed them on top of me, heading to my dresser for socks. "Just be a good girl and go to school."

"Just be a good girl. Just be a good girl." If I had been good, would that have changed anything? If I were good enough now, could I

make things better? I swung my legs over the side of the bed.

Mom sat down on the bed, socks in hand. "I thought going to school would help you get away from this." She uncurled the socks. "I thought it'd be good for you to hang out with your friends again and learn something new." Mom moved behind me to start brushing my hair.

"They're going to stare and ask questions. Or maybe they won't talk to me at all because they won't know what to say!" I said, finding it easier to talk when we weren't looking at each other.

She yanked one section of hair into a pigtail and started a braid. It was hard to explain my feelings, but I thought my reasons were strong. "Ouch!" I said, tilting my head away.

"Hold still!" She twisted the rubber band around my hair and started on the other pigtail.

I imagined the horror of walking in with all eyes on me. Would I cry? But if I looked happy, they'd wonder how I could smile after my brother died. They'd say I was like Matt, who had jumped right into football and parties and other things we didn't even know about. *What's wrong with Joel's older brother? Joel's brother hasn't shed a tear. Joel's brother is getting involved with the wrong crowd.* And if I left Mom alone with Dad, would she cry all day?

Mom finished the second braid and shifted so we both sat side by side on the edge of my bed. She looked at the clock and tapped her fingers on my bed as if playing the keys of the organ. The big first day was now five minutes away, and there was no way I'd be on time.

"Get your clothes on. You have art at nine. You can just slip in and everybody will be busy painting or drawing. Nobody will notice."

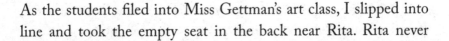

As the students filed into Miss Gettman's art class, I slipped into line and took the empty seat in the back near Rita. Rita never talked, so no one ever sat by her. We might be invisible together. Miss Gettman handed out big sheets of construction paper and crayons. Miss Gettman was short and serious. We always tried to guess why she was still *Miss* since she seemed so old and her name begged to "Get-a-man."

"Every summer has a story to tell," she began as she moved about the classroom. "A picture is worth a thousand words, so instead of an essay on 'What I did this summer,' let's make a collage of our summer memories.

"Rita, what's something you remember about this summer?" she asked as she made her way to the back of the class. Miss Gettman might ask me that same question in front of everybody, and everybody was going to be looking at me and trying to figure out what I would say. And if I wasn't so worried, I might try to figure out what I would say except I had no idea what kind of collage I could make about this summer.

Rita looked over at me and then began talking slowly, deliberately.

"I. . .liked. . .some. . .things. . ."

Bless her for stalling. If Rita talked any slower, the class would fall asleep.

"About. . .this. . .summer," she finished.

"Well yes, Rita. Why don't you tell me one or two of them."

Normally, Rita would have mumbled something and tried to stay out of the limelight. Rita paused and looked around the room. By now Miss Gettman was returning to the front of the class-room. I had eluded her gaze. Tim Neeves threw a crayon from his desk to the new boy sitting next to him and Rita's monologue was over.

"That's not what we do with crayons, young man, and that's certainly not a good way to start out your year." With that, she moved Tim to the empty desk in the back near me and I began a silent prayer that throwing a crayon would be the worst of his offenses.

"I'd like everybody to think of at least four events from this summer and turn them into a beautiful collage. *Collage* means a collection of objects that tell a story. It looks like the word *college* except it has an *a* in it." Miss Gettman sat down at her desk and smiled out at us. If only she knew what adding an *a* to *her* name could do for her. "You can begin," she announced as if we were starting a test. For me, it was worse than a test.

Heads turned as if in question. Shoulders shrugged and kids mumbled. At last Miss Gettman pushed back her chair so fast that it squealed on the floor. Kids giggled and she scanned the room as if hunting for the source of the laughter. Finally she resorted to yet another try at describing her assignment.

"Let's come up with ideas together." She headed to the blackboard and picked up her chalk. "For example, I went swimming this summer." She wrote *swimming* across the blackboard. "I took a car trip to Chicago to see my older sister." And she sketched a car, this time with someone holding a pennant out the window with a big *C* on it. "Can anyone add something?" She looked out toward the back, and I grabbed a crayon and began drawing furiously. Maybe if she thought I was on to something, she'd leave me alone.

The crayon I grabbed was brown. Brown is an ugly color and I hate brown. I don't wear brown, and I don't like to look at it. But somehow it seemed right for my summer picture. Then I picked up purple and began drawing swirls, then black circles, and I even tried yellow. My picture was a mess, but something felt good. One scribble broke the orange crayon; another scribble ran off the page and onto the desk. I could imagine that I was leaving dents on the desktop. I wasn't sure which swirl represented the night we watched fireflies on the front porch, or which swirl was the morning Mom cooked blueberry pancakes, or which jagged zigzag was when a car came out of nowhere and took away my little brother. Although my paper was filled with color, it was not bright. When at last my paper was consumed, I looked up to find Miss Gettman eyeing me curiously. As if, how could I be done already? I looked for a blank spot and pretended to put just one more touch on the page. She returned to her paperwork.

"Write your name on the back, because I'll be displaying these at open house next week."

I looked down at the mess of scribbles. This was not good enough. Joel could have done a better job with his eyes closed. If I ripped it in half, the noise would draw attention. Even if I folded it up, she might spot me trying to smuggle it out.

I carefully slid the sheet off the top of the desk and inside the open shelf. No one could understand my drawing. Not even me. I did not write my name on the back as she had instructed. No one would miss one picture from an entire class. Abby didn't have to have her name and art up on the night of open house. Amid a wall full of cottages and sprinklers and lakes and ice cream cones, no one would notice that Abby's summer was very different from the rest.

FIVE

"Hi, Uncle Troy," I said, opening the door wide and taking the plate of cookies from him. It was raining out, a real fall downpour. Uncle Troy collapsed his umbrella, then opened and closed it, shaking out the water. I was glad to see him again.

"Mary Frances sent those." Troy had offered the plate of cookies but stood there awkwardly as if waiting for something or someone.

"Come on in," said Mom as she joined us. "I'll make some coffee to go with these."

"When I called earlier, you said John was home?" Uncle Troy prompted. Uncle Troy wanted to talk to Dad? Was something wrong?

"Yes. I'll let him know you're here. He's in the basement."

Of course he was in the basement. Last week Dad set up two rectangular tables he had purchased at Salvation Army, hammered shelving behind them, positioned an old space heater near the tables, pounded nail-like hooks at eye level into all the studs, swept the floors, and dusted away the cobwebs. Dad was up to something, but it wasn't a sermon.

"Is there a problem, Troy?" Dad asked, emerging from the basement and closing the door behind him. I thought his question was odd, considering Dad wasn't taking care of anybody's problems lately. Uncle Troy stroked his chin as if about to make one of his serious chess moves.

"Matt didn't come by to rake the leaves," Uncle Troy began as Mom headed to the kitchen. That wasn't unusual; Matt dropped every ball except the one on the football field.

"Oh, so that's what this is about. I'll talk to him," Dad said.

"Actually, that's not why I'm here." Uncle Troy looked toward the kitchen and his cup of coffee. "I'll sit down and wait for Renee."

The grandfather clock ticked in the background. *One* one-thousand, *two* one-thousand, *three* one-thousand. Why couldn't they say something, anything? Matt took the stairs by twos, a bag tucked under his arm, and had nearly escaped before Dad called out, "Hey, Matt, Mr. Collins says you didn't rake the leaves. You need to do your job."

Matt nodded first to Uncle Troy and then to Dad, and raising his eyebrows in a way that would have gotten him in trouble if Uncle Troy wasn't sitting on our couch, said, "We *all* need to do our job," and shut the front door behind him. Mom returned with cream and sugar and two cups of coffee.

"Look, I know this has been a difficult time," Uncle Troy said. "The elders met and we're trying to keep an interim in place, but we also think it might be good for you to be around your congregation. The people who love you."

"I don't know when I'll be able to return," Dad said.

"I understand," Uncle Troy said. "Just remember, it might not be so much about the *church's* needs as *yours*, too. About how *you* might need the church, your friends," Uncle Troy continued softly. He adjusted his tie and took out a handkerchief to wipe his forehead. Uncle Troy looked stiff and uncomfortable.

"Troy, sometimes I don't even know if I can come back," Dad added. "Ever."

Mom frowned.

"I understand why you might feel that way now," Uncle Troy repeated as if he couldn't think of anything else.

"No, I don't think you do," Dad answered.

"Abby, why don't you go on upstairs?" Mom suggested.

"She can stay," Dad said. "This will be short." Then to Uncle Troy, he said, "Is there anything else?"

Uncle Troy took a deep breath. "Mary thought it might help if I talked to you."

"It won't," Dad said. "And it's presumptuous for you to walk in here and think you can fix things."

"John, maybe you should hear what he has to say." Mom looked over at Uncle Troy, who looked sadder than I could ever remember.

"Renee, he doesn't even have any children," Dad said. I was embarrassed. Dad never treated anyone like he was treating Uncle Troy. But Uncle Troy wasn't leaving; in fact, he had more to say.

"That's what I wanted to talk about." Uncle Troy hesitated. "Maybe I do understand a little. I've lost someone, too. So maybe it would help to share."

"But he wasn't your son," Dad said shortly.

"No, but I lost someone, too." Was Uncle Troy talking about Joel? It didn't sound like it. "It's a terrible thing to lose a child," he continued.

"You think you know?" my dad said. I bit my lip. I loved Uncle Troy, and Dad was being so mean. We all lost someone.

"You really think you know?" Dad repeated.

"I do." And with those two simple words he silenced my dad and created a huge gap only he could fill. We waited for whatever was coming. "We were pretty excited about having a baby," he said at last. "Took a long time, but then one day we found out we'd be parents," he explained. "Mary Frances quit working and we got ready for the baby.

"Our daughter was born in November. A beautiful baby girl. But she was stillborn. They don't know what happened. We named her Caroline Ann." Mom sat down slowly on the couch. Her face had gone from surprise to joy and then gently crumpled in pain as

Uncle Troy's words took on meaning. *Revelation.*

"Mary Frances was in the room for so long, and finally they came out and told me the baby had never taken a breath. I thought I couldn't breathe. I hurt all over. I didn't know what to say to Mary, so I just went in and held her."

"Oh, Troy, I never knew," Mom said sadly.

"Mary never wanted to go through that again. I would have liked to try. I wanted a child. I wanted another daughter. Or a son."

"I'm so sorry, Troy," Mom added. Dad stared straight ahead, unmoved.

"That's not the same at all," Dad said. "I had Joel for over three years."

I couldn't believe he said that. That wasn't my dad. Mom's face squinted in pain, and she took Uncle Troy's hand. My stomach hurt in a way it never had before.

"No, I don't suppose we can compare pain or grief. I just wanted you to know that I experienced at least a measure of it. I thought that by sharing. . ."

"Okay, that's enough." Dad stood up to indicate it was time for Troy to leave.

"John, he's trying to help," Mom defended.

"Well he's *not.*" Dad walked out and headed toward the back porch.

"I'm sorry, Troy," Mom apologized. "I know you meant well. Maybe after he thinks about it—"

"I was really angry back then, Renee," Uncle Troy interrupted gently. "Mary and I pulled away from each other. Those were hard times. And so when I see you two"—Uncle Troy looked at Mom and to where Dad had disappeared—"I feel like I'm reliving those days." Uncle Troy took Mom's hand. "We want to do whatever we can for you. You're like family." Then Uncle Troy let himself out the front door, but before he left, he turned once more. "People care; they just don't always know how to show it."

"Thank you, Troy. Give our love to Mary." After the door closed behind him, I ran out and gave him a hug good-bye. I wasn't Caroline, but I could be Abigail.

When I came back inside, Mom and Dad were arguing again.

"He had no business coming over here and telling me he knew what I was feeling."

"He didn't say *that*. He just said he understood."

"Same difference. And he can't understand. He had a daughter for a minute and maybe not even that."

"John, you're heartless! Sometimes I don't recognize you anymore. He's your friend, and he came to help."

"And that's what I'm saying. He *can't*." Dad was yelling now. "How is that going to help? How is *anything* going to help? I don't want to hear it and I don't have to."

And Dad showed her he didn't because he left us and slammed the door to the basement.

✳

When Mrs. Clevenger kept me in during recess for a talk, something didn't sit well in my stomach. I didn't dislike her, but she wasn't Mrs. Jennings, my third-grade teacher. After five weeks of school I didn't really know her and she certainly didn't know me or, more importantly, Joel.

According to the framed pictures on her desk, she had three kids who looked like they were in junior high or older. One picture of her husband and her boys was taken near a boat; they all looked happy, and the water in the background went on and on and on.

Out the window of our classroom I could see the kids on the swings. Back and forth, back and forth, higher and higher, crescendoing arcs like a pendulum nearly out of control. When the girl in the middle stopped pumping, the pendulum lost momentum. I wondered if that was how life ended, just a swing-set ride that slowed, slowed, slowed. The boy on the end let go and jumped clear over to the sandpile. The kids around him cheered. I smiled a faint ovation.

Mrs. Clevenger made some noise and said something I didn't understand. The jumping boy now swung off the rings. Mrs. Jennings, my old teacher, went over to check on him. She would do that.

"Abby, I spoke with Mrs. Jennings."

I turned back to Mrs. Clevenger. I loved Mrs. Jennings. I wandered by her room before school every morning and sometimes spent indoor recess there. When I was in room 32, I could sort of pretend it was still last year.

"She says you spend a lot of time outside her classroom." I hung my head. The two had conspired.

"Abby, can you tell me about these?" I looked up and my face warmed to see a stack of crumpled pages now smoothed: the homework I had never turned in, assignments I had wadded and left in my desk or the garbage can or maybe even hidden in my coat pockets. The newly uncurled pages revealed jagged scratches and scribbles and rips consuming the short story with a beginning but no end, the unfinished worksheet, and Roman numbers that didn't add up. How could X, L, V, I, and C be numbers when letters were for stories?

"*Can you tell me about these?*" No. Besides, I sensed she really wanted me to talk about something even bigger.

"Abby, do you ever feel like talking. . .talking about Joel?" Mrs. Clevenger asked. Could she read my mind? If so, I'd have to be more careful what I was thinking about. Or at least maybe throw out a tricky thought and see what happened. *Pink elephant. Pink elephant. Pink elephant.* "Because if you want to talk, I'm here," she continued without seeming to notice any pink elephants.

I bit my lip and shrugged. What else was there to say? He was gone, gone, gone. No one could bring him back, and the hole he left was consuming my family.

"He was three?" she asked.

"Almost four," I corrected. *Don't pretend you know*, I thought. Outside, the boy who jumped from the swing began scaling the monkey bar gym. My mom hated those metal cages. She was always afraid one of us would lose our balance, hit our head, or slip through the holes and fall to the ground.

"That's pretty rough to lose a little brother."

She couldn't know.

"You must miss him."

I thought about the empty crib in my bedroom storing our old stuffed animals. I considered the fuzzy monkey named George no one would touch because it was Joel's favorite stuffed animal. Even when Joel outgrew the crib, he wanted to keep it as George's cage. I wondered why Mom and Dad hadn't taken away the crib, and why I was stuck with that reminder. I wanted to be angry with Dad for not dismantling it. I wanted to be mad at Mom for ever putting Joel in my room in the first place so that I would feel his absence. So that I would miss the sound of his breathing at night, and his nose peering through the bars as he waited for me to wake up in the morning. "Play with me, Bee!" Dad needed to take down that crib. Dad needed to do a lot of things.

"How's your dad doing?"

She was reading my mind again. If she wanted Dad in here, she should call Dad in for a conference. He needed this little talk, not me. I didn't have to say anything I didn't want to. I was trying to be good, and if I did things right this time, we all might be okay. My heart raced and my head felt dizzy.

"I have to go to the bathroom," I said and stepped out, turned down the hall, closed my eyes, and let the stars fall into the darkness. *Why did she steal my papers? Why did she read them?* I clung to the door frame until the dizziness passed.

When my vision cleared, I saw the school secretary typing. She was *oblivious.* That was one of my favorite words Mom had taught me. Did I look as bad as I felt? In the bathroom, I ran the water until it was cold and waited, periodically splashing my face. The tingling in my hands subsided slightly as I shook them out, but my legs still felt wobbly. I gripped the gray marble sink to brace my weight and counted to sixty before I returned. Mrs. Clevenger hadn't moved, and all the kids from my class played outside. They were free.

"Abby, it's okay to be sad," Mrs. Clevenger said. "I watch you and sometimes..." She hesitated so long that I looked up. "It makes me want to cry."

Well, that made two of us.

"I just want you to know I'm here if you want to talk." She leaned forward and folded her hands across her desk. I felt like the little girls out on the playground who quit pumping. The pendulum wound down, and inside I was so tired and my head hurt and before I could control myself, I was crying.

Mrs. Clevenger pushed a box of Kleenex across the desk but didn't say anything. Neither did I. She tricked me. When someone says, "I care," or "I understand," it makes me cry even when I don't want to. Even though crying sometimes feels good and releases the pressure. So if I said anything right now, it would be all over and I'd have to say everything, and so I stopped crying and stopped talking and the pressure built and my head pounded. Enough to make me a little scared.

"And so you probably feel afraid?" she asked.

I nodded. I thought about all the nights Mom woke me up saying, "Shhh, shhh, it's just a nightmare." And then I answered in a whisper, "A little." *Pink elephant. Pink elephant, Pink elephant.* The lady was a mind reader. How maddening. I frowned so hard it hurt.

"Maybe angry, too?" she asked. I didn't respond. I wanted to leave. She wasn't Mrs. Jennings. She wasn't my friend. Maybe if I thought angry thoughts, I would not cry. *You are mean. You are mean. You are mean.*

"Am I the only one you're mad at?"

"No," I said, too easily.

"Then I'm in good company." She smiled slightly. She was not going to make me smile. "So tell me what's going on, Abby."

What could I say? Where would I begin? I stared beyond her.

"Give it a try, Abby." At last I sighed and blurted out something about everybody else.

"Dad's not going back, Mom's going on, and I don't know what Matt's doing!"

"I remember Matt." She smiled in remembrance. How nice to see somebody talk about Matt and smile. "He was the kid who could explain anything," she bragged. "Did you know that when I taught something new, I asked Matt to help the struggling students so they could understand?" Mrs. Clevenger paused. "I thought he'd be a teacher when he grew up."

She didn't need to convince me. When we unwrapped new games at Christmas, it was Matt who read the directions and translated them for the rest of us. He taught me to sound out letters and showed Joel how to pedal his trike.

"The funny thing about Matt was that he was a really good kid." And then she laughed and shook her head as if recalling a great story. "But he could really get himself into trouble." Her face sobered. "He's in trouble, isn't he, Abby?"

I nodded. Matt had always been accidentally in trouble. As early as I could remember, Mom and Dad would debate whether he deserved a spanking for his "accidents." But his naughtiness was so innocent, they just couldn't punish him.

Now he was not accidentally in trouble. He was deliberately in trouble. I knew it, but Mom and Dad didn't. Matt left at all hours with the wrong kids and acted like he didn't need any of us. What was I supposed to do? If I said something, would it make everything worse? But if I did nothing, would something bad happen?

If Joel were alive, this never would have happened. Matt would not have disappointed his greatest fan.

Matt not only passed down his mitt, foam baseball, and toddler-sized basketball; they came with loving instructions on how to catch, dribble, and throw. Joel proudly wore the hand-me-down glove as Matt carefully tossed the ball into Joel's extended mitt.

When Joel died, it felt like I lost two brothers. Mrs. Clevenger would never understand that. I wondered if Matt's truancy had red-flagged him, like a referee in a pickup game of flag football. If my grades were bad, Matt's could only be worse.

"And Joel?" she continued. She must have taken my silence as an unwillingness to talk about Matt.

"He's not coming back and I miss him." I looked down and closed my eyes as tightly as I could. I would not cry. I counted *one* one-thousand, *two* one-thousand, *three* one-thousand. . .and then blurted out, "He's not coming back and so nobody else can come back. It's sort of like reading a sad book I can't get out of my head."

I looked up at her and I held the tears back. I was almost proud of what I had said. It sounded so logical, and I didn't even cry.

"You did a good job of describing your feelings," she said,

confirming my analysis. A nearly imperceptible weight lifted, and I took a sudden breath in relief. "Mrs. Jennings showed me some of your stories from last year. You could be a writer. You have a way with words."

Any other day and I could have smiled. I did love words. Words that were magic. Words that could heal. Where were my words now?

"You haven't gotten to the end of the book, Abby," she reminded me. "And it doesn't have to be sad."

The school bell clanged and I winced. Neither one of us moved. The recess lady lined up the classes, and Mrs. Clevenger looked out the window to check on her students.

"Recess is over," she said at last. "Can we talk again another day?" I considered her offer and nodded. "Come in anytime you need to talk, Abby. Remember, you can't change anybody else. But you can write your own story differently."

SIX

The October afternoon was cold and quiet, and the half-naked trees surrounding our church cracked in the wind. The sidewalks leading up to the front doors were littered with leaves, and I wondered how long before they'd be covered with snow.

When we opened the heavy wooden doors to the sanctuary, Mom disappeared into the darkness and I slipped into the back pew.

Mom laid out the bulletin across the top of the organ and surveyed Sunday's assignment, her first Sunday back at the organ.

Mom opened *Organ Introits and Offertories* and played "Holy, Holy, Holy," stumbling so badly, she flipped to the second hymn. Mom's struggle with the notes made the melody unrecognizable. I had no idea what she was playing. Finally she resorted to "A Mighty Fortress Is Our God," as if she needed the reassurance. I made my way up the center aisle and sat beside her on the bench.

Because our organ faces forward, Mom's back is to the congregation. But with her personal rearview mirror, Mom can watch the bride make her entrance or spot the pallbearers arriving with the casket. When she plays the organ, she looks like she is driving a bus straight through the purple curtains at the front of Bethel Springs Presbyterian, and I'm sure there are many Sundays she would enjoy doing just that.

I leaned back and looked at her face in the mirror. Then I leaned forward, and I saw myself.

I don't look anything like her, which is not a good thing. My mother's dark brown hair is lush and thick and almost out of control. My thin brown hair is stick-straight. Her skin is ivory, and I have freckles. Mom's nose is little and turns up slightly at the end; mine is long and straight. Lots of the ladies at church say, "You'll grow into your features," and I'm sure it's not a compliment. Mom almost never wears lipstick because her lips are full and a rich shade of burgundy. My smile is all teeth like Mom's, but not nearly as straight and organized. And when I grin into the organ mirror, my lips nearly disappear in a thin colored-pencil line of pink. Her eyes are green and mine are a mixture of brown and gray, but when her eyes twinkle, I can almost imitate them. Especially if I practice. Sometimes the eyes tell me I am her daughter.

When Dad and Mom first came to Bethel Springs Presbyterian, one of the deacons asked Mom if she had any organ background, and she nodded yes. Unfortunately, no one has arrived to relieve her of the bench. The deacons probably have their regrets in "hiring" her, and I imagine finding her replacement is most likely an anonymous request on the church prayer chain.

I used to enjoy sitting with her on the bench. When I was little, I fussed so much in the toddler room that Mom bravely endured my busy fingers during church. In quiet moments she took my pudgy hands with her long, slender fingers and held them securely so I couldn't disrupt the service by plunking the key for the lowest pipe in the sanctuary.

I always tried to copy her hands as she played. Sometimes she would quickly brush my hand away while trying to keep pace with the hymn. Other times, she plucked my fingers off the keys between verses. But she gave up as I grew older and more experienced, realizing I was merely copying her notes an octave higher and we were playing a unison duet of sorts.

But I quit sitting on the organ bench in kindergarten when she tried to clean my face in the middle of a service. I vowed then and there I would never spit on a handkerchief and wipe egg off anybody.

Even today Mom could not play the fancy arrangement of "Near the Cross." Though the time signature is ¾, she had no feel for 1-2-3, 1-2-3. I tapped my fingers on the console to keep her on tempo. Usually the congregation can stay together if some brave soul stomps a foot to the beat. When Mom's foot slipped off the pedal, I decided I wasn't much help and that it embarrassed her having an audience.

"I'll go check out a book," I said and left her alone.

When I opened the door to the library, I was surprised to find Miss Mary Frances pasting neat rectangle pockets into new books.

"Can I help?" I asked, trying not to breathe in the smell of rubber cement. And then I remembered what Uncle Troy had told us and wondered if she knew that I knew or if Uncle Troy had relayed Dad's mean words.

"I can always use some help," Miss Mary Frances answered, almost putting my fears to rest. Maybe Uncle Troy had spared her. "Could you flip through the file cards and look for overdue books?"

I loved the file card holder filled with three-by-five cards. Date. Name. Returned. I loved the straight blue lines where I could sign my name. Once my goal had been to check out every book in the library so that every time someone took down a book, they'd see my name.

But today I knew to look for anything over a month after checkout and was pleased to pull six cards from the stack.

"Done!" I proclaimed. "Six late books!"

"That would have taken me quite a while, young lady!" Miss Mary said, smiling at me. "Now, how would you like to paste these stickers in the front of these books?"

I read "*Given in Loving Memory of* _____ " scrolled across the stickers.

"I don't know," I said. *In Loving Memory.* That was like old, dead flower arrangements. I didn't want my name at the front of a book and to be famous for *dying*; I wanted people to remember I *lived.* "Maybe I could file the returned books instead?"

"That's a better idea." She took the stickers back.

I studied the letters and the numbers on the spines and found their exact locations. The order and precision of the library pleased me. I scanned the children's books, knowing the little kids always stuck them back in the wrong places. One picture book about the life of Jesus was in backward. I opened it, remembering it was one of Joel's favorites, then flipped to the back pocket and took out the card. There was his name. The *J* was backward, but the rest was readable.

"I helped him," Mary Frances said, almost apologetically, as if she had cheated. "He made the *J*, but I wrote the rest," she added over my shoulder.

I smiled. Somebody would remember he lived.

When Mom came down, she looked surprised that I wasn't alone and stood hesitantly at the door as if an uninvited guest. Like me, she probably worried how much Miss Mary Frances knew about Dad's treatment of Uncle Troy. But as we filed the remaining books, Mom was drawn in and began surveying the typed categories Scotch-taped to each shelf: Old Testament. New Testament. Presbyterian History. Commentaries. Family.

"Death. Loss," Mom said, brushing her fingertips along the spines of another row. "Nothing on death and loss." I turned to Miss Mary Frances, who didn't even look up as she painted rubber cement.

"Try Grief," she said, and I wanted to scream, *We have!*

"Nobody says anything that helps." Mom dropped her hands to

her sides. I wanted to hide beneath the table. To be a kindergartner again.

"I know." Miss Mary pressed the *In Memory* rectangle across a page. "There really isn't anything *to* say."

"But you might share...," Mom prompted.

"No," Miss Mary Frances said sternly. Though I couldn't read Miss Mary's face, I knew she was not angry. "But I could *listen*," she concluded. "That's all I can do."

I thought about that. I wondered if anybody had ever wanted to listen to her talk about a baby who never took a breath.

Mom turned toward the window, her back to Miss Mary Frances, as if unsure how to begin.

"They just want to tell me why I *should* feel better so *they* can feel better. I'm supposed to get on with life." She sat down at the table across from Miss Mary Frances as if they were close friends, when the only connections they had were my piano lessons and two terrible and unexplainable losses.

"Joel's been gone two months, and yet it's almost like my friends have forgotten. Like it never happened. Why do you suppose that is, Miss Mary? Why don't people talk about him anymore?"

I knew the answer, and I think Mom did, too. They wanted the sadness to be over. If they mentioned his name, we would remember him, it might make us cry, and that would make them uncomfortable.

"Matt goes to school, Abby goes to school, and John goes to the basement or out to I don't know where. That's when there's no Joel. I miss him all day."

Miss Mary Frances took Mom's hand and put it between her paper-thin ones. Why wouldn't Miss Mary say something, *anything*?

"He was in his daddy's arms," Mom began slowly, really looking at Miss Mary Frances. "But it wasn't his fault." And then Mom retold the story in tears and gestures. Questions unleashed, questions I had never heard. But then, who could she have asked? The ladies from her circle, which Joel had called her "round" meeting? Certainly not. *"How could it happen? The car wasn't going that fast. Why couldn't John hang on to him? It was our first big family trip. Why then? What's going to happen to us now?"*

Too many questions. When Mom finally took a deep breath, she exhaled out all the weariness and exhaustion. I hadn't seen her cry that hard since that awful day in the hospital waiting room.

"They want to help you forget," Miss Mary Frances answered at last. "But you can't," she said with a sigh. "You never will forget. And the memory of him—even with all the pain—will always be sweeter than if you could."

That night, when I went to bed, the moonlight illuminated Joel's crib and his toddler bed nearby. I could see his stuffed animals, caged and lonely, some with their arms hanging out of the bars. I wanted to fall asleep and forget about the day, but when I said my prayers, I couldn't stop thinking, *"If I should die before I wake. . ."* I didn't want to die. Not yet. But it seemed so possible, especially when I had to stare at that crib. I tossed. If I fell asleep I might dream terrible thoughts.

Then the door opened a crack and light spilled in a long, thin strip across the floor. I wondered if Dad was thinking about me or the empty crib. And then I realized I was now the youngest child, the baby of the family.

"Good night, Abby."

If I said, "Good night," he would just leave. Not at all like my first memory of him when he used to rock me to sleep. Every first memory should be of being held. Maybe every last one, too.

"You used to read to me," I said and waited. Would that make him close the door, or would he stay?

"This is George. He lived in Africa," Dad began, sitting down on the bed. I held my breath. Joel's favorite story remembered. "He was a good little monkey and always very curious." We had grown to love Curious George because our own Curious Joel had brought the monkey to life. Dad stopped.

"Remember how Joel liked when Curious George fooled the fire department?" Dad asked. "How many times did Joel try dialing 1-2-3-4-5-6-7, just like George?"

"Too many." I laughed.

"Remember his birthday?" Dad asked. "He wore that silly bandanna hat the whole day. And everybody got a red balloon," Dad said softly. "Everybody got a red balloon, just like George."

I wondered if it was a good time to tell Dad about Matt. Or if I should tell him that tonight I would probably have another nightmare or that Mom cried when she went to the grocery store or that I had a lot of missing homework. Or that I had wasted the lunches Mom packed, the ones that cost us something when we had little income, throwing them away instead of bringing them home so Mom wouldn't ask for an explanation. But that would mean I'd have to describe a feeling in my stomach I didn't understand. I might be really, really sick and that worried me, too. Where could I begin?

"Dad?"

"Yes, Abby."

"You need to be nicer to Uncle Troy."

Dad sighed heavily. "I was wrong."

"And Dad?" I continued, trying to figure out how to say the next thing. He had listened once; he might listen again. "It's *my* room now. I don't want that bed."

His breath was a shuddery intake and he didn't say anything for what seemed like minutes.

"I can see why," he said at last, his voice gravelly. Then he cleared his throat and continued. "I'll take it down tomorrow." Dad didn't move off the bed, maybe contemplating the empty place in the room. Then he bent down to kiss me, and I felt a tear fall on my cheek. When he closed the door, the strip of light disappeared, but the crib was bathed in moonlight for one last night.

SEVEN

Before Joel was born, I started asking questions about having babies. So many that Mom sat Matt and me down to have a little talk. Mom was always direct and honest. She didn't show us any funny little pollywog pictures or talk about birds and bees or even read from *Wonderfully Made*. My mom had plenty of new words for us that day. *Intercourse* was one of them.

While Mom attempted the talk, Matt frowned and fidgeted. In a few minutes, I went from being curious, but happily oblivious, to understanding why sometimes ignorance is bliss. Asking a lot of questions might not always be the answer. I liked thinking it happened because of a watermelon seed, although I have to admit that in kindergarten when Kevin Moretti said his mom loved watermelon and never spit out the seeds and that's why he had four brothers, I stopped eating watermelon for a whole year.

"The baby grows for nine months and then when it's ready to come out, you'll have a baby brother or sister," Mom explained happily.

Matt rubbed his hands on his legs. I kept tucking my hair behind my ears.

"Can I go now?" Matt asked.

"Do you have any questions?" Mom sounded like my kindergarten teacher.

I shrugged, Matt looked up at the ceiling, and the screen door slapped shut. Dad was home for lunch. Perfect timing. "What's up with you three?" he asked, plopping down on the couch between us.

I looked at Matt and he looked at me and he kind of shrugged and then I giggled. I swung my legs back and forth, and Matt scratched his head. Mom bit her lip to keep from laughing. Dad raised his eyebrows and turned from Matt to me and back again, searching for an explanation.

"I feel kind of left out. Did I miss something? Is this some sort of secret gathering?"

"So I guess you had to do it three times? Huh, Dad?" I said.

"What's this about?" Dad asked, turning to Mom. "Renee?"

"Just explaining a few things, John. You can finish where I left off," she said, heading to the kitchen. "I'll make lunch." She winked at Dad, who turned back to us, shrugging, his eyebrows lifted in a question.

"She told us about the baby. About s-e-x," I whispered. "Ick."

Dad's face reddened.

"But she didn't say how the baby gets out," I added, knowing I was missing some of the information.

Dad could preach on Revelation, but he couldn't teach the facts of life. Matt said he had heard quite enough and marched upstairs, and so Mom finished our family life lessons the next day without Dad's help.

I was excited about a new baby, but Matt seemed apprehensive. That's when he told me about Mom's sadness. It made sense since there are so few baby pictures of me compared to the hundreds in Matt's leather scrapbook. I think of mine as unphotographed memories. The kind you don't want to remember.

There is one black-and-white photo where I'm on my mom's lap, but she isn't really holding me. She seems unaware of the camera, gazing beyond it. A bottle of milk sits on the end table and Mom's nightgown looks sloppy and unkempt. I finally took it out of my scrapbook and hid it in the bottom of my sock drawer. I found a few other photos—Dad holding me up to the sun, Matt tickling my nose with a feather, and a few of GramAnna holding me cheek to cheek.

I couldn't remember those days, but Matt could. He considered it another of God's failings. Matt hadn't wanted to relocate from Dad's first church in Madison, Wisconsin, to Bethel Springs, and he hadn't asked for a sibling. And then God failed the five-year-old boy who flicked the light switch on and off outside the bathroom door to try to get his mother to stop crying while his baby sister screamed from the end of the hall. God failed the kindergartner who stood at the bus stop alone on the first day of school because his mother couldn't push herself out of bed. God failed the boy who wanted to play catch with the dad who needed to heat TV dinners, change diapers, and then head out to visit the shut-ins.

When Matt told me the story, I apologized to the brother who was everything to me.

When Joel was born, Dad nicknamed him "the little pumpkin," and when he came home three days later, I thought he looked more like a squash. Mom called it jaundice, and they kept a watch on his color. And then everybody kept a watch on Mom.

Whenever Matt came home from school, he first ran to find Mom. Dad watched her as if out of the corner of his eye and never stayed at the office the whole day. He brought her special lunches from a restaurant downtown, and they took long walks pushing the stroller. Why wasn't Dad concerned now?

If for some reason I had previously been the cause of sorrow, Joel was the cause of great joy. When she sat in my bedroom nursing him, I looked longingly at the tender way she let his fingers curl around her forefinger as they rocked back and forth. She'd caress his head and press her lips to his forehead, and I knew that she really loved him. "Abby, do you remember this song?" she'd say and then begin the lullaby, "Have I Told You Lately that I Love You."

The melody and lyrics were unfamiliar and I couldn't remember her ever singing them to me. But I knew that if Mom loved this baby, she had to have loved me, too, and she still did.

It would be a lie to say I had always loved my brother. Once I nearly ran away from home because I didn't want to share a room with him, and another time I nearly lost him, quite accidentally.

The sanctuary had always been Joel's favorite place. When he was a baby and Mom practiced the music for Sunday services, he lay in a laundry basket on top of the organ, seemingly soothed by the low, rumbling tones. But when he learned to crawl and then walk, she brought me along to watch him. We had our own version of the game of hide-and-go-seek. Joel would always hide behind the pulpit and I would pretend I didn't know it.

"I wonder where Joel is today," I'd yell, louder than he needed, as Mom pounded a hymn on her console.

"Hmmmmm, I wonder if he's under *this* pew." And I'd stick my hand beneath and hear him giggle from the front of the church. "Joel? Oh, Joel?" I'd call out. "Oh dear, I think I've lost him."

That got him every time. "No, Bee, I here." And then he'd come out and run for a big hug and we'd play the game all over again with the same results.

But one day both Joel and I were lost until he was found.

"I'll bet he went up in the balcony," I said as I climbed the stairs, announcing to no one except the little boy crouched behind the pulpit.

I played my usual game but he didn't play his. When at last I popped behind the pulpit, he was not there. At first I wasn't worried; I figured he had finally caught on to the game and picked a new hiding place. I looked under every pew and table and increased the boundaries to include the entire second floor and then the basement, at last ending up in Dad's study, where I assumed I'd find him sitting on Dad's lap as they rocked or wheeled his office chair.

"What's up, Abby?" Dad asked as I sat down facing his desk.

"Joel and I were playing hide-and-go-seek and..."

"He's playing preacher?"

"No, I can't find him."

"Well then, let's go look together," he said, getting up.

"No, Dad, I've looked everywhere and I can't find him."

"Where's Mom?" he asked.

"She left to run an errand."

"Did she unlock the front doors when she came in?"

I shut my eyes, trying to remember entering the heavy sanctuary doors, and then ran to check. The front doors were unlocked; Joel could be anywhere. Within a half hour, our church friends were combing the streets looking for him.

Two hours later, I slipped back into the church. The lights behind Jesus were off and the sun wasn't bright enough to illuminate Him. By the dim-colored light from the stained-glass miracles, I could make out the benches and could hear soft breathing. Dad had just returned from his search and sat down on the front pew, bent over in prayer.

I quietly made my way up the aisle. It was my fault Joel was lost, and now everybody would hate me. I thought about all the times I was jealous of the attention he got and the times I was angry about the way our family had changed, but they were small in comparison to the way Joel had changed us for the good.

I felt a horrible coiling snake in my stomach that threatened to emerge from my throat. The skin of my face was prickly and my eyes stung. I tiptoed past the pulpit and took one more look behind it, as if I'd find Joel still hiding there. At last I collapsed on the back choir pew, right where the thick velvet curtains dropped to the floor.

And there he was, fast asleep, half-covered by the soft folds of purple velvet spilled around him. His sanctuary.

"Daddy, he's here!" I whispered.

"What?"

"He's behind the pew, asleep. We never checked the side pew in the choir loft." Joel had found a nook I had not discovered until now. He had really learned the game.

Dad walked slowly to the front, as if in disbelief, and then ran up the steps. We both stared at Joel as if he were a newborn, curled up sucking his thumb, his coat over him like a blanket. Dad reached over and picked him up. Joel's arms draped over Dad's shoulder as Dad whispered, "I found you. You're it."

✸

On October tenth, the day Joel would have turned four, Matt said he was going to the movies. I didn't think that was right. Mom never questioned what he was doing or who he was hanging out with or how he was paying for things, but I did.

We didn't have school the next day, so Rita had invited me over for a sleepover, but how could I leave Mom alone? As worried as everyone was about her with Joel's birth, somebody had to be concerned about his death.

"You're going," she said to me. "It's good for you to get out with Rita." She gave my shoulder a squeeze. "And Matt needs to get away, too," she rationalized. She needed to believe Matt was doing the right thing. How could I tell her the truth?

Mom couldn't know that the indoor theater was playing *The Computer Wore Tennis Shoes*, but Matt wasn't going there. Some of his new friends knew how to go to the drive-in without actually driving in. This drive-in was by the cemetery, and it didn't run Disney films.

The graveyard overlooked the big screen. Matt had told me kids climbed in the holes dug for upcoming funerals, poking their heads out for a perfect view of the big screen. He used to think that was morbid or disgusting. When *Psycho* played, Matt stopped taking showers for a few weeks. With all the talk around school about some scary shower scene, I figured he had gone to the pit. The last few Saturday nights he had spent behind a tombstone or in a hole in the graveyard. Tonight he was seeing *Rosemary's Baby*.

"What time is the movie over?" Mom asked as Matt threw on his letterman jacket. "Matt, that coat smells terrible!" she said. It reeked of smoke and Matt backed away, shoving his hands into his pockets.

"Mr. Paoletti is such a smoker," Matt said too smoothly, and Mom accepted his excuse too easily.

"So when are you coming home?"

"Nine, I think," Matt answered, looking away. I could tell he was lying. Couldn't she? Should I say something?

"Who's going with you?"

"I'm just meeting the guys over by. . .by the church," Matt stumbled. Lying wasn't always easy.

Mom not only accepted "the guys," but Matt's meeting place linked him with church friends, and so she didn't suspect a thing.

I bit my lip. Matt looked over at me and shook his head. I didn't know what to do. Maybe it was just one more movie. Still, that funny feeling in my stomach grew. All the times I hid a lie wound more yarn on my ball of guilt. I wondered if there was a way to pull at the end and free it all.

"Well then, let's go!" Mom said cheerfully. Matt frowned until Mom explained, "No, I'm not going to the movies with you!" She laughed at his open mouth. "I'm going over to Miss Patti's with Abby."

Then it was *my* look of surprise that made Mom smile.

"Don't worry, I'm not spending the night. Miss Patti invited me over while you and Rita play. But after that, I'm going home. I won't ruin your party."

I picked up my sleeping bag and overnight suitcase complete with stuffed animals, dolls, nightgown, and toothbrush, and then Mom and I walked next door.

Our Indian summer was lingering into October, with the leaves turning magnificent shades of pink, burgundy, orange, and gold. The leaves scratched at the sidewalk and swirled into a whirlpool of dancing colors. I stood in the center and watched the leaves surround me, each crackling a secret and magic whisper.

Rita came out with her Footsie and demonstrated how it worked, swinging the tethered ball in 360s while she hopped over the rope. Like jumping rope, it demanded coordination, but Rita was really good. I crunched the leaves along the walk, avoiding leaf-covered cracks. *Step on a crack, break your mother's back. . .* Mom and Miss Patti sat on the front porch, just within earshot.

"I like it that Rita has a friend like Abby," Miss Patti said. "It's good for all of us. Company is good." Rita and I ran off to play Barbies and Yahtzee. When we returned, Mom was still there, eating popcorn with Miss Patti.

Rita and I curled up under a blanket and talked about our Halloween costumes. I was going as a television set, and Rita was going as a ballerina. I had found an empty box in the church basement and painted a black square on the front, but I was still searching for antennae. Mom said we could untwist a hanger. She was always resourceful. *Innovative.*

"You're not going to be scared out there, are you?" Miss Patti teased.

"Of course not. We're almost *ten* now," I declared as if that were a cure for all fears.

"Well, I'm more than three times that and I still have a few worries," Miss Patti exclaimed.

"Well, I'm older than you are, so that means I have even more!" Mom added.

I never thought about Miss Patti being any age at all or that Mom was older than her.

"I thought big people didn't have so much to worry about," I said and immediately regretted saying *big*. "I mean big like old people. But you're not old, I just mean. . ." And then I stopped and shoved another handful of popcorn in my mouth. Rita nodded. She didn't seem to notice anything.

"Actually, I think we have *more* to worry about," Miss Patti said.

"Like what?" I said, cautious but curious.

Miss Patti paused for a minute and then too easily rattled off her list.

"We worry about burglars, our kids, paying the mortgage, losing our jobs, and. . .and other things."

"Now you tell me what *you* worry about, Abby," Miss Patti continued. I couldn't answer right away. Did she mean strange noises at night or that I might get hit on the playground or that Matt might get sick and die or that my mom and dad might not ever really talk again? Too much to consider. Mom frowned. What did Mom want me to say? Was anything safe? What could I tell her?

"Start with the hardest one," she said, as if reading my mind.

The hardest? How could I put my fears in order? I wished it were as simple as Mrs. Clevenger classifying the hardness of rocks from diamonds to talc. Ever since Joel died, there was a lump of fear that stuck in the center of my stomach, threatening to consume me. It was smaller than the ball of guilt, but it fought harder for space and was fed by thinking about everything that could happen to us. And sometimes I couldn't tell why I was afraid. How could I put something in order that didn't have a name?

Mom had stopped swinging and was staring at me. Rita was tugging at the threads of the blanket. They were waiting. I had to say something. Anything. I knew my *biggest* fear, but I couldn't talk about *that*. I looked straight at Miss Patti and tried to think of something to say. And then out came something completely unplanned.

"That I'd accidentally call you 'Fatty Patti.'"

My mother's mouth fell open but no sound came out. I could hear what she would have said if she weren't immobilized by shock. *How could you say that? Apologize to her. Abigail Renee, that was terribly rude. I can't believe you said that!*

I couldn't believe I said it, either. Out of the corner of my eye, I saw Rita. My cheeks burned. To embarrass my friend by humiliating her mother was beyond forgiveness.

Miss Patti was fixed on me. I didn't look away but pursed my lips together and frowned. She stared at me and nodded, a little smile, then a hearty grin widening between her full cheeks. Miss Patti had perfect white teeth and the most beautiful smile. And then out came her generous laugh. A deep bell-like tone resonated in the open air. Miss Patti seemed to laugh on both exhalation and inhalation.

At first I didn't join in, but then after nervously surveying my mom—who had thankfully joined in—and then finally Rita, I giggled slightly. Miss Patti was laughing so hard now, I wasn't sure she could stop. Mom kept gasping for breath, and just when I thought she could laugh no more, she started another round, tears streaming down her face. It was so good to see Mom not only smiling, but laughing. Laughing like she used to.

Sometimes, before Joel died, we'd play a family game like Twister or something and be laughing so hard we'd fall on the floor together, and then Dad would tickle us until we could giggle no more. That was a long time ago. *Hilarious. Exhilarating.* Those were the words Mom taught us back then. The word I learned on Joel's birthday was *juxtaposition*. My definition was "joy standing side by side with grief." I had realized that even though I was sad, I could laugh again.

And the strangest thing was, I no longer feared I'd call my best friend's mother Fatty Patti.

EIGHT

I wish I had a fancy name," I said, practicing *Abigail Abigail Abigail*. "A name like Kimberly or Cynthia or Pamela or *Sandra*." I licked my eraser and scrubbed my name so clean, I wore a hole in the page. Now I would have to throw away that paper, too. Despite my longing to learn cursive, the letters came out all wrong.

"Abigail is a nice name," Mom replied, her back to me as she peeled carrots at the sink.

"Dad just picked it because it's in the Bible," I said, pouting, now writing a new line of *Abigail* across the page, each name bolder and angrier.

"Nothing wrong with that," Mom said. "Abigail was an important peacemaker. Besides, he could have picked Dorcas or Huldah." She laughed as I frowned at the mess in front of me. "Or how about Hagar? Or Zipporah?" She turned to me briefly, then wiped the window with her towel. "Isn't practice usually over by now?" She peered out the window into the darkness.

Of course it was. It was over long ago. Matt never came straight home, and she should know that.

I held up my page, now pockmarked with erasure scars. It was an embarassment. I was supposed to circle the best words, but none were good enough.

"Besides, you weren't exactly named after David's wife." Mom put the pot on the stove and dried off her hands.

"But that's what *Dad* said." I scribbled out the last *Abigail* on the line.

"Well, I'm glad *he* thought so," she explained as she turned back to me. "But I wanted Abigail after Abigail Adams, who was married to John Adams, the second president. That makes her our *second* First Lady. A very strong woman." Mom rested her hand on my shoulder. "And you're my first lady." I felt her kiss the top of my head, but then she froze and I knew what she had seen as she quickly reached for my paper.

"Abby, why all the scribbles? What are you doing?"

I crumpled the paper into a ball before she could get it.

"Wasn't that your homework?" Mom grabbed my hand. "Weren't you supposed to turn that in?" She pulled my fingers apart. "Are you just throwing your work away?" Her voice was desperate. The homework was bad enough. What if she now found out about all the uneaten lunches she packed?

Mom uncrumpled my mess and smoothed it out on the counter. I couldn't turn that in and she knew it. There was nothing good in that line of Abigails.

"What's wrong, Abby?"

I shrugged. She wouldn't understand that Abigail wasn't good enough. And it wasn't just in penmanship. It was Roman numerals and rock formations, and keeping my room clean, and telling the truth about Matt, and my upcoming volcano project, which I was terribly far behind in. The project Dad had once promised to help me with much the same way he had with Matt's project years before. But if I said anything, Mom would be even sadder.

"Abby, this is serious. I don't know why you're doing this, but I want to help you."

Matt came in from the back door and dumped his football gear near the washing machine. The odor of dirt and perspiration threatened to overpower Mom's chicken soup.

"Oh, P-U!"

"Leave me alone, Abby." He picked up his practice jersey and put it under my nose.

"Yuck! Get that away from me!" I jumped off the seat. "You're late!" I tattled, thankful for a distraction.

"So?" Matt shrugged. "You wanna make something of it?"

"Don't start, Matt," Mom said. "You're supposed to come straight home after football."

"What time is it anyway?" Matt asked. Every clock in the house was off the wall and being cleaned. The clock on the oven was our sole navigation.

"No excuse," Mom said.

Matt poured milk over his Rice Krispies, his usual post-practice snack. I leaned over to hear them *snap, crackle*, and *pop*.

"Get your hair out of my cereal!"

"I'm just listening," I argued.

"You two stop fighting." Mom looked at the two of us with a slight smile, as if she might actually be pleased.

"Don't you have to *know* something about clocks?" Matt asked, opening the tool chest Dad left on the counter.

"Dad used to sit by his grandpa while he worked. By the hours." She studied Matt's reaction. "Those are his grandfather's very same tools," she added as Matt fingered the pieces lightly.

"Dad didn't want the farm; why does he want the clocks?" he asked.

"I don't know," Mom said. "Maybe because you can see what you're working with." She smiled as if pleased with her analysis. "I mean, I never liked vacuuming until I had kids."

"What does vacuuming have to do with this?" I asked, happy my homework was no longer the topic of concern.

"I like vacuuming because I can see a change. Nice smooth streaks across the shag carpet. I can see when I'm done." Mom sliced a loaf of bread. "It's different with kids. You never know if they get it." She pulled apart the slices. "And you're never done."

Clocks, farming, preaching, being a mom. I tried to make some sort of connection and wondered if it'd be one of those things I'd understand later. "Clocks were made to do something. They're precise. I think that's why he likes to work on them. Dad can fix them," she added with a sad smile.

Dad came in from his run. His face was flushed and he wore a sweatband around his forehead. Except for the fact that he didn't have fancy athletic gear, I had to admit he looked like a runner. We never questioned *why* he was running. Maybe we all knew the answer. We just didn't know *where*. "The usual route," was all he'd say.

"So you're the *Clock Doc?*" I teased. Dad tilted his head to the side.

"That's not a bad name," he said at last, nodding his approval.

And so that evening I ran downstairs to see what Dad was up to in the basement, hoping he'd help me with my science project.

Though Dad had turned into a recluse, he didn't seem to mind when I hauled over a stool and sat across from him. The room ticktocked with a variety of clocks hung on the nails in the studs. A few clocks lay on the shelves, some clocks were in mid-operation on one table, and a grandfather clock took up the other table.

"So what time is it *really*, Dad?"

"Hmm?" Dad murmured softly as he concentrated on where to squirt a drop of oil. He frowned so hard his eyebrows nearly met in the center of his forehead. I listened as the clocks ticked in *cacophony*. Mom's word for the week. In another ten minutes, the clocks would fight over the precise moment to announce the hour.

"What time is it?"

"Pick a clock," Dad said.

"But which one? How do you know the *real* time?"

Dad inserted what looked like a tiny screwdriver into the back of the clock, and I began to wonder if I'd have to wait ten minutes for an answer.

"Is there one clock that's really *right*?" I tried, hoping I wouldn't make him mad. Dad set the screwdriver down and set the clock upright. "Greenwich Mean Time. GMT, for short. Hourly signals are sent out. We coordinate by them." He spoke in shorthand. "The Royal Observatory in Greenwich, England," he added as if that would explain everything.

"Sort of like the North Star of time?"

"Good question, Abby." Dad smiled and nodded, removing the glass from the face and then oiling another part. I had asked a question and Dad had answered. It was sort of like old times. "Some clockmakers have a special clock to set their clocks by. Some have a Vienna regulator; it's weight driven. It has a constant source of power and is reliable," he explained. "I set my clocks by my grandfather's old clock." Dad showed me the Seiko 70 and then asked me a question. "Now, Abby, here's one for *you*. You asked, 'What *time* is it?' But I'm asking you, what *is* time?"

That was too easy. There must be a trick.

"Some people think it's measurable; some people think it's just a way of talking about measuring events," Dad continued.

"So how come you know all that stuff?" I asked. It was easier to ask questions than to answer his trick ones.

"Astronomy and a few philosophy courses."

"Astronomy has to do with time?" With my science assignment pending, this was a perfect lead.

"Well, they do kind of go together. The moon measures the seasons of time, but we need clocks to measure the minutes and the hours. Can you think of anything else that measures time?" I thought about the sundial at our grade school, but I was afraid to answer because Dad was talking and I didn't want him to stop.

"Sometimes people burned candles to measure time. Or how about an hourglass?" he asked. "A captain needs a clock to be accurate or he sails off course and can't determine his position. But for the high seas, it can't have a pendulum!" Dad almost—almost—laughed. And then he returned to his work and I watched. The ticking of at least five clocks measured time.

"I have a science experiment. It's about rocks and time and change. . . ," I began. "I might need a little help." *Or a lot of help,* I thought to myself. "We studied the hardness of rocks and the order from talc to diamond. We studied three types of rocks. Metamorphic and sedimentary and ig. . .igna. . ."

"Igneous," Dad finished.

"That, too," I agreed.

"You know, I think Matt had to do something like that once. Ask him about his volcano project. I'll bet he remembers."

Didn't Dad get it? Didn't he remember he had helped Matt? I felt embarrassed about asking for his help. I had thought if I could figure out something to do with clocks or astronomy or rocks, I could have Dad's attention and time. But I was wrong.

NINE

Look what I made!" I displayed an old T-shirt to Matt, on which I had written #72 in permanent black marker. It was a big weekend. Tonight was #72's sixth football game and the night after was Halloween. Dad hadn't gone to one of Matt's games yet, but Mom and I hadn't given up hope.

"Do you even know what position I play?" Matt ignored my shirt and turned to Dad, who sat behind the paper, drinking a cup of coffee. "Or my number?" he asked a little louder.

"Seventy-two!" I said, holding up the shirt. *Please don't fight. Please don't fight.* Tonight could be good.

"Offensive line and defensive tackle." Dad filled in the rest and then lowered his newspaper to point out an article from the front page. "There's been some vandalism at the cemetery. Some kids have been tipping headstones."

"How disrespectful," Mom said. "And #72, you'd better get your uniform out of the laundry room."

"I wouldn't want to hear about any of *my* kids doing that." Dad folded his paper and eyed the two of us. I thought of Joel's tombstone so solid in the earth. It wasn't going anywhere. Then I thought of Matt watching movies in empty graves. He wouldn't push over tombstones. Or would he? I studied his face. He didn't look guilty. But could I tell?

"Do you remember that volcano project you did?" I asked. "I have to do one this year." Fourth grade was a long time ago for him, but an exploding volcano had to be significant enough to remember.

"That was a mess," Matt said. Dad shook his head at the memory, and Mom laughed and rolled her eyes. I think she had misgivings about us doing it again.

"Could you help me with mine?" I pleaded first with my eyes, then mouthed *please* with my lips.

"Abby. . ." Matt drifted off and looked over to Dad, who was back in his newspaper. Mom gave Matt a go-ahead nod. "Well, it *was* pretty cool," he answered. "But I don't know."

"Matt, do you want to take Abby trick-or-treating tomorrow night?" Mom asked suddenly.

"Okay, I get it," he said. "I'll do the volcano, but I'm too old for the candy thing. Besides, I have a party."

"Oh really? Where?" Mom sat down with her cup of tea. Matt looked over at me, as if making some sort of agreement. "Some kids from the team are getting together." I had my doubts about what kind of party he was going to, but I didn't want to risk losing my tutor, even if he was only doing it to get out of trick-or-treating.

Matt slept in on Saturday, tired from the big win we didn't see. After I practiced my piano, he called me outside where he held out a bottle of Orange Crush.

"Thanks, but it's kind of early for soda," I said.

"It's not to drink. Hold your thumb over the top and shake it for thirty seconds." While I shook the bottle and counted in my head, he continued, "There are three types of volcanoes. We're going to make the caldera kind. It's the champion."

"Twenty-eight, twenty-nine, thirty," I said.

Matt waited a few more seconds. "Okay, take your thumb off."

The soda shot out, spraying into the air and foaming down the sides of the bottle. My hand was sticky and wet. "Cool!" I laughed at the orange mess.

"That's what happens when a volcano blows. But for ours, we'll use vinegar and baking soda. It makes a chemical reaction," he explained. "But first we have to build the volcano. And it takes lots of layers, so we need to get started now."

Matt took me down to the basement, where he spread out newspapers and a piece of cardboard. Then he told me to mix flour, salt, and water to make wet clay. Matt then set a bottle in the middle of the cardboard and we covered it with clay to form a mountain. Though it looked far from done, we left it for later. Matt said we'd add more layers over the next few days.

That night was chilly, but Mom took Rita and me trick-or-treating to the neighbors on our short street. If we hurried up one side of the street and down the other, we could do it without wearing coats—coats always hid our costumes. Whites', Henrys', Miss Patti's, Petersons', Scotts', Uncle Troy's, Morettis'—eight houses total, counting ours.

My favorite Halloween stop was at Uncle Troy and Miss Mary Frances's house, because they were always excited to see us.

"My goodness! Who's this?" Miss Mary Frances asked. "Troy, will you look here: a television and a ballerina. Who on earth could they be?"

Miss Mary Frances dropped a huge Hershey candy bar in each of our sacks.

"Well, Mary, we could give *strangers* another candy bar, don't you think?" And Uncle Troy dropped another candy bar in each of our sacks.

"It's Abby and Rita!" I blurted out, and we all laughed.

"In that case, here's *another* one for each of you!" Uncle Troy smiled, seemingly pleased with himself.

Then it was back to Miss Patti's, where she sat on a bench on her front porch, covered in a white sheet with holes for her eyes and arms. I've never seen such a large ghost. More like a cloud.

She was unmistakably Miss Patti.

"Whoooooooo's at my dooooooooor?" she hooted.

"She sounds like an owl," I whispered to Rita and we giggled. It was funny until she reached out and grabbed us both, holding us close. I knew it was her. But still!

Miss Patti gave out Dots and Milky Ways and invited Mom to stay while we finished off at the Morettis', where we collected a haul of Tootsie Rolls and a load of grief.

The Moretti house was really decorated. Fake spiderwebs dripped from their trees and porch. I had always thought spiderwebs were so pretty until then. The Morettis set skeletons next to their VOTE DEMOCRAT signs like dead people sitting on tombstones. Election Day was close but wouldn't compare to two years ago when we'd chanted, "Nixon, Nixon, he's our man, Humphrey goes in the garbage can." Of course, the Morettis reversed the chant. When I found out the Morettis attended the big brick Our Lady of Mercy Catholic Church on West Maple, I was surprised. Our church was so full of Republicans, I didn't even know Democrats went to church.

"So what're you doing *after* the party?" Kevin Moretti asked us as we left his yard of bones, his younger brother Kyle tagging behind.

"Just playing at Rita's."

"Wanna have some *real* fun?" Kyle continued. "We're goin' to the graveyard."

I thought he must be crazy. One visit to the cemetery was enough for me and certainly not on Halloween. Couldn't he just hang out in his own front yard?

"Abby's scared," Kevin taunted.

"I'm not scared." I looked to Rita, who was turned away and studying something hanging from the tree.

"But not in the *dark*." Kyle's voice rose and fell. "And not on *Halloween*," he said in his creepiest voice.

"What's the difference?" I asked.

"You have to be *brave* to go on Halloween," Kevin hissed.

"That's ridiculous," I said, my frustration growing. "You're just..." I couldn't find the right word. "Aggrascusting."

"What did you call me?" Kevin asked.

A word I had made up, combining *aggravating* and *disgusting*. He wouldn't know the difference.

"Aggrascusting," I repeated as if in a spelling bee. "The condition of being both aggravating and disgusting." Maybe Mom's dictionary game was paying off. Kevin and Kyle both looked insulted by my creation, though neither would challenge it. But they would retaliate.

"Your brother will probably be there!" Kyle taunted.

"No, he won't!" I answered too quickly, knowing full well he might be there already.

"Are you *sure* about that?" he sneered. Kyle knew enough about Matt. Maybe even more than I did.

"I'm sure *you* won't be there to check it out." I seriously doubted they were brave enough to head to the cemetery tonight.

"But your brother *will* be there," Kyle said slowly, daring me to say otherwise.

And then I had the perfect answer, but it had to have a well-timed delivery. I would call his bluff. I stared him down and let a long pause grow between us. When he assumed he'd won because I hadn't answered, I executed the one line to silence them both.

"Yeah, you're right. *Both* of them."

The Moretti brothers stood openmouthed. And for once they both shut up. I bit my lip trying to hold back the pounding in my head. I couldn't cry. Not now, so I turned and walked as slowly as I could back up the sidewalk, leaving Rita behind, but as soon as

I closed the door behind me, I ran to my bedroom, yanked off my television box, and flopped face-first on my bed.

I might have won, but I had lost.

TEN

I had almost forgotten that wonderful feeling of anticipation and how to look forward to something. That is, until the Ludemas' annual square dance and hay-bale maze, my favorite fall event. I was pleasantly surprised when revisiting good memories fueled a happy sort of expectancy. Hope snuck up on me.

The Ludemas' farm boasted the most beautiful barn in the county. Its base was rock and mortar, the sides were red planks, and the roof black tin. But my favorite spot was the silver silo that was a wonderful chamber hall.

When it was empty, my voice echoed off its tall metal and cinderblock walls. But in late spring, freshly mown grass was blown into the top of the silo. As the silo filled and the grasses fermented and settled, there was no space for an amateur alto or her legato echo.

Fastened along the exterior of the silo were metal ladder rungs, which Mr. Ludema scaled to reach the platform at the top of the silo. There he could check the height of the fermenting silage, his memorable balding head in the shadow of the silo's shiny dome.

Melody Joy Ludema was my good friend, second only to Rita. She was named Melody because Mrs. Ludema said she wanted to keep her in her head and heart. I hoped Melody wasn't too much of a disappointment, since Melody couldn't hold a tune.

One Sunday when we were seven, our Cherub Choir sang "In My Heart There Rings a Melody" for the choral introit. We had eight singers, but the other six usually didn't show, leaving me and Melody: the preacher's kid who sang alto, and the girl with the musical name who only mouthed the words while in performance.

So I sang with gusto, turning it into a harmony solo. Each time I arrived at Melody's name, I blurted MELODY in her face. Considering we Presbyterians sang all three verses and three choruses, her name was everywhere and I proudly announced it all fifteen times. With my less-than-cherubic behavior, I shouldn't have been surprised when she quit choir.

For tonight's potluck, Mom had made her favorite recipes of chili and corn bread, and that afternoon she and I had made three apple pies. The aroma of cinnamon, apples, and cloves made our house smell warm and loved. Mom let me roll out the dough and cut leaves to decorate the top of each crust. It amazed me how the combination of lard, flour, salt, and water could make such a flaky crust. Yet three of the same four ingredients were the base for my volcano, which was growing by layers in the basement and would never taste good topped by the apples picked from the trees in the Johannsons' backyard.

We drove out beyond town, where farmland replaced houses, and when we arrived at the Ludema farm, Dad parked on the grassy field near the silo. I jumped out of the car with one of Mom's award-winning pies to see how the barn was decorated.

"Be careful!" Mom called out. "Don't drop it!"

Red-checked cloths covered the tables, an area was cordoned off for square dancing, and Christmas lights hung from the rafters. The smell from the stalls on the floor below wafted up, and I inhaled deeply. It smelled clean and earthy. In the haymow above, a maze of bales would keep tunnelers busy all night. The annual Fall Festival was always a church highlight. The night should have been perfect.

I climbed the ladder to the top floor of the barn to check out this year's maze. The high school boys from youth group had stacked bales to form a narrow and intricate path with periodic holes where they could reach their arms through to scare an unsuspecting tunneler.

I crawled into the narrow entrance, and within a few feet I couldn't see a thing. The hay bales so muffled the sound, I could barely hear the children's laughter and their parents' voices. I inched forward like a mole, feeling my way along, making sure there were no sudden drops.

Suddenly there was nowhere to go. I had reached a dead end and had to get the line of tunnelers behind me to back out. I clawed at the sides until I discovered I had missed the spot where the maze made an upward turn. I braced my feet and climbed up into the darkness, feeling for another tunnel to take me horizontal again. After leveling off, I felt an opening and knew that to get free I had to descend farther into the darkness. Turning around was impossible. The girl behind me clutched my foot as if I were her only lifeline, and her ticket out. I inched forward, the straw scratching my face and hands. My face flushed and my heart raced. Which way next? "We're trapped!" someone yelled. I reached ahead to see if I could find anyone to lead me. Only blackness. I didn't want to descend any farther into the dark.

"Help!" I yelled. It didn't feel like there was enough air. "Get me out of here! Please help me!" I didn't care what the big kids thought of me; I just wanted out. "Help!"

Suddenly people pulled off the bales from above and light exposed the way. I closed my eyes against the brightness, only to reopen them. The barn roof curved high over my head, a protective sanctuary.

A congregation of high school kids looked down on me; a few smirked. "Sorry," I mumbled in apology as I headed to the ladder. The fiddles tuned and I heard the music begin. Shaking off my embarrassment, I descended to the square dance below.

On the middle floor, the dance was set up in the center aisle between the two rows of cow stanchions. Some of the church members wore denim and plaid and really got into the spirit. My dad was even dancing with Mom. They were do-si-do-ing, her curly hair bouncing with every step. Then Dad swung her around and she laughed, her cheeks a pink I hadn't seen in a long time. I hoped there were plenty more dances for them tonight. More than anything, I wanted them together. I stood at the punch bowl, surveying the happy crowd and occasionally looking out for Matt, who must have been off with his buddies.

When the caller announced a break and the fiddler put down his instrument, my dad headed toward the punch bowl, leaving my mom alone. Though the moment was over, I hoped we'd feel like a family again if we kept stacking pieces of happiness.

Maybe it was sort of like inflation. Once I asked Dad why the government couldn't make more and more money so the poor people would have enough, and he said it had something to do with inflation and that the value of the money would go down. It didn't make sense to me at the time, but now I wondered if that's how it was with happiness. If you had lots and lots of happiness, you didn't appreciate it; but if you had a sliver, it was worth so much more. Tonight we all had a sliver.

"Do you want some?" I asked Dad as I dipped the ladle in the punch bowl.

"Sure, honey," Dad said.

"Can I dance with you later?"

Dad smiled and I knew that meant *no*. "I'm afraid my big feet might get in the way," he confessed and then scanned the room as if to find me a better partner. "Where's your brother? I haven't seen him all night."

"Maybe in the maze," I answered, enjoying the fizzy orange punch. "It's really dark. I was scared, Dad," I confessed quietly. Dad stared ahead, a blank look on his face. Where was the dad who would have consoled? The fiddlers and guitarists began again and my feet moved in gentle motions beneath me, having a will of their own. I needed a partner. Was Matt tunneling in the maze over my head? It was strange I hadn't seen him. By now he should have been dancing.

"I need a partner!" Mom called out over the fiddles as she joined us. "Which one of you will risk your feet?" She eyed Dad, who turned toward me.

"Abby really wants to dance," he said. "Give her a spin." So Mom extended her hand in invitation, nodding her head eagerly. I didn't want to be Mom's second choice, but if I was, she didn't show it. Dad sat on a hay bale and sipped the punch like it was hot cider.

"The Virginia Reel!" the caller exclaimed, and I lined up across from my mother as we followed his instructions. The frenzy, the music, the spinning, the crisp night air capturing my breath before me, and my mother smiling—my heartbeat raced with exhilaration. Mom and I sidled to the front and suddenly it was our turn to run between two lines of arms forming an archway above us. Everybody smiled. Their outstretched arms pulsed with each beat, as if pleading for us to be happy. How badly we wanted to be happy. And I was.

But then the fiddles screeched like a car slamming on its brakes at an accident, the music dissolved, and the line of dancers formed new clusters at the barn windows for a view of whatever was happening outside. My heart pounded in anticipation. For a minute, I imagined it was something good, a surprise finale. A midnight hayride, fireworks, maybe even a bonfire and marshmallows. Then I heard my brother's name.

I raced outside to find Matt had climbed to the top of the silo and was swaying on the narrow platform at the top of the ladder near the opening of the dome. "We've gathered here together. . ." His words slurred. I rocked with his movements, like a mother with a fussy child, as parishioners commentated.

"Somebody better get him down."

"He's drunk."

"Get his dad."

And then all the mothers seemed to be looking for the missing band of high school boys they thought had been arranging hay bales, but in reality were doing whatever the preacher's kid was now guilty of.

Matthew hung on to the platform's low railing, a safety precaution designed for a farmer guiding loose hay up to the drop-chute hatch in the top of the silo, not for a drunken high schooler with little concern for his mortality. I knew he could topple over anytime. My only brother.

"Matt!" I screamed. "Come on down!"

"That's right!" he announced. "Come on down!" he mimicked and then began singing our Sunday school chorus—"For I'm going to your house today! I'm Zacchaeus up in the tree! Can you see me?" He laughed.

The large sliding doors on the second floor of the barn opened and there was Dad, standing at the edge, backlit from the lights of the party, looking up at Matt.

"It's time to come down now," Mom called from the bottom of the ladder. For some reason there was no panic in her voice. She was calm, even gentle. "Let's go home," she said, as if Matt had climbed a slide and the playdate was over. She waited and then with more urgency called out, "Matthew!" And then again like all mothers, she added the middle name. "Matthew John!"

He turned his head toward her voice, trying to connect with Mom, the woman who seemed to know the way home—maybe for all of us.

"Mom?" His voice cracked. "Mom?" He sounded young and vulnerable, just like Joel had when he was frightened.

Matt turned toward the crowd and his body whirled suddenly. One hand lost its grip, but the other hand clung to the bar while his foot stumbled on a ladder rung. The crowd gasped collectively, and I heard Mom suck in her breath. Matt recovered his footing and grabbed the bars with both hands to begin a clumsy descent down the ladder. I counted how many rungs to the bottom and prayed he would not slip. A few men stood at the base as if they could cushion his fall should he lose his footing. Uncle Troy was there. He was always there.

The crowd was strangely quiet as Matt's foot reached downward, searching for the next rung. We saw him readjust his hands and then stretch his leg as his foot sought a new foothold. Fifteen rungs to the bottom. The process painful and slow. When both feet landed on solid ground, we all breathed again. Matt stood alone in the dirt patch at the base of the silo until Mom pushed her way through the crowd.

"Oh Matt," she said and put her arms around him. His arms remained limp at his sides. "Let's go," she whispered to him.

"Let's go," he echoed softly. I followed them to the car. The party was most definitely over.

✳

Two nights later, nearly every fire truck in the surrounding three counties responded when the Ludema silo exploded into flames. A filmy haze sifted through the air, and the smell of smoke penetrated for miles around. The day after the fire was out, Sheriff Merchant made an unexpected visit.

"Hey, Abby, how're you doing?" he asked when I opened the door.

"Okay," I said. Always a safe answer.

"I need to speak with your father."

"Dad!" I called down the stairwell. "Someone's here to see you."

"Is your mom home, Abby?" he asked. I shook my head no. I felt like a mute; I wasn't exactly used to having a sheriff in our kitchen. Friendly Sheriff Bob came around to the elementary school for fire safety drills and to talk about drugs, but he didn't usually make house calls.

When Dad got to the top of the stairs, he raised his eyebrows at seeing Sheriff Merchant in the kitchen.

"Sorry about the intrusion, John." The sheriff extended his hand.

"What can I do for you, Bob?" Dad wiped his hand on a towel before shaking the sheriff's hand.

"I know things have been rough on your family these past few months. I'm sorry about what happened," he began, and Dad nodded in acknowledgment. "But we just need to ask you a few questions about the night of the party at the Ludema farm."

"Is there some reason you need to question *me*?" Dad asked.

"I've heard some rumors about Matt and want to lay them to rest. We'd like to ask you *both* some questions."

"Abby, run upstairs and get Matt, will you?" Dad asked. As I left, I heard the sheriff say something about a lawyer and Dad answer that he didn't think it was necessary. When Matt came down, he also looked surprised to see a sheriff in the kitchen.

"Matt, Sheriff Bob is here to ask some questions about the Ludema party." Matt nodded and looked down. I was embarassed for him.

"And Matt, should you choose, you could have a lawyer present," the sheriff continued. Matt frowned in confusion and then shrugged his shoulders.

"Son, I know these last couple of months have been rough on your family, and I don't want to make it any tougher. But the hard part of my job is asking questions, and I need to ask some about what happened at the Ludema party." Sheriff Merchant waited. Matt nodded slowly. I couldn't read his face. Then the sheriff continued, "I'm a part of the fire investigation. Unfortunately, I've heard some rumors. People are talking about that party. I'm just following up on some of the things people say."

"*Things people say*," my dad repeated quietly. "*Things people say* can't start a fire," he said.

"That's right, John. I'm not jumping to conclusions. I'm just asking Matt some questions." And then to Matt, he said, "We heard you were drinking and that you were at the top of the silo."

Matt nodded in agreement.

"I have to ask you, did you notice anything unusual about the silo that evening?"

"No, sir," Matt answered, the same blank expression on his face.

"Do you have any ideas what might have caused the fire?"

"No, sir." Matt looked from the sheriff to Dad and back to the sheriff. "Why are you asking *me*?" he asked. "Why do you think I would know anything?"

"We're just trying to determine a source for the fire, Matt," Sheriff Merchant said.

A source? Were they saying my brother knew the source? I looked at Matt and then at Dad and tried to figure out who would say something next.

The sheriff continued, "And it may not be *what* caused the fire but *who*."

"You're suspecting arson, Bob?" Dad asked.

"I don't know. This is just the hard part of my job, asking questions." The sheriff rubbed his forehead.

"Do you know the whereabouts of your son on the evening of November ninth?"

"No."

That was the truth. Dad could offer no alibi. He could not defend his son.

"Have you asked all your questions?" Dad seemed impatient.

"I believe so," Sheriff Merchant said. "For today, at least."

Matt looked to Dad as if in disbelief.

"Let us know what you find out. I'm concerned about what happened that night, too." Dad said it to the sheriff, but his eyes were on Matt.

"If you remember anything, give me a call," the sheriff said to Matt.

"Will do." Dad motioned the sheriff to the door.

✦

Every few days, following Matt's instruction, I went to the basement with a mixture of clay to add another layer to the bottle. Matt checked on my progress, and with each additional layer, he gave the same precautions about the clay.

"If it's too wet, it won't dry on the inside." He frowned. "Then it'll pull away from the bottle. You don't want that."

I nodded. I wanted it to work. I didn't want Matt to be mad at me or disappointed with our volcano.

"But if it's just a little wet and the outside dries and the inside expands, it'll crack the surface." He looked more serious than Matt usually does. "That's what happens with volcanoes, anyway."

"Cracks and bumps are good," I said. "Volcanoes have bumps.

So that'll be okay, right, Matt?"

Matt nodded and left me to work alone.

A week later the insurance investigators concluded the fire was caused by a problem with the hay. They gave us new vocabulary, words laden with meaning. They said "bacterial fermentation," "no external source," and "spontaneous combustion." Nobody was acquitted, no apologies, and no forgiveness.

But the dry whispers lighting the fires of blame were licking far more furiously. That fall I learned that sometimes even if you're not guilty, you still pay a price.

ELEVEN

After the flames died, the smoldering odor and damaging gossip hovered like a smoky haze.

"I'm not going to let it stop me from going to his game, and you shouldn't let it stop you either," Mom told Dad the morning of Matt's last game. Mom said we needed to go on with our lives and that this would prove we believed in the results of the investigation.

Pop Keeney Field was not only the site for the town's Fourth of July fireworks but also the home of the Bethel Springs High School Mustangs football team. That night, as team players ran behind the charging horses to break through the cheerleaders' paper banners, followed by the BS marching band in blue and green uniforms, I decided football games were better than fireworks.

"Regrettable." Mom sighed, studying the Bethel Springs acronym emblazoned across the uniforms of the musicians, athletes, and cheerleaders. "*Regrettable*," she repeated, as if that were the word for the evening. But for me this was not an evening for regrets: Dad had come to the game. Looking like a mysterious mountain man long in hibernation, his angular face covered by a closely shaven beard, Dad would be unrecognizable to most of the fans.

"Third and ten," Dad said, holding his cup of coffee to warm his hands. Second and eight, first and ten, fourth and fifteen, it never added up. I couldn't understand the numbers and the scoring, which didn't matter since I was more entertained by the cheerleaders' antics than what was happening on the field.

"They're on the forty yard line and they've got to make ten

yards," Dad explained, his arms extended as if line markers. My need for a tutorial must have been obvious.

"How come there are *two* forty yard lines?" I asked. "Why doesn't it go from zero to one hundred?"

"Each side has their own fifty yards. Each side counts down to the goal line," he continued. "You have four chances. They are called *downs. . . .*" The more he explained about chances and downs, and how sometimes a kick is worth one point and sometimes three, the less I understood.

The cheerleaders jumped and climbed until they formed a pyramid, blocking half my view.

"What about stealing?" I remembered when Matt's Little League team started doing illegal things and being cheered on for it. "Is that legal?"

"No, but there is a lot of hitting," Dad admitted with a smile.

"Too much. It's okay, Abby. Just watch for a while." Mom shook her head.

"GET on the good foot, uh-huh," the cheerleaders chanted in rhythm. "GET on the good foot, uh-huh. Get it, get it, get it ON. Get it, get it, get it ON. GET on the good foot, uh-huh."

"What does it mean to 'get on the good foot,' Mom?"

"Nothing. Absolutely nothing. They can't even tell we don't have the ball."

The girls stopped as if they had heard us, gazing up at the stands and searching the faces of their loyal spectators. They waved at their friends, giggled into their white gloves, and tossed their ponytails. With their backs to most of the game, I wondered if they knew what was going on. Even when they turned to watch, they couldn't see over the heads of the team members on the sidelines. After the cheerleaders huddled, they determined their next play.

"We're s-u-p-e-r, super is what we are. We're g-r-e-a-t. We're great as you can see."

At least they could spell. That was super. S-u-p-e-r.

Matt had been in the entire game except for a few plays. I could easily track him by the McAndrews and 72 across his back. I tucked our red plaid blanket closer, and Mom offered me the cup from our thermos. That hot chocolate tasted better than any I've ever had. Dad handed over a long red licorice rope and a bag of popcorn. I felt safe pressed in between them.

"This is a big play," Dad said. "We've got to score on this series." I looked away from the cheerleaders long enough to see my brother run on the field. Mom took out her binoculars. We were behind twenty-seven to twenty, and each second meant one last chance for our team to score, however they did it. Four downs, four quarters, everything seemed to be cut in fours. The way the clock on the scoreboard ticked down made my heart race. The teams rushed at each other harder and faster, the pounding clash of helmets and shoulder pads audible in the stands. Then everything changed and both teams were pointing fingers at one another. Flags flew and whistles blew and the men in the jailbird suits ran out to break up the problem.

Our players huddled in a circle around somebody who wasn't getting up. Then each member on the other team dropped to one knee as if in prayer.

The coaches ran on the field. "Who's down?" was the murmur from the crowd. It was someone in blue and green. Somebody said it was #12, but for a minute it looked like #72, until I found Matt on his knee. Everybody looked at their programs and "Danny Allemeier" was whispered throughout the stands. A man and a woman stepped down the bleachers and headed toward the sidelines. "That's his parents," I heard from behind me.

"Would Dr. Edmund Greenfeld report to the field?" the

announcer called over the loudspeaker, more as a command than a question.

Something felt familiar in a bad way, and that made me want to run. The crowd, the circle, the stretcher. But then as they took #12 away, he lifted his arm in a feeble wave, the crowd cheered in relief, and the game continued, electrified by angry parents.

"That was our quarterback. . . . Now it's going to be tough to move the ball. . . . That looked deliberate. . . ."

The referee returned and put his arm in the air, lowering his hand by his face, then crossed his arms above his head and pointed at the other team as if putting a curse on them.

"Roughing the passer!" blared over the loudspeaker. "Fifteen yard penalty and an automatic first down."

The scoreboard changed and the players took the field again, but this time they pointed fingers and punched their fists, and so did the people in the stands. It felt like the tense day on the playground when Brian Anderson and Karl Gorski started calling each other names and hitting each other and a crowd formed around them yelling, "Fight! Fight!"

Mom focused on Matt as the play began, but even without binoculars I could see something was very wrong. The players charged one another, but when the whistle blew and everybody stopped, Matt kept running into the player across from him, his helmet pounding against the other player's numbers. Flags were thrown and somebody pulled Matt off of the other player—the same guy who had hit the quarterback. Mom stood quickly to survey the field and I rose next to her.

Someone from behind us yelled, "What's wrong with him? Play's over!" To which someone argued, "That's the one that took out our quarterback!"

"Unsportsmanlike conduct?" someone speculated. "We just lost our gain and maybe the game."

There was a lot of booing from both sides of the field. It seemed everybody was mad at Matt, who now sat on the bench until the assistant coach took him out to the locker room. For him the game was over and so was the season.

"Where's your dad?" Mom asked as she sat back down and we both realized he was missing.

The referee held one arm out and struck it with his other arm.

"Unnecessary roughness!" blasted out across the field for all of Bethel Springs to hear. "Fifteen yard penalty."

Now with three minutes remaining, the coaches kept calling time-outs, the referees shaped *T*'s, and the clock stopped over and over. But there was not enough time for the Mustangs. When the clock ran out, the horses didn't race onto the field in victory. Instead our guys limped off as losers, and our mighty mustangs were quietly loaded back in the horse trailer.

That night, as I pulled on my flannel nightgown, I could hear Mom and Dad's voices coming up through my bedroom vent. Matt and I had long since discovered that after the weather turned cold and Mom and Dad no longer snuggled on the porch, they moved indoors. When the fan wasn't blowing white noise, we could easily hear their kitchen chatter.

We'd lie on the floor with our chins resting on our hands, hearing more than we wanted to learn.

"Abby lost another tooth; it's your turn to be the tooth fairy."

"What's the going rate?"

"A quarter. Matt keeps calculating inflation."

"You look more like a fairy princess—how about if you do it."

"Thanks, but you're not getting off that easily."

And at Christmas we discovered the truth about Santa.

"I thought I might ring a few bells and leave footprints on the hearth.

Joel and Abby'll get a kick out of that."

"Just make sure you eat the cookies we put out."

"No problem, Mrs. Claus. Somehow you always know what Santa likes."

I would stare at Matt wide-eyed. But he was never surprised. For me it was bittersweet. The truth meant I had to outgrow imagination and dreams. And so I held on to the love in their words. So much love.

Tonight the words floating up from the vent were just sad.

"He was in my arms. Why not me? Did I do something wrong?" Dad asked too many questions. I wanted to be the only one with the questions, and I needed him to be able to answer them. I wanted this to be a fun evening, but it hadn't been for Dad. *Regrettable.*

I didn't like to think it could be anybody's fault. And if Dad was blaming anybody, it ought to be the lady in the blue car. But maybe if Dad blamed himself, he wouldn't have to blame God.

"I just keep asking, 'Why? *Why* did it happen?'"

Mom didn't answer. The plates clinked angrily as she wrestled them into the water. I hoped she wouldn't turn on the faucet and drown out her response.

"Did you ever think there might not be a God?" Dad asked. Mom's hands were silent. I held my breath, as if Mom and Dad could hear me breathe down the vent.

"John," she said. "I wonder about a lot of things. About God, too." She waited. "I can't answer your questions. But even if I could, it wouldn't be enough. Could my answer just be that I love you and that I want to make us work?"

I couldn't hear anything. Were they whispering? *Say something, Dad. Please say something.* "I love you" was good. "I love you" would be enough.

"I lost Joel. I don't want to lose you, too," she added and waited again. What was Dad doing? I wished I could see them.

At last Dad answered, "Sometimes it feels like I'm in such a fog. I just can't think straight."

"I know. And it feels like our lives are unraveling," she said, and I nodded in agreement. Life was unraveling, and somebody had to rethread the pieces. "Matt is so angry. You saw him at the game. And what about the drinking? How did we miss that? And then all that fire business."

"You don't think he had anything to do with it, do you?" Dad asked.

"No, but your distance makes it seem like you think he's guilty." Mom turned the faucet on and I couldn't hear if Dad responded. Then she shut it off again. "I don't know what to do. I don't know how to make it better," she continued. "And Abby?" Mom asked. "I don't know about Abby, but we need to find out. She's not doing well in school and she has nightmares." Long pause. And then my mom, who hardly ever cries, was crying and there was nothing I could do.

Mom didn't know about me. I must be worrying her. I realized I was clutching myself, stifled by my own embrace, shrinking smaller and smaller. Dad couldn't take care of Dad, and Mom couldn't take care of Dad and Matt and me. What was going to happen to us?

"We just have to keep going, even if it feels like we can't," Mom said through her tears.

"I'm so sorry, Renee." Dad's voice sounded worn out and then he, too, was crying. Then he said something else I couldn't understand, his voice muffled. I stood perfectly still, my eyes closed, trying to listen, my arms still wrapped around me in a hug. I hoped they were holding on to each other.

"John, let it go. It's over." Over? What was over? Was somebody giving up? "Stop blaming yourself. It's over."

"It'll never be over, Renee. We're still here. We're still here."

"I know. The pain never goes away," Mom said. "I miss him, and I'll never get over that until heaven."

"And what if there is no heaven?" Dad asked. "What if this is it? What if we never see him again?"

Never see Joel again? I hadn't thought of that. No heaven? How could that be? I hoped Mom had answers. I didn't have to wait long.

"I know there is a God and a heaven and Joel is up there and one day I'll be there to see him," Mom said with determination. Then she paused and her voice thinned. "I just wish I knew we were going to make it here, without him," she added, before the air ballooned my flannel nightie into a ballgown and their voices were lost in white noise.

TWELVE

On the day before Thanksgiving, school was out at noon but I still had my piano lesson. As I ran out the door with my books, Mom reached into the grocery money jar, grabbed five dollars, and slid it into an envelope, which explained how Mom was paying for my lessons. What else was going to come out of the grocery jar and who would refill it? Mom wrote Miss Mary's name across the front. "Tell her I'll give her the rest later this week."

"It's with an *e*," I corrected. "Frances like *her* with an *e* and Francis like *him* with an *i*." Mom erased the offending letter and corrected the envelope that didn't hold enough money.

I had hoped we'd skip Thanksgiving this year since nobody was coming. We usually invited guests for Thanksgiving, but Dad said this year he didn't want any "strays." I looked at Mom in shock. What had happened to Dad? He had never used that word before. Mom took a poll about what we wanted for dinner, and Matt and I offered our suggestions—green bean casserole with the crispy things on top, turkey, stuffing, mashed potatoes and gravy, Mom's fruit salad with marshmallows, and please no sweet potatoes.

On Thanksgiving morning, Mom removed a leaf from our dining room table, bringing us closer together, and spread out a gold cloth that spilled over the shortened table. She found the thumbprint turkey place cards I had made in first grade and set out four. I don't know what she did with the one with Joel's name on it—the one I wrote with a backward *J*, before I really knew my letters. After she set out the Pilgrim salt and pepper shakers, she filled a cornucopia centerpiece and surrounded it with two candles, each cradled in a tiny pumpkin. Then she slipped napkins in the feather napkin rings Matt had made in third grade—the ones we had only four of anyway, because there were only four of us then.

The table looked beautiful but empty. Our table was perfectly symmetrical now—one side for everybody. I longed for our neighbors, Uncle Troy and Miss Mary Frances, Miss Patti, Rita, to make it full. Except for the decorations, this really wasn't any different from any other dinner. And this year we weren't giving thanks for much of anything.

Dad sliced into the turkey. That was always his job. Matt plopped a huge helping of mashed potatoes on his plate and began eating. That was always his job.

"Hey, we didn't say grace," I said.

"Grace," Matt said and laughed, taking another bite.

"God is great. God is good." I motioned for him to put his spoon down. "Let us thank Him for our food. Amen." Then I started singing my kindergarten song to the tune of "Frère Jacques." "*God our Father, God our Father, we thank You, we thank You, for our many blessings, for our many blessings. A-men. A-men.*" Mom joined in to make it a two-part round but not Dad and Matt.

"Thank You, God, for food and family, and. . ." I stopped. Nobody added anything. "And for our home," I added. "Amen." After overhearing some church members talk about the parsonage, I had questions that needed answering.

"Look at those sweet potatoes," Dad said as if they were the only thing he was thankful for. "They're my favorite." Matt and I exchanged frowns. No wonder Mom made them.

"Somebody said the parsonage isn't really our house."

"Of course it's our house, but we don't own it. It's for whoever is the preacher," Mom answered matter-of-factly as she spooned out ambrosia salad.

"Why can't we own it? I don't want to move. Ever."

"I know, honey. And as long as Daddy is. . . ," Mom began and then stopped.

"But he's not preaching. . ."

"Yes." Mom sighed, setting down the bowl. "We have a dilemma." *Dilemma*, the bad word for the day. Bad timing. Mom served me a huge helping of sweet potatoes, and then another scoop, staring down the table at Dad.

"I thought we were thankful for our home?" Dad said sarcastically.

"We are," Mom countered. "For however long it's ours."

"Thank you, Renee, for clarifying that," Dad said angrily, dropping the gravy tureen so hard it broke. Gravy flowed, dripping off the side of the table.

"You want someone to be angry with, and I don't want to be that someone," Mom said, tossing her napkin on the table as she stood. I stared at the pile of orange covering my plate. I had little room for anything else. "I thought the church and our home and *us* meant something," she continued.

Dad didn't seem to know what to say. Couldn't he at least say, *"It does! I love you so much! I'll go back to preaching. We can make this all work out!"* But instead he was silent.

"It's Thanksgiving," Mom said sadly. The gravy had spread across the table, saturating the tablecloth.

"Nothing's the same. We've all changed. Now's not the time for this," Dad said.

"When *is* the time? When *is* it time to stop running *away* and run *toward* something?" Mom continued, as if picking a fight. I almost wanted Dad to get really mad. I wanted to find out what made him tick.

"I'm not running away."

"You don't think so? You're tinkering in the basement with old clocks, avoiding everything and everyone." Dad scoffed and that seemed to incite her. "And this isn't the first time." She pointed her finger. "You also ran away from the farm."

"No, Renee, I wanted to be a minister."

"There are plenty of Presbyterian churches between here and Washington State," Mom pointed out.

"You wanted to live out there?" Dad asked, surprised. "And that 'tinkering' comment?"

"You know what I mean. When you avoid something, you get far away from it. I don't believe distance heals, and I'm beginning to wonder about time healing all wounds. Look around you. Other people are wounded, too."

"I think I'll just excuse myself," Matt said with a sarcasm that exceeded both parents. He picked up his plate and started for the kitchen.

"You can sit right back down and finish your meal, young man," Dad commanded.

"Why?" Matt called back. "So I can listen to the two of you argue about whether or not to go to church?" He faced Dad. "Who needs it, anyway?" And with that Matt turned his back and headed for the kitchen, where he dropped his plate in Mom's sink full of hot water and walked out the back door, which slammed like an exclamation point on the end of his sentence.

It was all my fault. I never should have said anything about the parsonage.

Now I had that nervousy-sick feeling. Would Mom cry? Would Dad call Matt back? Dad shot Mom a look of blame and Mom's eyes said it was his fault, and then I knew I would be sick even though I didn't eat the sweet potatoes. I didn't ask to be excused; I just ran upstairs to the bathroom as quickly as my stomach allowed.

My stomach now empty, I splashed water on my face, then dried it without looking in the bathroom mirror. I knew I wouldn't like what I saw. I shook out my arms and stamped my feet. The tingling was uncontrollable. My mouth tasted terrible. Then I went to my room and spread out on my bed. Why did they fight about that stuff? I flicked on the radio and heard "Vietnam." Always Vietnam. I changed the station to some unfamiliar song that could drown everything out.

"Abby?" I heard Mom say from outside my door, her hand on the knob. "Are you okay?"

"I'm okay," I lied.

The door handle seemed to hesitate and then turn, but not open. "Abby, the door's locked."

"I just want to take a nap, Mom. Okay?"

"I'm sorry, Bee," she said weakly. "It wasn't a great Thanksgiving." Sometimes her voice invited a discussion. Sometimes she would have said, "Can we talk?" But today she sounded tired, like she just needed to cry, but not in front of a fourth grader.

"Not right now, Mom," I said. "Please."

I didn't help with the dishes or come down for dinner. When Matt came home later that night, he knocked the "one-two-three" knock and I opened the door. He smuggled up two plates of stuffing and mashed potatoes and the puzzle Mom had bought for this Thanksgiving.

"You shouldn't have run away," I said, picking at Mom's creamy mashed potatoes. "But I know why you did it," I added. "You just wanted everybody to get along."

"Abby, you don't get it. You just do everything perfect."

"I left, too," I defended. "But I had to throw up."

Matt looked down at my plate of food, the new spoonful in my mouth, and then backed away.

"It's okay." I swallowed quickly. "I feel better now." I forced down another bite to prove that I was good.

"Go get us some salad," I begged. I wanted him to leave and then I would flush the food down the toilet. "You forgot the marshmallow stuff."

"And the pumpkin pie with whipped cream," he said.

"Punkee pie with whoopin' cream," I corrected, remembering how Joel pronounced his least favorite Thanksgiving dessert. Mom would have made Joel apple pie à la mode.

"Man, he really wrecked everything by dying," Matt said suddenly.

"Joel didn't ask to die." I didn't want salad or punkee pie anymore. I crawled up on my bed and stared at the ceiling, waiting for Matt to say something. He just lay there on the floor, then pulled out a cigarette and started to smoke.

"Matt, you're gonna get in trouble."

"No, actually, I'm not." And he was probably right.

I hated the smell and it made me even queasier, but he seemed to relax and I didn't want another fight.

"What do you think's gonna happen?" I said at last.

"Who knows?" Matt answered more as a statement than a question and took a long draw on his cigarette. He obviously knew what he was doing.

"It scares me," I whispered.

"I know," Matt said, and I didn't know if he meant he knew I was scared, or if he was saying he was scared, too.

"Why doesn't Dad go back?"

"I think he's mad at God."

"God didn't kill Joel," I said.

"But He didn't *stop* him from *being* killed."

Matt had a point.

"Dad's so different now," I said.

"Maybe he's mad at us, too," Matt wondered out loud.

"*We* didn't do anything."

"Exactly. But maybe somehow we *should* have done something," Matt said, his voice soft but heavy with guilt.

"Maybe we're not enough," I said, and Matt didn't set me straight.

"What about Mom and Dad? Do you think they still love each other?" I asked, afraid of the answer.

"They might still love each other, but they sure don't *like* each other."

"The Hanleys got divorced."

Matt was quiet. He had no reassuring words.

"Where'd you go this afternoon?" I asked, wondering where anyone would go on Thanksgiving afternoon when everybody has a home, and a Thanksgiving dinner, and a place card with a name at a special plate.

"Around." I waited. I didn't know where *around* was, but it probably wasn't good.

"Can we finish my volcano tomorrow?" I blurted out, taking advantage of our sudden bond.

"It should be dry enough tomorrow so we can paint it." He rolled my throw rug aside, dumped out the puzzle box, and began turning over the pieces.

"What is it this year?" I asked, grabbing for the box lid.

"It looks like Switzerland or something," Matt answered. "All that white snow is going to be hard."

The variegated whites and blues were near blinding. We'd need to make separate piles of blues and whites. I started the only way I knew how. I grabbed the smooth flat edges and tried to build a frame around nothing.

THIRTEEN

Thanksgiving night was our first big snowfall of the season. It doesn't matter how much snow we get in Ohio, the first snowfall always feels new. I opened my bedroom window to feel the chill as I let out the smell of cigarettes. The snowflakes danced in the glow of the streetlights and called me beyond the front porch, where I stood and caught snowflakes with my tongue. I didn't care how cold it was; I sat down on the bottom step and watched the snow cover the dirt and dry leaves of autumn with a clean, fresh blanket of white.

The front door opened and shut and Mom sat on the step beside me.

"Feeling better?"

"Yeah." I wanted to say it was something I had eaten, but I couldn't lie. Mom traced a line in the snow with her foot. "Maybe it'll snow enough to make snow ice cream. I know I've got some condensed milk," Mom suggested. "And Hershey's sauce, too."

I nodded. We could do it if it was deep enough to skim off the top and then scoop out a clean layer.

"Do you want to talk about this afternoon?"

I stuck my tongue out and caught a few more flakes. They felt refreshing on my face.

"Sometimes it just doesn't help to talk about it. I mean, nothing really works," I said.

"Try me."

I sighed. I wasn't getting out of this.

"Well, everybody says to 'start over.' But how do you 'start over' when nothing seems ended?"

"I don't know," she said, too honestly. "I don't know if we're beginning something new or trying to finish something old."

There were things that troubled me worse than that. "Do you ever wonder. . . ," I began and then stopped. I almost told her how many times I relived the event, trying to come up with ways to make it not happen. I almost told her I had a recurring nightmare about that blue car driving without stopping. Mom shivered as if she could read my thoughts and tightened her coat around her chest, then jumped up and returned with a quilt off the front porch. She didn't say anything, so I continued without finishing my first question. I couldn't even bring up my guilty feelings.

"Sometimes I wonder if I'll ever stop crying about all the little things that remind me of him. And that makes me worry one day I won't feel sad anymore that he's gone and then I worry maybe I'll feel guilty I'm *not* sad."

Mom nodded and traced a circle with her foot.

"Somebody said it would be so hard at first, and then it'd get easier, but that's not true. In some ways it gets harder because nothing really changes, except us." Mom added a smiley face and two eyes. She tried so hard. Something in that drawing reminded me that maybe she had lost more than I had.

"Losing Joel meant losing a part of me and finding a new me," she said.

"You're still *you* to *me*," I said, as if that might comfort her. Except, suddenly, I knew it wasn't quite true. She was my mom, but different than she was the seconds before Joel was killed.

"On the day you were born, I studied you closely, memorizing every detail." Mom pressed my nose as if it were a button. "I tried to figure out if you got Daddy's nose, or my eyes, or if you'd ever grow hair!" Her hand cupped my face, a face so unlike hers. "I wondered what you'd look like all grown up." Mom paused and took a shaky breath. "I'm so glad I have that with you, but I won't with Joel. I don't know who he would have been."

"He would have grown up to be a good kid."

"I think so, too," Mom agreed. "A lot like Matt." We were quiet. As if that were a heavy thought. The goodness in Matt so obscured beneath layers of cold snow.

✳

After five layers of clay and three days of drying, the day after Thanksgiving Matt finally let me paint my volcano with red and purple and a white snowy top. Dad kept me company as he worked on an anniversary clock in silence until a knock at the top of the stairs signaled another client. My handwritten CLOCK DOC sign was still tacked at the top of the stairs. Dad's basement business was growing by word of mouth, obviously filling some void in Dad as well as in town. Just how many broken clocks could Bethel Springs have— sitting around not telling time?

Today's guest visitor was Bruce Hanley. Mr. Hanley repaired cars and lived a block down the road. We didn't know him because he didn't have children, except on the weekends when he was always driving in and out of his driveway with two kids in the backseat. His daughter looked to be about my age, and I thought it'd be nice to play with her. Somebody explained that Mr. Hanley was divorced. He was the only one on our street who lived alone.

Mr. Hanley came down the stairs and shook hands with Dad almost apologetically. "I know you don't see me much at your house. I mean the *other* house." He looked my way and nodded a hello. Dad's clients included a lot of people I'd never seen at Bethel Springs Presbyterian Church.

"Don't worry about that, Bruce. I haven't been to the *other* house much lately either."

"And you won't see me. Not my style. But I heard you were fixing clocks."

"I'm trying," Dad answered. "What do you have?"

"I have this clock of my dad's. I think it might have been his grandfather's. I've never had anyone check it out. But now I was wondering if you could take a look at it. It used to run for a little bit and then just stop, but now it doesn't run at all."

"What kind of clock is it?" Dad asked.

"What do you mean?"

"Is it a wall clock or does it sit on a table? Or is it a grandfather clock?"

"It used to hang on the wall before it stopped working."

"Do you know the name on it?"

"I can't remember. What're you thinking might be wrong?" Mr. Hanley asked.

"I won't know until I take it apart. It could just be dirty. Could be a broken spring. Do you want to bring it by?"

"I have it in my truck."

"Then bring it in. I can't work on it right now, but you can leave it."

Mr. Hanley returned, carefully taking each step, carrying the clock in a cardboard box.

"Maybe it's unrepairable," Mr. Hanley said. I could hear my mother's voice in my head, correcting him—*irreparable*. "But then I thought how nice it'd be if Grandpa's clock could be fixed. It being so old and a part of my family." He took the clock out of the box and set it on Dad's table. "Maybe one day I'll give it to one of my kids." He shrugged. "It'd be nicer if it worked." Mr. Hanley blew the dust off and then stepped back as if to give it another look.

When Dad whistled through his teeth, I knew he would start work on the clock right then and there.

"It's an Ansonia Regulator A with strike on the hour and half hour!" Dad was obviously impressed. "I didn't get to see many of these back in Washington. There are fewer old clocks out west, except for family heirlooms. But this"—Dad pointed at the clock—"this is a piece of work." Dad reached into his toolbox and took out a screwdriver. He began unscrewing the back. "This could be part of the problem," Dad said as he tapped a spring. "Looks like the mainspring. And of course, there's quite an accumulation of grease and dirt."

"But you think it might be okay?" Mr. Hanley looked like it was important to him. You'd think he was talking about a patient. I glanced back at my volcano. I had been listening so long, a stripe of paint had dripped into an unusual streak.

"It's well made. It'll work again," Dad diagnosed.

Mr. Hanley smiled. Dad didn't look up; he was already cleaning pivots with something that looked like a toothbrush.

"You see this right here?" Dad pointed to a part. "That's a click spring." Dad took out a C-clamp and fastened it to the spring. "If I don't put on this clamp to hold the spring, the whole clock could just. . ." Dad's hands suddenly separated, as if the spring were a bomb.

"Is that so?" Mr. Hanley said in amazement, now bent over the clock, blocking Dad's light, absorbed by the inner workings of the clock.

"The mechanism is all wound up. It's under tension. You release it the wrong way and the spring just explodes."

"And you want to work on that?" Mr. Hanley asked, skeptical.

"I'll take a look at it."

"So these hands are in good hands?" Mr. Hanley laughed. I

didn't think the joke was funny, but Dad smiled anyway. I could tell Mr. Hanley liked Dad.

"I'll let you know about it in a few days."

"That'd be great, John," Mr. Hanley said. "I wrote my phone number on this piece of paper."

"Don't you have a daughter Abby's age?"

"How old are you, Abby?" Mr. Hanley handed the slip to Dad.

"Nine. Almost ten." I applied red streaks to the cracks and bumps on my volcano.

"Jennifer is ten. Almost eleven. Maybe you could come over some weekend."

"Sure."

"Not this one. She's with her mom for Thanksgiving." Mr. Hanley looked uncomfortable, almost embarrassed. "But maybe weekend after next."

"Just let us know." Dad nodded.

"Will do."

"Do you fix watches, too?" Mr. Hanley asked.

"No, my grandfather stuck to clocks."

"I heard there's a watch that went to the moon," Mr. Hanley said. "I think Neil or Buzz wore it on the *Apollo 11*."

"The Omega—*the watch the world has learned to trust*," Dad explained. "The Omega and the Patek Philippe will run till the end of time," Dad said with admiration.

"But who will be fixing watches *then*?" Mr. Hanley added with a laugh.

Mr. Hanley left, and before my paint job could dry, I sprinkled sand over it. I wanted to put in some trees and grass, but Matt said it would look fakey. Then he said we had to wait for the volcano to set. I could hardly wait to see it blow.

✦

"Come downstairs, Uncle Troy! The surprise is almost ready," I called out when he arrived. His timing was perfect.

Uncle Troy slowly descended the narrow wooden stairs, carefully holding on to the wobbly railing.

"So this is where you've been hiding out," Uncle Troy said to Dad, but with a smile.

"I wouldn't call it hiding," Dad corrected. "But it *is* my workshop."

"Where's this secret you want me to see?" he asked, and I led the way to the back corner. When Uncle Troy saw the monstrosity, he whistled. "Now, that's something else." He shook his head. "You did this by yourself?"

"No, Matt's been helping me."

"Good job, Matt!" Uncle Troy said proudly, looking over at Dad as he said it, but Dad had on his special clock glasses and was fixated on a few small pieces. "And just what is it made of?"

I ran my hand over the surface. "You wouldn't believe it, but it's just flour, salt, and water. It hardens like this."

"That's something else," Uncle Troy repeated and then cleared his throat. He looked back over at Dad's table and back to me. "I can't stay long, Abby," he said softly. "I kind of need to talk to your dad."

"Okay." I suddenly remembered he hadn't come over to see a volcano. I slipped up the stairs, looking back as Uncle Troy made his way to Dad's table.

"I wonder if I could talk with you before I leave."

This was one conversation I didn't want to hear, and so I clicked the door shut behind me and headed outside.

That night after dinner, Dad was back to working on Bruce Hanley's clock while I added black streaks to the volcano. I had even picked up some cotton balls to add near the top to make it look like it was blowing up. Matt didn't like it but I didn't care.

"Was that Bruce Hanley I saw today?" Mom said when she came down. She wrapped her arms around Dad's neck and leaned over his shoulder, studying his work. They looked like something I remembered from a long time ago.

"He brought this clock I've never worked on before. Amazing workmanship," Dad said.

"Uncle Troy liked my volcano!" I added.

"Uncle Troy was here?" Mom's voice tensed as she sat next to Dad. "What did he want?"

Dad didn't respond. The fluorescent lights buzzed and the clocks ticked.

"Something happen, John?"

"It's just church business."

"Church business is our business."

"It's about when I'm coming back."

"Did you have an answer for him?"

"No, I did not," Dad said shortly. And then there was another gap of only buzzing and ticking.

"Do I have to pull it out of you?"

"It's about the house and the timing and everything," Dad said. "Troy's working on trying to secure a short sabbatical—if we can get another interim. And if the new interim won't need housing, we can stay here. Maybe through mid-March."

Mom let out a sigh. But I wasn't sure whether it was relief.

"And then what?" Why did Mom have to keep asking questions? Wasn't it enough that we had a little time? "This just delays the inevitable," Mom said. "All this *staying*."

"Renee, you're going to have to let it go. I can't go back right now. So just leave it be."

"Leave it be?" Mom turned his command into a question. "I'm supposed to ignore everything?"

"He also claimed that attendance is down, the budget is suffering, and this interim doesn't do any visitation," Dad confessed as if an afterthought.

"Well, you're just full of good news," Mom said, her voice laced with sarcasm. "John, nothing's getting better when you just stay down here with all your clocks. You need to be around people. We need you," she said. "*I* need you," she added softly. Dad set the clock down and really looked at her. Mom continued, "How much time does this buy?"

"I don't know, Renee. Troy was going to work it out with the session and the presbytery."

Mom studied him and then said, "There's something more you're not telling me." She sounded suspicious.

Dad's expression changed to what Mom had once called exasperation.

The cuckoo snapped out from one of Dad's clocks as if curious what would happen next. Dad pushed back his chair, took the clock off the wall, and shut the trapdoor with such finality I was pretty sure the bird was a prisoner for life.

"There are some contingencies. . . ." He looked over at me, remembering I was at work in my corner. "They want me to see someone," he muttered.

"Hey, Abby, Dad and I need to talk," Mom said. "Do you think you could go upstairs for a while?"

No problem, I thought as I trooped up the stairs yet again. *Just keep moving Abby upstairs and downstairs and outside and wherever she can't hear fighting.*

"That's good, John," Mom said with more hope. "That's a good thing, honey."

But something about it wasn't a good thing because their voices got louder and louder. I'm sure if I went back downstairs I wouldn't hear the clocks or the lights, and I would be cowering by my volcano. Where was Matt?

Then something fell, crashing to the floor, and Mom gasped. Was she hurt? Did she cry? I wondered about the volcano I had just finished painting. We hadn't even gotten to put the chemicals inside and watch it erupt.

I don't know what was broken, but it didn't sound like it could be fixed. Irreparable damage. I flung open the door to hear what happened.

"John, something has to change," Mom whispered.

"I know," Dad said. "I know." More silence. "I was wrong. I can't believe I said those things." More silence. I breathed slow and quietly, but my heart raced as I waited for something else. When I couldn't stand it any longer, I let myself out the back door. But when I hit the steps, my legs felt tingly and I lost my balance. I couldn't get my hands out in front of me fast enough and my shoulder and chest took the brunt of my fall, knocking the wind out of me as I fell down the stairs. I lay facedown on the cold cement at the base of the stairs, surprised at how quickly it all happened. I didn't want to move. Did I break anything? After I brushed off the leaves and dirt, I slipped into the garage and sat in the station wagon to wait out the storm. I ached all over, but you couldn't see I was injured from the outside.

The next morning, I checked my volcano; it was in one piece, and whatever Dad broke was cleaned up like nothing happened.

Ironically, that Monday, Mrs. Clevenger asked for a progress report on everyone's science project. Somebody was making a magnet, someone else a sundial; Rita was creating a model solar system. Mrs. Clevenger pulled me aside before lunch to ask how my project was going.

"I haven't tried blasting it off yet," I admitted as we walked down to the cafeteria. "But it's painted and everything."

"Did Matt help you?" she asked.

"Yes, of course," I answered, and then worried that maybe he wasn't supposed to. Besides, how did she guess? Did she know *everything* about me?

"Good." She smiled and I smiled back in relief. "Matt loved that project when he was in fourth grade." As we entered the cafeteria, she inhaled and declared, "Spaghetti."

"And that means French bread, green salad, and apple crisp," I added. "It always goes together."

She had the class sit down and motioned for me to stay by the door. "Like I said, I'm glad Matt helped you." Her voice trailed off and then she tried again. "But how is everything else?" she asked. "I mean. . .are things getting better?"

I knew what she meant. She meant Dad and she meant Matt and Mom and maybe even me; and she meant, was our family coming back together? And I thought about the fight last night in the basement. But how could I explain it when I didn't even know what they were arguing about or what happened or if it even meant anything? There were too many layers of things happening or not happening. This wasn't a question I could quickly answer and then sit down between Rita and Melody and eat a peanut butter and jelly sandwich.

The spaces at the fourth grade table were filling up. Pretty soon I'd have to eat with the third graders. I rolled the top of my lunch sack up and down.

"I'll take that to mean there's room for improvement," she said, so knowingly. "I guess I'd better let you go find your seat." She put her hand on mine. "I'm here if you want to talk. Just remember, sometimes it helps."

I nodded thanks and escaped to my table.

That evening when Matt walked in the door, I begged him to let me blast my volcano. He dropped his backpack on the kitchen table and paused.

"Get on some old clothes. We'll blow it up," he said.

"Can you take it outside?" Mom suggested.

"It's pretty cold out there, and besides, it's way too heavy now, Mom. Abby put about five layers of clay on that thing." Mom sighed and resigned herself to whatever would happen in the basement. Besides, it was really Dad's shop now.

Matt carried the vinegar and a few Kleenexes, and I brought the dishwashing soap, food dye, and baking soda. It was hard to believe these few ingredients would really blow. When he tugged the string, the overhead bulb lit up the basement steps, revealing my volcano in the far corner. Oh, how I hoped it would work. And I could see Bruce's clock on the table. From the outside, it looked finished, but I knew better about clocks. It was the inside that counted.

Mom followed close behind with a stack of newspapers she added to the perimeter of my volcano. Then the three of us stood over the creation and awaited Matt's instructions.

Matt poured two cups of vinegar down the hole, then squeezed a few drops of Palmolive, and finally a few drops of red food dye. I closed my eyes.

"Abby, nothing happens until I put in the baking soda."

Matt put a few tablespoons of baking soda in a tissue.

"We're creating a chemical reaction with acid and a base. It forms a carbon dioxide gas." He twisted the edges of the tissue into a small packet, like a tea bag. It seemed to come naturally to him, and then I thought about the barn and my stomach felt funny. I deliberately focused on my volcano and his hands and the tissue and how nice my brother was to help me blow it up.

"Are you ready?" he asked. I plugged my ears and he shook his head. "It's not going to be noisy, but it'll be messy. Watch," he said. "Do you want to drop it in?" He handed the tissue to me. I shook my head. I was afraid. "If everything works right, we should be able to do it over and over and you can do it for your class, too," Matt said, and then dropped the tissue in the top of the volcano.

It took a while but then red bubbles began foaming over the sides. The dishwashing soap had done its job. The foam slid over the mountain and onto the floor. But that was it? Where was the fire? Where was the noise?

"Is that it?" I asked.

"What do you mean?"

"I mean, is that all it's going to do, or will it make some noise or fire?"

"That's it, Abby," Matt said. "Sorry to disappoint you."

"Isn't there something else we could put inside it?" It seemed like I had spent too many hours for it to just foam like bubble bath.

"I don't know." Matt frowned.

"It's good enough, Abby," Mom said, as if taking sides with Matt.

"But a volcano is fiery and explosive and this is not," I argued. "It needs something inside it to burn and blast off."

"And you think I'm the one to figure that one out?" Matt asked. "Sounds like trouble to me," he said as he walked up the stairs. Mom glared at me and cocked her head toward Matt, as if cueing me to do something.

"Hey, Matt, thanks," I said, late. Way too late.

✳

I don't know why I moaned in my sleep that night. There was something about falling, and the sensation that I wanted out of that nightmare but my eyes felt heavy.

"Abby, wake up. It's just a dream. Wake up." Dad's voice was near and I felt his hands on my shoulders and his whiskers rough against my cheek.

"It's okay now, honey. It's just moving pictures. It's just a movie. Turn it off." A movie? Hadn't I used those words? I felt a sudden dampness against my cheek and was surprised I had been crying. But when Dad pressed his unshaven face against mine, I realized the tears were shared.

"That's better. Now you're awake."

"Why does that happen?" I turned on my side, propping myself up on one elbow.

Dad ran his hand over my back and scratched from shoulder to shoulder. It felt so good to feel his touch again.

"I think maybe our day brain has too many thoughts that we don't know what to do with, and so our night brain tries to work them out. I don't know. If I did know, I'd stop them. For you. For me."

"It happens to you, too?" I said.

"I can't ever make the dream change. I want a different ending," he answered sadly. I didn't need to know what he dreamed about. I didn't even *want* to know. "I don't want it to be like this for you," he said softly.

And I don't want it to be like this for you either, I thought. *Or Matt or Mom.* We sat there together in silence for what could have been ten minutes, and then he got up.

"Good night, honey. Sleep tight." And I wondered if that would ever be possible.

FOURTEEN

The Bethel Springs Presbyterian Christmas pageant was scheduled for Christmas Eve. Christmas was on, though Dad's involvement was *dubious*. That was Mom's new word, whenever I asked if she thought Dad would let us do something. Like when I asked if we could put up the Christmas lights. "Dubious." Or if we could go to the town's annual Christmas parade. "Dubious."

The clear blue-sky days were gone and replaced with gray and cloudy. Though Mom and Dad didn't string any lights, thankfully the neighbors did. Our house wore its usual white porch lights, but everything felt colorless, as if we now lived in black and white when Christmas should be in color: green like a Christmas tree, red like holly berries. Miss Mary Frances gave me an early Christmas present, *Christmas Carols for the Serious Piano Player*, and assigned me two new pieces.

Mom always set up a village under our Christmas tree. Each house was made of cardboard and frosted with glitter. Every year since Mom was six, her dad had given her a house or a figurine. Since then, even when it wasn't Christmas or her birthday, people would come over with a miniature mailbox or a car with a tree on top, or a few carolers.

The village wasn't unlike Bethel Springs, except that it had one large mountain (not nearly the size of our own Terror Ridge), which began at the living room wall and flowed down to a tinfoil pie plate pond at the bottom. We had skiing and skating all in one perfect little village.

As a preschooler I lay under the tree, moving the pieces around and letting the girl figurines go next door to play with their friends. The Christmas Joel turned two, we thought we'd have to keep the set in boxes. But I pleaded with my mom and promised I'd watch him closely and teach him a reverence for the pieces.

We lay on our stomachs and I told Joel to lie on his hands until I was ready to hand him a piece. Joel dutifully obeyed. I told him the name of each person so there would be no confusion in future play; I was going to remain mayor of all village activity. And so, except for a mailbox that he accidentally sat on while I gave my demonstration (which I subsequently glued back together before my mom noticed), Joel shared my respect for our Christmas village. Would Mom set it up this year?

Mom usually shopped sales all year long and hid our presents in the hope chest in her bedroom. The hope chest seemed an appropriate hiding place for the things I longed for. Since no one at our house believed someone was coming down the chimney, there'd be no Santa this year. All reason for childishness left with the child. This December Mom even asked me to help her wrap all the Christmas presents, except mine.

As Mom retrieved the gifts, I calculated paper size and ribbon. She carefully laid aside the ones I wasn't supposed to see. And when she got to the bottom, Mom slowly pulled out a book and what appeared to be a flannel pillow. The book was *Curious George Rides a Bike*. She hesitated, as if she wanted to read it, but instead set it on her lap and smoothed the back of her hand across what I recognized as pajamas decorated with monkeys. I longed to press the soft flannel to my cheek.

Then she checked the label like she did on all the clothes she had ordered before we had time to grow into them, as if contemplating whether this was the best time to give the gift. The pajamas looked so small—was he really that little?

"I thought he'd like them," Mom said as she hugged the pajamas.

"He would have, Mom. You were right."

"We were going to give him the book and a bike," Mom explained carefully. "It was perfect." She opened the book and started to talk about the characters as if they were her friends. "Joel was still too young on his birthday, so Dad and I were going to wait and give him the bike for Christmas. One with training wheels. Maybe we should have given it to him earlier." She sighed in regret. "It would have been perfect." Mom picked up the book, turned to a certain page, and began reading about how the man in the yellow hat surprised George.

"'*He took George out to the yard where a big box was standing. George was very curious. Out of the box came a bicycle. George was delighted; that's what he had always wanted.*'" Mom would have gotten an A from Mrs. Clevenger for "Reads with expression." Mom turned to me. "We were going to put the bike in a big box in the yard."

"Good idea, Mom."

Mom hadn't talked about what would have happened if Joel had lived. When she opened the lid on the hope chest, it let something out in both of us.

"I miss him, Momma."

I hardly ever called her Momma anymore. That was reserved for scraped knees and bee stings.

"Come here, sweetie," she said, and I sat on her lap. I hardly ever sat on her lap anymore, either. Maybe too big for her lap but never too big to need her.

"When does it get better?" I asked.

"I don't know," she answered, and so I buried my head in her sweater. We both held on to the pajamas. Those soft, sweet, unworn pajamas no little boy would ever grow into.

"You're supposed to have better answers than that," I said gently, without meaning to blame her.

"Just because I'm your mom?" Her eyes glistened.

"I don't know," I answered. From the living room I heard "Away in the Manger" from Mom's favorite Firestone record of Christmas carols sung by Julie Andrews in her British accent. "Be near me, Lord Jesus, I ask Thee to stay. . ." Jesus seemed nearer when I was sitting on Mom's lap.

Where Does the Butterfly Go When It Rains? was one book choice on my first-grade Scholastic book order. I spent fifty-five cents and four weeks anticipating the answer to the title. But the book never addressed the question; instead it was filled with more, equally frustrating questions. Anybody could write a book of questions; it was the answers that I wanted. Where *does* the butterfly go when it rains? If the question can't be answered, does that mean it never finds a home? That book eventually joined the donation box of little-used or outgrown toys.

*

Matt was not happy about this year's Christmas pageant. He was too old for the performance, but when you're a preacher's kid and the sixth grader who's playing Melchior has the chicken pox, you have to fill in even when you're too old. Mom said it was a small role and at least the costumes were interesting. Matt suddenly became spiritual and claimed the kings didn't arrive at Christ's birth but perhaps two years later and couldn't he just wait two years and do it then? Mom didn't buy it. Matt dreaded everything about it except maybe being onstage with Mary, who was played by Christine Meyers.

I had always liked her until Matt seemed to, as well. She always got the good parts, working her way from a sheep with a solo, to head shepherd, to angel of the Lord, to the Virgin Mary herself.

Now I almost hoped Matt would go back to liking her instead of some of the girls I had seen him hang out with after school. But then again, a girl like Christine might not like Matt.

Joseph was played by Tim Granger, a new kid at church who didn't know what he was getting into. Melody Ludema was the innkeeper's wife because there was no singing involved, though Mrs. Buttery claimed it was because Melody was from a farm and would know how to herd the stable animals, namely all the preschoolers from BS Pres. The first through third graders were angels with halos, and the fourth and fifth graders were shepherds.

I was in fourth grade, and so I was obviously going to be one of the shepherds, or I could be a reader. Like Linus in *A Charlie Brown Christmas*, I could go to the pulpit mike and read from Luke, chapter 2, in front of the whole congregation. No costume, just the blue choir robe with the white collar. I could do that. When Mrs. Buttery heard my audition, she liked the way I pronounced "Gloria," and the part was mine.

My scriptures were about the angels visiting the shepherds. But when I really studied my part, I noted the problems with Mrs. Buttery's staging and let her know.

"Only *one* angel gave the message to the shepherds, Mrs. Buttery."

"Yes, dear," she said as she labeled the pews so the children would know where to sit.

I followed her down the aisle. I wasn't through. "A *heavenly host* isn't necessarily angels. Do you really think it's all *angels*?"

"I'm not sure, dear." She looked down the list of names on her cast list.

"Just how do you know what those heavenly host people looked like, anyway?"

"We're just doing our best, Abby," she said, as if patting my head.

I wondered what would happen if Mrs. Buttery didn't actually have the first and second graders put on coat-hanger halos and white sheets. What would happen if we admitted we had no clue what an angel looked like except that they really frightened everybody and their every appearance was followed by "Fear not!"? What did the "glory of the Lord" look like, anyway? Did she have any special effects in mind to pull that off?

"And why are angels always children, anyway?" I asked. "Couldn't angels have been grown-ups?"

Mrs. Buttery wasn't in the mood for making any major changes to her annual script. "Just read it," she said through clenched teeth as I climbed up into the pulpit for my first rehearsal.

The interim minister and the guest preachers had left a few old bulletins, a paper cup, and the mammoth Bible with print so large I could have read it from the front pew.

I opened its heavy front cover and landed in the Old Testament. Clutching another chunk of pages, I flipped to Matthew, Mark, and then Luke. The pages were thin and fragile and whispered like leaves falling from a tree.

That day I didn't even get to use the microphone, which was a great disappointment. I could shout to the balcony, but I really wanted to hear how my voice sounded amplified. I quickly read through the shepherd verse, charging ahead with great drama, "The angel said to them, 'Be not afraid; for behold, I bring you good news of a great joy which will come to all the people!'" But my favorite part was the ending when I got to all the glory stuff. I counted my verses from Luke 2:8–15. Eight of them. I had more than anyone.

On the night of the pageant, Dad was a no-show, Mom sat at the organ with the best seat in the house, and Matthew waited in the narthex for the finale. I hoped he wouldn't be late—two years late.

The preschoolers began singing "O Little Town of Bethlehem." A few lambs and donkeys were crying, and Mrs. Buttery's assistants tried to calm them down while other parents scooped their animals out of the pew, thereby rescuing the pageant. I spotted Ricky Sanders and Julie Sullivan and Stephanie Lambert and Bradley Grady. Joel would have stood next to Bradley. *Above thy deep and dreamless sleep, the silent stars go by...* "Their preschool voices weren't on pitch and half the words were muddled, but it still sounded sweet.

I remember my dad once preached that "O Little Town" was written by a discouraged minister trying to hold together a country divided by the Civil War. He took a sabbatical and spent Christmas Eve in Bethlehem and was never the same.

"The hopes and fears of all the years are met in Thee tonight," their childish voices sang, and I drew a quick breath. That was the first time I had heard it quite that way. Maybe that Civil War writer knew more than anyone else how hopes and fears can somehow coexist in the same holiday.

Then the animals sang and it was almost my turn to read. I looked back at my stained-glass Jesus sitting with His open hands reaching out to the children. It was backlit and each color was glorious. Maybe my Joel was up in heaven with all the hopes and none of the fears. Maybe my Joel was sitting on Jesus' lap right this very minute and not even missing me one bit. Maybe it was just us missing him and the way our family used to be. I was glued to my seat.

"Abby?" Mrs. Buttery had made her way to the choir loft. "You're next," she whispered.

Mom was at her bench, accompanying Elizabeth Winkle's perfect soprano rendition of "O Holy Night." I closed my eyes and I was in Bethlehem until Mrs. Buttery tapped me on the shoulder and I stood as if I had just woken up.

I could see my mom motioning for me to rise. The lights hurt my eyes as I strained to see who was out there. Uncle Troy and Miss Mary Frances had their usual third-row pew. Miss Mary's head was cocked and she frowned at me. Mom tapped the top of the organ three times for *I love you*.

The next reader pushed me along and I found my black patent leather shoes sliding between the choir pews toward the steps. The silence dragged on as the congregation waited for me to ascend. I tried to find the bookmarked section, but the words blurred on the page and all I could think was, *The hopes and fears of all the years are met in Thee tonight*. Tonight. If I read everything perfectly, maybe everything would be better. Tonight.

When I thought perhaps I had found Luke 2:8, my hands were sweaty and my fingers stuck to the page. I began reading, "Now while he was serving as priest before God when his division was on duty. . ." The verse seemed strange and unfamiliar. I heard Mrs. Buttery cough. I looked at the organ and Mom shook her head. Something was very wrong. I blinked again and saw I had read Luke *1*:8 instead. I traced my finger until I passed chapter 2 and began again. "And in that region there were shepherds out in the field, keeping watch over their flock by night." The microphone exposed how thin and weak my voice sounded, and Mrs. Buttery lifted her palm to get me to speak up. My heart beat wildly and I wondered if this was what it was like to have a heart attack like Grandpa. I stifled a sob in my throat. This was my big moment and I was falling apart. This was when I was supposed to be grand and wonderful and proclaim about the angel and the glory and everything, but I could only think about hopes and fears.

"And an angel of the Lord appeared to them." My voice was now a whisper instead of my practiced projection. I'm not sure my mother at her organ could hear me. I wanted her to play something, anything. I put my finger over the text and ran it back and forth. The words were blurring and I blinked rapidly as they came in and out of focus. My throat hurt and my mouth had turned to cotton. Worse yet, I had that terrible feeling I got right before I was going to throw up. The room seemed to spin; I grabbed the podium, focusing on the Bible in front of me. Seven verses was way too much. Everything was wrong but somehow I had to get it right.

"And the glory of the Lord shone around them. . ."

"And the glory of the Lord shone around them. . ." I tried again. "And the GLORY of the Lord shone around them." I paused and took a shaky breath. That horrible, shaky kind of breath that isn't deep enough; it just makes you sound as if you are going to cry, which was exactly what I was going to do. I squinted and saw Matt craning his head out of the back of the narthex, motioning for me to continue. *Come on!* he mouthed in exaggeration. I knew what he wanted; I just couldn't do it.

"And they were filled with fear." I choked and swallowed fast but not quickly enough. I tried to make it sound like a cough, and perhaps it passed, but I knew it was the beginning of a cry that might never stop, and I was about to do it in front of hundreds of people on Christmas Eve. Amplification was not working to my advantage. Each breath I took wasn't deep enough and the room started to swim. I was dizzy and burning up, but I couldn't even move to sit down or I'd faint. *Rescue me*, I thought.

And then I saw my favorite king make his way up the aisle, crown in hand. He marched right by the stable, stumbling slightly as he squeezed around Mary and Joseph, and then climbed Dad's pulpit steps. I kept my finger pointed on Dad's Bible. "2:10," I whispered. Matt held on to the podium and it was then that I could smell that he had been drinking. I hated that smell. It represented everything bad. But what could I do? He was here with me.

"And the angel said to them, 'Be not afraid; for behold, I bring you good news of a great joy which will come to all the people.'" Matt's voice filled the sanctuary with a kind of presence I didn't know he had. "'For to you is born this day in the city of David a Savior, who is Christ the Lord.'"

Savior, my *Savior*. I kept my head down until I peeked out the corner of my eye to see Mom staring at Matt. She looked so proud. Her eyes sparkled with tears. Her mouth was open as she silently gasped air. Tears dripped off her face and most certainly onto her hands and the keys. *I love you, Abby*, she mouthed.

And, suddenly, Matt arrived at what used to be my favorite verse.

"'Glory to God in the highest, and on earth peace among men with whom he is pleased.'" And then we heard the angels perched in the balcony sing "Gloria," their voices running up and down concluding in that funny "eggshells" ending. But I didn't feel *Gloria* as Matt escorted me back to the pew. I just put my head in my lap and cried. Mom should have mouthed *Thank you* to the king. But while Mom was fumbling with the running *Gloria* eighth notes, Matt slipped out the side door. There would be only two kings tonight. Matt had already played his part.

*

For me, the pageant was over. I knew no one would miss me, so when the next carol began, I snuck out the side pocket door, threw my robe on the floor, grabbed my coat off the hook, and ran into the night.

Snow had begun to fall and I could see my breath. The snow from previous snowfalls, now dirty and gray, lined the sidewalk, funneling me home. My black patent leather shoes were hardly up for the journey, but I didn't care. I just wanted to find Matt.

I paused and closed my eyes. When I opened them, I hoped I'd see the figure of my brother in the distance, but he was nowhere. The idea that it was foolish to walk in a snowstorm had not occurred to me until this moment. The idea that the house would be locked when I got there also had not crossed my mind. My feet were cold and wet and my toes felt numb and so I quickened my pace, running down the icy path trying to catch up to wherever he had gone.

"Matt!" I cried out. My echo hung unanswered in the still air. "Matt! Wait!" It was hard to run with my hands tucked under my arms, especially with the snow sticking on the sidewalk. The dream of Matt holding my hand and walking me home was just another illusion, and so I had but one realistic option: turn around and return to church to wait out the arrival of the two kings and the distribution of candy-filled stockings for all the good boys and girls of BS Pres.

That night in bed, I could see from my window the strings of lights on homes up and down the street. I held on to Joel's monkey, wondering where Matt had gone and why he still wasn't back. Christmas Eve, with its hopes and fears, was over, and that made me feel both sad and relieved.

FIFTEEN

Last year, when we said good-bye to 1969 and hello to 1970, Dad let us stay up until midnight and I saw how people in NYC rang in the New Year. We couldn't know that when the ball dropped, it would herald a year that would change our lives. When Dad turned off our Zenith, the small dot in the middle of the screen slowly extinguished 1969. And that's what I thought of this year, too; 1970 was faded and gone. Why celebrate?

Christmas Day thankfully had been uneventful, a relief after our tumultuous Thanksgiving and a reprieve from our bittersweet Christmas Eve. Now New Year's loomed, taunting us with other people's celebrations.

Our church always closed out the old year by praying in the new. But since most people couldn't stay up until midnight, parishioners stopped by the sanctuary in the afternoon and early evening and knelt by a pew to reflect on the past and pray for the future.

We dropped by the church before dinner. All four of us. I leaned forward and folded my arms along the top of the pew in front of me and bowed my head as if in deep prayer but secretly peeked out from under my arm.

Matt had his eyes closed, but I didn't think he was praying. My mother's head was bowed, her hair hiding her face. Dad sat straight up with his eyes closed. I couldn't tell if he was sleeping or in deep thought, or maybe he was praying. At least he was there; that in itself was sort of a surprise.

After prayer, we always picked up Chinese food and played games by the fireplace. Maybe that's why Dad had come tonight: to make sure we ordered his kung pao chicken. China King was the only Chinese restaurant in our small town, and nobody there was even Chinese, but they did make great pot stickers and egg drop soup. Matt wouldn't join us for Chinese food and games by the fire this year. Too determined not to be a preacher's kid for New Year's Eve, he had made other more exciting plans.

"Stay home with us," I had begged as I saw him stuffing bills in his wallet. "Don't do something that'll get you in trouble." I had no idea where Matt's stash of money came from, and that worried me, too.

"Have fun, Abby," he said and then drove off with a carload of guys I didn't recognize.

That left three of us. The wrong number for the four-person board games we used to play after Dad had put Joel to bed.

Dad and Mom and I played Chinese checkers. Mom and Dad had opposite triangles and I felt like an oddball, my marbles trying to navigate between their intersecting paths. By 9:00 p.m., the fire was dying and my dad's yawns signaled it was time for this year to end.

On the first day of January 1971, I awakened to see the same stuff of December: same clouds, same neighborhood Christmas lights, and same snow on the ground. Though we turned the calendar page, nothing really changed except the year. I slipped down the stairs in my nightgown, lured into the kitchen by the smell of bacon and coffee.

Dad's newspaper was left out and open to the obituaries. Date of birth, date of death, lots of names, and what people said about the deceased. I had never before noticed how many people died. Now it seemed so possible. People died any day of the year—maybe even New Year's Eve.

"Where's Matt?" I asked.

"He got in late," Mom said, scrambling the eggs. "And he doesn't feel well."

"Serves him right for skipping out on us."

"You could show a little charity," Mom said with an edge to her voice.

And then I remembered the pageant.

"I'll take him his breakfast."

When I set the tray on his bed, Matt looked like he was going to throw up, and I had to wonder about the wisdom of bacon and eggs.

"Yuck. Get that out of here."

"It's your favorite."

"Not this morning."

"The flu?" I asked.

"Something like that."

"You should have stayed home with us."

Matt grunted and rolled over. He was still wearing his clothes from last night.

"So you want me to take it away?" I asked.

"Yeah."

"Can I stay?"

"No."

"Do you need anything?"

Matt looked like he was trying to think up something that would help. I knew the feeling.

"Stop asking so many questions, Abby. Just go away."

But when I returned with the untouched plate of food, Mom immediately headed up the stairs and I followed in her wake, determined to learn what was going on. Mom knocked. That was odd.

"I said go away, Abby!" Matt yelled.

"It's not Abby." Mom let herself in. "We need to talk, Matt."

"Not right now, Mom." Matt groaned, holding his head. "I feel awful."

"That's exactly why we need to talk. You really need to remember why you feel awful so you won't do this again."

Mom never blamed me for getting the flu. But then I remembered another time Matt was sick, and I realized this might have something to do with the night Matt almost fell off the silo.

"It's no big deal, Mom."

"Maybe not to you right now, but it will be. And it is a big deal to our family."

Matt turned toward the wall and Mom sat down on the edge of his bed.

"I love you, Matthew." She stroked his head. "I don't know what you're doing, but it scares me."

"I'm okay, Mom."

"No, you're not. None of us are. And maybe it's about time somebody admitted it."

"Well, I'm not as bad off as Dad."

Mom smoothed Matt's hair, which had gone uncut for months and now covered his ears.

"We're each different," she said at last. "Dad handles it his own way."

Matt groaned and then turned and squinted his eyes as if trying to focus on his surroundings.

"Man, my head hurts."

"It will," she answered.

"Like you would know."

"I know more than you think I do," Mom said, placing her hand on his forehead. She sighed. "What does drinking do for you?"

"I feel better," he said. "Some of the time," he added softly.

I looked around the room at his team pictures on the wall, his trophies on the dresser, and the framed photo of Matt helping Joel hold a bat with Joel wearing a Chicago Cubs jersey.

Matt scrunched his eyes and then released and opened them.

"What's *she* doing in here?"

"She might as well stay," Mom said.

"Well then, why don't we just bring in the whole family for one big therapy session," Matt scoffed.

"I *would* if Dad weren't driving that grandfather clock to Cleveland today."

"It works? How about that! They get their *timepiece*. Or is it a *clock*?" he asked, mimicking Dad's instructional tone. "Just in time to count down to a new year." Matt shook his head in disbelief. "Never thought Dad would get that old thing working."

Mom took his face in her hands, turning it toward her.

"Back to you."

"Mom, I'm not going to do it again."

"I remember you saying that two months ago. After a certain silo episode."

"Yeah, but this time..."

"Yes. *This* time things are going to be different." Mom's voice took on a steely edge. "I'll take you to school if I have to. And you won't be going anywhere at night unless I drive you, and then I'll wait and take you back. Otherwise, you're at home. And while you're at home, you're going to start working on those grades."

Matt moaned.

"Matt, you've always been a good student. Cs and Ds are below you. If you're going to college..."

"I'm not."

"Well, whatever you do, you'll need better grades than that."

✳

As soon as Dad came home that afternoon, I went downstairs to read while Matt watched his Buckeyes play Stanford in the Rose Bowl. The basement was dark except for the overhead bulbs focusing on Dad's workspace, one cozy circle of light. Though the winds howled and the snow was flying sideways, inside we were warm and sheltered.

The background ticking of clocks made the room sound active. No wonder Dad never seemed lonely. A cuckoo popped out, and Dad looked up again to cross-reference the bird's entrance with the other clocks hanging on the wall. That greeting announced I had been down there for forty-five minutes.

Dad had two clocks in front of him, and a grandfather clock lay open on a nearby table. I tried to think of it as Dad's patient, instead of the casket it appeared to be. Dad slid his finger against the minute hand of the smaller clock, gently nudging it clockwise. As he moved the long hand, the little hand followed in synchrony.

Dad stared at the face of the clock and I wished I knew what he was thinking, or that he could look at my face that way again.

"Can you tell the difference?" Dad said at last.

"They both look like clocks to me."

"One's a *timepiece*; one's a *clock*," Dad said. I smiled, remembering how perfectly Matt had imitated Dad's description.

"Don't they both tell time?"

"One of them needs winding," he explained. "And, you see, with *this* one you can take the big hand *and* the small hand and move them wherever you want. It won't harm the clock." He moved the smaller hand around the face. "But this one? You just move the big hand." He slid the big hand clockwise and the little hand followed.

Dad adjusted his special eyeglasses then opened the back, took out his fine pen oiler, and began placing drops of liquid on certain parts inside.

"Why are you doing that?"

"I'm oiling it," he said. "With whale oil."

"Why *whale*?"

"It's more pure than the earth's oil," he explained. "I need to oil the pivots. This is the verge." Dad pointed to a part shaped like a boat anchor that moved back and forth. "That's what makes the ticking noise. This is the pendulum bob, and this is the bezel that holds the glass face. This pin holds the hands in front." Dad took out an old leather purse and removed from it an assortment of files, screwdrivers, and wire cutters.

"This clock over here is losing time." Dad slid his chair toward another patient. "It's winding down. It has what's called a variable source of power and needs rewinding." Dad pulled up another chair. "Here, do you want to wind it?" he asked and handed me a key. When I heard the door to the basement open, I looked up and saw Mom backlit at the top of the stairs.

"Did Abby tell you?" Mom's steps were slow as she descended.

"Did Abby tell me what?" Dad asked.

"About Matt's not-so-happy New Year."

We were having a good time until Matt interrupted it. Again.

"Matt was pretty sick this morning. He got drunk again last night. Abby knows. She's seen him," Mom said. "I think we all know he has a problem." She paused and then added, "And some of my jewelry is missing." Could Matt steal from Mom?

"What's gone?"

"The necklace you gave me on our anniversary."

"I'll talk to him."

"He needs more than a talking-to."

"What do you suggest?"

"I don't know. I don't like where he's headed."

"I don't either," Dad agreed, frowning.

"I told him he's grounded and that I'd be accompanying him everywhere, but that's not a long-term solution. Something else is going on," she said sadly. "I was thinking he needed to talk to someone. What if he. . ." Mom stopped and took a slow breath. "What if we *all* went in for counseling?"

Dad went back to the clocks.

"Don't do that, John," Mom said. "That clock thing. It doesn't help us figure out what to do. We need to talk."

"I *am* talking. Maybe Matt could see a counselor at school or something."

"Oh, I see. Matt has a problem, but not *you*," she said, tapping the table on *you*. "And Abby? You want me to make an appointment for her, too?" I winced. "Fine," she said, and headed back upstairs.

Dad polished the exterior of the wood case, oiling it, then wiping it in silence. One side section had been damaged, almost as if someone had hammered it. Dad had sanded the wound and begun restoring the wood. I wished Dad could do the same with us.

On the first Sunday of the New Year, Mom said we needed fresh air, so she made Matt and me walk to church in our boots. Grooves of frozen muddy water made the trip a challenge. Because it hadn't snowed since Christmas Eve, we were surrounded by the melting and refreezing remains of stained brown slush. No hope for a fresh flurry, just bitter-cold temperatures. How I longed for a good snowfall. The snowball-packing kind that covered the ugliness with white. The sky was dark, heavy, and overcast, so typical for January in the Midwest, and nearly as dense as the depression hovering over us.

It was too cold in church for me to take off my coat. Something had exploded in the boiler room, so there would be only one service that Sunday.

No sunshine illuminated the stained-glass windows, making the church dull and dark. So dim that during the singing of "In the Bleak Midwinter," Matt ducked out of the sanctuary without Mom noticing. Though I had never before understood how winter could be bleak, I did now. This was Reverend Davidson's first Sunday, and I had to confess some relief at his rough start. He was our third interim; the previous two looked like they had retired twenty years before. So far, nobody could rival Dad.

After that cold Epiphany service, Reverend Davidson announced Mrs. Tinsley wouldn't be teaching my fourth-grade Sunday school class anymore. She had slipped on the ice and broken her hip. Did parishioners want to bring in hot meals? Being out a Sunday school teacher at the first of the year wasn't a good omen. Hadn't Mom called that *prognostication*?

Two weeks later, when Matt's first semester report card came home, we learned Matt was not only skipping church but school as well, and so Mom called a family conference in the dining room. I wondered if she thought I was somehow his accomplice. And in my silence, was I?

"It says Matthew John McAndrews was absent four days in November and six in December." Mom held the report card at arm's length. Matt couldn't alter a typed report card mailed home. "I know you were sick once, but the rest of this is a problem."

"I'm disappointed, Matt," Dad added.

Matt raised his eyebrows. It was the face of a dare, beckoning Dad to fight.

"Do I need to drop in periodically to check and see if you stayed in school? Or shall I go with you to class and hold your hand?" Mom suggested.

"No, Mom."

"I didn't think so."

Matt stood up and pushed in his chair, "Look, no other guy is grounded all the time. I'm fifteen but you treat me like a kid." He stopped. "Like Abby," Matt concluded derisively.

"Abby's showing more maturity than you are right now," Dad said.

I didn't like being a part of the comparison and exhaled through my teeth.

"Don't do that, Abby," Dad said and then returned to Matt. "The reason we treat you like a kid is because you're acting like one. You're not ready for responsibility."

"We can't trust you, Matt," Mom chimed in. Had she talked to him about her necklace?

"As you earn our trust, you'll get more responsibility and then more freedom," Dad concluded.

I looked up at Matt. He was rolling his eyes but they missed it. Why was he doing that? I didn't want to be in this much trouble— ever.

"You can go upstairs and start on your missing work. Now."

My perfect packing snow arrived that evening. I had been testing each snowfall with marginal results. But after rolling a snowball from the foot of the steps down the length of the front walk, I had the base for an enormous snowman that could greet any passersby. This was not just any snowman, either. This was a *fat*man. A corpulent, obese snow creature who was more than rotund. I then ran back to the house and rolled a second ball in a parallel line. I strained to lift its weight, but it wouldn't even budge.

"Matt!" I yelled. "I need help!"

Matt opened his window and looked out.

"What's up?"

"I can't lift it."

"I don't want to make a snowman, Abby. Besides, I've been banished to the tower."

"Just put this ball on top, then I'll roll the head and you can go back inside. It's really good snow."

I remembered a time we'd made a fort. And another time we'd made snow creatures and lay in the snow, teaching Joel how to make angels. Mom had Joel so bundled up he could barely flap his arms up and down, so Joel's angel wings were small. When I helped him stand back up, we accidentally stepped on the design. Still, Joel stood in awe as if it were a real angel. Then Joel wanted to make our angels hold hands. And so we lay in the snow with me in the middle, holding Matt and Joel's hands as we swished our arms up and down to make wings. Did Matt remember?

"Please, Matt?"

"Oh, all right. But only for a minute."

Though it was bitterly cold, Matt only put on gloves and a hat. Either he was trying to be like his friends—underdressed and cold—or he meant it. I had one minute.

Matt struggled to heft the second mound on top and floundered. Some of the snow chipped off, so I began patching our snowman.

"He'll be even taller than me," Matt calculated. Did Matt actually sound proud?

"How do you know it's a *him*?"

"Oh, shut up," he swore.

"You're not supposed to say that."

"You gonna tell?" Matt dared. He knew I wouldn't.

"It's a *her* anyway," I argued.

He tried again to lift the snowball, his face reddening with the strain. I lifted from my side until we had the ball slightly above the first snowball and then we lowered it. As I began gluing the two balls together with handfuls of snow, he turned to go.

"Where's the head?" I called out.

"Oh yeah," he said reluctantly, and waited.

I rolled a third stripe through the yard, stopping at Matt's feet. Matt easily picked it up and then raised it above his head to set it on top. Our snowman was now much taller than Matt. Then he began pressing two snowballs across the front of what now would be a *her*.

"Matt!" I said in mock horror, my face warming.

"You said it was a *girl*," he reminded as he stood back and surveyed the stout lady.

"You've been watching too many of those bad movies in the graveyard."

He shrugged and headed back to the house.

"Can't you stay?"

"It's cold."

"Then put something on."

But Matt kept going. He kept moving away like always. I picked up another ball to start a friend for my snow lady, but instead fired a shot at his head. I'm usually a pretty bad aim, but that day I was Davy to his Goliath.

"Hey!" he yelled, batting the snow off his head and neck.

"You taught me how," I said, giving him the credit.

Matt rubbed his head and took off his hat to shake the snow off. By then I had fired three more shots, two direct hits—one strategically nailing him on the butt.

If he was cold, he had forgotten. But now he was mad. Matt picked up a handful of snow and pitched it with his usual baseball precision. I ducked and narrowly missed a pitch to my head. But I wasn't so lucky with Matt's next four. Each time I bent over to make a snowball, he fired off another two shots. The scrape of snow on skin slashed like glass.

I retreated behind the hedge, but he lobbed them over. My face smarted from the last hit that nailed me in the right eye.

"Cut it out!"

"You started it!" he said as he shot another volley over the hedge. It was harder for me to make it over but I returned fire for fire. Or ice for ice.

Then I noticed Joel's red wagon beneath the hedge and began filling it with ammunition. After ten snowballs, I moved down the sidewalk toward the tree and started firing them off, one-two-three-four-five-six. I had no idea what I'd do when I ran out, but I knew I'd go out in a blaze of glory.

I moved in on him, pulling the red wagon. Our flurry of snowballs quickened as we pummeled each other at close range. I always lost a snowball fight, but this time it felt good. I was *in* the fight. At close range I could nail him nearly every time. And though everything he threw at me hurt, it hurt better than not feeling anything. It hurt better than being invisible.

Finally I stormed the last four feet and ran squarely into him. The surprise jolted him so much, he staggered and nearly fell over. Just as I stepped back to plunge forward for a second attack, instead I ran up to him and wrapped my arms around him. At first he wrestled with me, but I wouldn't let go. I buried my head into his sweater and locked my fingers together around his back. With the rhythms of a wrestler out of season, he slowed until he stopped. And then we stood there, not speaking.

"Hey," he said at last.

I wouldn't let go. Actually, I *couldn't* let go.

"It's okay." Until he said it, I hadn't realized I was crying. Or maybe I started crying because he said it. Who knows? "Let's go inside now."

I didn't want to let go. He was listening to me and he had played with me and I thought maybe he still loved me. I squeezed him tightly and then dropped my arms. He took my shoulders and surveyed me at arm's length.

"Oh Abby," he said, his voice thick with emotion. "Is that why you're crying?" Matt tugged off his glove and stroked my cheek. There was blood on his hand. "I hurt you. I'm sorry, Abby. I didn't mean to."

How could his touch ever hurt? The warmth of his hand brought life to my scraped cheek; I could feel the sting and it felt good and right.

"We gotta get inside and put something on that," he said, putting his glove back on and taking my hand. But then he stomped his foot and pulled away. "Shoot, Mom's going to kill me."

"I'll tell her—"

"You tell her the *truth*," Matt interrupted as he turned to me. "You tell her that *you* started it and I'll *still* be in trouble." He shook his head. "I wasn't even supposed to be down here. Now I'll probably have even more sessions with that counselor." Matt slumped in defeat. "Oh, what does it matter?"

"I'm sorry, Matt," I said. But I wasn't sorry. This was the best thing that had happened this whole year. Even if it was only a few days old.

"No, *I'm* sorry," he said.

I smiled up at him. Complete forgiveness.

"People always get hurt, but never me." Matt kicked at the snow.

I took off my scarf and wound it around his neck.

"It was my fault," Matt said.

"No, it wasn't. I started it!" I would have laughed, but Matt looked so sober, staring at the snow. A brutal wind whipped across the yard. I shivered and wiggled my toes in my boots and clenched my fingers tightly, then opened and closed them over and over.

Matt muttered something inaudible.

"What?"

"I said that's not what I meant."

I blew warm air down my gloves and rubbed my hands together.

"I shouldn't have let Dad carry him."

I stopped, frozen by his words. Was he serious?

"Matt, it wasn't your fault. It wasn't anybody's fault. Except maybe that lady driving the car."

"Abby, Joel wanted *me* to hold him—" Matt's voice choked. "It's all *he* wanted. He just wanted *me* and I let him down. Literally."

I didn't know what to do with his words and thought if only Matt could tell somebody else—maybe Dad or Mom—it might help. But then I realized that telling them might not make it better. Dad had pulled Joel out of Matt's arms, and Mom had told him to.

"It was an accident. You couldn't know," I said desperately. I felt like I was losing a brother. Again.

"Do you remember what happened?" he asked seriously, intently.

"Well, yeah," I answered and thought, *Unfortunately.*

"Where was *I*?" Matt stood without shivering.

"What do you mean?" I asked, shaking even though I was the one wearing a coat.

"Where was I when it happened?"

I stomped my feet in the snow. I could barely feel them anymore.

"Well, you weren't driving the car," I snapped. I felt like he was trying to trick me or something.

"No, really, Abby, I don't remember. I don't remember *anything*. I don't remember seeing it happen, and I don't remember anything about the road or the ambulance or anything." Matt's face begged for information. "It's all a blank. I just want to know what I did."

"You tried to get a doctor," I answered quickly.

"But that was *afterward*. WHERE WAS I WHEN JOEL GOT HIT?" he pleaded.

This felt like when the sheriff came to our back door. An interrogation.

I remembered Dad unfastening Joel from Matt's back and carrying him, and I remembered thinking how nice that looked, and then I remembered a blue car and how it seemed like it was coming at us and I felt my mother push me and I fell and I saw the car hit Dad and then there was Joel and the windshield and then there was no Joel.

But there was no Matt.

I played the whole awful scene in my head over and over, but I couldn't see what was happening beside or behind me. After the accident, Matt was running to Joel and Matt was running around, yelling for a doctor and pounding on car windows and begging people to do something, but there was no Matt when the car hit. I closed my eyes and let the snow fall on my eyelids. I didn't have peripheral vision, and I couldn't see something that wasn't on the screen.

"You see? You can't find me there either," he said softly.

"So? What does that *mean*?" I asked.

"I ran. I must have run," he decided. "I could have done *something. Anything*. But I didn't see anything because I was a *coward*. Maybe the car was headed for *me*." Matt's eyes were a watery cold blue.

I kicked a clod of ice. I wanted to say something. I wanted to hug him, but that wouldn't help because I didn't know the truth. I only knew that even if he ran, he hadn't done the wrong thing. Did *anybody* do the wrong thing? Did anybody do the *right* thing?

The longer Matt stood there, the more frozen he appeared. He would be a statue soon—unmovable, a solid ice sculpture. He stared at me in silence. I didn't know what he was thinking, but his face looked cold and sad. I felt something trickle, the dampness of a tear, except I wasn't crying. I touched the side of my face. My wool glove was stained with blood, but nothing hurt because I, too, was frozen. Matt's eyes softened and he took off his glove again. His hand was warm when he touched my cheek. He touched my wound like I wished I could touch his.

Sixteen

"We have a little over a month, John. Then what?" Mom asked over breakfast. The kitchen table suddenly seemed small and confined. When February began, we knew time was running out on Dad's sabbatical, and our home. We tried not to talk about the obvious, but sometimes Mom brought it up. Usually at meals, when family time became fighting time.

"I can't return just because of a deadline. There has to be a reason," Dad said, adding two pancakes to his plate.

"What about *three*?" Mom asked, looking around the table. Matt acted like he wasn't listening and pushed his scrambled eggs around with his fork.

"I'd be faking it. Every single day."

"That sounds familiar." Mom punched the words and then gained momentum as she paced the short length of the kitchen. "Every single day I get up and I pass the door to his bedroom and I think about getting him out of bed or I think about surprising him with pancakes or I forget and set the table for *five*. Every single day I'm home but he is not here. Every single day I say good night to Abby and then I turn to go to his bed and touch his sleeping face. Every single day. You want to talk about faking it? Give it a try sometime."

Mom's voice held anger and tears. I wasn't afraid of her anger, but I feared her sadness, and the only thing I knew to do was throw my arms around her like she would throw her arms around me—but I just couldn't.

Mom began clearing the table, although it was obvious most of our plates were full. Maybe she knew we weren't hungry anymore. She scraped the plates into the garbage can and then dropped them in the sink with such force I heard something break. I cringed but nobody else looked worried. "And how about this? I've always hated playing that church organ. Did you know *that*? But I've done a pretty good job of faking *that* for all these years."

Matt smiled and turned away.

"And what's so funny about *that*, young man?"

Matt shrugged, trying to hide his half smile. "Well, I'm not sure it was such a good fake job."

Mom's face made an "ah," but nothing came out.

"I mean, well. . . ," he stammered. "You didn't *fake* playing that well."

Dad's eyes widened. Mine must have been saucers. Then even Dad smiled and I got the giggles. The nervous kind because you're not supposed to. Like during prayers of repentance when a big belly laugh comes out of nowhere.

"Laughter at my expense?" Mom asked as she threw up her hands and turned to leave.

"Don't feel bad," Dad called after her. "The organ and the clock are the two most complicated mechanical inventions prior to the Industrial Revolution."

We three made eye contact, shrugged shoulders, and sat in silence like scolded schoolchildren, united by memories of dissonance and discord. But she wasn't through.

"Tell me again why I'm still playing that obsolescent monstrosity?" she asked, returning as if an idea was forming. I think it was a rhetorical question, which was a good thing because we had no answer.

The next day, while I watched Saturday morning cartoons, Mom announced, "You've got a new Sunday school teacher."

"Really? I thought nobody wanted our class." I stopped spreading peanut butter on graham crackers, my pre-breakfast appetizer. At that moment the Road Runner slapped a false train tunnel on the side of a mountain, foreshadowing doom for Wile E. Coyote. "Mrs. Tinsley's out for the rest of the year?"

"Who's the brave one to take on the Class of 1979?" Matt asked. as he came in with a bowl of cereal.

"It's not Mrs. Johnson, is it?"

"No," she said slowly.

"Please tell me it's not Mrs. Ludema!" I begged.

"It's not," Mom answered, biting her lower lip.

"Well who is it then?" I asked, running out of ideas.

"It's me," she said, looking at Matt and then finally at me.

"You're not disappointed, are you?" she asked at last.

"No, but you *can't*. I mean, you have to practice with the choir during Sunday school."

"No, I don't," Mom continued. "I'm not the organist anymore," she announced. Mom stood taller, prouder. "I now teach fourth-grade Sunday school."

Mom had officially resigned as church organist.

That Sunday Mom's first lesson was on Paul and the early Church. Mom found a way to get us under the church, to pretend we were apostles hiding in the catacombs. The boys in their Sunday best, and we girls in our dresses and black patent leather shoes, trekked through dark, gritty corridors, past cleaning supplies, drippy pipes, the old furnace and the new boiler, and ended by emerging out the basement window to our salvation and the sunny parking lot above.

Our class loved her—especially the boys. But their parents probably preferred Mom back at the organ, looking like she was driving it straight through the altar.

When we arrived home after Mom's debut, I raced downstairs to tell Dad all about the mysteries of our church basement. Dad sat, alone, with the monotonous ticking of clocks. Mom had followed me and, upon hearing the end of the story, smiled shyly.

"Do I rename you Apostle Renee?" Dad asked. Mom cocked her head to the side as if unsure whether he was teasing her. "Sounds like Abby enjoyed Sunday school," Dad reassured, and she was drawn down the remaining stairs.

"Well, at least she wasn't in the library under the table," Mom said. How did she know about that?

"Anything else to report?" Dad asked. I was surprised at his interest.

"The Fitzsimmonses had a baby boy, and Mrs. Sycolin's dog got bit by a raccoon, and Angela's grandma is taking her to Florida for spring break," I said, all in one breath.

"And Greg and Carol got engaged on New Year's Eve, and they asked if you were still doing weddings," Mom added quickly.

"They can get married at the church," Dad answered.

"But Carol doesn't want just *anybody* doing the service."

"I don't know," he answered, which really sounded like no.

"I could understand not doing a funeral, but you could do a wedding," Mom continued.

"It might send a message," Dad said, adjusting his Clock Doc glasses.

"What kind of message?" Mom questioned. "That you're back in business?"

Dad concentrated on the back of the clock, a miniature screwdriver in his hand. Mom leaned over the table until she was nearly face-to-face with him.

"Or does it have something to do with the institution of marriage? Is that something you question, too?" she whispered. She must have thought I couldn't hear.

"Renee, I don't question marriage—yet," he muttered, glaring at her persistence.

"We've got a couple of weeks, John, and then I don't know what we're doing. I don't know if we can make it on this clock stuff. And why would they allow us to stay in the house? The attendance is way down after those first interims. The church is struggling, John. People need someone to do weddings, to do funerals. To do *life.*"

Dad looked grim.

"Please tell me you have a plan." And with that she turned quickly and trudged upstairs.

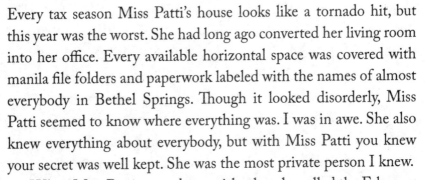

Every tax season Miss Patti's house looks like a tornado hit, but this year was the worst. She had long ago converted her living room into her office. Every available horizontal space was covered with manila file folders and paperwork labeled with the names of almost everybody in Bethel Springs. Though it looked disorderly, Miss Patti seemed to know where everything was. I was in awe. She also knew everything about everybody, but with Miss Patti you knew your secret was well kept. She was the most private person I knew.

When Miss Patti came down with what she called the February flu, Mom took over. Miss Patti said she felt so awful, she couldn't get up the stairs to her bedroom and instead collapsed on the couch of her office, the one place not yet occupied by files.

"Renee, you really need to leave. I don't want to make y'all sick."

"You need some help, Patti. Tell me what to do."

"Only if Abby leaves," Patti said. Mom nodded in agreement

but I didn't move. I knew she wouldn't notice one way or the other. "Maybe if you could hand me a few files, I could work on them here on the couch. I need to get started on some of these right away," Miss Patti added, vaguely waving her hand in the direction of a stack of files. Miss Patti looked flushed and unable to focus.

"Tell me the names," Mom asked, eager to help.

"Hindrichs. Try the third drawer down in the file cabinet. And then pick up that blue notebook from the end of the table." She wiped her sweaty brow and Mom frowned.

"You don't need to do anything right now except get better," Mom said. "You should take it easy."

"It's tax season," Miss Patti argued. "I can't."

"Then you're going to need help," Mom said. "I think I can do it." To me she added, "Abby, you need to go home now. Miss Patti's right. You might get sick."

"And I'm paying you," Miss Patti said, as if not giving up without getting her way. "We're both getting a deal out of this." She sighed and leaned back on the couch. Rita nodded at me. We were getting a good deal, too.

Mom began spending each day at Miss Patti's, leaving our house after making breakfast for Matt and me. Miss Patti was down for days, and then had to play catch-up. She had Mom typing, filing, running numbers, and filling out forms. Mom's heels would click across the floor, and Patti would roll her office chair to various file cabinets, opening and shutting drawers with a *swish* and a *click*. Mom didn't come home after school, and so I often joined her at Miss Patti's, where Rita and I did our homework at her kitchen table.

Most of the time, it was quiet in the living room, but sometimes the two of them laughed. And when they did, we tried to listen in but were always too late for the punch line. Mom was efficient and organized, and finding accounting a better fit than accompanying. When Miss Patti said Mom was a natural, Mom beamed as if it were her first compliment.

After homework, Rita and I played board games, read books, and sometimes watched television. They often sent us to run certain files to clients' houses and even do special pickups for elderly customers. Miss Patti even paid us. But the more time Mom spent at Miss Patti's, the less she spent at our house with Dad. The more time I spent with Rita, the less I spent with Matt. Five minus one divided by two equaled two, but we were lonely twosomes. If we were talking accounting, the minuses outweighed the plusses, and I missed being a family. Though I didn't want to think about it, I couldn't help but remember how the Hanleys alternated holidays, and that made me worried.

Valentine's Day fell on a Sunday. Mom and I went to church together and heard Reverend Davidson speak from the love chapter about fourteen ways to say "I love you." I wished Dad had been there to hear it. I wondered if Dad would take Mom out later, but when we got home, Mom heated up Campbell's soup and made tuna melts, which didn't seem like much of a Valentine's dinner.

"Twenty Questions," I began. "I'm thinking of something. . ."

"Is it bigger than a bread box?" Mom began so obviously.

"Yes."

"Is it bigger than a car?" Matt continued.

"Yes," I answered. I didn't know if my idea counted since it was kind of tricky. They'd probably say I was cheating.

"Is it bigger than a building?" Mom asked.

"Yes."

"Is it a place?" Mom asked.

"No." They were starting to catch on.

"Well, it's certainly not a person!" Matt laughed.

"Is it an idea or emotion?" Dad asked.

"Yes," I answered, looking up at Dad. He was on to me.

"That's five," I said, holding up my hand.

"Is it *love*?" Dad asked softly.

"Yes," I answered, nodding.

"That was a good one," Mom said gently. "How'd you guess it so easily?"

"Well, it *is* Valentine's Day," Matt said sarcastically.

"It was our verse today," I said, nodding to Mom and then repeating what she had given me a star on the chart for just an hour before. A verse about the height, breadth, depth, and width of God's love. When I finished, I added my own conclusion: "God's love is immeasurable."

Matt shook his head like he was disgusted.

"That's not really fair," Matt argued, even though I knew he didn't care about the game. "Love isn't really a *thing*."

"Person, place, thing, or *idea*," Mom corrected. "Let it go, Matt."

"Okay, so here's mine," Matt said suddenly, more to me than anyone else. "Why didn't God just *make* us love Him so we wouldn't mess up?"

"And then, if God's love is so great," Dad added, "why do bad things happen?" We became quiet. This wasn't the way to play Twenty Questions. He was breaking the rules. His question couldn't be answered with a yes or no. Or maybe couldn't be answered at all.

I felt confused. I had always been the one to ask where the butterfly goes when it rains, or why God bothered making mosquitoes, or how places in the world are in different times or even different days, and suddenly I was very scared my dad didn't have the world figured out.

"So if it's okay to ask questions, then okay," I said. "Why are we here? Why would God bother making people who would sin? And why did God create people when He had angels? And why did Adam get to name the animals? Eve would have come up with something better than *dog* or *cat*." I said it in one breath. I didn't have answers but I wanted to prove I had questions, too, and that just because I had questions didn't mean there wasn't a God.

"Bravo, Abby!" Matt said, clapping slowly as if capturing air between his hands.

I blinked quickly, hoping I wouldn't cry. I didn't dare look at anyone. Finally Mom broke the silence.

"My turn." She looked straight at Dad. "Do you wish Joel had never been born?"

Dad stopped suddenly.

Mom and Dad stared at each other as if in a no-blinking contest.

Had Dad not heard? I could repeat the question for him. I could scream, *"Do you wish that Joel had never been born?"* But I didn't and neither did Mom. She waited and so we all waited.

"That's hard to answer," Dad said at last. And then the silence built up a pressure so strong that the idea of a lifetime of no Joel hit me like an ocean wave, threatening to knock me off my feet. Joel was not erasable. I couldn't just stop and rewind my life like when Dad made the family movies go in reverse. We couldn't rewind to before Joel's birth, throw away the reels, and then go forward never knowing him. It was so impossible, it was ridiculous. We could never forget.

But now Mom's question had to be answered. Good or bad.

"I would answer that question differently at different times," Dad concluded. "So much joy, so little sadness. We weren't unhappy before, but look at us now. Ask me again in ten years. I'll have a better perspective."

I felt like Dad had hit me in the stomach. Or that maybe I should hit him in his. He couldn't have actually said that. This was Joel we were talking about. But nobody spoke until Mom drew a deep breath.

And at first I thought I imagined Mom's response because my head was ringing with that question and it didn't sound like her voice. This voice was steely.

"You mean right now you'd say you wish Joel had never been born?"

Mom said the words *never* and *been* and *born* with huge spaces in between. "What else are you planning on wishing away?" she continued. "What about all of *us*? What if one day *we* bring you grief?" Mom had way more questions than I had and they kept coming. "And does that mean you wish we never married because then we'd never have had Joel?"

I bit my lip so hard I tasted metal. I licked the blood away and swallowed hard, trying not to cry.

"You asked me a question," Dad said.

"I did. You're right. That's fair," she admitted. "But your response to life is unfair. It's like you can't or won't make any new memories and we're supposed to live with someone who's stuck with only regrets. I *can not* do it." Mom separated and spliced *can* and *not* with great enunciation. *Can not* had never seemed more deliberate. What did that mean? Was she giving up on Dad? Or was it just that she could not do something anymore? I was confused.

"STOP IT! JUST STOP IT! I hate it when you guys fight," I yelled. Everything inside of me after months of quiet was churning and incensed. I wondered how many of Mom's not-so-nice vocabulary words gleaned from the newspaper I could remember and spew unguarded and unchecked. *Insidious, detrimental, catastrophic, menacing, horrendous.* I searched for a word that would describe the hateful way we treated each other. "I *despise* it when you fight." I jumped out of my chair and screeched it across the floor. I searched for a word. I needed somebody to be at fault. The only thing I was sure of was that it wasn't Joel. He didn't ask to die. Matt had a smirk on his face. What was *wrong* with him? Was nobody on *my* side?

"You care more about *Joel* than you do about *us*. He's dead, but we're still here," I blurted out and then gasped. I couldn't believe I said that. Matt's eyes widened. The smirk was gone.

"Quite a *question*, Renee," Dad said, as if to blame Mom.

"Quite an *answer*, John," she said. They hadn't listened to me. Mom looked at Matt and then me. She sighed and I could see *I'm sorry* written on her face. "We love you. We'll get through this," she said. I wasn't convinced. Mom reached for Matt, who backed away. She got up and hugged me, but it seemed as forced and contrived as her words. I kept my arms at my sides until she let go and then ran upstairs and away from the questions. Something was very broken and somebody needed to fix us, fast.

I practiced my piano differently that day. I really pounded the keys and it felt good. I turned each legato song into staccato and each pianissimo into forte. The pieces were now unrecognizable, and I liked them that way.

That night Mom came into my room to put me to bed—something she had rarely done since Joel died. I pretended I was asleep but she tucked in my covers anyway. As she turned to leave, I whispered, "Are you going to leave him?" I knew about these things. Jennifer's mom had left her dad.

Mom paused in the crack of the door, backlit by the hall light.

"Why would you ask, Abby?" she answered, without turning around. I was afraid she couldn't face me. "Are you worried about that?" She didn't come right out and say no, so I knew leaving him must have crossed her mind.

"You've thought about it," I pointed out. And now that I'd vocalized it, it was something I had to consider, too. Who would I live with? Would Dad be able to take care of me? Would Mom have to go back to work? Where would we live? Would Mom get one kid and Dad the other? Did losing Joel really have to mean losing our family?

"I've thought about a lot of things," Mom said, shutting the door and cutting out all light. "And sometimes leaving seems easiest." She sat on my bed. "Your dad can't move on, and I have to. But that doesn't mean I'll be able to move on by leaving him. Some things you can never leave behind; you have to work through them instead."

The possibility hovered like stagnant smoke. I needed more reassurance than that. I wanted to know we could have a happy ending, even if I couldn't imagine how.

"What will you do?" I persisted.

"Abby, let me explain something." She lightly stroked my hair. "When you were born, I loved you, but I cried a lot. I didn't think I'd ever be a good enough mom. Everything just seemed too much to handle. It was like being in a dark tunnel, and I wondered if I'd ever get out of it. But I did." She paused and took a long, slow breath. "Your dad walked me through that tunnel, and thank God I was able to become a mother to you and Matt," she said with new energy. "I feel guilty about some of those weeks—months. But what can I say? I did the best I could. I'm sorry." Her fingers continued playing with my hair, but her words stopped. I was pretty sure she was done.

"Mom, you don't have to be sorry." I turned to face her. "I don't remember it." My eyes had adjusted and I could see her silhouette. I reached for her hand and laid mine on top of hers.

"Well, that makes two of us," she agreed. "But you see, I think maybe Dad has his own tunnel now." Mom explained it as if to reassure herself. "I need to cry, but I can't," she confessed, looking to where Joel's bed had been. "I *can't* because Dad *can*. Dad can take this time-out, but somehow I have to keep everything moving forward. I have to get Dad through the tunnel." I wondered if Mom had any idea how long the tunnel could be, and then as an afterthought, she apologized. "And here I am dumping on a nine-year-old."

Mom's words were sad, but there was something almost hopeful in the way she said them. Sort of like what we had learned about oil paintings in Miss Gettman's Great Masterpieces unit. She had shown us a painting of a room with heavy drab colors but one area strangely illuminated. She asked us to determine the direction of the light source and to speculate about what it could have been. After that, whenever I looked at a painting, I looked for the source of light.

"It's okay, Mom. I like talking to you." I leaned against her. "Sometimes at night I used to talk with Joel. We'd whisper to each other in the dark. I still do. I don't know if he can hear me, but it makes me feel better."

Mom was quiet. I wondered what she was thinking about my talking in the night. I frowned in suspense.

"That's good," Mom said at last, and I relaxed. "You can talk to anybody you want to, Abby." She stroked my arm. "And maybe it would help for you to talk to the counselor at school—if you want."

And then Mom took both my hands in hers and said, "Every day I feel a little different. I have new feelings that aren't always good, but they're new and I'm feeling something. And sometimes in that mixture of feelings there's hope."

If Mom had hope, then I knew our painting had a source of light. I didn't know what it was, but something made the drab colors brighten.

She squeezed my hands tightly. "Abby, for now all we can do is hope."

SEVENTEEN

"Twist and Shout" blared over the gym loudspeakers, and so that's exactly what fifty-three fourth graders did. Our PE class plus Mr. Lemke was really shaking it up, and it wasn't pretty. Mr. Lemke loved blasting his Beatles music as loudly as he could get away with, so that's what we exercised to at every PE class.

Not only was Mr. Lemke going prematurely deaf, but he didn't look anything like Jack LaLanne, my television model of fitness who swam the Golden Gate Channel towing a twenty-five-hundred-pound cabin cruiser and who could do one thousand chin-ups when I could only do three.

I didn't feel like jumping jacks today. I felt sluggish and couldn't make my muscles move. Like most nights, I had tossed most of my sleep away and awakened tired and worried.

Despite the lyrics, I wasn't working anything out in my life or on the gymnasium floor. Rita jumped and I flapped my wings apathetically. Then as if on cue, we pointed to each other, exclaiming the lie that we really looked good, and we twisted and shouted in a frenzy until my head spun and everything was tingly and dark and the next thing I remember was lying on the floor with Rita hovering above.

"Are you okay?"

"What do you mean?"

"You fell down or something."

"I'm fine," I said quickly.

"Are you sure? I should tell Mr. Lemke."

"No, Rita. Don't. I'm okay, really."

I was pretty sure I'd fainted. People fainted all the time. It was not a big deal, but if Rita made it one, everybody would be looking at me and then Mom and Dad would have to know and tonight I had plans.

The song ended and Mr. Lemke said it was time for cooldown and stretching, so Rita joined me on the gym floor as he played "Puff, the Magic Dragon," one of the most depressing songs I've ever heard.

"Can you come over after school?" I asked.

Rita looked around as if Mr. Lemke could hear us talking. But his ears were already ruined by rock and roll. She didn't answer. I could tell she was having to think about it.

"Well, maybe. . .but wouldn't you rather come to *my* house?" she asked. "Or maybe we could go sledding down Terror Ridge?" I wondered if she was offering other choices just in case I wanted to get out of my house or if she didn't like coming over anymore. I had to admit, playing at my house wasn't like it used to be.

"We can sled," I said at last, rather weakly, too tired to argue the merits of a playdate at my house. I'd play with her this afternoon, but tonight was special. I had to bring my palm branch to the Ash Wednesday service.

Last year on Palm Sunday the preschoolers had run in with their palm branches, and the elementary school kids had followed singing the "Hosanna" song. Last year, Dad had told the congregation to wave their branches like a banner and imagine they were in Jerusalem. He explained that Jesus' followers didn't want somebody to heal their wounded hearts; they wanted a battle warrior. They were saying, "We want a king! Down with Rome!" He said that maybe the only ones who were truly innocent in their praise were the children.

Joel loved it all. I thought we had a picture of Joel waving the palm branch and almost dancing up the aisles. Probably only Joel could have gotten away with that in our decidedly Presbyterian church. I can almost hold the snapshot in my hand, but after I looked all over for it, I had to admit it was only in my head. The picture we never took.

Dad challenged everybody to save their palms to be burned the next year. I liked the way Dad planned it out, my palm branch recycled, everything coming full circle the way the hands on a clock go around and return to their spot and the way seasons come and go.

The ashes from last year's Palm Sunday branches would mark our foreheads on this year's Ash Wednesday. We would wear the mark of a sinner and the remembrance that we were forgiven. *Absolution.* After church that day, certain women in the Hannah Circle twisted and tied the palm branches into crosses and handed them back to us.

The two palm frond crosses were still pinned to my bulletin board. Now I had to find somebody to take me to the service.

After sledding the afternoon away with Rita and then doing homework adding up Roman numerals and memorizing a list of spelling words, I climbed on my bed and took down the two yellowed palm crosses. I kept them behind my back as I headed downstairs, where Dad was in the kitchen making what I hoped was dinner.

"What's cookin'?"

"The Whites' clocks," Dad said. "I've got one on the burner and one in the oven."

"I don't get it." I pulled up a chair near the oven, feeling the warmth from the boiling water and the heat from the oven.

"They said these clocks didn't work. But they really just need a cleaning," Dad explained.

"But won't the oven wreck them?"

"No, they're full of dirt and grease. I took a toothbrush and some gasoline and scrubbed the mechanism. Now it's getting a boiling bath." Dad pointed to the clockworks on the front burner. "But if I don't dry it off, it'll rust, so I put the boiled clockworks in the oven on low."

I shook my head. Looked risky to me.

"But I can't do that with a clock with wooden gears. Just the ones made of metal."

"So will that take all night?" I asked.

"No, just another hour or so. Why? Did you have something in mind?"

"Sort of. . ."

Dad drew up a chair, sat down, opened the oven, and gave it a peek.

"Want some dinner?" he teased. Mom was working late again at Miss Patti's and we were on our own.

"I'm not hungry for clock," I said softly. "Besides, we probably don't have *time* for dinner," I added, almost stalling, knowing time was easier to tell than the truth.

Matt came in the back door and slammed it behind him.

"What's cooking?"

"Time," Dad said.

"I want to take my palm branch back." I offered up the two crosses from last year.

"I see." Dad stood then, lifted the pot from the stove, and poured the boiling water into the sink. The steam enveloped his head and I couldn't see his face. "I can't, Abby." He put the clockworks on a pan and slipped it in the oven with the other piece.

"Then I'll go by myself," I said.

"It gets dark too early. I don't want you out alone."

"I'll take her," Matt said. I turned in surprise.

"You're on probation," Dad reminded him.

I looked at Matt quizzically. Did he say he'd take me just to get out of the house?

"It's only a few blocks. You can trust me to get her to church."

"And back?" Dad asked.

"And back," Matt answered.

"Well, I suppose it wouldn't hurt for you two to spend an hour together in a familiar pew," Dad said, baptizing the next clock in boiling water.

That evening as Matt and I neared the church, we were welcomed by a glowing fire. I watched people place their frond in the fire barrel and I handed Joel's to Matt. We dropped our fronds into the fire, the sudden burst of flame lighting Matt's face. Then we headed to the balcony where we sat alone, invisible. I counted twenty-three people, six bald heads in the congregation. I wasn't really sure I wanted to wear an ash smudge, but I did want to see what happened to the twenty-three palm branches; and unlike other churches with morning services, we only had a few hours to bear the mark.

"In the Old Testament, ashes have been associated with sorrow and remorse," Reverend Davidson began. I wondered where he was going with this and didn't know whether I'd like it or not. Reverend Davidson always did church in a new way, which both interested and concerned me. Would people like him better than Dad? Would our vague housing extension continue long enough for Dad to come back? "'Roll in ashes; make mourning as for an only son,'" he read from Jeremiah 6:26. "But in the New Testament, we know that our sins were forgiven by God's only Son's death on the cross."

I gave Matt a sideways glance. Was he listening? I wished Dad was here. Dad was more "associated with sorrow and remorse" than with New Testament forgiveness.

"On Ash Wednesday, we wear the cross. The ash cross on the forehead was a practice begun in the twelfth century. Ashes from burned palm branches were mixed with oil and smudged on the Christian's forehead as a reminder that we are sinners needing forgiveness." At this point, someone brought in the ashes and dribbled oil into the bowl.

"As we sing 'Amazing Grace,' please make your way to the altar to receive the mark of the cross."

One by one, Dad's congregation came forward to be touched by Reverend Davidson. Matt and I filed down the winding balcony stairs and into the aisle. I knelt and lifted my face to receive the powdered cross on my forehead. Looking down the altar rail, I could see Matt wearing the sign of the cross. We returned to the balcony with our mark, the last to be seated.

"Today we're going to do something different," Reverend Davidson continued. "You see the mark, but do you understand the *inner* significance?" he asked. "We need to walk out with the mark on the *inside*. Turn to your neighbor and wipe off their mark. And as you leave tonight, carry the mark *inwardly*." I was glad Mom wasn't there. She would have spit on her hankie and ruined it.

But when I looked at the cross on Matt's face, I didn't want to wipe off his mark. And I wanted mine to stay, too. I shook my head no and he nodded that he understood. Matt already wore the mark inwardly for a reason neither of us could explain.

✳

After the third big snowstorm followed by a layer of sleet, the hill behind the junior high, dubbed Terror Ridge, was a sheet of ice. Each day after school, Rita and I would walk the half mile dragging our toboggans to sled away our afternoon. When we tired of that, we built an ice fort at the bottom of the hill by peeling off sheets of ice from the top of the snow and stacking them in layers for the walls. Even the older boys helped us construct the fort. Though we sometimes sat inside to get out of the wind, it was much more fun to build than to play in it. We called it the icehouse because it took buckets of water splashed between layers of ice to make the house freeze solid. Now whenever we sledded too far, we hit the gouged area missing its surface of ice, making the ride so rough it felt like we were in a paint shaker at Nichols Hardware.

One night when the moon was barely visible, our friends decided to go night sledding and we ran home with the news, begging Mom to let us join them. Dad came in from the kitchen with a hot cup of something to nurse whatever he was coming down with and, after hearing our plea, was unmoved.

"I don't want you kids out there on that ice," Dad said.

"But Dad, we've been doing it for the last two afternoons."

"That hill behind the junior high?"

"*Everybody* does it."

"That's steep and there's a stream at the bottom," Dad argued.

"We never go that far."

"Yes, but it's too slick now. It's like sledding on glass."

"It's just ice, and it's the same ice we sled on by day."

"Then why go at *night?*" Dad asked. "If it's the same ice you sled on by *day.*"

"But Dad, *everybody's* going there tonight. *Please?*" I begged.

"We don't have to do what *everybody's* doing."

"But why not?" Matt questioned matter-of-factly.

"I told you it's not safe. There has to be an adult."

"*I'm* going," Matt countered as if that counted.

Dad shook his head.

I wasn't sure Matt was helping my argument. I could already hear the answer: "*All the more reason for an adult. . .*"

"It's probably the only time they're gonna do it, Dad," I continued, not about to give up.

"There will be more snowstorms," Dad predicted.

"But it's perfect right now. Pretty soon it'll melt and then it'll be all slushy," I said.

"What if *Mom* went?" Matt asked. Mom sat in her favorite easy chair, her feet extended toward the fire. She'd never leave her cozy corner.

"I'd still say it's the *same* dangerous hill and the *same* dangerous ice."

"I just thought it would be fun," I said softly, in my best disappointed voice.

Mom stared at me for a long time, twirling her slippered foot. "It might be fun," she said at last.

Dad looked at Matt and me and then at Mom, shook his head as if in disbelief, and left the room.

That night we could barely see the path from the back of the gym to the bottom of the hill. With too much speed, the only danger was shooting off into the creek below. Each run sounded like one long scrape scratching down a sheet of ice. I've never sledded faster.

We had one sled, one toboggan, and two inner tubes, and they all worked great on the ice. Matt borrowed someone's saucer, and one of his friends twirled him so many times that Matt shot down the hill faster than anything I've ever seen.

"He's a bat out of hell!" Matt's friend Jimmy yelled out. Matt skimmed beside the icehouse and, despite the churned layer of ice, overshot it by twenty feet.

"Matt, that seems too fast," Mom cautioned when he returned panting from the climb. "It worries me."

"Mom, everybody's doing it. It's fine," he said. His breath hung like a cloud of fog. "Don't worry, I never get hurt." And then he took off down the hill with a running start, leaping into the air and flying onto the crest of the hill.

I looked to Mom, whose worried brow said she wished she knew what was at the bottom. "Invincible!" Matt yelled. "Look out beloooooow!"

At last Mom joined in and tested the ice on an inner tube. Matt spun her and she sailed down the hill, laughing. The snow shimmered and glowed in the darkness, the evening set in black and white.

Rita and I took the toboggan and I could hear my dad's precautionary voice even though he wasn't there. *"Don't get your legs caught out to the side or they'll be pulled back."* I tucked my legs securely on top and we shot down what felt like a cliff.

"Look out below!" we called as kids scurried out of our path. We stopped short of the icehouse and the creek below. The next time we formed a chain. Everybody grabbed a hand or foot or the side of someone's saucer and we whipped down the hill together like a snake on the snow, never knowing if the head or the tail of the snake would arrive at the bottom first.

"You wanna ride the saucer now, Abby?" Matt asked. "I could give you a real spin!"

I wasn't so sure about that. I hated being out of control. I was the last one to learn to ride a bike, not because I was scared to fall, but because I hated the feeling I was *about* to fall.

"I think I'll just do the inner tube a few more times," I said, checking to see if Matt was disappointed in me. Matt shrugged his shoulders and took another flying leap, catapulting down the hill. Mom shook her head. "He's crazy!"

When Matt came back I asked to borrow his saucer.

"It's fast," Matt said. "Do you want me to push you?"

"No. Don't do anything. Let me just try it by myself first." I carefully sat down on the saucer, and before I had a chance to even push off, I began slipping. "Woo-hoo!" I squealed as the saucer took off, clinging to its handles as I spun in circles. The wind whipped my face and I closed my eyes, wondering where I was headed. When I opened them, the world was still turning, and I was flying faster and faster. I was dizzy and disoriented and heading down backward. Then I hit the rough path where we had disrupted the surface and I clenched my teeth as I bumped through it. But I did not stop. I heard yelling and I wondered why, but it was too late.

My head hurt, my back ached, and my face was numb. I heard mumbling and somebody saying my name over and over; it sounded sad and I wondered if I was dead, so I opened my eyes to find out if I was. Mom stood over me, a blur, saying my name, but I couldn't answer. I was pretty sure this wasn't heaven.

"Abby, are you okay?"

"I'm okay. I'm fine," I said, before I really knew if I was. I didn't want her to worry.

"Abby, count my fingers," Mom said, holding up her hand. But I couldn't focus right away and everything seemed as dizzying as the spinning ride down the hill. Rita was crying.

"Can we go home now, Mom?" I said faintly.

"I don't want you standing yet, honey," she answered. "Let's wait a minute. I think they're calling an ambulance."

My eyes widened in fear. I wasn't *that* hurt. I *couldn't* be *that* hurt. People who went in ambulances died. I tried to get up but my head hurt too badly and I felt like I was going to throw up. My pillow was the icehouse. *A cracked windshield. Shattered glass like a punctured spiderweb. Fragile.* I had run smack into a structure I had once sprayed solid.

"Did I break it?" I asked Rita, and everybody laughed but then abruptly returned to concern.

"No, but it nearly broke *you*," Matt said, and he wasn't being funny. He looked big as he towered over me. I wanted him to pick me up and carry me home. "I shouldn't have given you the saucer," he added.

I wanted to tell him it was okay, but everybody was talking too much.

Finally, one of the kids who lived nearby ran and got his dad, who was a doctor. By the time he arrived, I was sitting up.

"She's suffered a concussion," Dr. Hutchinson concluded after asking me a few questions and feeling my head. "I see these things all the time," Dr. Hutchinson assured my mom. "Just keep waking her up every hour and asking her questions. It's probably not serious, but she shouldn't do anything that might bang her around for a while." Sledding was over for the night and, I feared, the season. "And Renee?" he said softly to Mom. "Her face is awfully thin. Is she eating enough?"

Mom searched my face as if she hadn't seen me before.

"I never should have let you go," she said.

"No, Mom, I wanted to go," I said, my head pounding. "It was really fun. I shouldn't have taken the saucer. It was just an accident." Matt was strangely silent. I was so relieved he hadn't pushed me down the hill. He didn't need to feel guilty, too.

"You really had me scared, Bee," Mom said softly. "I don't know what I'd do if I lost you."

Matt and Mom carried me to the car, my arms draped over their shoulders. After we got home, Dad threw open the door and raced out without a coat. "I can't believe you took them out. What on earth happened to her? Did she break something?" Dad's voice was full of anger.

"No, Dr. Hutchinson says she's going to be fine."

"Fine? Fine? You're carrying her home and she's fine? I heard she hit her head and couldn't walk."

"He said we need to keep watching her through the night. In case it's a concussion," Mom explained.

Dad was quiet. I hated the silent treatment. It was worse than getting yelled at.

"I don't know what to say," Mom apologized. "I. . .we were having a good time. But maybe I shouldn't have taken them out. Maybe it *is* my fault." Mom's voice was as thin as a crack in the ice.

Dad shook his head and took me in his arms. "I'll take her upstairs to our room," he said at last.

Mom and Matt stayed at the bottom of the stairs. *I'm okay,* I mouthed as Dad carried me away.

Mom came up a few minutes later and then Dad left. Mom helped me get on my nightgown, tucked me in their bed, turned out the light, and then crawled in beside me. Light from the hall spilled into the room until it was darkened by Dad's silhouette.

"I'm sorry I yelled. It was wrong of me to blame you for what happened."

"I was so scared," Mom said softly. "I mean, when we were on the hill."

"I can imagine," Dad answered back. "Actually, I don't *want* to imagine it. I feel like I was there somehow."

"Maybe it was just too familiar," Mom concluded. Her arm made long, stroking motions across the top of her quilt in the place Dad usually slept. "Sometimes it seems like the only thing we share is watching our kids in pain."

"I don't want to think about that right now," Dad said, coming toward us. "Tonight I'm going to sleep on the floor on the other side of Abby. We'll take turns waking her up and checking on her." Dad set a pillow on the floor and unfolded a blanket off the foot of the bed.

That night, I slept in their bed next to Mom, Dad beside me on the floor. I was between them. Every hour after their alarm went off, I'd find them both hovering over me, asking who was the president or how many fingers they were holding up or what day it was. "Richard Nixon, four, February twenty-seventh," I'd answer. When I passed the test, I closed my eyes and got to sleep for another hour.

Only one time did I have trouble falling back asleep. Dad kept coughing and turning and rustling his covers.

"Renee?"

"Yes?" Mom whispered back quickly. She wasn't sleeping. Whispering always seems louder to me than talking and sometimes even louder than shouting, and it certainly gets my attention.

"Couldn't she see where she was going?"

"She was spinning and she was backward."

"I'm going to go knock that icehouse down," Dad said.

"Shhh, John," Mom said gently.

"What if someone else hits it and breaks their neck?" Dad asked.

"I'm sure someone did something to it after we left. Everybody knows what happened."

I did my pretend deep breathing to keep them thinking I was asleep, but they didn't seem to have anything more to say. The next hour when I awakened, I said, "Peter Pan, fourteen, and Christmas Day," and opened my eyes just enough to see Mom and Dad look at each other, wide-eyed, and then I heard their laughter. With them being together again, I didn't think I had ever felt more loved.

EIGHTEEN

I thought we were making progress," Mom said. Their bedroom door was cracked open, and I could see Mom sitting up as Dad pulled a sweatshirt over his head and then sat back down on his side of the bed.

I leaned against the wall surrounded by framed family pictures that told our ages by our teeth. Matt without teeth and then Matt with teeth and then Matt with braces. My biggest smile sported two missing top teeth. Most of the pictures had bluish-gray backgrounds and were taken at school. All except Joel's pictures. There was one of him barely able to hold his head up, another holding his favorite monkey. When we first came home last summer, Mom took down Joel's pictures. But a faded outline of each frame, a silhouette, remained on the wall, making the absence greater, and she put them back up.

"I thought last night was different," Mom said, her knees up to her chest, her arms cradling her legs. "That whole thing with Abby. Even though it brought back. . ."

"I can't think about it. That's something I don't want to relive."

"But then we're back to nothing. We're stuck again."

There was a long silence. No response. "You're in the basement every day," Mom continued, as if explaining her point.

"While *you're* at Patti's," Dad countered, looking at her then turning away.

"I have to do *something*, and we need the money. At least *I'm* not trying to avoid anything or anyone."

"Are you sure you're not going to Patti's to avoid thinking about him?" Dad said.

"*Him?*" Mom asked. "*Him?* He has a name," she corrected over his shoulder. "And maybe I am. But just because I'm trying not to think about *Joel* doesn't mean I don't remember Joel each day."

Dad jumped up and grabbed a tennis shoe from under his side of the bed.

"Running again?" Mom asked. She picked up the shoe's partner from a pile of clothes, but when Dad reached for it, she pulled away. "Where do you *go*, anyway?" she asked. "Can you tell me *that?*" Dad responded by snatching the shoe and sitting down to put it on. That he wouldn't even answer Mom made my stomach hurt. Mom shook her head and closed her eyes. "I don't understand you anymore, John." Her voice was not angry, but full of sadness.

I stepped back from the door and headed down the hall before Dad left the room. After last night, we weren't going to church. This would be a good day to be at Miss Patti's. Maybe we were all running. And maybe there was really nothing that could bring us back.

"Morning, Abby," Dad said as he passed my room, as if everything was all right when it was so very wrong.

✦

That afternoon I left Rita's early. I had a plan. As I looked up and down the street, I could see which houses had their television sets on by the lights flickering from their windows, calling me home with the hope that maybe tonight our family would sprawl across vinyl beanbag chairs and shag carpet and share an evening brought to us by NBC. I had forty-five minutes before Tinkerbell lit the castle to convince them.

Every Sunday evening, as the Baptists convened at Calvary Chapel, I said a very quick thank-you that God had called Dad to presbytery. For if I had been fully dipped like the Baptists who go to church all morning and night, I would have missed congregating with my family for an evening of Mutual of Omaha's *Wild Kingdom* and *The Wonderful World of Disney*. On those Sunday evenings I felt that all was well with the world—or at least the Magic Kingdom, if it was indeed a real place and not just something magical coming out of our black-and-white Zenith. After all, when you're from Ohio, California seems like a huge leap of faith.

I opened the door to find Dad in the kitchen laying out bread and butter for grilled cheese sandwiches. Mom came down the staircase with a stack of bills in her hand.

"You want to watch *Wild Kingdom*?" I asked. "It's about to start." I liked Marlin Perkins and thought it was a nice warm-up to Disney.

"I have to finish this, Abby. But maybe Matt? Where is he, anyway?"

"Dad?" I asked, hoping he might want to join me. I knew he'd say no, but I'd make him say it.

"You know what, Abby? I think I will," he said, much to my surprise. "Let me finish this and I'll be there."

"Jiffy Pop?" I suggested.

"Dinner first," he said as the butter sizzled in the pan.

"It's not an easy year with the taxes," Mom began. "Patti's trying to help me."

"Do we owe?" Dad asked, immediately concerned. He buttered the bread and set each slice in the hot fry pan.

"Actually, I can't tell. I'm not far enough along."

The doorbell rang, and when I saw Uncle Troy I thought the more the merrier, but when he and Dad left for the living room, I knew I was running out of time. We were going to miss the animals, but we could still watch Disney if the discussion was short.

Fifteen minutes later, Dad came back to the kitchen and his very melted cheese sandwiches. Dad explained to Mom that since the interim minister was local and had a house nearby, he didn't need the parsonage. But the church would begin a search for a new pastor, and when he was selected, we would need to move. In the meantime, they thought it best not to rent out the house, under the circumstances.

"*Under the circumstances?*" Mom asked. "You mean like pitying us? Or do you mean because they don't want bad renters?"

"They can't pay two salaries, but they're extending the housing through August." Dad set a sandwich on each plate. "They hope to have a new minister by then."

"I don't want one," I said, pushing the sandwich plate back. It was quarter till and we had to hurry.

Dad found the popcorn and pulled out a pot, pouring a thin line of vegetable oil into it. He wasn't making Jiffy Pop.

"So, are you glad about this extension?" Mom asked. "Because I'm not."

What was she thinking? An extension was good; I didn't want to move.

"I'm afraid this extension means we're still in limbo," Mom said. The oil began to sizzle, followed by a few lone pops before Dad clamped the lid shut and the percussive rattle followed. Dad shook the pot as tiny explosions released the sweet smell of popped corn. Dad focused on listening and shaking, listening and shaking. But Mom wanted an answer.

"At least you *know* you have doubts, and you question how to live out your faith. Maybe that takes the *most* faith," she suggested. Dad didn't respond, so she continued. "There are a lot of people who are searching; maybe you're the person to point them in the right direction."

"If I only knew what that *was*," Dad answered. "I'm not exactly a beacon of light."

"Then, by the strength of God, step back into that pulpit and preach something that might start making sense to somebody, somewhere. If it doesn't work, hell, we'll just move to Washington State and you can take over the farm." Was that a challenge or a threat? Or was she daring Dad to say something? Anything. Just like she did that morning. Dad grimaced, perhaps at the thought of farming. Or perhaps at Mom's uncharacteristic vocabulary.

"Mom, you really shouldn't swear," Matt chided as he came in the back door and headed for the refrigerator.

"Dad made grilled cheese." I pointed to the remaining plate.

"You're serious. Farming?" Dad asked. "You'd be a *farmer's* wife?"

"Depends on who's the *farmer*." Mom smiled playfully. Dad didn't.

"Dad, farming? No wonder everybody's upset," Matt added, taking out a jar of peanut butter from the cupboard. I hoped Matt wasn't going to spread it on his grilled cheese.

"Or if you'd rather be a clock doc, then let's move to Chicago and find some masterpieces to work on," Mom suggested.

"I'm not moving," Matt interrupted.

"I don't know that we have to *move*—" Dad began.

"Of course we have to *move*," Mom interrupted. "Somebody has to *move*, or move *on*, or move *out*."

The conversation that began with simple suggestions and teasing took a sudden turn. Matt and I needed to leave, now, but instead I found myself glued to the table even though I wanted to be glued to the TV. But if I stayed, at least I would know exactly what they said, and then maybe they wouldn't say all of it. Maybe I could keep something bad from happening. Matt turned his back, opened the bread box, and pulled out a loaf of Wonder Bread. He was working in slow motion, as if he, too, needed an excuse to hear the rest of the argument. Matt stuck his knife into the peanut butter, slid it out, and licked off a thick glob.

The popping increased, and Dad shook the pot harder, until it slowed and then stopped, and he took off the lid, releasing a cloud of steam. A few kernels escaped the pot. Something smelled slightly burnt.

"I've been waiting for change, but nothing happens. Now I don't even know what I'm waiting for anymore," Mom said. "You don't have to know how to put the whole puzzle back together right now; just start with a few pieces." I imagined our annual Thanksgiving puzzle. It was as if we'd lost the box-top picture.

Matt picked up his grilled cheese and his peanut butter sandwich, grabbed an apple from the bowl on the counter, and headed out the screen door, which slapped appropriately. Dad and Mom didn't even seem to notice. Mom just stared at Dad.

"All I know is that you're taking your time while your family is falling apart." And then she took a deep breath and said quietly, and too calmly, "Maybe we need some time apart to figure out where we're headed. A little distance. A separation of sorts."

Distance? A separation of sorts? *Estrangement?* Where was the mom who said divorce wasn't in our vocabulary? Where was the dad who once ordered me to unpack my knapsack and take off my coat and boots, because McAndrewses never joked about running away? Mom had her boots on and her bags packed, but I wasn't sure where she was going.

Dad took down only one popcorn bowl, filled it, and planted it in front of me. It was five minutes to seven and our show was about to begin.

"Go on ahead, Abby. I'll be there in a minute."

When I stepped out, their volume increased.

"Your answer is to just keep busy. Stay distant," Dad said.

"*I'm* distant?" Mom sounded appalled.

"Quit a job, get a job, stay away. There are plenty of ways to avoid facing what happened," Dad said.

"*Facing what happened?*" Mom repeated. "Just say it out loud. 'Joel died.' No more euphemisms, no more hiding the truth or hiding away," she said. "I'm not the one holed up with clocks in the basement," she said. "I can't play with time, but I'm living in the present and have some hope for the future. It's *time* to move forward."

Dad walked out but he didn't come join me in the living room; instead he headed for the front door. "You're not there for us, John," Mom called out after him. "Somebody has to move on, even if you call it running away." The front door clicked shut, but Mom finished her thought. "You've got to figure out what you need to do, but I need to go on."

Mom disappeared upstairs and I watched television alone, but it wasn't NBC.

✳

The next day marked the beginning of a new month. While I was at school, Mom moved into one of Miss Patti's extra bedrooms, but I didn't know about it until dinnertime, when Miss Patti took out her tuna casserole, set two plates on the table, then held out two more, awaiting Mom's response.

"Abby, I'm staying *here* tonight," Mom said. Something was different. Working late at Miss Patti's wasn't unusual, but tonight Mom seemed strange and awkward. "It's tax time and we've got a deadline and Miss Patti needs me more often." Mom's explanation came too easily, as if rehearsed. And besides, she usually went home to eat with Dad and Matt. What would they do now? "You can go eat with Dad and Matt, or you can stay here with us. I'm sleeping upstairs."

I wanted to believe this was just a sleepover so that I could run next door, grab a sleeping bag, say "hey" to Dad and Matt, then return for a fun evening with Rita. Four plates at Miss Patti's, two plates at home—that is, if Matt stayed. Matt might not be there that night. Or maybe Dad wouldn't eat. Or maybe I needed to make it even, three at home, three at Miss Patti's. I couldn't decide.

"You're welcome to stay with me tonight," Mom offered.

I frowned. How generous. Miss Patti set one more plate down and held out the last one. Which plate, which house? Was this an ultimatum, or was I supposed to be thankful for the invite? My face grew warm, and I felt angry I had to make a choice that felt significant. What happened to *"Some things you can never leave behind; you have to work through them"*?

"I don't know," I said at last and slipped from my seat. Rita followed me out and took my hand. Not knowing what to do, I headed back home. If I didn't pretend this was only for one night, then I would have to admit something was very wrong.

Rita sat on our back porch while I went into our kitchen. Two cans of unopened Campbell's tomato soup stood on the counter. A strip of light escaped through the crack at the bottom of the door to the basement. Dad was working, but I didn't see Matt. I wanted to go downstairs, but I didn't know what to say and I felt guilty for eating at Miss Patti's and for what I was about to do. Quietly, I slipped upstairs to my room and opened my drawer. I hesitated, then finally picked out a nightgown and pants and a shirt and one pair of underwear. This was only for *one* night.

When I came back down, I paused at the top of the stairs, opened the door, and threw my clothes behind it.

"Hey, Dad," I said as I headed down. I tried to read his face like he read the faces of his clocks. His eyes looked tired, but he smiled at me.

"Hey, Bee," he said. I came beside him and he folded me into his arms. "You doing okay?" he asked, then corrected himself. "No, I guess that's a silly question."

"Daddy?" I began, my face muffled against his shoulder. "Maybe you could. . ." And then I couldn't think of anything to say. I hadn't really figured out a way to fix this. I really needed to think about it. "I love you," I said at last.

"I love you, too, Bee," Dad said, and he took in a quick breath. He didn't want to cry and I didn't want to see him cry. I wanted to make him feel better, but I should have known that wasn't possible.

That night, I went to bed alone in the room that wasn't mine, while Mom worked downstairs with Miss Patti. I heard the chairs roll across the hardwood floors and the wind whistle in the attic above. A few minutes later, the door opened.

"Abby, are you awake?" Mom asked in a whisper.

"Yes."

"Then I'll come to bed now."

"It's cold in here, Momma."

"I know. We're at the end of the hall. We have to remember to keep the door open during the day."

Their guest room was perhaps the most nicely furnished room in Miss Patti's house. Rita said it was her grandmother's furniture, and that we were the first guests to use it.

This was where Rita played our telephone game. She had a tin can at her house and I had one at mine. My telephone hung from the window of Mom and Dad's bedroom. We strung yarn across and talked to each other on chilly fall afternoons or warm spring Saturday mornings, having more fun than we could have had with a real telephone.

But today the phone line would not have worked. The language spoken between the houses was foreign, and I was no interpreter.

Mom's nightgown slid over her thin body. In the moonlight, I could see her silhouette and I knew that even if she weren't my mom, I would think she was beautiful. She ran her fingers through her hair, fluffed it gently, and then leaned back as she massaged her head. I imagined what that felt like. She put cream on her face by the moonlight illuminating the dressing table. I wondered what she saw in the mirror. Did she know she was pretty? Mom tiptoed to the bed and tucked her slippers beneath it. She peeled back her side of the crisp cotton covers and slid in next to me, spooning her body with mine.

"Now you'll be warm," she murmured in my ear as she stroked my hair. I felt her heartbeat and soft, rhythmic breath against my neck. I closed my eyes and tried to make our breathing one, but we were too different.

"How many people have you lost?" With my back to her, I could ask that question.

"I know lots of people who have died," she answered.

"But did you really *know* them?"

"Some..." Her voice drifted.

"Does it ever get easier?"

"No. And I suppose that's a good thing," she said. "If it got easier, it would mean I loved less."

"What was it like when Poppa died?"

Mom's breathing changed, slowed. And then she sighed.

"Different," she said at last. "Poppa was older. I was more prepared. But it was still sad."

I remembered when Joel was a baby, Mom left for Poppa's funeral. She took Joel with her and was gone for three days. When she came back, it took her a long time to smile.

"What about your mom?"

"You're sure curious tonight," Mom teased, tickling my side. I grabbed her hand and put it on my arm. I loved the gentle caress of her fingers.

"I was just a baby. I didn't know she died," she answered.

"So that one didn't hurt."

"It hurt. But in a different way. Everybody always had a mom except me. I always missed her even though I didn't know her. I had to imagine what she was like. I had to *pretend* things about her." Mom rolled to her back and I copied her. She folded her hands across her waist and I did the same. We stared at the ceiling.

"I always wondered what it would be like to have a mom," she said at last. Mom bent her face to her shoulder to dry her eye. "And then when Matt was born, I realized how much I had missed," she said softly. I could see the other tears sliding down her porcelain face. I touched her cheek and traced the liquid trail with one finger and then the next finger, until I had touched away most of her tears and my fingers were damp. "It hurts no matter what. It just plain hurts to lose someone."

"I wonder what your *dad* felt like," I offered cautiously. "I'll bet he missed your *mom*."

"This isn't what I wanted, Abby," she said.

I thought about my dad and wondered if Mom thought about him, too. I leaned toward her and kissed her cheek. Mom reached out and pulled me close, and that was the beginning of our first sleepover.

NINETEEN

When I awakened, I wondered why light was coming in from the wrong direction and the wall had moved. That's what I hate about sleeping in a strange room. My stomach remembered before my head that something bad had happened. We weren't at home anymore and we were hardly a family. *Separation. Estrangement.*

Mom's side of the bed was empty, the comforter turned back, exposing the white sheets, which were cold to my touch. I shivered in the morning air.

After school that day, I wanted to head home to see what Matt was doing. What did he think about us? I assumed Matt would stay with Dad. Each parent would have a kid, but would Matt miss me? Did he care?

What about Dad? Did he miss us? Should I talk to Dad about it? Could I ask Dad about what Mom did, or should I go home and act like everything was normal when it was so awkward and strange?

"Hey," I said, coming in the back door.

"Hey, Abby," Matt said, running his fingers through his hair. "You doing okay?"

"I guess," I answered. "Did Dad say anything?"

"No. He just went downstairs and worked late. I fell asleep before he went to bed."

"So you didn't even *talk*?" I asked, remembering my conversation with Mom.

"Why would we?" Matt asked. "We never do anymore."

I shrugged. Matt made it sound so hopeless.

"Well, maybe she'll come home tonight."

"I don't think so, Abby."

"You don't *know* that!" I snapped.

Matt shrugged, picked up his backpack, and headed up the stairs.

"Don't go," I said, "I'm sorry."

"It's nothing to be sorry about, Bee. It's just the way it is."

"Doesn't it make you feel bad? Don't you ever get sad?" I asked, trying to remember a time he had really cried about Joel. What was wrong with him, anyway? "Don't you ever feel like crying?"

"Maybe," he admitted. "Sometimes."

"Well, why don't you?"

"I don't want to."

"I can't stop it when it happens," I confessed.

"You just have to be angry," Matt said, as if divulging a secret. "I just think of something that makes me really, really mad and then I don't cry."

But what do you do when the thing that makes you mad is also the thing that makes you want to cry? Who knows, maybe he's mad at me and that keeps him from crying.

Maybe Dad is mad now, too. I almost didn't want to go down to the basement to find out, but it might be better than imagining the worst.

"Hey, Dad, I'm home," I called down the stairs.

"That's great, honey. You want to stay for dinner?" he called back. Was Mom expecting me? What would Dad make for himself? Not that it mattered. I just wondered and I worried. The pause must have signaled my answer.

"It's okay, Abby."

No, it wasn't okay. It wasn't okay that two plus two no longer equaled four. Nothing was okay and everybody was pretending it was. I headed down the steps to find Dad putting aside his project, as if waiting for me.

"I don't like this," I said.

"I don't either."

And then I felt sort of sad for him and sad for me, and my nose started to sting. I scrunched my face to stop from crying and then remembered what Matt said and tried the angry trick. I got mad that Matt didn't seem to care and that maybe Mom did this to us. But then I felt guilty and quickly discovered that guilt also stops tears.

"I'd better go," I said.

"Okay, Bee," he said as I headed up the stairs.

✳

Miss Patti's table was set for four.

"Today is Dr. Seuss's birthday," Miss Patti explained. "He's sixty-seven years old. Tomorrow we'll celebrate in Mrs. Clevenger's class." Miss Patti hefted a stack of Dr. Seuss books into a cloth bag. "I have a lot of cooking to do tonight, so y'all need to do your homework upstairs."

By 8:15 the next morning, Miss Patti had her buffet breakfast set out on two long tables under the window in Mrs. Clevenger's room. Everything was labeled: Green Eggs and Ham, Sneetch Frankfurters, Oobleck, Blue Goo, Pink Ink, Moose Juice, Goose Juice, and Green Grape Cakes. Though skeptical, I filled my plate with a rainbow of foods. Most kids wouldn't eat anything that looked weird, but I tried everything so I wouldn't hurt Miss Patti's feelings.

"Don't miss the Wumbus milk; it's my personal favorite," Miss Patti said with a wink as she spread out a pile of books and let us choose what we wanted her to read.

I had heard the stories before, but I loved to be read to, especially by Miss Patti whose voice made everything sound warm and safe. She began with *Green Eggs and Ham* and went through *If I Ran the Circus, The Cat in the Hat, The Sneetches and Other Stories, Happy Birthday to You*, in honor of Dr. Seuss, and ended up with Horton.

Rita looked shyly proud, and I felt happy for her and proud she was my friend. Miss Patti's house wasn't home, but Pink Ink and a good friend helped.

✦

My best excuse for going home was to practice my piano, and so I began practicing. A lot. I felt like a Ping-Pong ball bouncing between two houses that didn't feel like home. But after two and a half weeks, it was obviously not a sleepover and I needed a plan.

"Maybe we should do something about Mom and Dad," I said to Matt, after I had finished practicing and started my homework.

"Do you have any ideas?" I asked Matt, opening the oven to check on Dad's brownies. The smell of rich chocolate filled the kitchen and I was really glad I hadn't given up chocolate for Lent. Matt sat at the table poring over a book. This was one of the first times I had seen him study in the last few months.

"Like what?" he asked.

"Maybe they could have a date or something."

"Valentine's Day is over," Matt said unromantically.

"Then what do you think's gonna happen?" I asked. Matt seemed unusually gloomy. Maybe it was his calculus, but he didn't look hopeful.

"I don't know, Abby. It's really messed up."

"I don't want to live over there forever. I miss you and Dad." I was tired of straddling my afternoons and my parents, and I didn't want us to become the Hanleys. "I just want it over," I said, opening my notebook and taking out pencil and paper.

"What do you want me to do about it? How do you think I can fix it?"

"Can't you say something to Dad?" I asked. I knew they were spending a lot of time in the basement, where Dad was teaching Matt the trade.

"Can't you say something to *Mom*?"

He had me there. Matt slammed his book shut. "I hate this class." He rubbed his forehead as if he had a headache. "What good does it do to be over *there*?" he asked, as if I had any choice.

"I don't know. I don't want to be over *there*. But for some reason, she can't be *here*," I reminded him.

"Maybe it's *me*," Matt said with a laugh, before he frowned.

"That's silly, Matt."

"I don't know," he answered.

"It's not you. It's more about Dad and stuff."

"I suppose," he said with a shrug.

"Really, Matt, you gotta think of something." I tapped my pencil on the table.

"Abby, it's bigger than you and me. It's not like that *Parent Trap* movie with those sisters getting their parents back together."

I knew he was right. But I had to admit I had spent a lot of time trying to remember what the Hayley Mills twins had done to get their parents reunited. We sat looking at each other, saying nothing until we both smiled. It made me realize how much I missed him and how much I missed us being a family.

"Are you coming to my recital?" I asked. "Saturday night?" I hoped he didn't have any plans, as I really wanted him there. He needed to sit between Mom and Dad.

"If you want me to," he said. Which was not what I wanted him to say. I wanted him to say, "I *want* to be there."

"I mean, you don't *have* to go. I just sort of hoped you *wanted* to."

"Remember when Uncle Troy fell asleep and started snoring?" Matt said and laughed.

"I felt embarrassed for him."

"What about Miss Mary Frances? I wonder what she said to him at halftime."

"Intermission," I corrected.

"Maybe something funny like that will happen again."

"You never know," I encouraged. Then the back door opened and Mom came inside. Mom only came home when she needed to talk with Matt and she knew Dad was busy, or when she had something to tell Dad, something better said in person than on the phone.

"Hey, what're you two up to?" she asked.

"Just finishing our homework," I said, pointing out how Matt was doing the right thing. Perfect timing for a discussion. I kicked Matt under the table and he frowned in confusion.

"Something smells good in here," Mom said, and then opened the oven door, releasing the chocolaty aroma of Dad's brownies. "Since when did your dad start baking, anyway?" I hated it when she called him *your dad* instead of just *Dad*. It felt like what divorced parents said about each other.

"I guess we're missing out." I nudged Matt's foot.

Matt nodded and asked, "Yeah, what's so great about living over *there* anyway?"

Mom tested the top of the brownies and then licked the brown batter off her finger.

"It's not *better*. It's just *different* over there," she said as she closed the oven door.

"I can imagine," Matt said in his mocking voice.

"Don't make fun of her," Mom corrected. I assumed they were talking about Miss Patti.

"I'm not," Matt defended. "But *why*, Mom? Why over there?"

"Dad needs time, I need space," Mom answered.

"That sounds pretty philosophical. When do time and space meet?" he asked. "Ever? I mean, what's it gonna take, Mom?"

"I don't know." She looked him straight in the eye. "I don't know anymore," she said very slowly as she sat at the table. Her resignation gave Matt momentum.

"Whenever Abby and I fought and I said I hated her, you said love was a choice. You *made* us make up. You said I *had* to love Abby because she was my sister. Doesn't that work for you and Dad?"

I didn't need to chime in. Matt was doing a great job. I just nodded my two cents.

"I suppose it should. But it's not exactly like we're mad at each other or that we aren't making up. We just don't know how to go on together. It's so much work. I don't have it in me." Mom looked worried. She had said too much, and I could tell she knew it.

"Look, I didn't really come over for such a serious talk," she admitted. "Changing the subject," she said very deliberately. "Baseball. Matt, did you decide to try out?"

Matt stared ahead as if deciding whether to drop the subject so easily.

"I don't know if I'll do a spring sport."

"That's probably a good choice. You could use the time to get your grades up."

"And I have driver's ed. Somebody has to take me out driving." Mom winced. "I'm not *that* bad, Mom."

"I'd take you out with me, but. . ."

"I know, Mom, you're not really ready for that yet."

"Are my brownies done?" Dad asked as he came up the steps, then stopped when he saw Mom at the kitchen table with the two of us. Almost like normal.

"Abby's piano recital is Saturday night, but they're having a dress rehearsal this Friday," Mom said, and then added softly, "At the church." She looked at me and then Dad and then back to me. "Miss Mary Frances wants Abby there at six thirty. Patti and I need to meet with a client after he gets off work. Can you just stay there with Abby? Or at least drop her off and pick her up?"

I'm not sure why, but I felt like the dry cleaning.

"I could do that."

"I mean, I know it's the *church* and everything. . .but thanks."

"I miss you, Renee," Dad said suddenly. I think I gasped, but nobody noticed. Mom did not answer but took a long, slow breath from her nose and then bit her lip. It felt like someone had said, *I love you*, but no one heard it—so no one answered back. *Be nice*, I thought to Mom. I willed her to *just be nice*.

"I'm going to the recital," Mom added, and I wasn't sure if it was a warning or an invitation.

"I'll be there, too," Dad said.

Sit together, I thought loudly. *Sit together*. I could picture it now. Matt would be between them. Nobody would have to know about us. If Mom and Dad and Matt all came and I played my best and we were a family again, well, that would be nice. Maybe that was a good plan.

On Friday afternoon, Dad took me to the dress rehearsal but didn't stay. I wasn't surprised, knowing he'd feel strange sitting around the church, waiting through "Country Gardens" or a Bach prelude. But he was there to pick me up promptly at eight o'clock, and since it wasn't a school night, he asked if I wanted to come home and spend the night. It felt strange calling Mom and asking her if I could spend the night at home, but she didn't seem to notice. After I got in my jammies, Dad made some hot chocolate and we sat in the kitchen with only the little light on over the stove.

"What's it like without me?" I said, almost whispering.

"Lonely," Dad said soberly, teasing me with his dramatics. "Terribly lonely."

"Seriously, Dad, don't you miss us?" I snuck *us* in very softly. There was a difference between *me* and *us*.

"I miss you. I miss Mom and I miss *us*. Our family," Dad said, carefully explaining everything so I wouldn't be sneaky anymore.

"Then why don't you do something about it?" I asked.

"It's not that simple, Abby."

"But you always tell *us* to say 'I'm sorry' and 'I forgive you.' Can't you do something like that?"

"Sometimes things happen that aren't anybody's fault," Dad answered and then took another sip of his chocolate.

I wanted to ask if he was worried about what was going to happen. I wanted to ask whether he cared if we got back together. I wanted to ask so much more, but what if he didn't have any answers?

The next night was Saturday, March twentieth, the first recital of the year for all twenty-seven of Miss Mary Frances's students. I helped set up one hundred folding metal chairs in the social hall and imagined what it would look like when they were filled. I would play the first movement from the "Moonlight Sonata." I liked it, because I got to use a lot of pedal to connect the notes. Miss Mary Frances said it was sort of a lamentation. That fit my mood. Miss Mary Frances said it got its name because it sounded like moonlight on Lake Lucerne. That was a picture I could hold in my head.

Miss Mary Frances always began with the younger students and ended with her best pianists. Each year of piano lessons, my name dropped farther down the program, which increased the time I had to be nervous, and didn't allow my family a side-door escape at intermission.

This year, I was more than halfway down the program, just after intermission. I counted the people in front of me. It seemed to take forever to get to my turn, but then suddenly I was up. As I sat down on the black piano bench, I looked out the corner of my eye and found Dad, then Matt, then Mom, in a nice row of three. They smiled, but I pretended I didn't see them. Miss Mary Frances had taught us stage etiquette.

I placed my hands on the keys and began very softly. Pianissimo. Connected triplets, rolling arpeggios. For a few minutes, I actually forgot about everything except the music that was somewhere inside me; I just had to pull it out and let everybody else hear it. Miss Mary Frances called it memorizing, but I called it *playing by heart.*

Pretty soon it was just me and the piano and the pedal and sitting tall on the bench and legato and the ostinato pattern and more pedal. I could delay a note and a resolution until the perfect moment and hold the audience in suspense, connecting everything with my pedal. This was my favorite Beethoven piece, even if Beethoven didn't think it was his best. Miss Mary Frances had told me Beethoven was deaf at the end of his life and still writing music. I couldn't imagine not hearing the pitches ascend and descend. And then my piece was done, and there was a hesitation to clap until I looked out and stood to take a bow. Dad was smiling proudly and Matt nodded at me like I had done something really special. Mom was even leaning over Matt to tell Dad something.

Maybe all my practicing could change something. Maybe if my music was beautiful enough, it could draw them back together. Maybe the word *legato*, which Miss Mary Frances defined as "smooth, connected," was perfect for the evening.

But that legato lasted for one magic night. On Sunday after church, Mom was whispering on the phone. That was never a good thing. If I had thought that beautiful music could change everything, I was wrong.

"There's not enough in there for the electric bill." Pause. "Nothing," she answered. "Well, there was Matt's school yearbook and he needed new shoes." I waited and tried to imagine how Dad was filling in the gaps.

"I'm not," she said quickly. "She's not taking anything for food or rent. What are *you* spending?" The pauses shortened and Mom's words grew louder and angrier.

"I can't pay for something with nothing, and I don't want to bounce a check." She waited a few seconds. I had no idea what Dad could be saying. "Then tell them to pay now. Then let me know when the check clears." Mom hung up without saying good-bye. She never let me do that.

"Abby, can you take this over to your dad?"

I wasn't sure I wanted to go over there right then. "What is it?"

"Don't worry about what's inside; just take it over," she said, shoving it toward me. "And tell him it's due on the twenty-second. Monday."

"No," I said. "*You* take it over." I didn't move. I'm not sure who was more surprised by my disobedience. It took her so off guard she didn't make me head next door.

The next day Rita and I watched television all afternoon. From

Brady Bunch to *Speed Racer, Gilligan's Island, Green Acres,* and *Petticoat Junction* and then finally *Leave It to Beaver,* who had the perfect family. Beaver Cleaver's parents would never separate; why did mine? Then we just sat around in the living room watching Mom and Miss Patti writing and adding, writing and adding.

"Do you have a key for that clock?" I said at last.

"I don't think so," Miss Patti answered.

"My dad could probably fix it," I suggested. "Or maybe even Matt." Mom raised her head and took note. She must not have known Dad had an apprentice. For as long as I could remember, Miss Patti's Regulator clock hung silent on the wall. I had stared at it long enough, waiting for her to wind it.

"Some things don't want to be fixed," Miss Patti answered.

"How do you know it doesn't want to be fixed?" I asked, almost irritated.

"Sometimes *people* don't want things fixed," Miss Patti clarified.

"But it's a *clock*. It's not telling time."

"Well maybe I don't want it to tell time."

"That's weird," I said. She wasn't making any sense and I didn't feel like losing the fight. "That's just weird."

"Not really. Just to you." Miss Patti seemed uncharacteristically grouchy.

"You don't really even need it then," I pointed out.

"It was my *father's*. It's still special."

"Then why don't you want it to tell time?" I asked, and then I noticed Mom's stern face and her finger pointing at me with that look that said, *Don't pick a fight, young lady. Let it go.*

"I'm not worried about the time, Abby," Miss Patti continued. "And besides, I can't stand the noise. I had to listen to that thing tick TOCK, tick TOCK. Then I'd straighten it and try to find the perfect level, but it would TICK tock TICK tock. Drove me nuts.

A room should be quiet when you want it quiet and noisy when you want it noisy. I want it QUIET," she said, as if maybe that's what she wanted right then. "So, NO, I do *not* want your dad touching that clock." Was it my imagination, or did "your dad" sound like she was angry?

"Let's go to *my* house," I whispered to Rita, but she shook her head. Fine. They could all stay with that clock that didn't tick or tock, but I was leaving. Finding our back door locked, I checked the birdhouse for the hidden key and let myself in.

"Dad? Matt?" No answer. I opened the door down to the basement, but since it was dark, I closed it quickly, almost certain something would come up the stairs after me.

The house felt hollow, empty. Now Dad and Matt were usually together since Dad was teaching him how to fix clocks and drive the car, and in charge of getting the responsibility and freedom thing worked out. Mom had taxes and me.

I sat in the living room and let myself feel good and lonely. Where were they? Had they gone out for dinner? Why didn't they invite me? I wandered upstairs, where my bed looked strangely inviting. Feeling a bit like Goldilocks, I lay down on my bedspread and rubbed my fingers along its soft chenille tracks. Maybe tonight I'd spend the night at my real house even if it didn't feel like home anymore. I needed something to be *mine*. My blanket, my pillow, my room.

I was awakened by activity in the kitchen and my heart raced until I realized it was Dad and Matt. How long had I slept? My room was dark and I couldn't see the clock. They didn't even know I was there. I listened to the pleasant rise and fall of their voices without understanding what they were saying. Their words came into focus as I wandered back downstairs.

"I forgot my history book," I overheard Matt say as I stopped at the bottom of the staircase and played with the finial that would never be fixed.

"Do you need it for tonight?" Dad asked.

"I have a test tomorrow," Matt answered.

"Matt, this is one of those times you need to be more responsible." Dad took a deep breath. "But, son, I *am* glad you're studying." His voice was gentler now. "So let's go back." I hurried down to the kitchen so they wouldn't leave without me.

"Hey!" I said, bursting in on the scene.

"Hey!" Dad imitated with a smile. "We didn't know you were here," he added, giving me a hug. "How're you doing, Bee?"

"Fine. Can I go, too?"

"All right."

"Maybe we can go to Ruby's for dinner," I suggested.

But after Matt retrieved his textbook, Dad didn't go to Ruby's; instead, he headed down a rural road and into a cornfield, where he stopped the car.

"This isn't the way to Ruby's," I pointed out, hanging over the seat between Dad and Matt. My stomach growled.

"Here's the key," Dad said to Matt.

"Key?" Matt asked.

"It starts the car," Dad said. "I thought we could take a drive. Especially since your mother gets nervous even thinking of practicing with you."

Mom? What about me? I wasn't excited about this field trip.

"I haven't had much practice." Matt scratched the back of his neck and looked away.

"You don't really need it here," Dad said. "Here's a little responsibility. Let's see how it goes."

"You've got a lot of confidence in me. A cornfield?"

"We have to start somewhere. It'll take time."

"Time." Matt laughed. "Good one, Clock Doc." *Be nice*, I willed. Why couldn't they just talk to each other nicely?

Dad tossed Matt the keys and I wondered whether I'd be safer sitting in the middle of the field out in the cold. At first Matt didn't move. I couldn't figure out why he was so reluctant. At last he opened his door.

"I thought you'd want this, Matt," Dad said. "What's gotten into you?" Dad got out and they switched sides. I scrunched deep in the back. "Feels like you're always mad about something." Dad slammed his door shut. Matt's door slam confirmed his point.

"What's gotten into *me*?" Matt asked. "You're asking about *me*? That's kind of like that Bible verse about the speck and the log."

"Okay, so I was right that you're mad. And you're mad at *me*. Just get it out."

Matt started the car. I held my breath. "Three on the tree," Dad said gently.

More silence.

"Left foot is for the clutch. Right foot for the brake. You can't use the stick unless your left foot is on the clutch." The car made a terrible grinding sound. "Your left foot has to be down." The car hopped or jumped over what remained of the corn stubble. I buried my head.

"Okay, so now you need to shift down." Then there was a repeat of metal scraping against metal. Sitting on frozen cornstalks was starting to sound safer and quieter. "Use your left foot when you shift."

"DAD!" I yelled from the back.

"Does she have to be here?" Matt yelled. "I mean *really*. It's bad enough."

"Abby's fine," Dad said without looking back. "Just try following the rows."

Matt was fine when he drove at one speed. It was when he reached for the stick with the knob that I winced and plugged my ears. Now he drove the outer mowed circumference.

"Okay, shift down," Dad instructed. I plugged my ears again, but there was no scraping sound and the car did not jolt, so I cautiously released my hands.

"Now, Matt, tell me, what's with the act?" Dad asked, as if trying to make Matt angry or give him a driving lesson to help with concentration and focus. "You can't exactly claim you're upset I'm not preaching when you don't even want to go. You've got a lot of anger and I'm not sure why you direct it at me."

"Don't start on me now!"

I cringed. Dad's face was stoic. "So, it's something else?" Dad continued. "Try stopping here."

Matt put his foot on the brake and the car hiccuped to a stop and died.

"You have to put your foot on the clutch both to shift and to stop," Dad said. "Start the car again, but don't forget the clutch." Matt turned the ignition but the car didn't screech. "Maybe you don't really know why you're mad at me," Dad said as Matt concentrated on the circumference and kept a steady speed. Matt's shoulders were tense and hunched. I leaned forward, growing more comfortable with the circular path. "Well?" Dad asked, awaiting his answer.

"I don't know, Dad," Matt said, and then sighed.

"Then how about if I give you a big long list and you can take your pick?" Dad asked. "I can think of lots of reasons you might be angry."

"You can think of lots of reasons that *I* might be angry?" Matt repeated. In a few years would I talk to Dad with that tone of voice?

"You're fifteen. That's a pretty good reason to be angry." Dad began counting on his fingers, and Matt began to press down on the accelerator. "You're mad that life isn't like it was when you were *fourteen*." Dad added his forefinger to the reason on his thumb.

I could relate to that. Some birthdays brought privilege, some regret. There were lots of times this year I just wanted to go back to being a kid again. PJ, pre-Joel.

"I don't need a sermon, Dad," Matt said as the car bumped over stubble. Now we were going faster than I thought we should.

"You said you didn't care if I was in the pulpit or not," Dad reminded him. "So I'm in the pulpit right now."

"Just shut up," Matt muttered.

"Slow down, please!" I said from the back.

"You're mad that Joel is dead." Dad looked straight ahead, never checking Matt's reaction. "You're mad that it takes so long to get over the *fact* that Joel is dead. You're mad at *yourself* at how badly you want to *get over* that Joel is dead." With each new point Dad's voice got louder and Matt's driving became more erratic. I didn't think Matt was as mad as Dad was by this point. Dad had never been one of those fire-and-brimstone preachers, but he could have fooled me right then.

I hoped Matt didn't feel me over his shoulder as I tried to catch his reaction in the rearview mirror. Matt's mouth was a tight line.

"You're mad that your dad couldn't hold on to Joel tight enough to keep him *from* being dead. And you're mad that *God* didn't stop the whole thing from happening."

Matt slammed his foot on the accelerator and the car screamed across the stalks as he clutched the steering wheel.

The anger of Matt's silence was far worse than any of the swear words I'd ever heard him speak. I gripped the seat to keep me steady as Matt mowed down the iced stubble.

"Stop it!" I screamed. My heartbeat raced faster and faster with the pitch of my moans until I was screaming. "Let me out! Let me out!" I reached for the door handle. "I can't breathe!" *I will throw myself out of the car. I will get away. I can do this.*

The stalks scraped the bottom of the car, and on muddy, half-frozen patches we slipped around unsteadily. "Stop, stop, stop!" I screamed as my door flew open and the corn stubble scratched my arms. Then Matt slammed on the brakes and turned to see me hanging out of the car, my fingers gripping the handle.

My breath came in short pants, and I couldn't say anything and neither could they. Though I wanted to run, I couldn't. A moan escaped me and I closed my eyes so I wouldn't see anything.

"Get back in, Abby," Matt ordered from the front, and I pulled the door shut and slid to the middle of the seat. Matt cranked the wheel and headed out of the pasture and onto the road. I never sat up; I just hoped there were no other cars on the road.

Slowly, carefully, Matt made his way along the country roads back to our house. I made no noise. All the life had been sucked out of me.

"You forgot one point, Dad," Matt said at last, but his voice wasn't angry. It was low and steady—rehearsed. "How about that I'm mad that everybody probably wishes it had been *me* instead of Joel," he said. His voice was sad. I wanted to give him a hug around the neck. We were now a block from home. "How about I'm mad at myself that I felt glad it *was* Joel and *not* me." And then Matt slowed and methodically pounded his fist against the steering wheel. "But now I'm mad that it *wasn't* me."

His words hung in the air, but no one knew what to do with them. We didn't talk as Matt turned into the alley behind our house. We were home.

"Well, now you know," he said, handing Dad the keys. Matt closed his door and walked in the house. I wasn't surprised Dad didn't stop him, because I knew Matt had spoken a truth and there just wasn't any answer.

With Dad immobilized in the front, I felt like a prisoner, forgotten in the backseat. At last he got out and shut his door, leaving me alone and wondering what to do.

Twenty

The three of them were finishing dinner, but after that ride, I wasn't hungry. I knew if I stayed I might scream or cry or who knows what. Plus I didn't want Mom thinking Dad hadn't fed me, so I headed right past them.

"Hey, honey, I missed you." Mom hugged me as I tried to slip out of the kitchen. "Next time tell me where you're going."

She couldn't be serious. I stopped and turned back.

"I just went next door, Mom. Remember that place we used to call *home*?" Miss Patti started clearing the plates. I continued, "That place we should go *back* to. It's been almost a month." My sarcasm felt surprisingly good and so I didn't quit. "How much longer is it gonna be, Mom? Pick a date. Let's go home."

Rita stared straight ahead, her mouth open but nothing coming out. I guess nobody expected that to come from me. Including me.

"Are you okay, Abby?" Miss Patti asked.

"Did something happen?" Mom asked.

I rolled my eyes and plopped down in my chair. If they only knew.

"Oh brother," I said disgustedly. *Oh brother, indeed*, since it was really all about brothers.

"I guess we can take that for a yes," Miss Patti said.

"I just want it over. I want it to go away."

Mom nodded her head. "I know. I want to forget about the pain."

"Everything, Mom. I want to forget it all," I said angrily. "Except. . ." I didn't know what else to say because my eyes burned and I felt so tired and sad.

"You're afraid you'll forget *him*," Mom said. But I didn't know if I agreed. I was almost to the point I actually wanted to forget him. Everything was measured PJ or AJ, pre-Joel or after Joel. Maybe *PJ* was better than ever having Joel and living in AJ. Maybe now I understood why Dad couldn't answer whether he wished Joel had never been born and maybe I should forgive him. "That's why I wish I could see him again." Mom reached out and took my hand. "So I won't forget. So I can remember everything about him."

"You won't forget him," Miss Patti said softly. "You won't." And I knew with a painful certainty that I couldn't forget him either, but I also couldn't imagine our future with his memory.

"Why did they say I shouldn't see him?" Mom asked, pulling her hands away. Her voice was eerie and transparent. "Everybody said it was just a body." Mom stared off as if talking to someone out the window. Mom's hands seemed to be holding an imaginary child we knew was Joel. "But it wasn't just a body. See? I gave birth to him. That little body was the one I bathed at night, dressed in jammies, and rocked to sleep. I counted his toes and tickled his tummy. I loved the feel of his soft face against mine."

Patti was strangely silent. Mom leaned forward on her elbows as if the weight of the memory was too great, her hands folded. I had unleashed something by my anger, my questions, my sarcasm.

Mom kept going as if she didn't expect an answer.

"I sat in that hospital room and I caressed his little arms. I held his hand. I knew he was dead, but something of him was still there, and I knew it would be the last time I'd get to see him or touch him."

Nobody moved. We all sat at the table together, holding the picture of a mother with her son.

"At least you *got* a body," Miss Patti said.

Mom turned. Patti's tone was reprimanding, and Mom seemed unsure how to respond.

"Patti?"

I looked at Rita, but she wouldn't look at me.

"What is it, Patti? I don't understand," Mom asked.

"I didn't have a body," Patti said. "I would have liked to have held him one more time or I'd like to hold him again. But I don't even know if there *was* or *is* a body, because I don't even know if he's dead."

"I don't think I understand. . . ," Mom interjected. That made two of us. I looked over to Rita, but she wasn't looking at me.

"I'd wear the bracelet if it fit on my wrist. Is he POW or MIA? I gave it to Rita."

As if on cue, Rita got up and left. Was I supposed to leave, too? Who was Miss Patti talking about? I wanted to ask, but it didn't seem like I was supposed to.

"Actually, I just need to know if it's over or not. Should I keep waiting?"

Waiting for what? What was this about? Something was wrong but I couldn't figure out what it was.

"What are you trying to say?" Mom asked my question and Patti cleared her throat and continued.

"He may never come home, and I may never know if he's dead or alive. That's what I live with."

We waited for more story, but it was as if Patti didn't know where to begin.

"We have a bracelet. It says POW and his name. Jeff Carson. That's my husband. He was military. We met in Raleigh and got married. Then we had Rita." Patti paused and looked at us, as if considering whether to go on.

"Rita doesn't remember him. She was just a baby. He only held her a few times before he got sent over there."

No wonder Rita would never respond when I asked about Mr. Carson. *Where is your dad?* It never occurred to me that questions don't always have an answer.

"I don't even get to know if Rita will *ever* meet her dad. It's been going on eight years since he's gone missing, and nobody can give me any more information. He's MIA or POW. No body, no funeral.

"I don't have a tombstone to visit, and I'm not always certain whether I should grieve or whether I should hope and pray. I'm not sure what facing reality really is because, what is my reality?"

"I'm sorry, Patti. I never knew," Mom said.

"No way that you could," she said without blame. "But I'll tell you what *not* having a grave can do," she continued. "You don't look down to the ground." She met my mom's eyes. "Some look *up*, but I just plain had to look *out* for us." Patti's voice had a steely resolve. "At first everything familiar was sad but somehow comforting. Then it became just plain irritating. Every place reminded me of him. I couldn't get restarted and I was depressed." Miss Patti paused and then pointed to all of us, as if there was a lesson to be learned. "But I had an accounting degree, and there was no reason I couldn't use it. So with the little money we had, we left North Carolina and came here.

"Maybe the reason I don't tell everybody is that I don't want to relive it over and over. Nobody here needs to know, anyway. But when you say you wanted to touch the body, I know what you mean. I really do."

Mom didn't have to say anything. This time it was *her* arms around Miss Patti, an embrace that said *I'm so sorry.*

Patti subconsciously twisted her finger where a wedding ring should have been and then pulled a necklace from beneath her sweater. A small diamond ring and a band hung from the chain.

"It doesn't fit anymore. When I moved here I didn't wear it. I didn't owe anybody an explanation." She dropped the ring back inside her dress. "But just for the record, I *am* married. Or *was* married."

Mom nodded, holding Patti's hand in hers.

"So, Renee, sometimes there is no finality. Sometimes you just have to start over." They sat there for an uncomfortably long time. "Well now, at least you know my side of it," Patti said at last.

"But what if you can't escape the past?" Mom asked.

"We don't *escape* it. We live *through it* and then we start over."

"*You* left. *You* started over," Mom pointed out.

"I did it for *her*. For *me*," Miss Patti answered. Mom nodded. "And I didn't say you had to *leave*," Patti clarified. "You have more reasons to *stay*."

"What if we don't want to start over? Or we can't? Or what if it feels like I'm just burying something?" Mom asked softly.

"You mean, like Joel?" Miss Patti asked.

"Yes."

Rita came back downstairs fingering a heavy, oversized silver band. In capital letters across the bracelet read JEFFREY CARSON. Rita traced the letters with her finger. I guessed this was her only link to her father.

Rita slipped the bracelet over her tiny wrist, then extended her arm with the silver band dangling from it. Somehow we were united. She could understand. She had lost someone, too. Maybe she knew what it felt like to have a father who was missing in action. My *comrade*. Maybe she knew how subtraction emptied a family. And maybe she knew how our friendship was more than playing the Game of Life.

TWENTY-ONE

Early the next morning I awakened to the sound of Matt knocking on Miss Patti's kitchen door. That was a first. I stood there in my pajamas wondering what he could possibly say to me at this hour. Maybe an apology?

"Get in the car, fast," he whispered insistently.

"Are you out of your mind?" I asked. "After last night?"

"Dad is going for a run. Quick, we can follow him."

"You really are crazy." I shook my head. "It's six a.m. and I just want to go back to bed."

"Abby, don't you want to know where he goes?" Matt asked. "I do."

Actually there was a part of me that was curious. Dad always said "my usual route," but no one ever knew what that was. But to get in a station wagon with Matt when the feeling of trying to throw myself out of it was still vivid?

"Abby. Please." His words said, *I need you. Help me.* He wasn't a bad driver when he wasn't mad or trying to prove a point, and for some reason he wanted my help. He needed me.

"Let me get dressed first."

"We don't have time. He's leaving. Just grab your slippers."

The car was cold and I shivered as Matt put in the key.

"I'll do better this time," he promised.

"I should hope so."

Matt killed the engine and restarted three times.

"Matt! Quiet! Someone is going to hear us!" Slowly we rolled out of the alley and toward the street.

"When Dad goes out the door, we'll follow at least a block

behind," Matt said, focused on the road.

I felt like we were spies on a mission as we stalked him block by block. Occasionally we waited for Dad to gain a stronger lead, but I'm not sure it mattered. He seemed oblivious to everything.

Driving without a license was against the law, but I doubted many residents of Bethel Springs knew Matt's age or qualifications. I waved my best beauty queen wave so that I looked like a happy traveler instead of a hostage.

Dad turned and headed outside of town, away from people. Traffic was light and when Matt drove slowly and stayed in first gear, he did pretty well.

"Not bad," I admitted. Matt smiled at me and then looked in his rearview mirror. A few construction trucks came up behind and Matt pulled over on the shoulder to let them pass since we were only going about eight miles per hour. The car died and when Matt put it back into first, it made a terrible noise. I looked ahead but Dad had a long lead.

The road narrowed and fell off sharply to the right; Matt concentrated on keeping the car between the lines. We caught up within a quarter mile of Dad, never saying anything. I studied Matt, who was intent on trying to get everything right, his hands gripping the wheel. "Keep your eye on *Dad*, Abby," he reminded me just as I watched his face change.

Matt swore under his breath.

"Matt, what is it?"

"I think I know where he's going." And then Matt's stony silence.

"Where? What are you talking about?"

A dump truck and two garbage trucks came up behind us. The sign read 25 mph, but without a shoulder, we couldn't pull over and let them pass. The truck driver laid on his horn and I looked ahead to see if Dad had noticed. "Matt, you have to speed up."

"But then we'll catch up to Dad."

"Then turn around."

"There's no place!"

"Matt, do something!"

"I'm going to have to pass him."

"But he'll see us!"

"Or hear us." Matt grimaced. He was right—if he sped up, he'd change gears and alert the world that an underage driver was stalking Dad.

The truck honked again. We had no choice. Matt put his foot on the clutch and we both took a deep breath as he shifted into second. We were gaining on Dad when Matt shifted into third. It was strangely silent as we passed him. I turned to see Dad's reaction to his purple station wagon driven illegally by his only children.

If a bomb had gone off by the side of the road, I'm not sure he would have noticed. His face was frozen, his eyes in a trance, every muscle of his body moving forward to God only knows where.

Now we were ahead of him, and then I understood as I saw the gates to the cemetery. Matt pulled in and parked behind a tree.

"We can go home now," he said.

"Joel. It's always Joel. It will always be Joel," I said sadly. For months Dad ran out on us for the memory of a dead person. "I hate him. I hate him. I hate him." I didn't really know which one I hated, so I left it open for interpretation. All I knew was that the people who lived were less valuable than the memory of the one who died.

We waited for Dad to pass by before we could turn around and go home. I looked at my pajamas and slippers and at my chauffeur hiding a purple station wagon under a tree while we stalked our own dad, who was running to see a tombstone. "This isn't normal," I said.

Dad finally got through the gates of the cemetery.

"We'll never get beyond Joel," I said as we turned around and headed home.

✳

That week dragged on, and I didn't practice my piano until Friday afternoon. Miss Mary Frances warned me everybody would groan whenever I practiced "Für Elise," and she was right. When Dad came home, I called out over the annoying half-step pattern played by my right hand.

"I think Mom misses you," I said, my left-hand arpeggios outlining a somber key.

"You do, honey?" he said, stopping under the arch.

"Yeah. She looks really tired and sad," I said, trying to concentrate on the notes and my fingers, but knowing I had Dad's attention.

"She's working long hours, isn't she?" Though he stood behind me now, I didn't turn around.

"Yeah, but she seems lonely. I think she needs you to come over and visit." I played the wrong key, looked down, and lost my place in the music.

"Dad, don't you miss us?" I turned around and made room on my bench so Dad could sit down.

"I do, Bee."

Then say something. Do something. Miss us as much as you miss him, I thought to myself.

"You want to play that duet?" Dad said, picking up *Bach Duets for Beginners* and opening to one we used to play together. We synchronized our notes but the music sounded as mechanical and precise as Dad's collection of clocks. At the end of the piece, Dad went back downstairs. Solo work.

Later, I heard the back door slam and Matt yell down the stairs, "I'm ba-ack!"

"Where's Mom?" Dad called out from the basement.

"Next door," Matt answered and then asked, not so nicely, "Where did you *think*?"

"Don't be sarcastic, Matt," Dad said.

I could see now why Matt thought he couldn't fix anything between them. Matt threw open the refrigerator and dug out a piece of cold pizza.

"Everybody's going to Joe's later tonight after the game. I need you to drop me off." Joe's was a popular pizza place for high school kids. Matt was off restriction, but I was pretty sure his activities were still limited.

"Looks like you've got pizza *here*," Dad said with a laugh. "Who's going?"

"Just a bunch of the guys."

"Who's in this bunch of guys? And what're they doing?"

"They're cool." Matt pulled out a bottle of soda. "I can pick my own friends."

Dad drummed his fingers on the table. I could tell he was vacillating. He might have said yes, but the line about picking his friends swayed the verdict.

"What do you want, anyway?" Matt's attitude was not helping his case. "I raised my grades and I haven't gotten into any trouble."

"Matt, you've got a ways to go," Dad answered.

"You know," Matt began, "maybe it's not *what* you want. Maybe it's *who* you want. Somebody else."

Ouch. That stung. Now is when I thought Dad should tell Matt how special and unique and important he was, but Dad was quiet. Maybe I knew why. After the drive to the cemetery, we knew the truth.

"Matt, I don't like your attitude. Maybe you need to go upstairs and cool off," Dad said tiredly, almost void of emotion when he should have been angry.

"I am *not* going to my room," Matt responded, matching Dad's calm and control. "I want to hang out with people. And at least I *do* want to hang out with people," Matt added in a mumble. As he popped the top, the soda fizzed over and he mouthed a swear word Dad didn't see.

"At least you *what?*" Dad asked, as if he didn't hear.

"I want to hang out with *people*," Matt repeated louder. "Mom runs next door and you go to the basement." And then he paused and I almost wanted Matt to add, "Or run to the cemetery," but he didn't. "Can't blame a person for wanting to hang out with people," he finished. Of course, there was *me* to hang out with, but somehow I didn't count. Matt leaned back and took a swig from the bottle, and something about it bothered me. Maybe Dad recognized it, too, and that finalized his decision.

"Nobody's running away and you're not going anywhere either."

"Nobody's running away?" Matt scoffed.

"What's really bothering you now, Matt?"

Here was the perfect opportunity. Somebody needed to say it. *You run to the cemetery and run away from us.* Maybe Somebody should be me, but I looked to Matt. Would he say it? I let Matt continue.

"How long are we supposed to live in lockdown around here?" Matt fired back.

"You're not in lockdown. I just said to go upstairs. It's not going to kill you." I frowned my disapproval. I didn't like that word, and neither did Matt, by the scowl on his face.

"You didn't answer my question, Dad. How long are we supposed to live in lockdown?" They held a stare-down. I couldn't tell who would break it. *Tell him, Abby. Dad needs to hear. Tell him.* My mouth was dry. "It's always a funeral. I want to live before I die."

Matt turned away as if to leave, then spun back around and added, "I'm beginning to think that Joel has it better."

"You're out of line." Dad's voice was the calm before the storm.

"*I'm* out of line? Of course! I'm *always* the one out of line." He turned from Dad to me. "But I'm *not* the only one who feels this way," he continued. "Just ask Abby. She's sick of it, too."

Though I knew what he meant, I hated him for putting me in the middle. We had a problem, but I did *not* know the solution. *You run to the cemetery and run away from us.* I nodded my head in silent agreement, but Dad was staring at Matt, uninterested in my opinion.

"You can go upstairs now before anybody else gets hurt."

"Before anybody *else* gets hurt?" Matt repeated. "Everybody's hurt." And instead of running up the stairs, he took them slowly and deliberately.

I was supposed to have said something, but Dad had completely ignored me. Where was my allegiance? I wanted to join Matt, but I couldn't figure out where I belonged, paralyzed between Matt's defiance and Dad's decision.

"You should go up and talk to him."

"I will," Dad said. "Later." And so I left. After all, he never asked me to stay.

The next morning, Mom and I came home to get the car. Except the car wasn't there.

"Where'd you put the wagon?" Mom asked Dad as she ran in the back door. Dad was sitting at the table with the paper and coffee.

"Good morning, dear. The coffee smells great—mind if I join you for a cup?" Dad said from behind his Saturday paper.

"We're late," Mom answered, as if in explanation. I pulled my sweater closer about me. "Where's the car?"

"What do you mean, 'Where's the car?' *You* drove it yesterday afternoon." I didn't like the way Dad answered. I didn't like the way they talked to each other.

"I put it back in the garage."

"Then it's in the *garage*," Dad responded, much the same way Mom answered when I asked where my shoes were. *"Wherever you put them."* But the tone wasn't just frustration. Something was wrong. Mom looked around suspiciously.

"Have you seen Matt this morning?" she asked. It was about Matt again. I took the stairs in twos, slowing at the top, afraid of what I might find.

I opened Matt's door and saw myself reflected back in his mirror, then tiptoed inside. Clothes were strewn all over the floor like usual, but his bed was made. Nobody had slept in it last night. The dresser and desktops were bare. A pile of trophies, certificates, and pictures littered the carpet and filled the trash. I could imagine Matt frustrated, angry, sad, his long arms swiping everything off the surface, his mementos crashing to the floor. He did it alone and nobody heard his outburst, and somehow that made me feel all the sorrier for him. There on the top of the pile was my favorite picture of Joel in his Chicago Cubs jersey. Matt is smiling as he helps Joel hold his bat, but Joel looks like he's trying to be tough.

When I returned to the kitchen, my face said it all and my parents flew into action.

"Just start calling his friends," Dad said to Mom.

"This was in the trash," I said, showing Dad the picture of Joel and Matt. "And this, too," I added, holding out a clear bag with shredded green leaves.

"Get out the directory. The Whites, the Davises, the Petersons," he said curtly, taking both items from my hands.

"Those aren't his friends anymore," Mom interrupted. Though I knew she wanted them to be. Dad should have known who Matt was hanging around with, but he didn't.

"Well, then call the guys he *is* hanging out with," Dad said, matching the edge of her voice as he set the bag and the picture on the table.

"I'm not your personal secretary. Here's the phone. You can start with the Burtons." Mom stared at the picture of her two sons and then at the bag of something she didn't want to recognize. What a difference between the past and present.

Dad frowned and exhaled slowly, the receiver in his hand. He was used to answering other people's problems, not phoning *with* the problem.

"Is this Sharon Burton?" Dad began. "This is John McAndrews. Sorry to bother you so early on a Saturday morning, but I was wondering if your son. . ." Dad stumbled for the name. I mouthed *Mike.* "Your son Mike was. . .or I should say, were your son and my son Matt. . ."

This was awkward. Painful. However Dad worded it, it was obvious he didn't know where Matt was and was accusing somebody else's son of getting into trouble. And he was still the minister, sort of. That didn't go over well.

As Mom and Dad alternated down a list of names, no one had seen Matt and he had never gone to the party.

"What happened, John? What did you do last night that caused this? Did you have another fight?" Mom's voice wasn't angry, just heavy, as if weary from battle.

"It wasn't that different from any other night. He wanted to go out but I said no."

"That sounds pretty normal," Mom said with a sigh.

"Maybe it was more than that, though," Dad said slowly. "At

first he was defiant, but then he gave up. Way too easily."

Mom waited for more information. Maybe this is where I was supposed to tell them that we had taken the car one morning and followed Dad to the cemetery.

"I went to the basement and had some clocks to work on. His light was out when I came up. I never checked his room. I should have gone in and talked to him, but the door was shut."

"We need to call the police," Mom said.

"And we need to get out there and start looking," Dad countered.

"And we need to get everyone we know out there looking. After all, we don't even know how long he's been gone. Maybe since last evening." That realization gave way to miles of possibilities. "Just where do you think he could be, John?" she asked, turning to Dad, a sliver of fear lacing her voice. Dad scratched the back of his neck.

"Stop worrying about what it *looks* like and just call the police." My stomach tightened. "They can find him."

"It's not a game of hide-and-seek, Renee. If he doesn't want to be found. . ."

"If he doesn't want to be found, it's because he's lost. *Really* lost," Mom said. "Maybe he can't come home because he's hurt. And it's time we did something about it instead of sitting around." *Sitting around* was directed at Dad with an edge I'd never heard before.

"And I suppose this is going to be my fault? Or should I say my fault, *too?*"

"This is not about Joel and this is not about you. Everything is not about *you*," Mom said. "This is about Matt. He's gone and we need to find him before he's hurt. Unless of course he's *already* hurt." And then her voice changed. "Oh John, I can't stand that thought. What should we do?"

"He wants to be found, Renee. That's why he ran. He wants our attention and he's got it."

"You're acting like he's only pulling a prank," Mom snapped back, the cold chill back in her voice.

"Renee, I love him. You *know* I love him," Dad repeated.

"I know you do," she said. "But that's not always enough," she added softly.

I hadn't done enough either. I didn't speak up last night in his defense. If I felt alone, maybe Matt felt even more that way. I knew I had to find him. I needed a brother; maybe he was gone because I wasn't a good enough sister.

When Sheriff Merchant arrived, he had a battery of questions. "What kind of a state was he in?" he asked, writing notes on his black notepad.

"State?" Mom asked. "I don't know, I wasn't at home." She reddened. Did people know Mom and Dad were separated?

"What are you getting at, Bob?" Dad asked. It felt like the Ludema fire interrogation revisted.

Sheriff Merchant answered by firing off a list of questions, and Mom and Dad stumbled at the answers.

"Was he angry? Did something happen that made him want to leave? Do you have any idea when he left? Is there anyplace he might have gone? Who does he hang around with?"

The questions targeted Matt as an angry runaway. It was a guess, but if it was true, he could be all the way to New York.

The day inched along with no Matt and no car. Then later that afternoon the sheriff's car pulled up to the house.

"We found the car. Have a seat." Sheriff Merchant motioned my mom and dad to sit down. That was never good. There was something else and it was going to be bad.

"The car is in the river," he began slowly, rubbing his forehead. Mom gasped. "It's sustained a lot of damage. Looks like the driver lost control on 282 and plunged over the guardrail."

"But what about Matt?" Dad asked as Mom gripped the table.

"The car is full of water, but the good news is that there's no body," Sheriff Merchant said.

"That's *good* news?" Mom exclaimed.

"It's possible the driver escaped."

"Escaped? After a crash?" Mom asked. "Bob, why aren't you out there looking?"

"We've got officers walking the riverbank. And. . ." The sheriff paused. "And we're sending a team of divers."

Mom took a deep and shaky breath and then stood. "I've got to be there."

"I understand, but we have enough people working the site."

"Where are they?" she asked, pulling on her coat as if she hadn't heard a word he said.

"You can't go, Renee," he said more firmly. "I'm sorry to say this, but we're dragging the river."

Mom froze and then slowly sat back down. Dad took her hand.

"Right now the best thing you can do is to stay here. If Matt was the driver, and if he got out, and if he's cold and injured, he'll come home. Somebody needs to be here for him." *If. If. If.*

"But we do have a few more questions." These questions weren't about a teenage runaway, and I could have answered them all.

"Did your son say or write anything? What was his state of mind?"

"I want to live before I die. . . ." Was Dad going to tell them that?

"Has anything like this ever happened before?"

Once in the cornfield at high speed.

"Did you say anything that might have triggered this?"

"It's not going to kill you."

"Did anything happen recently that might have disturbed him?"

It's always going to be about Joel.

I couldn't hold it in anymore. "We went to the cemetery. We took the car and we followed you."

Mom turned to me and then Dad. "The cemetery? You were at the *cemetery*?" Her look made me question if I should have told. After all, they'd search the cemetery, but they'd never find him there.

✳

The afternoon dragged on. The longer the wait, the less hope. And yet, maybe no news was good news. If they didn't find his body, he had to be alive, didn't he? I couldn't picture how you dragged a river. I wondered how many people were walking the river's edge, scanning for signs of life downstream. Some called it a waste of time and speculated he had run away, ashamed of what he had done to the car. If he was alive, he didn't have any money or dry clothes. *If he was alive. If he was alive. If he was alive.* He had to be lonely. Scared.

I had to do something, but what? *Hide-and-seek. Hide-and-seek.* He was lost. Did he really want to be found? *Hide-and-seek.* It was not a game. I slipped away, knowing I would not be missed in the confusion, and ran all the way to the lamp by the side door of the church, where I retrieved Dad's hide-a-key.

The church was cold and dark and eerily quiet. "Matt?" I said, tiptoeing through the social hall. "Matt?"

I ran up the steps to the sanctuary, where we had crawled beneath the worn oak pews while Dad worked on his sermons. Was our childhood playground once again Matt's safe haven?

"Matt?" I called. "Come down!" I tiptoed to the balcony, where I could survey the entire church. The tops of the hanging lights were dusty. Sunlight streaked through the stained-glass windows and lit the perfect bands of magic sparkles hanging in the air. Straight ahead hung the three wooden crosses united by a circle, and behind the pulpit was the stained-glass window of Jesus and the children.

I left my balcony and searched the dark halls behind the sanctuary. I needed to find him before anybody else thought of this place.

"Matt? It's me. Abby," I called out in a stage whisper, hoping the janitor wasn't nearby. Then I yelled just to see what it sounded like. I yelled the familiar name from our game of hide-and-go-seek. The name of the brother who would never be found.

"Joel!" His name echoed and reverberated throughout the empty rooms. "I wonder where Joel is today?" I yelled, imitating our childhood game. How strange that I could pretend I was looking for him. That I could make-believe he was just hiding from me and that in my play he could be found.

Matt's hiding places were less predictable, more challenging but perhaps less researched than mine. For nearly every Sunday of my childhood, during Dad's sermons, the moments on the organ bench, and even during Sunday school, I considered my next hiding spot. That's how I dreamed up the perfect hiding places. Once I stood on the men's room toilet for over an hour while Matt searched the rest of the church in frustration. He came in the bathroom once, but he never checked the stalls.

The next time we played, I took a pair of boots and pants out of the missionary donation box and designed what I called "Mr. Phelps" in one of the enclosed bathroom stalls. When Matt opened the main door to the bathroom, I heard him mutter, "Excuse me," and close the door. I stood on the toilet with Mr. Phelps for what seemed forever, but at least I had a book. What I couldn't know was that Matt also had a book he was reading while he waited for me to give up my secret location.

Wherever Matt hid he always popped out at me when I least expected it, right when I was about to discover him. The anticipation was thrilling and terrifying and caused wild thumping in my rib cage. I couldn't decide if I loved or hated it.

"Matt? Come out! Please!" I yelled as I headed out of the sanctuary. "Everybody's looking for you! We're worried about you!"

A voice down the hall said, "Can't imagine why."

"Matt!" I exclaimed, running to find him in a small office down the hall, sitting in the dark, but unhidden. A figure behind a desk, leaning back in an office chair.

"They're all looking for you. What happened?"

"I just went for a drive," he said as I flicked on the light.

"Oh, Matt, you're hurt," I said, pointing out the obvious. He had sustained a long cut across his forehead, his face was bruised, his clothes were wet, and he held a stack of paper napkins to his head that was soaked in blood.

"It was an accident."

"An *accident*?" I asked.

"Yeah, an *accident*," he snapped back.

"You *accidentally* took a car?" I asked. "Did you *accidentally* drink? Or what about that green stuff?" I sounded like my mom. First she'd rush over and comfort us, and then she'd yell at us to never, ever do that again. "And did you *accidentally* drive into the river?"

"Does it really matter?"

"No," I said. "No, I mean *yes*," I corrected. "I want to know. Were you drunk?"

"Would you believe it if I wasn't? I really *wasn't*," he said. "I had one beer, but nobody else will believe that. So what does it matter?"

"I'd like to think my opinion matters," I said.

"Wouldn't we all."

"Stop it. Just stop it. You took something that wasn't yours and you wrecked it. You don't care about anything or anyone."

"Look, I just went for a drive, but I slipped on a patch of ice and slammed into the side of the railing and went over the edge. It was awful but I survived. I always do," he said as if that wasn't a good thing. "Then I needed time to think, and I didn't know where to go."

"How about home?" My voice didn't sound compassionate.

"How'd you find me?" Matt asked, as if it had suddenly dawned on him that I had accomplished what the police had not.

"I remembered playing hide-and-go-seek."

"That seems like a long time ago," Matt said.

"I wish we could just go back to when we sat in the balcony and counted bald heads. Remember that?" He couldn't have forgotten.

"Ratios," he said and smiled sadly.

We could never go back. I wanted us fixed, but I didn't know how. I shook my head. If only I could have stopped him from taking Dad's car. But then again, maybe some things were just meant to happen.

Matt started pulling hymnals off the shelf and lining them up across the table.

"So now I gotta go home," he said, positioning them like a line of dominoes.

I wanted to tell him how I'd go with him and how I'd explain what happened and that it would be okay, but I knew better.

"Prodigal son," Matt said, naming himself. "Do you think they'll kill the fatted calf when I return?" he asked as he added another hymnal to his line.

"Mom has Chinese takeout in the fridge at Miss Patti's," I teased. He returned my smile.

"I didn't set the Ludemas' barn on fire," he said suddenly.

"This isn't about the barn."

"It might be to everybody else," he answered, the line of dominoes almost ready to tumble. "You didn't really say you believed me."

"What difference does it make whether I do or not?" I asked. "You said it yourself."

He stopped standing up hymnals long enough to look at me. Really look at me.

"Maybe you're right. I'd like *you* to believe me, but what I really want is for *him* to."

You haven't given him much reason to, I thought. Matt touched the first hymnal and they began to tip over one by one, until the last books toppled off the desk and fell open on the floor.

"And I need for him to believe that I really didn't want Joel to die. That I should have kept him on my shoulders."

"But that would make Dad guilty," I said softly.

Matt began picking up the fallen hymnals, returning them to the bookshelf, then adjusting their spines until they were in perfect alignment.

"Do you really think anything's going to change?"

"You mean about Mom and Dad?" I asked. "Or about Joel? Or about all of us?"

"I don't know. Maybe it's not even about Joel anymore," he said and then looked up quickly. "Wouldn't that be awful? Maybe we don't even know what needs fixing anymore."

That was too big for me. It probably was *not* about Joel. But to figure out what it *was* about was even bigger than trying to figure out who we were as a family without him.

"Do you think Joel can see us?"

"Not if heaven is perfect," Matt answered quickly.

Matt was probably right. Seeing us would make Joel sad.

"They're really worried," I said, thinking about Mom and Dad.

"Yeah, yeah, yeah."

"And I should have said something last night." Matt looked up at my words. "You were right," I admitted, nodding my head.

"Now what do we do?"

"Dear Abby," he said, invoking the name of the advice columnist with all the answers. "*Dear Abby*, always wanting to fix everything." He wasn't making fun of me; his voice was kind and gentle.

"You can't fix this, Abby. But one thing I know: someone needs to notice *you* need some fixing."

He couldn't begin to know the feelings in my stomach or in my head and how I had so little control over them. But with all his problems, how could he ever make anyone see mine?

Matt got up and headed for the door. When I followed him, he turned and looked at me as if I were a puppy on his heels and so I stopped.

"Don't worry, I'm not coming with you."

But I knew I'd go part of the way—just far enough to make sure he actually went home. I didn't want him ever running away again.

I waited twenty minutes by the side door, then headed home, arriving just as the police were leaving. When I opened the front door, I heard Dad and Mom and Matt in the kitchen talking about leaving for the hospital. Did anybody even notice I was missing?

"Uncle Troy will be here any minute. What are we going to do about Abby?" Mom said, unaware I was standing behind her.

"Where have you been?" Dad asked as I stepped forward.

"That doesn't matter right now," Mom said. "We just need to get Matt to the doctor. We can talk about this later."

I guess Matt hadn't told them the whole story. Maybe none of us ever did. Maybe that had to change.

"Matt didn't light the fire," I blurted out.

That pretty much changed the topic, and everybody stared at me. I repeated it very slowly. "Matt did not light the fire."

"Nobody said he did," Mom answered.

"But nobody said he *didn't*, either," I pointed out.

Matt looked down, Dad cleared his throat, Mom's face wore a question mark. I don't think anybody knew what to do next.

"Right now we need to focus on what happened *today*, Abby," Mom continued. "We have to deal with what happened *today*."

"The Ludemas' barn is about today," I said, not backing off.

Matt wouldn't look at anyone. He stared beyond me at what I assumed could be the clock or Mom's farm calendar. Maybe I shouldn't have brought it up after all. Maybe Dad really did blame Matt.

"Does anybody blame Matt for the fire?" Dad asked. I looked over at Mom, whose face questioned Dad.

"Are you accusing me?" he asked.

"No one's accusing anyone, John. Abby brought up something important, and maybe we didn't handle that whole thing right."

"Look at me, Matt," Dad said. Matt slowly turned his head and swallowed hard. Was he going to cry? My throat felt suddenly dry. Thick.

"I know you didn't light that fire," Dad said. We all nodded in agreement about his innocence. "But what about the other stuff?" Dad continued. "Were you drinking when you took the car?" Matt was expressionless, a soldier answering his superior.

"Yes, I was."

"Have you been doing drugs?"

"Yes, I have."

"And my pearl necklace? The one from Dad?" Mom asked.

"I sold it."

"You stole it," Mom clarified. And this time I could see his eyes water and his face crumple.

"I'm sorry. I'm sorry for all of it," he said.

"Stop. That's enough. I don't need to know any more," Dad said softly as Mom wrapped her arms around Matt. Dad clapped his hand on Matt's shoulder. He was back. But would he really quit drinking and smoking and stealing? Of course he wouldn't be driving, but how hard was that now that we didn't even have a car? It didn't feel safe to hope for a happy ending.

"You said some people run away and they don't want to be found," Dad said, turning to Mom. "You said some people are lost." Mom's eyes grew misty as Dad continued. "Maybe that's me." Dad's voice quivered but he kept going. "One thing I know for sure: Without you *I'm* lost." I could see his eyes watering.

"And maybe you're lost, too, but I think you want to be found," he continued. "And you know the way home, Renee." Mom's face softened. "Come home, Renee. Come home," Dad whispered.

My nose tingled like it does when I'm about to cry. Maybe I was lost, too, and maybe I needed to be found. Maybe I had a lot of questions and doubts, but the one thing I was sure of was that she was not coming home.

TWENTY-TWO

Holy Week begins with Palm Sunday and concludes with Easter, which always brings out the "A and P" Christians, short for ashes and palms. Holy Week is also spring break, which, until this year, was Dad's busy season. But even this year we weren't going anywhere for all the obvious reasons: death and taxes. Good Friday is a part of that week, and if you ask me, it's an *oxymoron*. What's so good about a day you remember someone's death? Hadn't we spent months now doing that? And look where it got us.

But Mom and Miss Patti were hosting Uncle Troy and Miss Mary Frances, Dad, Matt, and me for Easter dinner, and so on top of doing her taxes, Mom was getting Miss Patti's house ready and planning Sunday's menu.

On the Wednesday before Easter, Rita and Miss Patti were already up and dressed and ready to go somewhere. Rita said she couldn't play and Miss Patti told Mom she didn't need her that day. Nearly two months of sleepovers had gone by and maybe they were tired of us. Mom argued they had work to do to make the April 15 deadline, but Miss Patti and Rita had a resolve I couldn't understand. "Go work on your dinner plans."

"It's a special day for us. Something we do every year," Rita explained. I must have looked hurt because then Rita spilled the secret. "It's April seventh. It's Daddy's birthday," she whispered. I raised my eyebrows. *Daddy's birthday?*

Patti then filled in the gaps. "Jeff restored an automobile. I keep it in the garage. It's about all we have left of his. We take it out on his birthday and Father's Day. We keep it alive. Or *him* alive. It's just something we do."

Mom nodded, but I could tell she looked confused. A hidden car?

That afternoon Miss Patti and Rita headed out the back door toward the alley. Miss Patti opened the garage and they disappeared, only to reappear in the most amazing car I had ever seen. Mom's eyes widened. It was a shiny red and white automobile with huge fenders, whitewall tires, and no top. Truly, it looked like it could fly.

Miss Patti gave it a real honk and then Rita leaned back in her seat and wrapped her scarf around her neck like a movie star.

"What *is* that?" I asked Mom.

"I don't know, but I think they call it a speedster." She shook her head in amazement. They blew by us and I felt a sense of longing. I wanted to race the wind with them and bring someone back to life with the turn of a key. Oh, to be riding along in the most incredible automobile in Bethel Springs. Especially since we didn't even have a car anymore.

Mom and I could have gone back inside, but instead we sat on the front steps, waiting for their return. Uncle Troy came down the sidewalk, whistling through his teeth.

"Now that's somethin' else," he said, staring down the road. "A 1936 Auburn Boattail Speedster. I thought I saw one of those once before. Maybe even on this street." How did Uncle Troy know something about everything?

"They take it out once or twice a year," I said, as if I also knew something about everything. He whistled through his teeth again and then looked at Mom in that serious way he did before a church talk.

"Look, I want to help you out however I can, and I don't think most people know," he began. "But I know you're *here*, not *there*." He nodded at Miss Patti's and then the parsonage.

Mom bit her lip and then looked from me to Uncle Troy and back at me.

"I'm going home. To *our* house," I explained. "I'm going over *there*," I added, as if I needed to, and left them talking.

"You feel okay?" Matt asked when I slammed the door behind me.

"I should be asking you that question," I snapped. He had stitches in his forehead and one broken rib, but the doctor said otherwise he was in pretty good shape and a very lucky guy. For some reason "very lucky" had made Matt look sad. What made some accidents *unlucky*?

I followed Matt to the washing machine, where he proceeded to put everything from his laundry bag in one load. He could do it his way. What did I care?

"Miss Patti has a 1936 Boattail Speedster she keeps in her garage."

"No kidding," Matt said. "I've never seen one of those."

"I don't know why I told you that."

"I'm not going to steal it."

"That would certainly get everybody's attention."

Matt poured detergent in the machine, turned the dial, and dropped the lid with a bang.

✳

That Sunday morning, right before church, Mom put a ham and scalloped potatoes in Miss Patti's oven. In between tax returns, Mom had also baked hot cross buns and made Matt's favorite marshmallow and mandarin orange Jell-O salad.

Last year we had hunted for eggs and even Matt had participated. He hid our decorated eggs for Joel and me to find. I avoided the obvious eggs, knowing Matt had "hidden" them for a three-year-old. But some were clearly *my* eggs: the ones high in the branches, the one in the downspout, and the one in the mailbox. Mom helped Joel find the eggs, but he only wanted the orange ones, disappointed by all other colors.

That same Easter someone had asked Dad about whether it was appropriate to have Easter egg hunts and Dad smiled. "New life," he added. "Finding new life in Christ." Back then Dad always had an easy answer for everything.

This Easter, we didn't decorate any eggs. This Easter, Dad wasn't in the pulpit, but he did join us in the balcony. "You can see everything from up here!" I encouraged, hoping he'd see church the way I did. Miss Patti and Rita sat in my row, both wearing dresses, which was rare. Once pants were allowed in school, Rita had never looked back. Now she scratched at her legs as if her stockings were eating holes in her skin.

The sanctuary was crowded with men in suits, women in new spring dresses, and little girls with hats and gloves. I've always worn hand-me-downs from the Douglas girls. This year's installment was a yellow gingham dress with puffy sleeves.

"Christ is risen!" Reverend Davidson announced with cheer.

"He is risen, indeed!" the congregation answered.

"Let us now sing 'Christ the Lord Is Risen Today.'"

"Alleluia!" I whispered to that. I wanted Rita to like the hymns. Christmas Glorias and Easter Alleluias were my favorites.

Miss Patti stood next to Mom and mouthed the words. Rita tried to figure out the music staff. I giggled each time she read one line and dropped to the wrong verse. Matt stared down at his hymnal, but I sang out, hoping Dad would, too. Most of all, I wanted him to like church again.

"He is risen!" Reverend Davidson repeated.

"He is risen, indeed!" the congregation echoed. When we sat down, I pointed out where we were in the program to Rita and

Miss Patti, who were not very good at the Presbyterian stand up/ sit down stuff. And as a matter of fact, Miss Patti had pretty much decided she could stay seated and sing instead of getting up and down all the time.

Though I wanted to doodle or play games, Matt had his eyes closed like he was about to fall asleep, and Dad was watching everything as if he had never really been to church before.

Reverend Davidson assumed the podium and opened his Bible with the rustle of onionskin pages. I loved that familiar sound. The scripture reading for that Sunday was about Mary Magdalene's arrival at the tomb and how she didn't recognize Jesus.

"Did Mary Magdalene go to the tomb to find a risen Lord?" the minister said. "No, Mary Magdalene came to anoint a dead body," he said. "Mary was so certain Jesus was dead that she didn't recognize the resurrected Lord when He appeared in front of her." What about us? Would we be able to recognize Joel in heaven?

Heaven frightened me. Each time I imagined *on and on and on* with no end, my stomach rolled and I felt dizzy. There was something good about day and night and seasons and stops and starts. What would it be like to spend eternity without any control over time? I tried to picture the happiest day of my life and imagined it going on forever. Was heaven like that?

And what would we be *like* in heaven? Would Joel be a kid and me an old lady? I sighed and Dad looked at me and mouthed, *What?* I shook my head and looked down. Maybe we could talk about it later. Then again, maybe not.

"In what ways are *you* returning to tombs with gloom in your heart when we can claim victory on Easter Sunday?" Reverend Davidson concluded, his voice rising in power and volume. I wasn't sure he needed a mike.

Mrs. Tangan was listed for special music and I looked down

the pew toward Matt and we both rolled our eyes. Mrs. Tangan's hair was ratted so high, a bird could have lived inside, which might have explained her high soprano warble. We used to mimic her on the way home from church, increasing the vibrato with each verse. Today she sang her annual special music selection, which began with *"Low in the grave he lay,"* a dark and ominous verse that erupted into the happy chorus *"Up from the grave He arose!"* and an ascent that scaled a full octave. *"Hallelujah! Christ arose!"* Mrs. Tangan sang, beaming.

Reverend Davidson's message about Mary Magdalene was just about as good a message as he had ever delivered. It was Easter Sunday and my greatest hope was that it had resurrected something in Dad.

"Can you girls put the napkins on the table?" Mom asked when we got home. Rita and I began folding each pale blue square, setting one at each plate.

"That rose and gravy song was kind of interesting," Rita said, a teasing lilt to her voice.

"What are you talking about?" I asked, taking the bait.

Rita smiled playfully. She was the nicest friend anyone could ask for, but she was mischievous, and because we sometimes read each other's minds, it just happened.

"Up from the GRAVY a ROSE!" we belted at the same time but different pitches, loudly and proudly, until Miss Mary Frances reprimanded us for not respecting Mrs. Tangan's God-given talent and courage. After that, even the sight of Mom's potatoes made me bite my lip.

"Uncle Troy, would you say grace?" Mom asked.

Uncle Troy looked at Dad and then around the table and bowed his head. At his "Amen," I cased out my favorite dishes.

"So, what did you think of Reverend Davidson's message?" Miss

Mary Frances said. "And please pass the scalloped potatoes," she added with equal importance.

"Thank goodness we're not having *gravy*," I whispered, and then Rita and I got to giggling. Miss Mary Frances frowned.

"It was nice to have the focus on a *woman*," Miss Patti answered, smiling at Miss Mary Frances and then shaking her head at the two of us. "Seems to me that the men always get the most press in the Easter story, but this story is really about a *woman*," she explained as she passed the hot cross buns to her right. "Can I get anyone some jam?" she asked. "That's why Mary Magdalene's my favorite."

"How about you, Matt?" I asked, looking down the table. "Who's your favorite?"

"Judas," he said without missing a beat.

"Seriously, Matt."

"Okay, then maybe the guys around Jesus on the cross," he answered.

"Which one?" I persisted. "Please say the guy who goes to paradise."

"That one."

Maybe there was hope for Matt yet.

"I like Peter," Miss Mary Frances piped in. "Even though nobody bothered to ask me," she scolded, and then paused so we'd have a chance for a follow-up question.

"Why *Peter*?" Mom asked politely.

"Because Peter hung around," Miss Mary Frances said. "He denied Him, yes, but he stuck closer than those other cowardly disciples."

Miss Mary Frances always had a fresh way of seeing things.

"But don't forget John," Uncle Troy said. "Jesus asks him to be Mary's son."

"As if anyone could replace *Jesus*," Mom said.

"John is Jesus' beloved friend. That's what I'd like to be." Uncle Troy spoke honestly.

"This is nice," Miss Patti said. "I think I could go to church if people were allowed to ask a few questions like we're doing right now. And I think I might listen to someone who didn't act like he had all the answers."

"Those potatoes look delicious, Renee," Dad said, changing the subject and offering Mom a smile. "Could you pass them down?" That triggered the gravy song, and I forgot Miss Mary Frances's warning and started humming it until Rita kicked me under the table. Dad took two heaping helpings on his plate; he had obviously missed Mom's cooking as much as Matt had.

The room went quiet as we all enjoyed our favorites except Rita, who seemed to be trying to decide what she wanted next. "I guess it's not so bad to lose someone if He comes back in three days," she said. Quiet Rita. The one-who-rarely-talks-Rita, piping in with some deep thought, when before all she could hear was gravy and roses. I nearly choked on my hot cross bun.

Dad, who had been strangely quiet about anything except food, nodded an unspoken understanding.

"Now that's a thought, Rita," Miss Patti said to fill the space widening the table like a leaf added for holiday dinner.

"But I think even if we knew the plan, it'd still be hard to watch someone suffer and die," Dad concluded.

Even Miss Mary Frances was silenced. Uncle Troy took another bite so he wouldn't have to say anything. Mom took the empty ham tray to the kitchen, and I pointed to the ambrosia salad that barely made it back around the table to me as everyone served up generous portions.

"And what's next on the church calendar?" Miss Patti asked from her end of the table. That could be taken a lot of ways.

"Ascension, then Pentecost," Dad answered from the head of the table. "The gift of the Holy Spirit."

"The one Jesus called the *Comforter*, am I right?" Patti asked, looking straight at Dad. She was right and she knew it, and her point was not lost on any of us.

"They lose the Son and gain the *Comforter*?" she repeated. I remembered Pentecost as tongues of fire now aptly demonstrated over Easter dinner.

Miss Mary Frances's eyes widened, Uncle Troy cleared his throat into his napkin, and Rita hummed our song as Mom passed the ham for another round.

"And the beginning for the Church," Miss Patti added, to my surprise. By her firm tone, this was not a definition but an encouraging proposal.

My Easter was about being lost and found. It was about a Comforter. About hope and life, and the birth of a Church, and resurrecting dreams even when nobody quite knew how. But we were together and we were talking. And something about that felt—for now—almost good enough.

TWENTY-THREE

Mom opened the mail, sorting bills into one pile, dumping junk mail in the trash, and saving handwritten envelopes for last. With her head bent over and her face in deep concentration, I noticed for the first time that she had some gray hair. Matt and Dad watched the news side by side on the couch. Matt looked like a younger version of Dad, without all the creases.

"Grandpa and Grandma are coming," Mom announced, letter in hand.

"Yeah!" I squealed, then stopped in disbelief. "Really?" I didn't ask the obvious question. *Why would they come now?*

"You've gotta be kidding. They never come," Matt said, turning from the news.

"They came *once*," Dad corrected. "After Abby was born."

"They say they're coming for your birthday," Mom said, looking toward me.

"No, they're coming because we're so messed up," Matt corrected.

"Matt!" Dad scolded.

"He's right. They're coming to fix us," Mom agreed.

"They'd better hurry," I said, and then everybody laughed.

"Do they know Abby and I don't live here?" Mom asked. Dad kept watching the TV. Soon Grandpa and GramAnna would see that everything was broken.

"You could come home for a week," Matt suggested.

"Matt has a point," Dad said.

"Not now," Mom said simply.

Not now. Not now. Then when?

"I'm glad that new counselor's been helping Matt, but we're not all at the same place," Mom pointed out.

Matt was seeing a new counselor? I wasn't sure if that made me feel better or worse. He was getting help; that was a good thing and it probably explained some of the positive changes I had seen in him, but what did it mean for me? Would somebody make me say why I had weird feelings and strange thoughts and anxious "what-ifs" about bad things that could suddenly happen to us?

"We can't work on things when we're not together," Dad said.

"But we weren't working on things when we were together, either," Mom pointed out.

"It's about the job, then. You won't come home until I go back."

"No, I don't care about the job anymore," she explained. "If you can't do it, then find another career. A new minister would give the church an opportunity to start over, and maybe we could restart and move on, too."

"Seems like you already have," said Dad.

"Maybe I have," Mom agreed. "I don't want to be the same person I was. I can't." She didn't apologize; Mom stood tall, her voice confident and persuasive. "Now maybe you should go seek that pastoral counseling the elders were talking about."

"Would that really change anything?"

"I don't know," she said honestly. "I don't know."

＊

Though I had always wanted to be done with nine so I could have a double-digit birthday and hold up both hands and answer, "Ten!" I no longer wanted a celebration and I told Mom that.

I also told Mom I didn't want a lot of friends over or a cake or games or even lots of presents to open. Unfortunately, Mom didn't get it. She hadn't gotten to do Joel's fourth; and for his sixteenth, Matt said he just wanted money or a car, and we all knew that wasn't going to happen since we were still borrowing a used loaner to get around.

And so on May fourteenth, when I came home from school, nine girls screamed, "SURPRISE!"

Mom had planned a bowling party. My first time bowling. Ten years, ten bowling pins, and ten girls. She had it all worked out: Rita, Melody, Phyllis, Marci, Barbara, Maureen, Kris, Linda, Tonja, and me.

"But it's not my—" I began.

"Not *yet*. I had to do it early so it'd be a surprise!" Mom hadn't looked this excited for a long time. She gave me a big hug and then scooted us out the door to caravan to the Spare Room, the only bowling alley in town. *Oh joy*, I thought. Hadn't she heard me? Didn't she understand? I didn't want a birthday.

The boy at the counter rolled his eyes as we shouted out our shoe sizes. At first I thought he deliberately gave us the dumbest-looking shoes on the rack until I realized everybody had clown shoes. Barbara and Rita looked down at their feet and started tapping away. My shoes were too big, but I didn't care.

"Once my uncle Ed took me bowling!" Tonja bragged.

"Have you ever knocked them all down at once?" Linda asked.

"That's called a strike," Marci explained knowingly. She had brought the pink bowling ball her grandparents had given her last Christmas.

"This is gonna be fun!" Barb said, taking my hands in hers. I didn't share her enthusiasm, and headed down to the end of the bowling alley where Mom had the #10 station decorated with streamers and a big sign reading A HAPPY TEN FOR OUR ABBY! She thought of everything.

"Let me go first!" Phyllis begged.

"No, please, I want to!" Melody said.

"Abby should. After all, it's *her* birthday," Marci pointed out. I looked down the other nine lanes, where people got to bowl anonymously.

"Well, at least let her pick who goes *first* then," Kris said, seemingly aware I wasn't fighting for that honor.

"Go reverse alphabetical," I suggested, and then I wandered off as if in search of the right weight ball, leaving Barbara lining everybody up reverse alphabetically in two lanes.

I slipped between the popcorn machine and a huge tank of stuffed animals where you could put in a quarter and a claw would grab at the animal you wanted, and I watched the party that was supposed to be for me. Silly, crazy, screaming girls who, except for Rita, couldn't understand me. I was dying inside.

If I were somebody else, I might want to be one of those girls bowling in lane #10, their names and scores on the board: Tonja, Rita, Phyllis, Mom, Melody, and Maureen on one team: Marci, Linda, Kris, Dad, Barbara, and me on the other.

Dad bowled a strike, but the only other person who knocked down all her pins was Linda. We were just plain awful. My turn awaited. Finally, Barbara bowled and I was next.

I returned with a black ball. There is nothing graceful about a skinny almost-ten-year-old girl hurling a six-pound globe down a narrow aisle. The only grace we bowlers experienced was in getting a spare, which Dad described as a second chance.

Suddenly, Maureen rolled a strike and everybody screamed. I covered my ears, watching for their mouths to close so I knew I could take my hands away. I came with a headache that was only getting worse, compounded by Neil Sedaka, the smell of hot dogs, rolling balls, crashing pins, and fourth graders.

Tonja dropped her six-pound ball on Mom's foot, Kris spilled her soda all over the floor, and Barbara was mopping it up with Dad's coat. I slumped low in my plastic chair and stretched out my feet. Stupid blue, brown, and yellow shoes. I hadn't even taken off my coat. Could we go yet?

"It's your turn, Abby," Phyllis said. "Hurry and go!"

I wished I could get my turn over faster, but I had never been able to knock down more than four at a time.

"Who's the birthday girl?" I heard from far away, pretending it wasn't me and praying there was someone else with a birthday.

"It's her," someone said, pointing at me.

"Who's the birthday girl?" I heard again as the man brought over a pink T-shirt with the words *Knock 'em dead on your birthday.*

"Put it on!" my friends encouraged, but I shook my head in such a way they didn't force me. The man looked disappointed. The whole thing was ridiculous.

"Abby, that was kind of rude," Mom scolded. "What's gotten into you?"

Dad tried to help me with my swing, but gave up quickly.

Every time Marci threw the pink ball, I thanked God for the padding on the side of the lane. We always moved behind the scoring table, knowing she could throw it backward or sideways and take out any one of us. I looked at the scoreboard. Nobody had rolled over an eighty. Wow. Time for a break.

Mom had made a cake with ten candles and frosted lanes. The girls argued over who would get the bubble gum bowling balls lining the sides. I didn't really care.

I opened my presents and got a Troll doll, Barbie, turtleneck sweater, smiley face clock for my bedroom, and poster of David Cassidy. I thanked them all. Then Linda handed me a soft package. I ripped open the wrapping paper to discover a large stuffed monkey.

The girls started laughing and I felt my face burn. Did they know? Who would give me a monkey, knowing Joel was the one who loved monkeys?

"I thought he looked like Curious George!" Linda said, shrugging. She didn't look guilty. But *Curious George*?

"Abby, open another present," Mom said as she handed me a bright pink package obviously from Marci.

"I don't really want to," I said at last.

"C'mon, Abby, at least open what I got you!" Phyllis begged, yelling over Jefferson Airplane.

"And me, too! You didn't open mine!" said Melody. What was the big deal anyway?

"It's just. . ." I stuttered. "I don't know. . ."

"Maybe it's time to light the cake," Rita said, granting me a temporary reprieve.

Mom lit one candle and, with it, lit the other nine. Blue- and pink-colored wax dripped over the frosting. On cue, they sang "Happy Birthday" as badly as they bowled, Melody Ludema's nasal pitchiness sticking out above the rest. It was better when she didn't sing.

And then, because she just didn't get it, Linda picked up that stuffed monkey and added, "Happy Birthday to you, you live in a zoo, you look like a monkey, and you smell like one, too!"

"Blow them out! Blow them out!" the girls chanted. "All at once!" Kris said as if I needed instructions. "All TEN!" Phyllis added. "Make a strike!" Mom cheered. I bent down close to the cake and tried not to breathe deeply. The Spare Room smelled of cigarette smoke, hot dogs, pizza, stale popcorn, catsup, and mustard.

As soon as I blew out the candles, Mom pulled them out and began cutting the cake.

"I want the pink gumball!"

"Can I have a piece with lots of frosting?"

"I want the blue piece."

"I only want *cake*, Mrs. McAndrews."

I wanted to yell, *SHUT UP!*

"Which one do you want, honey?" Mom asked. "Which part of the cake?"

"I don't care," I said. And I meant it. As at most birthday parties, the girls scraped off the frosting, took a bite of the cake, and then went back to play.

We bowled one more set. The ball felt so heavy, weighted. Once Linda threw the ball and it flew in the air and came down with a thud. I looked for a dent in the floor and checked the ball for damage when it returned.

"Try for *ten* on your *tenth*!" Barbara squealed. I rolled my eyes. That was pretty original. No, a strike would not improve my attitude.

"Maybe you should try the *green* ball, Abby. I think it's *lucky*!" Melody claimed.

"You can try my pink one if you want. But only *you*," offered Marci. I grabbed the green one shooting out and flung it quickly down the lane. It skimmed the padding and missed every pin. I did it twice. I didn't think anybody was a bigger zero.

Rita was next. Whenever she threw the ball, it took forever to reach the pins. The girls started counting the seconds. "One-two-three-four-five-six!" Linda and Kris began blowing as if they could huff and puff the ball down the lane. "Twelve-thirteen!" The ball slowed like a clock winding down. "Fifteen-sixteen-seventeen," they continued. "I think it's gonna STOP!" Marci squealed. "What would happen if it *did*?" Their eyes widened and they laughed, as if that would be the most hysterical thing they had ever heard of. In another time and place, and on another birthday, I would have thought this was great fun.

At last the ball clipped a pin on the count of twenty-five. They were having such a good time. Mom had tried so hard.

I left for the bathroom, knowing I had three girls before my next turn. No one ever knocked anything down with one ball. I had plenty of time.

Pushing open the bathroom door, I took in the cracked tiles, peeling paint, and dingy odor reminiscent of Matt's football uniform and I lost it. My birthday lunch went down the toilet.

The stall doors held so much graffiti. *Joyce loves Brian.* Hearts and flowers. Peace symbols, smiley faces, *Have a Happy Day.* Lots of words I didn't understand but pretty much figured out had to be bad. I wasn't the only one who had hidden out here.

I left the stall to rinse my hands and splash my face with water. My legs felt weak and I leaned against the bathroom wall, slowly sliding down until I landed on the floor. This was not how I thought I'd spend my tenth birthday back when I was little.

When I was nine, I was safe. I could catch lightning bugs, run through the sprinkler, and share a bedroom with a little brother. But now I wasn't a kid anymore, and I didn't want to celebrate like one. Now I had to be careful because accidents happen. I checked for dangers like radiators and electrical cords and whether Mom turned off the oven. I felt cheated out of the kind of childhood everyone else had—except maybe Rita. And now that Joel wasn't having any more birthdays, I didn't think I deserved one either.

"Abby, are you okay?" Rita asked, swinging the door open with a rush of cold air. I shivered.

"I'm okay."

"Then you have to come back."

"Do I?"

"You've been gone a long time. Everybody's wondering where you are. I thought maybe you were sick, but you're just sitting here."

"I know."

"It's your birthday party," she pointed out, sitting down next to me.

"Duh!" I sounded so rude.

"Why are you acting like that?"

"It's too hard to explain."

Rita frowned. I could tell I had insulted her.

"It just doesn't feel right somehow," I said. "You know, without Joel."

"I've never had a birthday with my dad. But you have *that*. And you have a brother, too. That's something."

I thought about that. She was right. She didn't say very much, but when she did, she was almost always right. I hugged my knees to my chest and rested my head on one knee, studying the haphazard pattern of chipped and missing tiles.

"Do you think you'll ever know what happened to him?"

"Mom hopes so. But I don't think so," she said, looking up at the ceiling. One panel was missing, exposing pipes and insulation. I timed the intervals between the drip from the leaky faucet accompanied by the buzz of the fluorescent lights. One. Two. Three. Drip.

"Marci threw the ball down the wrong lane."

"Really?" I said. "Or are you just saying that to make me laugh?"

"She almost hit these two guys in the next alley. Someone yelled, 'Look out!' Talk about clearing the place." Rita laughed softly.

I shook my head. Marci and her pink bowling ball.

"Everybody thinks it's kind of cool having ten pins and ten friends," Rita said.

"Yeah. I guess my mom had fun planning it."

"So maybe you should have some fun, too."

The door swung open and my mom rushed in, looking puzzled to find the two of us on the floor.

"What are you doing in here? Everybody's wondering where you are!" The door began to swing shut and Rita scurried out before it closed.

"I don't like it out there."

"It's your birthday. I thought this would be a fun event."

"I know you tried," I said.

"I did more than *try*. I wanted your tenth to be a great year. It's something *new*, Abby. You're not *nine* anymore; you're double digits."

"Nine wasn't a good year."

"Exactly. That's why we're trying to move on," she said.

"You're getting pretty good at it," I said under my breath.

"What do you mean? Here I am, trying to celebrate that you're a year older, but you're acting all depressed and angry. Honestly, I don't know what I did wrong."

She didn't say it to make me feel guilty. I could tell she had just about had it, but I didn't really care. I wished I could explain why I felt so weird, but that would mean I understood something I didn't. She started to head out the door, but then spun back around with renewed purpose.

"Just what kind of birthday party did you want, anyway? How did I let you down this time?"

"I didn't really *want* a birthday party," I said.

"So if you didn't really *want* a birthday party, and I hadn't given you one, wouldn't I still be the bad mom who forgot you turned ten? Are you telling me you wouldn't have been mad at me for that, too?" I tried to run that statement around in my head, but it turned out to be really confusing. "That's a pretty big risk for me to take," she added, before I could figure out what she had asked.

"Maybe it's not really a good year to celebrate."

"Maybe *last* year was not a year to celebrate. Okay, I agree. But when do we *start* celebrating? How about if *this* year is better?" she suggested. Then her voice softened. "Abby, how about we start to move forward this year?"

How? The way *she* had already moved forward, leaving so many behind? I *did* want things to change, but I also didn't want to leave things behind. I *did* want to celebrate and be happy and get out of lockdown or whatever anybody called it, but I *didn't* want to celebrate my birthday. And that was that. Maybe I couldn't explain it, but I just didn't want to have a birthday this year, and I wanted somebody to hear me and understand me even if it didn't make sense.

"I didn't want it!" I said, louder than I meant. "And I don't want to move on. I want to move back home. I want to go home!" I yelled. "I want to go home!"

My head throbbed as if my brain wanted out of my skull. I banged it on the tile wall as if that would help.

"All right, let's just pack up and go," Mom threatened. "Tell your friends the party's over."

"I'm not going back to Miss Patti's. I want to go home. I want to go home." When I banged my head on *home*, for a split second a new pain overpowered the old. So I just kept saying, "HOME HOME HOME," pounding my head against the wall with increasing intensity.

"Abby, stop that. You'll hurt your head again!" Mom tried to grab my shoulders but I fought her. I think I heard her screaming, but maybe it was just me.

The door swung open again but I just kept beating my head against the wall, screaming, "HOME HOME HOME!" Louder and louder and louder.

"Abby, STOP it!" Dad shouted, kneeling down and pulling me into his arms. I couldn't think of how I had arrived on a bathroom floor yelling, "HOME," but here I was. A small, tearless rag doll.

"Abby, I'm so sorry. I'm so sorry."

I touched my forehead where there must have been a bruise. Everything was out of focus.

"Your mom can't come home, Abby."

That was it? The reason we weren't going to be a family?

"Your mom can't come home unless I make some changes. Abby, I'm sorry. I'm so very sorry."

The water dripped, 1-2-3. I could hear muted cheers outside, but inside only the buzz of the fluorescent lights. No one spoke.

"Presbytery has a grief counselor. A retreat for pastors who've lost a loved one." Dad took a deep breath and continued. "And I'll talk to Uncle Troy about the church. I'll work something out for all of us." He held me at arm's length and I could feel him looking at me and really seeing me. "Abby, you need to talk to someone, too. That's not a request. I'm so very sorry we waited this long." Dad took my hand and pulled me off the floor.

I looked at Mom. Dad was making a step. Was this enough? I knew she couldn't go back, but could we go forward?

"Let's go home, Abby," she said as she took my other hand.

TWENTY-FOUR

I slept in my own bed that night. Though I had gotten used to sharing with Mom, I liked having my own room again. It was strange and yet familiar to wake up in our house, bumping into one another on the staircase. I smiled at the thought. We all had so many adjustments. It wasn't perfect, but somehow it was going to get better.

We moved back just in time for Grandpa and GramAnna's visit. We all went to the airport to pick them up. None of us had ever flown, not even Grandpa and GramAnna, so this was huge. Dad pointed out the airplane as it landed and taxied to our gate. One of the stewardesses at the desk pinned some Delta wings on us and said after the plane landed we could go in the cockpit and meet the captain. Matt was pretty interested, but I just wanted to see Grandpa and GramAnna.

"You know they'll want to have a birthday dinner," Mom reminded me as we stood at the entrance. I nodded. *Unavoidable. Inevitable.* She had taught me those words long ago.

"No cake and no singing," I said, without looking at her.

"No cake and no singing," she agreed.

I counted forty-three people and then came Grandpa and GramAnna. I ran to give them both a hug. It was a strange hello after such a sad good-bye. As if a dotted line had been drawn from Washington State all the way to Ohio, a line from the day after Joel died to the present. What would we talk about? Did it have to be about Joel? Please no.

On the ride home, Matt and I squished in the back of the

station wagon and listened to Grandpa and GramAnna talk about what it felt like taking off and landing, what it looked like above the clouds, and the airplane food.

"I hope you're not too full, because we're having a nice birthday dinner tonight," Mom warned. I knew no matter what they served thousands of feet in the air, it wouldn't compare with Mom's beef stroganoff, homemade rolls, green beans with almonds, and Waldorf salad. Actually, I hated Waldorf salad; mayonnaise and apples don't go together, but it was Grandpa's favorite.

"You feeding that kid?" Grandpa asked Mom as he studied me in the back of the wagon.

"Trying to," Mom said softly.

"How does it feel to be a decade?" GramAnna turned back to ask.

"A few days older than nine," I answered honestly.

"Smart kid." Grandpa laughed. "I'm just a whole lot of days older than nine."

GramAnna brought two packages to the table at dinner, Mom had two hidden in the corner of the dining room, and Matt had a small package under his chair. The invisible birthday wasn't quite invisible.

"John, would you pray?" Mom asked. When Dad hesitated, I was afraid he'd say no, but then he bowed his head and we followed. I glanced out of the corner of my eye and as far as I could see, no one else was peeking except for Matt, who shook his head at me, and so I shook my head right back.

"Lord, we thank You for this day and for the little girl You gave us ten years ago. And for family near and far, all together today. Bless this food. Amen." The food began a round of clockwise motion and we filled our plates with stroganoff, green beans, and rolls. Grandpa took plenty of salad.

"Do you remember the time John said grace and Matt bowed

his head and covered his ears?" GramAnna began. "Matt never heard John say 'Amen,' so we let him stay that way until we had all loaded our plates!"

Matt looked a little surprised. Obviously, I wasn't the only one who hadn't heard that story. "How old was I?" he asked.

"That was after Abby was born," GramAnna said. "I guess you were about five. Just going into kindergarten. We were here for August."

I didn't look over to Mom. That was probably a time she didn't want to remember.

"Did we have fun?" Matt asked.

"I guess you were too young to remember much," Dad said. "Grandpa would take you to the playground almost every day, and GramAnna would put Abby in the stroller and push her around Bethel Springs."

"It's hard to believe that was ten years ago," Mom said softly.

"Abby, when you were born, you didn't cry much," Dad said to me. "So the doctor had to spank you. After that, we couldn't get you to stop!" *Thanks, Dad, for bringing that up.* Maybe that had something to do with Mom's sadness and the reason Grandpa and GramAnna came out for a whole month.

"But that didn't last long," GramAnna defended. "And her big brother could always get her to stop." I looked over at Matt, as if he could remember, but Matt was quiet. "Never saw a boy who could hold a baby as long as you could hold your little sister."

"But you probably wanted a brother, didn't you?" I asked.

"No," he said, shaking his head and frowning. "I wanted a sister. I remember that. I didn't want to share a room or my toys, like the Moretti brothers. I prayed for a sister and that's what I got. And I think I got one of the best I could ask for."

I took one of those sudden short gasps. He didn't need to give me the small box under his chair. This was gift enough.

After a dinner of successfully avoiding anything Joel, GramAnna followed Mom to the kitchen. As we cleared the plates, Mom leaned over to GramAnna.

"I need to know. Why did you come?"

I was surprised. Mom's question seemed sort of sudden. Unwelcome.

GramAnna's face didn't change. She looked hard at Mom. Somehow I knew the answer wasn't as simple as "We love to see you!" or as special as "For Abby's birthday!" Finally, she answered, "Lots of reasons. We wondered about you two. Something seemed wrong. Something still seems wrong. I'm not sure how you're doing."

"I'm trying."

"I can see that. I wasn't *blaming* you. I think you're doing better than *he* is," GramAnna admitted quietly, and then continued. "And we just needed some sort of closure, I guess." *Resolution.* I knew what that meant. Mom nodded and GramAnna plunged her hands in the soapy water as Mom took her place beside her. Then GramAnna rinsed a pan and handed it to Mom to dry. "And maybe I felt guilty. I felt bad for pressuring John to come to the wedding. The timing of it all. *If only.* . ." Mom set the pan down heavily and frowned.

"Why is everybody living *if only*? You all try to put a bunch of puzzle pieces together to see if you can figure out how this happened!" she exclaimed. "It *happened*! Why is everything about *blame*? Why does everybody have to think they're at fault?"

GramAnna didn't have an answer, but I did. *It has to be somebody's fault, because if nobody is to blame, then the world seems terribly out of control. If nobody is to blame, then maybe God is.* Right now, we probably didn't need answers; we just needed to keep going.

"I see some presents that need to be opened," Grandpa called from the dining room. Mom looked down at the plates in the sink. GramAnna dried her hands and I set the last of the plates on the kitchen table. As soon as I opened the presents, my tenth birthday would be over. At last.

I opened GramAnna's first. "Your mom said you liked pink and purple," she said as I unfolded a long afghan she had knitted in my favorite colors. I thought about my bedroom, baby blue like a nursery, but I smiled anyway. This was soft and warm and it didn't matter that it didn't match anything.

Matt's present was a charm bracelet with one charm on it, a tiny emerald stone.

"It's your birthstone. Every birthday I can get you another charm," he explained. "It'll be a great bracelet—when you're about twenty," he added almost apologetically.

"Thanks, Matt," I said. "I think it's a great bracelet right now."

And finally, Mom handed me two boxes. I went for the big package first and it was a purple and pink quilt. Now I had two things that didn't match my room.

"Now open the little box. Then you won't be so confused," Mom explained.

The box held a note.

Abby,
It's time to make your bedroom special. We'd like to paint your room and take you shopping for a few new things to make it pretty.
Love, Mom and Dad

There are two things I thought I knew: I didn't want a birthday party, and I didn't want birthday presents. But there was one thing I didn't know: I really wanted a new bedroom. If someone would have asked me before, I would have been afraid I was somehow painting Joel out. But the reality was that he was gone and now it was my room and *only* my room. If Mom and Dad were actually letting me change it, even giving me *permission* to paint over it, then I wanted it. And this was something they knew I needed before I did, and that made me feel very good somehow. Like I was really home and that it might stay ours at least for a while.

"Do you think you'd like that?" Mom asked, putting her hand on Dad's.

"Thanks, Mom. Dad," I said, and I couldn't say anything else because there was a huge lump somewhere in my throat, and I didn't want to cry. They already said I cried too much when I was born.

"I told your mom I wanted to help. I'm good at painting and even better at shopping," said GramAnna.

"Anything else you want to do on your birthday?" Dad asked.

"Hey, why don't we go out and shake the trees?" Matt suggested. Grandpa looked confused.

"Ohio-style," Dad clarified.

"But it's such a mess...," Mom cautioned.

"It's Abby's birthday, remember," Dad said. "It's her call."

"You're right." Mom smiled. "And purple does seem to be the color tonight. It can be dessert."

I grinned, thinking about mulberry cobbler. That was the only answer needed. Matt knew the drill and got out a sheet of plastic while I found a large plastic bag. Then we headed to the lot next door with its two mulberry trees laden with reddish-purple berries. We'd have to move quickly; the sun was starting to go down. Matt spread the plastic blanket.

"I get to shake first!" I yelled as I climbed the tree and shook the limbs as hard as I could. At first it sounded like a rush of wind rustling the leaves. Then the tree rained mulberries and it sounded like a summer storm. Only the ripest fell. We popped berries into our mouths, and soon our hands were stained with purple deliciousness. I checked the bottom of my bare feet and they were purple, too.

Matt tipped the plastic to the center until a valley formed in the middle with a hill of dark mulberries. Then we picked up the corners of the tarp and poured the berries into the bag. Matt readjusted the tarp and I climbed back up and resumed shaking. Grandpa and GramAnna just laughed.

"Beats blackberry picking with all those thorns."

"Yes, but these trees are a mess." Dad picked up his foot and revealed a purple sole. "Ask Renee how she likes cleaning up after the kids when they play in the field." Dad grabbed a branch and began shaking it, the rustle of leaves and branches drowning out whatever else he had to say. After ten minutes, the tree was clear of its ripest produce and Matt and I sat down to eat mulberries. I liked to suck on them and squish them against the roof of my mouth with my tongue, then swallow without chewing so the seeds wouldn't get stuck in my teeth. By the end, no matter what we did, our fingers and faces were purple with the sweet juice. Grandpa just kept smiling and laughing. I could tell he was getting a big kick out of mulberry picking, Ohio-style.

"Do you still use that camera we gave you?" Grandpa asked.

"You want to get a picture of the purple people?" Dad asked.

"I was thinking about the *movie* camera and that projector."

"I haven't used it lately, Dad."

"Do you suppose we could have a movie night? Maybe see some old films?" Grandpa was never one to ask for much, so he had Dad's attention. "I feel like I missed a lot," Grandpa added, his voice full of regret.

"We could do that. I'll talk to Renee," Dad said.

Mom must have thought it was a good idea, because the next day, after GramAnna made fettenballs and Sinterklaas cookies (even though it wasn't Christmas), we settled into the living room to watch old family movies. I'm not sure why, but we only shot movies on holidays and at big events, never the ordinary ones.

Each reel ushered in another year of holidays and guests. Thanksgiving arrives and so do the guests, and then the camera pans to everybody at the dinner table and then there's Matt and me by the tree opening gifts. We could trace our ages by the presents opened: a plastic doll, a book, a tricycle, a bike.

Easter comes and I am dressed in the Douglas girls' dresses and a white hat and gloves, and then we are running around the backyard picking up eggs. Grandpa and GramAnna, Mom, Dad, Matt, and I all laughed and chattered and added our own sound effects and narration. The short reels of us have been spliced together, each event separated by a white flicker at the end of the tape, and a clicking sound, and then suddenly we are celebrating something new and we are a season older.

In a few minutes, we watch Matt go from a baby in the hospital to sitting up in a house I don't recognize. Then Matt is wobbling, then walking, then running away from Mom. Dad is swinging him upside down, and then Mom comes over to stop Dad. Just when I'm almost bored of baby Matt, the tape flickers and there I am at the hospital and Dad is holding me. But then there is a skip in time and I see GramAnna and Grandpa with me, and then there's Matt at the bus stop for kindergarten. When at last I see me again, I am walking.

Dad stopped splicing reels together after that, so Dad has to keep stopping every three minutes to put in a new one. Each time he changes a reel, he rewinds the previous one. We beg him to let us watch ourselves go backward and sometimes he lets us, but most of the time he tells us it's hard on the machine. Sometimes I don't know if I can believe him. Is it really hard on the machine, or is it hard to know we can't go backward in time? While the reel rewinds in darkness, we talk about what we've just seen and try to guess what's coming.

When the next reel pops up, we see Mom, Dad, Matt, and me projected on the living room wall, our mouths forming words that nobody can hear. Sometimes I can read lips. And then one year we are about six and twelve and someone is about to enter the picture and change our lives.

There is a baby and Mom is holding him in a hospital bed. He's wrapped in a bundle and the camera seems to close in on his tiny face. The picture is as shaky as Dad's hands on the day of Joel's birth. Then we are at home and Dad is on our front porch holding the baby, and Matt is pointing to the baby and I run up the sidewalk to see him for the first time. I scrunch up my nose and look back at the camera. There is a long pause and I know what everybody is telling me to do, but I frown and shake my head instead until at last I obey. I bend down and kiss the baby and then pop back up and scrunch up my face again.

Everybody in the living room laughs at first and then they stop. Unsure. Now all the events on the wall have a baby in them. And that baby is the center of everything, whether tugging on the Christmas tree and being pulled away, or planting his chocolate birthday cake all over his face, or ripping into presents. And then he's on his tricycle and smiling and waving hello or blowing kisses good-bye.

And then there is our car, loaded and packed like we're going on a trip. But what we don't know yet is that we don't want to take that trip. Dad straps the last suitcase on top, waves, and gets in. I am jumping up and down, but Matt is standing still with his hands in his pockets. Joel is the second-to-the-last one in the car and he crawls into the front on the floor. The doors slam and the car slowly drives away, except I know the camera has to stop and that Mom must later join Joel in the front seat. I look to Dad, wondering how much is on that reel and whether we can finish it, and whether I even want to. In our living room, the tears are running down Dad's face.

There is a motel swimming pool in Iowa where we're standing in our swimming suits, and then a geyser at Yellowstone, where we stopped for an hour. Then there is Grandpa's barn next to the river, cows grazing in the field, roses lining the walkway to a white house. Mom smiles shyly and waves the camera away. GramAnna is wearing an apron and her thick gray hair is bundled in a bun on the back of her neck, and Grandpa has on a plaid shirt and jeans with suspenders. He's a short, stout man, and he's scratching the back of his head the same way my dad does when he's nervous. Dad does a slow pan of the animals in the field and then the camera quickly returns to Matt, who has climbed on Grandpa's tractor. He waves at us.

And then we are at Birch Bay, and we are playing in the sand and I remember Mom filming from the shore. I know the camera will soon stop shooting, and I don't want it to stop. Joel stands there with a piece of kelp and all at once I have returned to the place where I was happiest and saddest, and then there is no more and the reel goes to white and the end of the tape keeps going round and round, making a sound like a card stuck in the spokes of a bicycle wheel.

We didn't talk. The projector hummed, leaving a white circle on the wall as our only light. After a long time, Dad shut off the projector, the room fading to black and the fan quieting.

"When was that developed?" Matt asked at last, so softly I could barely hear him. And then I considered what that meant. Nobody had taken our picture in almost a year, but somebody had touched the camera. Dad looked to Mom.

"I did it," she said softly. "I just wanted to see him again." She leaned back on Dad and he put his arm around her.

"I'm glad you did, Renee. Thank you." And Dad bent down and kissed her. We had looked back and we had survived.

✦

Before they left, GramAnna had repainted my room "lavender sunset," bought me a new Lava Lamp, cut out pink and purple wallpaper flowers and glued them on my walls, and made new hot-pink floral curtains. Matt said he'd have to wear sunglasses in my room. *My room.* Best of all, Grandpa got me a dark purple bean bag chair. It was my room, and decorated the way it was, it didn't feel so much like somebody was missing.

On the day they were leaving, Grandpa and I had breakfast together, and then I ran upstairs to get my homework. When I came back down, Dad and Grandpa were talking seriously and Mom was making breakfast for GramAnna.

"You can come back," Grandpa said kindly, his eyes warm, and his smile so soft and kind. I liked everything about my grandpa, and I'm not sure why his heart was bad, because it seemed to be functioning quite well that morning.

"Dad, you know I can't. I didn't want it then and I don't want it now. I'm sorry." Though his words could have sounded mean, his voice was gentle.

"Well, what exactly *do* you want?" Grandpa asked.

"What're you guys talking about?" I interrupted.

"None of your business, Miss Nosy," Mom said.

"Your ears are too big for your head," Dad added.

"I'm just curious."

"Well, let's just say Grandpa and GramAnna would have preferred my caring for a *herd* rather than a *flock*," Dad tried to explain. The weight of it seemed heavy, until my father suddenly stood taller, straighter, and the two of them headed out the front door.

On this cool, misty spring day, there was the promise of afternoon warmth. Memorial Day had come and gone; summer was coming.

"Did you know those are from GramAnna's garden?" Grandpa asked, pointing out the budding rosebushes lining our walk. I shook my head. I had no idea they could be transplanted from so far away. I wished my grandparents weren't visitors, and that they would transplant more than their rose cuttings, but I knew they couldn't stay. I didn't want to think about it, but a part of me knew I would not see them for many years. Or maybe never again. When I was nine, I learned that these things happen.

The car was loaded with their suitcases and ready to leave, even if I wasn't ready for them to go.

"Say good-bye to Grandpa," Dad said, but I couldn't. Was it my last time? As Grandpa opened his car door, I ran to give Grandpa and GramAnna another hug. Good-byes and hellos are unpredictable.

"I love you," I said again. The words everybody wishes they'd said when life is fragile and they don't get another hello. I returned to the front porch where Dad pointed to the roses, which were tipping ever so gently. And then I noticed from one stem to another a delicate spiderweb, highlighted by dew.

"Gossamer," Dad said in a whisper, and I startled in recognition of a long-ago word from a long-ago time.

"Gossamer," I agreed, smiling back at him. "Gossamer."

TWENTY-FIVE

Each day in June was warmer than the last, and I found myself increasingly drawn to the coolness of the basement—and my dad's company. If Dad was concentrating on a clock, I could ask him the kinds of questions I used to ask him before Joel died. Sometimes he had answers to questions I didn't know to ask. I didn't know that the roots of a weeping willow reach out as far as the branches above it or that it takes sixteen hundred light-years to fly to a constellation.

And so I spent the last afternoons of school in Dad's basement, surrounded by time and something more.

"How come grown-ups don't like birthdays?" I asked.

"Oh, it's not that we don't like them," Dad said. "Some of us still believe a person needs one day a year to be recognized." Dad smiled. "But some of us don't want to be reminded we're getting old. Or maybe I should say *older*."

"But the party," I said; then the cuckoo clock behind him interrupted by announcing the half hour. "You and Mom don't care about having a party or getting presents at Christmas. How come?"

"The party and presents are nice, but that's not what's important. The people are." I thought about my party and how the bowling, cake, and stuffed monkey were not what was important. Just my nine friends—even if they were a little crazy sometimes.

"Maybe I'm getting old," I said, resting my elbows on Dad's worktable, my chin in my hands.

The basement was almost as good as the crawl space under Miss Mary Frances's library table or the hollow beneath Miss Patti's front porch. I tried to think of some other topics. Anything that would keep Dad talking and listening.

"I used to look forward to holidays," I continued. "Back when I was a *kid*. But then the big day is over and there's just a big letdown."

"I remember that. It's almost like everything before December twenty-fifth is more fun than the actual day of Christmas."

"You think so, too?"

"Of course," Dad said, looking up. "And I'm not even a *kid*," he added. "But we're not really talking about *Christmas*, are we? We're talking about *birthdays*."

"Well. . .sort of. . . ," I admitted, feeling my face flush.

"It's okay to look forward and celebrate your birthday again," he said softly. Dad rubbed his forehead and then sighed. "And Abby?" Dad looked down sadly. "You're ten, but you're still a kid. Be a kid for as long as you can."

I shrugged my shoulders. Now *I* was the one who didn't want to talk. My eyes stung with the faded longing to display ten fingers. Now it seemed like such a silly gesture.

"Did you know the daily rotation of the earth is slowing slightly?" Dad said, changing the subject. "It kind of feels like this year slowed down, didn't it?" he asked. "Like there's a lot of gravity. The more gravity, the more time slows down."

That made sense. Things had been pretty grave around here and definitely slow. Gravity.

"And how about this one: Time slows down the faster you go. As you approach the speed of light, time approaches a standstill." That sounded backward, but I nodded as if I understood. "So what about when people say, 'Time flies when you're having fun'?" he asked.

"This year sure hasn't flown! It took forever."

"Not every year will be like this *last* one," Dad said. "Please be my hopeful little girl again."

"Hopeful *big* girl," I corrected.

"Please look forward to things," he encouraged. "It reminds me to do it, too." Dad pulled me to his side.

"What do *you* look forward to?" I asked. "I mean, when you're old, do you still look forward to things?"

Dad paused and then fingered the hands of the anniversary clock, looking to the clock on the wall for reference before setting the big hand.

"First of all, young lady, I'm not *old.* And second..." Dad paused. He was starting to sound like his old preacher self, with three points and all, and it made me smile. "Second, when you get *older,* you appreciate each day a bit more because they all go too fast."

I studied him, the man who could move time.

"I didn't really answer your question, did I?"

I shook my head.

"I haven't been looking forward to *anything.*" Dad took out the oil pen and put a pin drop on the mechanism. "But I'm going to *try,* honey."

"What's the third point?" I asked suddenly.

"What do you mean?"

"Dad, you always have *three* points. What's the third point?"

"You know me too well," Dad said with a laugh, and then admitted, "I guess I do have something I look forward to." Dad set his tools aside and dusted the top of the clock. He squirted something on his rag and then polished the brass until it was shiny. I waited.

"I think I've forgotten Joel's voice. I just want to hear it again." Dad's voice had a ragged edge to it, as if snagging across polyester. "Sometimes I try to imagine the sound of it, but I can't hear it anymore." He stared up at the basement door as if Joel might come running down. "How could I lose his voice?" Then he looked at me and very deliberately added, "So when I get to heaven, I know I'll see Joel come running and I'll hear him say, 'Daddy's home!'" His voice cracked, and if my heart could break, it did.

"I wish you felt the same way about me," I blurted out.

"Oh, Abby, I love you. I love you so much!" He looked at me with sad eyes. "I just love you *differently*. You are special in different ways." He paused, then quietly added, "You've always lived up to your name."

"Oh, I don't know." I rested my head on his shoulder. "I don't know much about that *peacemaker* stuff."

"That's not what your name means," Dad said. "It's Hebrew and it means 'A father's joy.'"

A father's joy? *A father's joy.* My name meant something. Abigail was her *father's joy*. Abigail was also speechless.

"If I miss Joel and his voice, it isn't because you're not enough," Dad continued.

"And *Renee*?" I asked, pressing for more.

"Reborn," he said in a whisper. I put the meaning of my name together like pieces of a puzzle. I didn't feel so small and invisible. I was *a father's joy reborn*.

"I was so excited when Matthew was born. A *gift from God*. I loved him so much that I worried whether I could love another child as much as him. But then you arrived. I was so happy to have a little girl, a *daughter*." He smiled in remembrance.

"What does *Joel's* name mean?"

Dad tilted his head, as if carefully considering what he was about to say.

"'Yahweh is God,'" he said at last.

Oh, how I wanted to give him back Joel's voice. I had seen Joel's fingerprints, his toys strewn around the house, the crib in our bedroom. I thought of his voice, but I couldn't imagine the sound. I closed my eyes and tried to imagine a color—orange, but it, too, disappeared. I could *think* words Joel would say, but I couldn't *hear* them.

The clocks ticked in the background, absorbing the silence with their cacophony. "I was having a good day yesterday," Dad began. "I was going in to pick up something your mom wanted at the grocery store. There was a clerk I used to see. An older lady. Kind of forgetful sometimes, but very sweet. She said, 'Where's your little friend today?'" Dad stopped, his voice high and thin, and fragile. "She didn't know." His voice now faint as he held back the tears. "I was having a good day. But I couldn't tell her."

"So what *did* you say?"

"I said, 'He's not with me today,'" Dad whispered, and wiped his face with the back of his sleeve. "Maybe I'll write her a note sometime to explain."

"You didn't lie."

"No, I didn't."

"Joel was happy," I said, trying to make him feel better.

"This is what I know," Dad began, as if he'd thought a lot about what he was about to say. "Joel only lived long enough to know good things. He didn't see evil in the world. He didn't have any bad memories. Even his death was so sudden that he never knew what happened. I take small comfort in that." Dad sat back in his chair. He was done. As if rested. Maybe even at peace. I wanted a little of that.

"I saw a boy on the playground, Dad. He had thick blond hair and overalls and a shirt with green stripes. I yelled, 'Joel!' but it wasn't Joel. Some people turned and stared at me. I waited for the kid to turn around. But up close, the boy didn't even look like Joel."

Dad nodded his head. I knew he understood. Maybe something

like that had happened to him.

"Do you ever wonder what happens when he's been gone longer than he was alive?" I asked.

I watched Dad set the clocks in motion and turn time backward and forward until everything seemed to match. And as he lovingly adjusted the hands, I wondered why clocks had hands and faces but no eyes.

"We won't forget, Abby. We won't forget. A part of him is still alive."

Death had made only some things past tense. I knew then that I'd never say Joel *was* my brother. He *is* my brother and will always *be* my brother. And I am Joel's sister.

Still, though we had pictures of Joel, and even some home movies, they were mute. I longed to give my dad the one thing he wanted. My dad, whose big voice used to fill a sanctuary, needed to hear his son. And then my heart began pounding with a little idea and a big hope.

"Just a minute," I said, jumping up from the table.

"Abby?" Dad questioned as I bolted up the stairs.

On the card table in Mom and Dad's bedroom was a Dictaphone Dad used for dictating sermons. His handwriting was illegible, but Sherrie the church secretary could "read" his voice. Dad would use a foreign language when he spoke into the microphone, ushering in each new thought with a "New Paragraph" and ending each sentence with "Period."

When we interrupted him, sometimes he'd let us tape our voice, and he'd play it back for our amusement. When my father played back his own voice, it sounded the same as when he recorded it. But it was not the same when I heard *my* recorded voice—so unfamiliar and childlike. Matt said it had something to do with hearing through your bones.

The Dictaphone sat among a pile of notes and reference material from Dad's last sermon. It was dusty and I assumed it hadn't been used in the last year. I unplugged it and hugged it close as I returned to the basement. I set it in front of Dad and plugged it back in. Dad looked like he was about to say, *Not now, Abby*, but I pushed the lever to the left and the tape swished in reverse. If I left it on PLAY I could hear the tones go backward over the tape heads. It was so inconceivable to me that sound could be captured and replayed. I didn't understand how it worked and I didn't need to know. It could stay magical, and with it I would rewind time.

I pressed PLAY and heard Dad's resonant voice.

"The seed was sown in different ground. Period. What ground are you today? Question mark. In other words, comma, quote. How's your dirt? Question mark. End of quote." This was Dad's last sermon before we went on our trip. I remembered sitting through his oratory thinking we would soon be at Grandpa and GramAnna's farm with all of its dirt and his message would make more sense.

Dad looked thoughtful as he listened. Then I fast-forwarded until I hit Dad's closing prayer. "Heavenly Father, comma, we want to be the good earth. Period. We want to be planted with Your Word and to grow in You. Period. Nourish our faith so that we might weather the storms, comma, the temptations, comma, and the heat. Period. May we bear fruit for You. Period. Amen. Period." There was a *click* and then I hoped there was something more. I held my breath. Silence, then a clicking and rustling.

"Just count down. Say anything." It was Matt's voice.

"Anything," I repeated.

"Very funny, Abby," Matt scolded, then added, "Okay, just count."

"1-2-3-4-5-6," I said. "Now play it back and let me hear it."

"No, say something else," Matt ordered.

"Testing, testing. 1-2-3. Testing, testing." There was my voice again, thin, high, young. It didn't sound like me. Was it really me? No, it was that *other* me. I was so much younger then. "Okay, Matt, it's airtime. Let's do it."

"And now for *The McAndrews Radio Theater*, hosted by Matt McAndrews," Matt's voice boomed. We were ready with a script and a collection of sound effects, but we were *not* ready for an interruption.

"Me, too! Me, too!" Joel said, and I could almost see him running in. My heart beat like the ticking of one of Dad's clocks. I think I stopped breathing, and Dad's eyes widened as he stared at the recorder controls. It looked like he thought Joel might climb right out of the Dictaphone.

"Joel, not now. This is *our* show. Go find Mom," my voice said. I can't believe I asked him to leave. I felt a useless guilt. "Just turn it off, Matt," said that selfish me on the tape. *Don't turn it off. Don't turn it off. Don't turn it off*, I prayed, unable to remember what happened next.

"I pway, too!" Joel begged in his toddler voice that we laughed at, never correcting his dropped letters. When Joel asked Mom to "please pray," it always came out, "Pweeze pway." Not only did Joel drop his *r*'s and *l*'s, but his *t*'s often became *f*'s. Someone said he'd outgrow it. He never had the chance.

"Joel, say something into the microphone," Matt said, suddenly accommodating. Joel went uncharacteristically speechless.

"Say 'I love Abby,'" I suggested.

"I wuv Bee," Joel repeated. I smiled but I couldn't look at Dad. Why didn't I ask him to say, "I love Daddy," or "Daddy's home!" But then again, how could I know?

"Say 'big truck,'" Matt coached.

Joel loved trucks. But he couldn't pronounce the word, and Matt knew just how it would come out. I forgot about this part of the tape. My hand reached for the OFF button, but Dad shook his head and pulled my hand away.

"Say 'big truck, big truck, big truck.'" Matt could barely talk he was laughing so hard.

"Matt." I heard myself scold in that unfamiliar voice, and now as I listened, I found myself mouthing his name in correction a year later. Out came the words in Joel's little voice, but not as Matt had dictated.

"Big truck, big truck, big truck!" Joel obeyed enthusiastically, and Matt laughed and hit the table with his hand. Joel joined in the giggling, unaware of what was so funny and that he was the source of our laughter. I frowned now just as I must have then.

"Oh, it's *funny*, Abby," Matt rationalized.

"Do you wanna hear it now, Joel?" Matt said, and then the machine clicked off and there was nothing. Nothing but silence. Nobody had recorded anything since July 1970. We had never finished our radio show, and Dad had not preached another sermon.

I tried to remember that day and what was left unrecorded, but somehow it had blurred together with all the other days I didn't hold on to tightly enough. With this Dictaphone recording, I only had sound. No picture and no real memory of the event. I could barely remember speaking into the mike. The entire episode couldn't have taken more than thirty seconds.

Dad nodded his head.

"It sounds just like him. I remember now," Dad said softly. "Thank you, Bee."

And then I wasn't sure why I asked the question, but I had to know.

"What happened in the ambulance? Did he say anything?" Dad didn't answer at first. He just sorted the remaining clock parts and carefully put them in four different boxes. "You don't have to tell me if you don't want to."

"Well," Dad began slowly, "nothing, Abby. That's just it. They worked on Joel and asked me questions about my leg. I said I was fine. At first they spoke a language I didn't understand, and then they didn't talk much at all. It was like they already knew something I didn't want to know. I felt so helpless. And the whole time that siren was ringing in my head."

"So you didn't get to talk to him?"

"I talked to him. He might have been alive, but I don't know if he heard me," he said as if that still bothered him. "I said, 'Hang in there, kiddo, I love you.'" Dad looked like he was thinking hard. I patted him three times so he could feel my "I love you." Dad unconsciously patted the clock as if it were Joel. "I hoped he'd say 'Daddy.'" He closed the face of the anniversary clock. I had no idea if it worked now or if he was finished, but I had an idea that was as much as he could relive. "I *needed* to hear him say 'Daddy,'" he continued. "It would have sounded like a prayer."

Dad put the clock on a shelf with the other works in progress and clicked off his desk lamp. "Thank you, Abby." He rested his hand on mine.

"Daddy," I said, hoping I could be my father's joy. Hoping my voice would sound like Joel's. "I love you, Daddy," and then I started crying. Just softly at first, but then it got louder until I was sobbing. I couldn't make my dad happy by saying what Joel would have said. I couldn't be my father's joy or anybody's joy.

"I can't be Joel."

"Abby, Abby." Dad pulled me close. "You just need to be Abby."

"But I can't even do that good enough."

"You're wonderful just like you are."

"No, I'm not. I don't get Roman numerals and I. . ."

"What does it feel like to be you?"

"My stomach hurts all the time and I think about things so much harder than everybody else, and I'm scared, and I don't know how to stop worrying."

"Well then, that makes two of us," Dad said at last. "Are you looking forward to talking to Matt's counselor next week?"

"Not really." I wiped my tears and laughed. "But I guess that's what you do when your fears get too big for your heart."

I had to begin somewhere. Mrs. Clevenger had said that the end of the movie didn't have to be sad, and that I might get a chance to write it differently. She knew I had something to say. And so I knew I would talk and I would relive the last year and I might find help and hope in the process. It might all begin with telling my story.

TWENTY-SIX

I'm in charge of the Fourth of July," Dad said rather suddenly on the third of July. We all looked to Mom, who smiled. "I'm packing a picnic and we're going to town." We were three weeks into a summer that, though not perfect, wasn't terrible. Dad went on a grief and loss retreat, and I had been seeing Matt's counselor.

At first I didn't want to talk. Where could I begin with someone I hardly knew? Mrs. Sherman wasn't a bad person. Actually she was rather grandmotherly and wore glasses on a string around her neck, her hair graying slightly around her face. When she said, "I hurt for Abby McAndrews. It must be hard to be her," something happened and it all broke loose and there was more babbling than anything else. She had an interesting way of repeating what I said but in a new way. It was sort of like paraphrasing but adding some kind of information I hadn't thought of. And it was that piece that tugged my heart in sad but happy ways. She always made me feel like I was smart and clever and that I had nothing but hope in front of me.

The last time I talked to her she gave me a leather journal. "You have quite a vocabulary. *Expressive*. Write down your thoughts. When it's full you can always throw it in the back of your closet and discover it years later for an interesting read." At first I wrote slowly, but now my journal was almost full.

And so Dad, Mom, Matt, and I all changed. Individually. Personally. Sometimes we did our own things, and sometimes our things came together. I hoped the Fourth of July would be one of those things and that our Fourth wouldn't be too independent.

To start our Fourth, Mom made blueberry buckle and served sliced strawberries with whipped cream for breakfast. "A little patriotism," she explained as she arranged our red, white, and blue breakfast. When the three of us came home from church, Dad had the picnic ready. Mom said we needed to dress in red, white, and blue for the town parade and gave us red, white, and blue flip-flops and baseball caps. We wore them to humor her, knowing we looked silly, *ludicrous*. Mom did not have to give me that word for the day; I knew it fit.

Most of the buildings on the parade route had red, white, and blue buntings hanging from their awnings. We stood at the edge of town and watched children pedal by on decorated bikes with flags hanging off the back end like tails. The Shriners drove by in their little cars, followed by happy- and sad-faced clowns that scared the smaller kids. Next came fire trucks and police cars, their sirens nearly overpowering the BSHS band marching in wool uniforms. The Rotary Club came from behind in a truck loaded with kids throwing candy to us.

After the parade, we went to the Kiwanis barbecue and ate baked beans, corn on the cob, fried chicken, three-bean salad, and watermelon. And for dessert, we enjoyed bowls of red, white, and blue: strawberry shortcake with ice cream topped with blueberries.

The parking lot at the Food Mart had a few rides and concession stands, and so we spent the afternoon with the ten tickets Dad gave each of us. I wouldn't ride the Leap Frog with its sudden plunging drop, but Matt did. Some of the people coming off looked as green as the mascot. Thankfully, because there weren't any other wild rides, Matt stayed with me, making this one of the best Fourth of Julys I could remember.

It was so hot and humid, Matt and I rode the Egg Scrambler three times to cool off. Then we headed to the arcade, where we laughed at the crazy mirrors that made us look short and fat, or long and skinny. I looked so thin. Was that really me? The barker challenged Matt to hit the hammer and make the bell ring—but only if he was strong enough. Matt eyed his remaining tickets, but I shook my head.

"Win a horse for your girl!" another man called out. It looked simple enough; Matt just had to pitch a ball at a circle to win me a stuffed pony.

"I could do it, Abby," he claimed. "For you."

"Let's go ride some more rides," I said, pulling him away. I didn't need another stuffed animal, or for him to prove himself. I just wanted for him to be with me.

After we ran out of tickets, we searched Pop Keeney Stadium, where Mom and Dad had spread a quilt on the field at the thirty yard line, ready to hear the band from Columbus followed up by an evening of fireworks.

Dad unpacked the dinner of Italian subs, peaches, Bugles, Orange Crush, and Pecan Sandies. Nothing very healthy, only good old-fashioned junk food. And then he gave us another dollar in case we wanted to go buy a corn dog or a sno-cone or even a long red licorice rope.

"What did you use your tickets on, Abby?" Mom asked, as I poked Bugles on my fingertips to look like claws.

"I rode the Bumble Bee, the bumper cars, the Egg Scrambler, the merry-go-round, and the Ferris wheel," I answered. Dad nodded and I looked away, remembering the last time I had ridden the Ferris wheel—and that he was with me. "Matt rode them with me," I said, shooting Matt a smile of appreciation. This day would not be sad. Matt would turn sixteen at the end of the month, and that sounded so much older than ten. He was almost a grown-up. I wanted this happy day to last forever.

I finished off all ten of my bugles.

"I wish there had been a roller coaster, though," Matt said.

"I think I've had enough roller coasters," Mom said softly. "This whole year." Mom bit into a perfect peach and, without dripping, ate it.

"This band is supposed to play some forties tunes," Dad said. "You think we can dance?"

"Everybody is pretty close together." Mom scanned the football field, now a patchwork quilt of blankets.

"Forties?" Matt asked. "I thought it was a *band*. A *real* band."

"It's a community event, Matt. The Who won't be here tonight. These are the Good Notes. Ever hear of *big* band?" Dad asked.

Matt groaned and I laughed. "Dad and I used to go dancing," Mom explained. "We were pretty good."

"For *Presbyterians*," Dad added as a disclaimer.

When the Good Notes began, they played what I called "happy music." Dad took Mom's arm and they held each other's hands and rocked back and forth in place. Dad swung Mom and she twirled in the space of grass between blankets. Whenever they made a mistake, Mom tossed her head back and laughed until Dad caught her up again in his arms. He wouldn't let her go. They danced one song after another. Any other day I would have been embarrassed because hardly anybody else was dancing. But people were clapping and pointing, and not making fun of them: Mom and Dad were fun to watch, and something said that their audience, like me, was happy to see them on their feet and in each other's arms.

Then the color guard marched out onto the field, and the announcer told us to stand for the national anthem. Seventh grader Jackie Monroe from Bethel Springs Junior High began her solo, but then modulated whenever she began a new phrase. After her battle with pitch, I could appreciate *the flag was still there*.

Then the Good Notes continued with mostly patriotic stuff: "My Country 'Tis of Thee," "You're a Grand Ol' Flag," "Battle Hymn of the Republic," and a desperate closing attempt at the *1812 Overture.*

"Let's go for a walk," Dad suggested, and Mom answered by offering her hand as Dad helped her up. Matt and I watched them walk away, tiptoeing between blankets.

"Where are they going?"

"Don't know," he said. I looked across the last thirty yards, trying to find anybody I knew. "Remember how we always used to come here for the fireworks?" Matt continued.

"Sort of," I answered, the memory a shadowy recollection.

"We always had a picnic and ate all sorts of stuff Mom never bought at home. Kind of like today," Matt said softly. "And once a piece of a firework landed on our quilt."

"Seriously?"

"If you look I'll bet you can find the hole." Matt stood up and took out our flashlight and ran the beam over the log cabin pattern until he found the blackened hole. "Look right there!" The singed mark made it real, even if I couldn't recall the wounding.

"Why did we stop coming?"

"Joel didn't like the noise. Plus it was too late for him." Matt looked serious, as if remembering something I didn't want to know about. Was there something else I had to dread?

"Do you ever feel sort of guilty when you think of something that. . .that might be all right, since he's gone?" Matt asked me quietly.

I knew the feeling. And whenever I thought of something like that, I *did* feel guilty. I remembered when Joel was born and how I felt mad that we couldn't ride bikes and go hiking and roller-skating as a family. Now we were going back to our lives before Joel, and I wasn't sure if it was okay to be happy. It was hard to explain.

"I was dreading sharing a room with a preschooler," Matt admitted at last. "That makes me feel bad now."

"I know what you mean." I had spent three years with Joel, and sometimes I had looked forward to the day he'd move out with Matt and I'd have my room back. And once I sent away for "Amazing Instant Life," a sea monkey kit advertised on the back of Matt's Marvel comic books. I had to wait six to eight weeks (sixty-one days to be exact) before it arrived. But Joel flushed it down the toilet before I could see my crustacean in suspended animation turn into a humanoid creature like the advertising claimed. I was really mad at him.

"Joel never really got into trouble."

"And he never will," Matt said. "Not like us, anyway. We'll never be as good as him because he didn't live long enough to be bad. Even though you're near perfect, you can never be as good as the *memory* of Joel." Matt spoke so softly and gently. He wasn't mad at me or anyone else. It was just a truth Matt had figured out. "And even though I know I shouldn't feel angry about it, I still do."

What could I say to that? *But that's not what killed him,* I thought. But grief and guilt were killing us.

"Now I've said it, and nothing awful happened," Matt confessed as he shrugged his shoulders. "I guess talking about it does feel better than holding it in my head."

I wanted it out of his head. I wanted Matt to keep talking and talking. I probably needed to hear him say things more than he needed to say them.

"Matt, what did you think was the worst part? I mean, over there in Washington." In a sentence, I was back on the boardwalk with the car and the ambulance and the long drive home.

"The hospital," he answered easily. Too easily. The hospital was the sad memory that came back uninvited. The place where hope was extinguished. "We stood around waiting and waiting and then the doctor came and told us he was already dead. They should have a better way of doing that."

"You mean saying someone's dead?" I asked. "Is there a good way?"

"I don't know," he answered. "I guess you *do* have to know."

"Miss Patti and Rita don't know. They still have hope, sort of."

"But they never get to move on, either."

I shook my head. He was right. We could move on with a different kind of hope, maybe even today.

Dad and Mom returned and sat at the other end of the blanket. Mom handed over a bag of popcorn in a paper sack and a cold bottle of Grape Crush. She leaned back against Dad as he held her in his arms. Something so new and yet so familiar. *Reborn.*

"You're a *gift from God,*" I whispered to Matt.

"Gee, thanks." Matt laughed.

"No, really. That's what your name means," I explained. "That's why Dad named you Matthew."

We were silent for a long time, staring up at the sky. I longed for the first blast, wondering where the fireworks could fit in with a sky riddled with stars. Mom and Dad murmured softly.

"Did you like Birch Bay?" I asked him.

Matt sighed. "I don't know. It's hard to take the good out of the bad. I remember we were having a fun time before, and it felt like we were a family."

"Would you go back?"

"Never."

"Me neither!" And we both laughed at the same time, as the first rocket shot into the sky with a whistling sound. Independence Day. The *Fourth.* The day after the *third.* Almost a year ago.

"That's a twizzler!" Matt shouted, and then I remembered our naming game. We had all sorts of names for the various fireworks. Sort of like how God knows all the stars in the sky by name.

"I like the noisy ones," I shouted. "The big bangs."

"I like the fizzy ones," Matt admitted.

I felt nervous and I couldn't explain why. The blasts continued, but I was silent. A triple-decker, a rainbow, buzzing bees, and then sparklers.

"What's wrong, Abby?"

"I don't want them to be over," I said. I knew that the bigger and better the fireworks, the closer we were to the grand finale. I tensed for the end, when no more fireworks would light the sky.

"Abby, they just *started*!" Matt said, too loudly. "Relax! Just watch them!"

A twizzler and multicolored sparklers were followed by a series of booms we called heart attacks. I waited through the thunderous noise and then asked again. "Do you think we're at the grand finale?" A *snap-crackle-pop* went off.

"We're a *long* way off!" Matt sat up and pointed to the new spectacle. "Awesome triple pop!"

"Tell me when we get to the finale."

"Abby!" Matt sounded disappointed in me. "Stop it!"

"But I want to *know*, Matt," I pleaded. "Just tell me. I *need* to know."

"I'll try." He turned to look at me. "But I can't always tell." I must have looked worried, because he reached out his arm. "Just hold my hand, Abby. Enjoy them, and I'll give you a triple squeeze when we hit the finale."

My brother was holding my hand, and he had ridden the rides with me all day, and instead of heading off with his friends, he was staying with me for the fireworks. I wasn't sure it got any better. He probably even remembered that a triple squeeze meant "I love you." And maybe this was what heaven felt like: when you wanted a moment to go on forever.

I hurt all over from the absence of Joel, the brother who had made me a middle child, then left me as the baby of the family, but my hurt suddenly seemed so different now. Tonight was good because even though there was hurt, there was hope.

Twenty-Seven

D ad came to church with us the next Sunday. And the next. For two Sundays in a row, we sat in the balcony and I counted the children in the colored glass. I knew by then that nobody could escape the picture, but when I could count on something being constant, I felt reassured.

"I used to wish I could be in that picture," I said to him.

"That would be nice, wouldn't it, Abby?" Dad put his arm around me and rubbed my shoulder with his hand. He looked sort of sad as he studied the children, and I wished my dad wasn't too old to join them at Jesus' feet. Dad's eyes were moist, so full that when he looked down at his congregation, he brushed his eyes with his hands. I looked away.

"This is my last Sunday in the balcony," he said. I frowned, wondering if this meant we weren't going to church anymore, but he leaned over and whispered in my ear, "If God's still here, then I've got to find Him."

Where did he plan on looking?

On July nineteenth, the Bethel Springs Presbyterian Church readerboard read:

SUNDAY, JULY 25, 1971
SERMON: WHEN GOD IS DEAD
REVEREND McANDREWS PREACHING 10:30

I ran all the way home to ask what it meant.

"So you think God is *dead*?" I asked Dad, breathless with

anticipation and my run home. "*Everybody* is wondering." I threw in *everybody* for emphasis.

"*Everybody* is wondering, huh?" Dad smiled. "Then I guess *everybody* will have to come find out!" he said, nodding to me.

"So you're not going to tell us what it's about?" Matt asked.

"Something tells me you'll be with *everybody* at church on Sunday," Dad said, and Matt shook his head and grinned. Dad had him. "Front row balcony?" Dad teased. "Sounds like attendance will go up!"

Dad returned to his church office the next day. I watched for signs of what God being dead meant.

I knew if Dad was going to say God was dead, we were finished at Bethel Springs Presbyterian. I considered the move and imagined a different house and a big backyard. I tried not to think that Rita might not be my neighbor. But if there was a chance Dad's sermon title was what Mom called a "teaser," we might have hope.

The return of the reverend was the talk of Bethel Springs, and that week was the longest month of my life.

On Sunday, Matt returned to the balcony with me. And pretty much *everybody* was there. We could see a lot of the people we saw at Christmas and Easter. Matt counted more than four hundred heads, most of whom I didn't recognize. But I spotted Dr. Hutchinson, the Monroes, Mr. and Mrs. Gorski, and even the Morettis, who decided not to be Catholic for the morning. Uncle Troy ushered in our neighbors the Whites, and even Bruce Hanley with his two kids. It looked like most of Bethel Springs had turned out for Dad's "God Is Dead" sermon, and the spillover was filling my balcony pews.

The bulletin listed songs and verses but didn't hint at the last agenda item, which would determine our future. We could hardly wait for the sermon. That was a first.

As we sang "Near to the Heart of God," I scanned the verses for clues.

"There is a place of quiet rest. . .there is a place of comfort sweet. . . there is a place where all is joy." We sang it faster than usual, as if in a hurry. Either that, or we finally had an organist who could play it at the right tempo.

Then Mr. Rodecker came to the pulpit to read from Deuteronomy, one of those books so full of rules I couldn't relate to it. But today it felt strangely familiar and I followed along in my Bible, searching for clues from what Moses told the Israelites.

I liked when Mr. Rodecker read that God would go before and fight on their behalf, and as I underlined it, he continued, "'In the wilderness where you saw how the LORD your God carried you, just as a man carries his son. . .'" And then I stopped. There was more after that but I couldn't focus. *Just as a man carries his son. Just as a man carries his son.* I kept thinking about that until Dad returned to the pulpit for the responsive reading and instructed us to open to the back of our hymnal.

"'A Time for Everything,' from Ecclesiastes 3," Dad began. "Please join me in reading the bold lines."

"For everything there is a season."

"And a time for every matter under heaven."

"A time to be born, and a time to die."

"A time to plant, and a time to pluck up what is planted."

A time to die? The congregation kept reading, but I couldn't join in. Something followed about a time to heal and a time to weep and a time to speak and much more. But *a time to die?*

When there were no more bold lines about time, Dad continued alone.

"'What gain has the worker from his toil? I have seen the business that God has given to the sons of men to be busy with.

He has made everything beautiful in its time.'" Then Dad raised his head and continued, by memory, from his heart, looking at us. "'Also he has put eternity into man's mind, yet so that he cannot find out what God has done from the beginning to the end. I know that there is nothing better for them than to be happy and enjoy themselves as long as they live.'" Dad paused, as if waiting for the weight of the words to sink in, then closed the massive Bible and placed his sermon on top. Only one page.

"Someone once said that 'time heals.' I've discovered it doesn't. There are wounds too deep to be erased by the passage of time."

I shuddered. Dad was giving up. I looked quickly at Matt, who sucked in suddenly, as if preparing to hold his breath.

"But time measures seasons. And now it's *time*," Dad began slowly. "Time for a new season. It's time to plant and build and dance and mend. And if you'll have me, it's time to embrace. I have had time to search and a time to give up, a time to keep and a time to throw away. I've had time to gather stones. I've had time to be silent, and now it's time to speak. And so I tell you today, that when God is dead, it may be that He only *seems* dead."

I exhaled slowly; maybe my dad still believed. But what did that mean? I had come to realize I believed whether *he* did or not. But what would his *time to speak* mean for our family? Did it mean a new cover for a new puzzle, and could we put us all together differently?

"I don't have any answers today. I have understood the burden, but I cannot comprehend the beauty. I'd like to be able to tell you that I can fathom God because of what I've felt this past year, yet I cannot. I'm still searching. But I have eternity in my heart. I have time to grow."

I looked over at Matt and shrugged my shoulders. This was not Dad's usual sermon.

"The books and the counselors say you feel shock, sorrow, grief, and numbness. I think I experienced all of that. And it took a lot of time. I'm a little slow." He looked up and laughed. That was not in his notes. We all laughed as if to say it was okay. "So I need to thank you for being patient with me. But even more so, I need to thank my family. For any of you who have been through a dark tunnel, you know what it means when someone takes you by the hand and leads you to the light." Dad looked straight at Mom and she held his gaze. "That's what Renee has done for me." I squeezed Mom's hand. I was so proud of her.

"My son, Matt, he's all that I could ever ask for in a son. That's all I'll say." Dad looked down and waited. For some reason those two short sentences took nearly everything out of him.

Then he popped back up with a smile. "And Abby?" he asked in a happier voice, finding my face in the crowd. "Abby was everything constant. Through a time of sorrow, she reminded me there could be joy." Dad smiled up at me and I smiled back, and then I turned to smile at Matt and Mom. It didn't really matter what Dad said now; we were going to make it.

"You knew Joel." Dad cleared his throat and then his voice became congested. "I loved him and I still love him and I thank God that I had him for three years." Dad nodded reassuringly toward Mom. Though we are four, we have always been five and he knew it.

"But this loss changed us. I've been asking lots of questions lately. I even asked, 'What if there isn't a God?'" Dad waited as if to let it sink in. "I asked, 'What if there is no heaven?'"

My lip hurt from biting it so hard. I felt the eyes of Dad's congregation searching the pews for our family. Matt questioned me with his elbow. Without even looking at him, I acknowledged Dad's confession.

"Don't act so shocked," Dad continued. "I know each one of you has asked questions like these." I turned to see the other members of the balcony. Some pursed their lips as if they were angered by his suggestion, but many were nodding their heads in reluctant agreement. I looked back at Dad, who was smiling up at me like he didn't care what anybody thought.

"During this time of doubt, it occurred to me that because I wasn't talking to God and He wasn't talking to me, I assumed He was dead. But I found out that just when God seems dead—it might be when He's coming back to life."

It was summer, but it felt like spring, Easter Sunday. *Resurrection.* We had been about death, but now we were about life.

"Like the Israelites in today's reading, I have been carried like a father carries his son, and yet I have not trusted Him. Still, I know He has gone before and He will show me the way, if I will follow. I have faith, just a little, but I still have it. I pray daily God will help make it grow. Now more than ever, when faith is the hardest and the least likely, it's the most needed. And it's the best way for me to say I love God. And I think I do."

Dad pulled out a handkerchief and wiped his forehead. He never did that during a sermon.

"I'm back up in the pulpit. Be patient with me. I have more questions than answers. If you'll work through them with me, I'll do my best for you. I'll try to be the minister you need." Dad picked up his page and folded it in half. "I love you all and thank you for your prayers."

And then Dad did something really shocking: he just sat down. I saw heads turn and women dab their eyes. What had happened? I turned to Matt, but he had no explanation.

"Three points?" he whispered, holding up three fingers. I shrugged, and my frown gave way to a silly smile. I tapped my watch and held up five fingers. Dad had only spoken for five minutes, and I had actually paid attention the whole time. Matt shook his head and exhaled.

I craned to see Mom's reaction. What was she thinking? The organist made a hasty return to her bench, unprepared for the brevity of Dad's message. Her first notes sounded dangerously like Mom at the keyboard, but nobody minded: Reverend McAndrews was back.

"*This is my Father's world,*" the congregation sang out, at first hesitantly and then growing in fervor. "*All nature sings and 'round me rings the music of the spheres.*" I fumbled with my hymnal, unable to find the page number, too stunned and excited to join in. Beside me Matt sang really loud; I couldn't look at him or I'd cry, but not because I was sad. And then I remembered the words on Joel's tombstone, HE SHALL WIPE AWAY ALL THEIR TEARS.

I could have danced in the aisles, but then again we were Presbyterian—that would never work. I wanted to run down the steps and fly into Dad's arms. He was home. We were all home.

When the postlude began, Matt stood and turned to go. Standing tall, he put his hand on the small of my back and urged me forward, as if escorting a date.

"It's good to have your dad back," said Mr. Henry.

"Shortest sermon he's ever preached!" Mr. Siemens laughed, and then added gently, "I heard every word." He tapped his hearing aid as if I might have forgotten.

"I don't know when I've been so moved. It made a lot of sense," added Mrs. Corning.

Dad made a lot of sense by not making any sense. He hadn't answered any questions, except to say that it was all right to question. Waves of people headed toward him to shake his hand.

"I forgot my bulletin," I said, excusing myself. As the balcony emptied, I returned to the front pew and sat down.

I know God is everywhere, but for me, He was especially in the balcony that Sunday. I was home. The sun streaming in the side windows blinded me, so I closed my eyes in its warmth, rested my arms on the railing, and folded my hands.

Maybe it was a prayer, maybe it was a resolve, but I knew from then on, wherever I went to church, I'd find the balcony and rehearse the questions I'd ask God when I got to heaven. Maybe after Joel died, Dad had had time to do that, too. Maybe the balcony was a good place for a man who was only used to the pulpit.

As the church emptied, I headed down the back stairs with the bulletin I wanted to keep forever.

Dad looked different. Softer, gentler, and strangely at peace. He knelt down and talked to the children who came to him. He gave Miss Mary Frances a hug. He listened carefully when Mr. Rohatsch told him yet again about his bum leg. And then the line of people came to an end, and Dad looked from the stained-glass window back to the balcony, surveying the church, as if God's house was a thing of beauty. He opened the pocket door to his study and we followed.

"Let's go *home*," Mom said, as if we hadn't been there for months. "I know you told me not to worry"—Mom slid the door closed—"but I wondered what you were going to say," she said with a catch in her voice. Dad pulled her close and she sighed, her worry squeezed out in his embrace. They held each other for a long time. Usually Matt would have squirmed, but he stood in silent respect.

"I don't have any answers." Dad stepped away to take off his robe. He hung it on the familiar hook behind his door.

"Questions are okay, too," Mom answered.

"Let's go home!" I said, anxious to celebrate. "Mom made your favorite!" I could already smell the rosemary and thyme Mom had pasted across the roast, potatoes baking beside it. The green beans fresh from our garden would be steamed, and the molded Jell-O salad in the refrigerator was a special treat. And mulberry pie for dessert.

We left the room that would once again be Dad's office. A warm midwestern wind blew, and Mom planted her hand on her hat. Matt stretched his arms as if in a yawn. "Good day for a drive," he offered tentatively.

"A Sunday drive...," Mom began dreamily, and then awakened. "Well, it *was* a good day."

"Easy on him, Renee—it *is* a good day for a drive. Matt's getting to be quite a good driver."

Dad stopped at the roses, fully in bloom, and we all paused when he cleared his throat and announced, "I asked for one more Sunday off."

"More time?" Mom asked, looking concerned.

"They said yes, Renee."

"I guess they liked the sermon?"

"I was thinking we need a family vacation. This year has been no vacation."

"I'll second that," Mom said. Matt and I silently acknowledged a third and fourth.

A year ago, we had left everything familiar for our first family vacation. I hadn't known then how it would change us. Now I was more than a little scared.

"Where would we go?" Mom asked.

"I'm not sure." Dad shrugged his shoulders. Dad didn't know where we were headed, and he didn't have a plan. That was strange. "I'm open to ideas," he continued. "We have the next eleven days."

"Can we go *east*?" Mom asked softly, and Matt nodded in agreement.

"Or maybe even north," Dad answered. "Remember Lakeside, Ohio? On Lake Erie? We could take the ferry to Putin Bay and spend a day at Cedar Point."

The wind blew my hair about my face and Dad brushed it aside. "You're quiet, Abby. You don't want to go?"

Yes and no. This would be our second family vacation. I wanted everything to be safe, but I also wanted something different. I wanted new experiences and to make more memories, but I also wanted to hold on to this moment and many more—if they were all good.

Dad turned my shoulders to face him. "Abby, I can't promise you that nothing bad will happen. But we survived this, didn't we?"

I nodded and looked up at Mom, who smiled. She looked so happy. Matt's eyes met mine and he nodded back.

It was now almost a year since Joel had died. Time had gone on, even when we could not. But somehow we had made it and we were together, and we were willing to try again. Did Mom have a word for that? Was there a word bigger than *hope*?

EPILOGUE

I remember an idyllic evening I wish I could have saved in a jar. Instead, we collected the next best thing—the fireflies lighting our front yard.

At dusk, Dad hauled out the sprinkler and pretended to give the lawn a shower. But we knew the water fireworks were for us, and so Joel and I ran to put on our swimsuits. Matt didn't run through the spray, but Joel and I skipped back and forth through its rainbowing arc. When I picked up the sprinkler and turned it on my dad, he laughed and lay back on the wet lawn. Dad let Joel stay up later than usual. Time hung heavy in the humid air as we stretched dusk into dark.

Mom had mixed frozen lemonade, and it tasted as good as homemade. Dad disappeared and returned with a bowl of his popcorn. He sometimes put Parmesan cheese on top.

"A meal in itself." He tossed a few kernels in the air and caught them in his mouth. Matt and I sat on the front porch, its paint peeling in layers of white, green, and then black, its wood warped beneath our feet. Mom, Dad, and Joel sat on a cheery orange-and-blue pinwheel quilt that Mom left on the porch swing for cooler evenings and brisk mornings.

Now, as the sun slipped behind the neighboring houses, leaving a ribbon of pink, the grass began to shimmer with fireflies. Especially in the vacant lot next door—thick with unmowed grass.

"What can you see, Abby?" Dad pointed to the night sky.

"The Big Dipper and the Little Dipper." They were the most obvious. Some of the other formations were a stretch for even my vivid imagination.

"Too bad so many people have their lights on; otherwise we'd see more," Dad said with a sigh. "Maybe one night we should take my telescope to the Ludemas' pasture."

"Or your folks' farm. It's dark there," Mom murmured, leaning into Dad.

"I don't want to take it on vacation with us." Dad pulled Mom close, capturing her in his arms as the porch swing rocked.

Dad looked up at the night sky as if for the first time. "'When I look at thy heavens, the work of thy fingers, the moon and the stars which thou hast established; what is man that thou art mindful of him, and the son of man that thou dost care for him?'" Dad quoted so naturally, it sounded like he had made up the question himself. The psalmist and my dad probably would have gotten along very well.

Joel stirred and then leaned away from us.

"Twinkle, twinkle!" he yelled as he tried to keep up with the on and off bursts lighting the air. God's version of fireworks for preschoolers without all the noise. Fireflies.

"Get a jar," Mom said to Matt as she took Joel's hand and swiped at the air. Joel squealed.

"Shhh! Joel, you'll scare them away," I warned. Joel jumped up and down in his wet bathing suit, silently trying to grab at the mysterious hovering lights.

Matt returned with an empty mayonnaise jar and the little net we formerly used for his fish tank. That is, before the fish died.

"Catch fish?" Joel whispered.

"No. Catch *lightning*," Matt answered. And sweeping his wand through the air, he captured a lightning bug, pushed the netting through the opening, and quickly refastened the lid. "There you go, Joel. He's yours." Matt handed the glass jar to Joel.

"Honey, don't have him hold the jar. He might drop it and cut his foot," Mom warned.

"Put it on the step, Joel," Dad said.

"More! More!" Joel yelled, forgetting about scaring them away. I scooped the air and captured a lightning bug in the hollow of my cupped hands. Occasionally I saw the light flicker through my fingers. I transferred it to Joel's hand. He stared at the twinkling light.

"Fwashwight," he said and giggled. "More, more!" Joel pointed to the lot next door.

Indeed, it seemed the fireflies had escaped to the nearby vacant lot, and so we all followed Joel's lead, Matt carrying the glass jar at the end of our processional. Even Mom swept the night sky with her hands, capturing lightning bugs and adding them to the jar. Sometimes the jar sparkled enough to be our own personal lantern, a flashlight with an inconsistent battery.

The air felt warm and thick, like a blanket wrapping up all of High Street. Every step released the pungent smell of forgotten flowers. And among the weeds, Matt even found a few misguided Wiffle balls from long-ago games.

"Did you do this when *you* were a kid?" I asked Dad.

"We didn't have fireflies in Washington. I guess that's why I think they're so neat." Dad reached out with both hands to capture a flicker.

"Then can we take some to Grandpa and GramAnna's, so they can see them?" I asked.

"They wouldn't live, honey," Dad said, pulling me close to him. I was still in my wet bathing suit, but he didn't seem to mind. "Time for pajamas," he said at last to Joel, letting go of me and taking Joel's hand. "This little monkey is going to bed."

"No bedtime!" Joel shook his head.

"Yes, bedtime," Mom countered. "It's *way* past your bedtime,

Curious George. Come back and say good night after you brush your teeth."

"Even entomologists need sleep," Dad said, resorting to carrying Joel. "I'll take him upstairs, Renee."

"I'll bring the lantern after you put your jammies on," I promised. Joel waved good-bye and nestled his head on Dad's shoulder. I watched the two disappear into the darkness and into our home. A trail of light traced their journey. The front porch lit up, followed by the front hallway and the stairs going up to our room. I saw the light in the front bedroom window click on, and shadows behind the curtains, and then the center light from the bathroom sink where Dad would brush Joel's teeth.

I am like Joel. I never want good things to end. When I unwrap Christmas presents, I dread opening the last one. At night, when Mom scratches my back, I don't want her to leave until her tender caress soothes me to sleep and into my dreams. And how can I enjoy the Fourth of July fireworks when each explosion of color might mark the grand finale? It's almost as though I need to know exactly how long the light show will last so that I can anticipate the dark.

Dad called out from the front window, "Joel wants his twinkles." And so I brought the flickering lantern to meet Dad and Joel on the front porch. For Joel, the fireworks could continue; he had obviously talked Dad into another round of good nights and good-byes and hugs.

How could I have known that even now I'd wish for one more?

Dad tickled him until Joel couldn't stand it anymore, and then Dad tipped him upside down to swing like a pendulum.

"Oh, John, I don't like it when you do that," Mom warned, but failed at shielding a smile when Joel's giggles began.

"It's TIME!" Dad said, mimicking the clock. "Hickory, dickory, dock!"

I rocked my head back and forth in rhythm with Joel's world, until he pointed insistently.

"Daddy! Daddy! Look!" Dad stopped with Joel hanging upside down, his outstretched hand urging our eyes to follow his vision.

"Stars in the grass!"

Dad flipped him aright and back in his arms, and we studied the grass covered with shimmering dots of light. It was a silly thing to do, but we all lay down on the porch with our heads on the step below, for a moment looking at the world upside down to see what Joel saw. Joel's world, and now ours, was lit with twinkling lights flickering through the grass, a miracle simple enough to grasp in our hands and our hearts.

And sometimes, even now, I hold on to that evening. I remember how later that night, from our bedroom at the top of the stairs, I could see the stars out the window almost as clearly as the lightning bug lantern on Joel's dresser. It was magic. Almost as magic as holding fireflies, their glow illuminating yellow lines between our fingers. And I think about the five of us lying on our backs on the worn porch under the night sky. And I remember that when the world seems most upside down, sometimes, if you look, you can see stars in the grass.

Dear Reader,

Stars in the Grass began as a short story for a creative writing class at the University of Michigan over twenty-five years ago. It was told by a preacher's daughter in her church pew looking to her father in the pulpit below. Though I wrote *Seeing from the Balcony* before I met my husband and we had two daughters, losing a child was my greatest fear. I think I subconsciously hoped if I worried about the subject on paper, I could somehow keep it from happening.

Because I loved Abby's voice and wanted her to share more about her family and friends, I knew it could be a book. As my life experiences, friendships and family expanded, so did the story. There is a lot of me in Abby, maybe you, too. Who hasn't experienced loss, guilt, or estrangement, and in grief and anger asked difficult questions? In reading, may you, like Abby find hope in your own story.

Ann Marie Stewart

STARS IN THE GRASS
DISCUSSION QUESTIONS

1. Do you, like Abby, remember a time when you thought life was idyllic? What changed that perception?

2. What made Renee such a strong character and more able to move forward than the rest of the family? Who was the slowest about moving forward and why?

3. In what ways do Matt, John, Abby and Renee change over the course of the novel?

4. What was the impetus for Matt's behavior?

5. Why do you think Uncle Troy's tragic story was so poorly received by John? Why was Miss Patty's story received differently?

6. What was the significance of hide and seek?

7. Each family member dealt with loss and guilt differently. Whose story do you relate to? Whose do you not?

8. Why do think John retreated into fixing clocks?

9. Why did Miss Patty not want her clock fixed?

10. Why was the crisis of faith so crucial to this family? Have you ever had such a crisis?

11. What symbolism do you see in the book and how does it affect the story?

12. Abby's teacher tells her "You can't change anybody else. But you can write your own story differently." How does Abby do this?

13. "They want to help you forget," Miss Mary Frances answered at last. "But you can't," she said with a sigh. "You never will forget. And the memory of him—even with all the pain—will always be sweeter than if you could." How are Miss Mary Frances' words true?

14. "God didn't kill Joel," I said.
    "But He didn't *stop* him from *being* killed."
    Why does this question always surface after an accident?

15. As in Abby's Christmas Eve service, how are hopes and fears so often intertwined?

16. Why did Dad provoke Matt on his driving lesson in the corn fields?

17. Why did following Dad to the cemetery cause Abby to react with such hatred?

18. How does looking back at the movies help them all look forward?

19. How does Joel getting in the last word with the Dictophone provide healing?

20. On the Fourth of July, Matt and Abby come to a conclusion about their guilt and grief. "I guess talking about it does feel better than holding it in my head." In what ways do we offer a support system to those needing to deal with a variety of emotions?

21. If the final sermon had gone another direction, what would have happened to the family?

22. How is the setting of 1970 Bethel Springs, Ohio, integral to the plot and theme of the novel?

23. In the movie version, who would you cast in each role?

24. What question would you ask the author?

25. "What I couldn't know then, but try to remember now, is how fragile and delicate are the moments we most treasure, and if they break into pieces, repairing means seeing anew." Have you experienced a difficult season and come out of it seeing anew?

ABOUT THE AUTHOR

Ann Stewart and her husband, Will, raise two daughters and a flock of sheep on their Virginia farm where fireflies light up the sky on warm summer nights. Music, theater, teaching, and an MA in Film and Television, propel Ann's creative storytelling.

Ann originated the series and wrote three of AMG's *Preparing My Heart books*, and writes "Ann's Lovin' Ewe" for *The Country Register*, contributes to *Mentoring Moments*, and has written for *Proverbs 31*.

More Historical Fiction that You'll Love

The Captive Heart by Michelle Griep
Paperback / 978-1-63409-783-3 / $14.99

The American wilderness is no place for an elegant English governess on the run from a brutish aristocratic employer, yet Eleanor Morgan escapes from England to America, the land of the free, for the opportunity to serve an upstanding Charles Town family. But freedom is hard to come by as an indentured servant, and downright impossible when she's forced to agree to an even harsher contract—marriage to a man she's never met.

Backwoodsman Samuel Heath doesn't care what others think of him—but his young daughter's upbringing matters very much. The life of a trapper in the Carolina backcountry is no life for a small girl, but neither is abandoning his child to another family. He decides it's time to marry again, but that proves to be an impossible task. Who wants to wed a murderer?

Both Samuel and Eleanor are survivors, facing down the threat of war, betrayal, and divided loyalties that could cost them everything, but this time they must face their biggest challenge ever. . .Love.

Michelle Griep's been writing since she first discovered blank wall space and Crayolas. She seeks to glorify God in all that she writes—except for that graffiti phase she went through as a teenager. She resides in the frozen tundra of Minnesota, where she teaches history and writing classes for a local high school co-op. An Anglophile at heart, she runs away to England every chance she gets, under the guise of research. Really, though, she's eating excessive amounts of scones while rambling around a castle. Michelle is a member of ACFW (American Christian Fiction Writers) and MCWG (Minnesota Christian Writers Guild).